SOVEREIGN ORDER

Macomber, James,
   Sovereign Order / James Macomber

First Edition
10 9 8 7 6 5 4 3 2 1

SOVEREIGN ORDER©

BY

James Macomber

Scorpion Books

1

The "hadduta" was ready for pick-up.

"Hadduta". Get it?

Who says terrorists don't have a sense of humor?

"Hadduta", you see, is Arabic for "children's bedtime story". Something that puts the little innocents to sleep. Sends them off to dreamland.

In this context, however, 'hadduta" was code for something else. Something that would put innocents to sleep. Lots of them. Not just children, though. Men, women, children. Hundreds. Thousands. Tens of thousands.

An entire country even.

To sleep. For a long, long time.

Maybe forever.

Rashid al-Nassef felt liberated — which in a sense he was — as the car pulled away from the plush compound owned by the Iranian Revolutionary Guard general in the Sharak-Gharb section of Tehran, Iran. This was a long time coming.

The General's driver took al-Nassef to Imam Khomeini International Airport south of Tehran for the one-stop flight to Kloten Airport in Zurich where he rented a car using an assumed identity and drove the 130 miles south to Lugano. He exited the A2 highway at Vezia before reaching the city proper and drove eastward to the exclusive Castagnola area and the luxury villa overlooking the breathtakingly beautiful Lake Lugano.

He spent the night in the luxurious villa owned by financier Ottah Younis. The next morning, he turned over the car he'd driven from Zurich as well as the papers he'd used to rent it to another man who would drive the vehicle to its stated destination in Milan. A short while later, al-Nassef and Younis stood at the window of the villa's library and watched as a small container was loaded into the trunk of a different car, this one not rented but acquired by a remote third party just for this trip. A brief conversation, a short handshake and al-Nassef continued on his way.

He headed south out of the city of Lugano spurning the major highways and opting instead for secondary roads which wound through a series of picturesque villages along the shore of Lake Lugano. Even the hardened al-Nassef couldn't ignore the incredible beauty of the deep green waters of the lake country with the foothills and mountains beyond. But for him it was a sterile observation much like how he would look at a well crafted bomb. Things should have a purpose, he felt, and so he noted the beauty and then disregarded it as not presently useful.

He reached the Swiss-Italian border at the tiny village of Ponte Tresa where, as expected, the crossing was guarded, if one could call it that, by a single border guard from each country. An enclosed wooden structure straddled the actual boundary line but both the young female Swiss guard and the thirty-ish Italian man were chatting casually on the Italian side in Lavena Ponte Tresa. Even though Switzerland was not part of the European Union and Italy was, Rashid knew that at most of the small rural crossings, vehicles were more often than not simply waved through without inspection or question.

But not this time.

The Italian border agent halted al-Nassef with an upraised hand.

"Purpose of your visit, signore?" the guard asked after al-Nassef had rolled down the window.

"Holiday, Brigadiere," he answered in slightly accented but fluent Italian as he handed over his passport.

"Grazie, but my rank is appuntato, signore," the guard said examining the document. When he was finished, he pointed at the windshield. "Your vignette is expired, signore," referring to the annual toll permit sticker required in Switzerland. The Italian looked smugly at the quite attractive young Swiss woman, clearly seeking her approval.

"I did not realize that, appuntato," al-Nassef responded, "but this is a rental car and…"

"Yes, I see that," the Italian said curtly. "May I see the rental papers, please?"

Al-Nassef took them from the glove box and handed them to the guard. Trying to control his irritation, he explained, "But I am no longer in Switzerland, *appuntato*. And the vignette is not required in Italy. Indeed, it is not even required on secondary Swiss roads. Only the major highways."

"That is quite true," the Swiss sentry said with an amused smirk. She'd been dealing with the Italian's air of macho superiority for days and really didn't care to have him doing her job for her.

"I am aware of that," the Italian said through gritted teeth. He thrust the papers back at Rashid. "Please open the trunk, signore."

Al-Nassef shook his head slowly.

"No?" the *appuntato* asked in a challenging tone. He pointed to an open space by the guard shack. "Back your car in over there, signore, and get out."

In fact, al-Nassef wasn't shaking his head in refusal. He was shaking it in chagrin, thinking, "This fool will never know that he could easily have lived through this day." He did as he was told. As the two guards approached, his right hand wrapped around the butt of a 10mm Glock 29 semiautomatic pistol that was wedged between the driver's seat and the center console. Opening the door with his left hand, he looked around and saw no one. A further quick glance revealed no surveillance cameras either. As he placed his feet on the ground outside the car, al-Nassef brought the weapon around from behind his back and pointed it at the guards, gesturing with it to herd them into the small wooden building.

The Italian was armed. The Swiss was not. Once inside the cramped space, al-Nassef pointed at the woman with his left hand and instructed her to remove the Italian's sidearm from its holster. Slowly. Carefully. By the butt. With thumb and forefinger only. She laid it on the counter as instructed. Al-Nassef picked it up and immediately jammed it into the chest of the Italian guard and pulled the trigger.

Even before the shock completely registered with the Swiss, al-Nassef slammed a powerful backfist into her forehead stunning her. She slid to the floor. Checking the area again to make sure he remained unobserved, he placed both weapons on the counter and leaned over the stunned woman. He began with a vicious right to the side of her head and continued to hammer her face until it was bruised and bloody. Then he covered her mouth and nose with his hand until she stopped breathing. He reached down with both hands and tore her shirt open, then grabbed the front of her bra and ripped it off. Then he roughly pulled open the top of her uniform trousers and pulled both the pants and her underwear halfway down her hips.

He turned to the already dead Italian and pulled him over and placed him on top of the Swiss woman. Then he picked up the Italian's own weapon, cleaned it thoroughly of his own fingerprints, and placed it in the Swiss woman's hand where she lay under the Italian. Wrapping his own hand around the woman's he pressed the muzzle of the Italian's gun into his chest very near where he had first shot him. He gave another quick look around the outside area and, seeing no one still, pressed the woman's finger onto the trigger. The Italians body bucked only slightly and then both were completely still. Al-Nassef checked both for a pulse and then examined the structure for any signs that he had ever been there. Finding none, he casually exited the building, got in his car, and headed for Torino.

2

Law Offices
Loring Matsen & Gould
Washington, DC

The spacious main conference room at the Washington law firm of Loring, Matsen and Gould was crowded with several dozen men ranging in age from their late thirties to their seventies. Among them, there were two Medals of Honor, three Army Distinguished Service Crosses, three Navy Crosses, an Air Force Cross, eleven silver stars, an average of more than one Bronze star per attendee, most with 'V's' for valor, and more purple hearts than anyone could count — or care to remember.

One of the two recipients of the Medal of Honor was also the host for this quarterly gathering of the Washington DC chapter of the Special Forces Veterans Association. Senior Partner John Cann, a former Green Beret had earned the nation's highest military decoration when his "gallantry and extraordinary heroism at the risk of his life above and beyond the call of duty" saved the lives of more than twenty men and retrieved the bodies of three fallen comrades following an ambush by a regiment of NVA regulars in a country near Vietnam where none of them were supposed to be.

Most of what had happened that day was still classified and even most of the attendees did not, could not, know the details. Someone who did know was Arthur Matsen, the most senior partner of the law firm who, along with fellow former OSS operative Gordon Loring (Gould came later) had founded it following World War II. Decades later, the firm still maintained very close connections to the military and to the intelligence community and, as it had with Cann and others, did a good deal of their recruiting from those communities. Indeed, in some circles it was reputed—and in others it was known—that Loring Matsen and Gould was more than a law firm and many of its associates were more than lawyers.

Cann, a fit, good looking fifty-something man who looked somewhat younger, moved around the room sharing current news as well as reminiscences with the others in attendance. He knew most of them, some by reputation but most on a personal and professional level. All, by history, experience, and deeds were part of a very special band of brothers.

Cann was standing off to the side of the group when a dark-skinned man of medium height and rugged build joined him with a broad smile on his face and an outstretched hand. "I understand congratulations are in order, John," the man said. "I hated to miss the engagement party but I was in Colorado until this morning."

The congratulations were for the recently announced engagement of two of Washington's most notable attorneys not to mention two of its most eligible singles, John Cann and Katherine Price, also a senior partner at Loring Matsen & Gould. The party the man referred to was the one given for them by Arthur Matsen at his Georgetown home. Cann and Price, being essentially private people, would not, left to their own devices, have had anything like an engagement party. But the elderly Arthur Matsen was more than merely the head of the firm. He had been mentor and father figure to both Cann and Price over the years and was delighted at their finally getting together. "How many people," he'd asked them when they gave him the news, "get to play father of both the bride and the groom." Matsen, who was now in a wheelchair much of the time. had accepted Cann's warm embrace around his shoulders while Price placed an affectionate kiss on the top of the old man's head.

"I understand, Mr. Justice Santi," Cann replied taking the offered hand. "Thank you."

"Oh, please," Santi said rolling his eyes. "If you appear before me on the bench, Okay, but anywhere else it's still Arturo."

Santi had recently been confirmed — after a bruising partisan battle — as the first Hispanic Justice on the United States Supreme Court. But more importantly, he and John had been the closest of friends for many years. Santi was another one of the few who knew the details of Cann's Medal of Honor, in his case, because he was there. And would not be alive today if John had not been.

The two men exchanged nods.

"Katherine's a lovely woman, John," Santi went on. "And an excellent advocate. She appeared before me several times when I was on the Appeals Court and, I'll tell you, I was mightily impressed. I don't take sides, of course, but there were times I actually felt sorry for her opponents. Some of them, I think, didn't even realize how badly they were having their asses handed to them."

Cann gave a small laugh. "Yes, Katherine can be formidable," he said.

Santi gestured toward the door of the conference room indicating the law firm in general. "Is she here? I'd love to say hello and give her my congratulations personally."

"I'm afraid not. She's in London. A previous commitment. I'm flying over to join her in a couple of days. We were going to spend the week in London but Robbie Foster called a little while ago and invited us to be his guests at the Monaco Grand Prix. I haven't had a chance to run it past Katherine yet."

"Well, that's quite an engagement present, I'd say." Santi knew Sir Robert Foster was now head of the Sunbritech Formula Racing team. But he had also known him in years past when "Robbie" was with the British Secret Air Service. The Special Forces fraternity is truly international.

"Well, please give Katherine my best wishes when you see her." Santi clapped Cann on the shoulder.

"I will, Arturo. Thanks again."

The SFA gathering began to break up just after 6:00PM. When the last of the warriors had left, Cann locked the conference room and headed back to his office. He crossed to a window that faced east and stared at nothing in particular for a moment then turned his gaze to a photograph of Katherine on his desk.

He looked at his watch.

6:30 PM here in Washington.

Going on midnight in London.

She was probably in bed already, he thought. The bilateral negotiations on the new extradition treaty between the US and the

UK were generally cordial with few sticking points, but the schedule started early in the day so… And they had talked earlier.

But still…

He left his office and walked down the hall to another one that had a bronze plaque by the door with the words, *Katherine Price, Senior Partner*, on it. He had a key — she had one to his office as well — and let himself in. Katherine's office smelled like her and he breathed her in. He crossed over and sat in her chair feeling her presence there as well. His eyes went to a photograph of himself on the desk. He smiled and was looking at the phone, thinking maybe he should call anyway when it rang.

First he wondered why the switch board would be putting a call through to Katherine's office. Everyone knew she was in London. But then he noticed that the light that was flashing indicated the call was coming in on a direct private line. He leaned forward and looked at the caller ID. A London number. He picked it up.

"Katherine Price's office."

"Hi," Katherine's voice said. He was amazed at how warm and fuzzy he got just hearing it.

"Hi," John said in return. "I've been sitting here fighting the temptation to call you. I thought it might be too late."

"I know. I felt it. And I knew you'd be afraid you'd wake me. So I called you."

Things like that seemed to happen a lot.

"How'd you know I was in your office?"

"I tried your office first. Then mine. I'd have tried your cell phone next, then home. But I got it in two."

"Good."

Neither said anything for a moment then Katherine said, "I didn't really have anything new to tell you since we talked earlier. I just wanted to hear your voice and say good night."

John smiled. "Well, I'm glad you did. I miss you, Kath.

"Miss you, too." A long warm silence lingered in the air.

"Oh wait, there is something new…," John said. "Robbie Foster's invited us to be his guests at the Monaco Grand Prix."

"And who is Robbie Foster?"

"Sir Robert Foster, actually. I knew him way back when but now he's Team Principal — sort of a general manager — for the Sunbritech Formula Racing team."

"When is it?"

"Not this weekend coming up. The following one. Actually, it really starts on that Thursday. Usually a race weekend is Friday practice," he explained, "then a second practice on Saturday morning followed by qualifying Saturday afternoon and then the race on Sunday. In Monaco, though, the first practice is on Thursday then nothing on the track Friday so business can be conducted. Then it's the usual schedule on the Saturday and Sunday. I'm already booked on Saturday's BA flight to London so we'll have the weekend there and can fly on to Monaco on Monday or Tuesday."

"The Monaco Grand Prix, hey?" Katherine said with amusement in her voice. "Well, I have to give you credit. I know you weren't crazy about my plans for the Royal Ballet and the British Museum but, really… Monte Carlo? I mean most men would just say they had to work or something."

John chuckled. He loved Katherine's wit. But then he loved just about everything about her. She was beautiful, smart, tough, strong, funny… and the fact that she'd once saved him from being beheaded by terrorists didn't hurt either.

After a moment, Katherine said, "But you know what would make me feel better?"

"I'd like to think I do," John responded playfully.

That elicited a throaty chuckle from Katherine but she stayed on course. "I mean professionally."

"What?" he asked.

"A licensing issue keeps coming up in the Tele-Orizzonte merger I worked on the last few months. What if we fly into Turin on the way to Monaco. I could sit down personally with the Orizzonte chairman and maybe get things finalized. Then we could go on to Monaco the next day or so. We have the time."

John exaggerated an exasperated sigh so she could hear it over the phone. "You do realize you're entitled to enjoy some free time without working, don't you. With me," he added pointedly.

"I know," she said soothingly. "But we'll be right there. Not taking advantage of it could set a bad example for the associates."

"You're a senior partner, Kath," John countered. "You're *supposed* to set a bad example. It gives the associates something to aspire to."

Katherine laughed aloud. God, he loved that laugh.

9

"You don't really mind, do you?" she asked.

Actually, he did. But only a little. "No, Torino's a beautiful city," he said using its Italian name. "It'll be a nice quiet interlude before all the excitement begins."

3

Via Cottolengo
Torino, Italy

The 'martyrs' came from many different places. On arrival, each was taken to the mosque on Via Cottolengo then dispersed to various other locations nearby. They were not allowed to interact with each other in any respect. Indeed, while they knew there were others and that there was a common mission, they didn't know where or what it was or their part in it. Except they knew they would be martyrs.

Their ages varied from early twenties to middle-age. All were educated, some highly so and almost all were professionals. There were two women among this group, one the young wife of a man in his thirties. That couple had a very small child. He, too, would be a martyr. None were Arab or Maghrebi or even Middle Eastern. Not what the world typically thought of as Islamic extremists except, perhaps, for the one of Pakistani extraction.

The stereotype of the poverty-stricken, disaffected lone bomber was no longer the norm. In truth it never was. For a long time, many of the suicide bombers were the very young or poorly educated who were recruited and indoctrinated in the righteousness of martyrdom and promised heavenly rewards. Sometimes the indoctrination took hold. When it didn't, the truly poverty-stricken might be offered what seemed like a vast sum for his family and persuaded to do it out of family or tribal loyalty. Many so-called suicide bombers, characterized in the press and hailed by the terrorist organizations as highly ideologically motivated were in fact duped into it, like the six year old who was fitted with a suicide bomb vest and told to walk into a group of soldiers and press a button on the vest which, he had been told, would spray flowers on everyone. Or others who were told that their job was only to carry the bomb and place the explosive which was then remote-controlled detonated while they were planting it. And still others who were bluntly forced and blackmailed into it — told they would be killed in any event and, if they did not choose to die as a suicide bomber, their families would be killed as well.

But here, now, these martyrs gathering in Torino — these *shuhada* — were ideologically or politically or religiously driven, fully aware of what they had committed to do and fully committed to doing it. Even they, at this time, didn't know the details, the where or the when or the what — they just knew the why.

Jihad.

Porta Pallazzo
Piazza della Repubblica
Torino, Italy

The Via San Giuseppe Benedetto Cottolengo is one of more than a half dozen streets in northwest Torino that converge into the octagonal shaped Plaza della Repubblica, site of the Porta Palazzo, reputed to be the largest open air market in Europe. But it is not entirely open air. Quartered by the Via Milano running north and south and the Corsa Regina Margherita running east and west underneath the Plaza, each of its four segments has a large permanent structure which houses indoor shops and vendors. Outside the permanent structures, the available ground is covered with more transitory shops and stalls, some covered in gaily colored fabric, others, truly open to the air.

Gabir Koude's stall, one of the outdoor covered ones, was located in the northeast quadrant of the sprawling marketplace, right on the sidewalk abutting the Via Milano. It was a good location and Koude did a brisk business selling finished leather goods, shoes and sandals, coats and jackets, belts and gloves, as well as raw, treated and tanned leather.

The streetside location also made deliveries easier and Koude watched as the yellow Iveco Eurocargo truck pulled up directly in front of his stall and stopped. Ignoring the instant cacophony of blaring horns directed toward his having blocked a perfectly good driving lane, the driver engaged the emergency brakes and got out, leaving the diesel engine running. With a nod to Koude followed by a sharply tossed hand gesture to a particularly vociferous objector to his parking spot, the driver crossed to the back of the truck and began to untie the ropes holding the canvas top down.

There was a second man sitting in the cab of the truck looking at Koude out of the corner of his eye. The leather merchant stared at the man inside until he turned toward him. Koude gave a single brisk nod and walked to the back of the truck. The man inside the cab opened the passenger door, got out, and walked around the front of the vehicle and disappeared into Koude's stall. Neither Koude nor the truck driver paid any overt attention to the man's movements as they unloaded the shipment of leather goods. When they were done, Koude paid the bill and joined the other man inside his stall.

Two stalls down where she sold flowers, real and artificial, Khalida Tahri observed the activity. As the newcomer crossed toward Koude's stall, Tahri took out her cell phone and put it to her ear, positioning herself so that the lens of the camera in the phone was pointed at the man. With her thumb, she pushed 'select' and captured the image. She then pressed a single speed-dial digit and then 'send'. As the live low-resolution images were being transmitted, Tahri kept the phone properly positioned against her ear. After a moment, a voice came on at the other end of the phone. The young flower vendor listened briefly, then spoke. "Yes. I believe so." She listened for a moment, then answered. "Leather goods. A truck from Bosnia. Iveco. Yellow. White canvas back." She relayed the license plate, listened for a few more seconds, then clicked off without saying more.

Tahri returned to her work but continued to keep an eye on Koude's stall. After a few moments, she saw two dark-skinned men come around the corner and approach the leather goods stand. Both men wore kufi skullcaps and one was dressed in a thobe, the traditional loose flowing Arab garment. The other man was in jeans and a leather jacket. Tahri knew who they were. As the men went inside the stall, the one in the leather jacket looked over at the flower stand. Tahri turned quickly away.

After a brief time, the men emerged with the newcomer between them and walk away to the north. Tahri saw the movement out of the corner of her eye but avoided looking directly at them. As a result, she didn't see the man in the leather jacket look back at her just as he turned the corner.

Moments later, a minivan with darkened windows came up the street and veered across against the traffic and pulled up directly in front of Tahri's stall. The side door of the van slid open and the man in the leather jacket got out and crossed quickly to the flower vendor. He gripped Tahri's arm and leaned over and spoke softly to her.

"The Imam wishes to see you."

4

Polizia di Stato Questura
Via Egidi Pietro
Torino, Italy

"So, what do we know about these so-called 'martyrs'?" Capo Ispettore (Chief Inspector) Pietro Mastrota of the Italian State Police asked the two men sitting across from him. "If that is even what they are."

"Almost nothing," the man on the right answered. "The talk on the street is that several outsiders have arrived over the last few days..."

"Outsiders?" Mastrota interjected. "What makes them outsiders?" The Capo Ispettore insisted his people take nothing for granted.

"They are not Arab, Ispettore..."

"So why is this suspicious?" Mastrota again interrupted the undercover police officer. "Because they are not Maghrebi? This is the Porto Pallazzo," he continued. "We have people from all over come every day."

"Si, Ispettore, that is true. It is not their nationality or appearance. Not by itself, anyway. We are told that they arrived at different times and places over the past several days but were all met by the same two men — two of Bagy's inner circle — and taken quickly and directly to the Imam's residence behind the mosque. That is what is unusual."

Mastrota nodded, accepting the premise. The Arab immigrant population in Italy and in Torino in particular was overwhelmingly from North Africa — Morocco, Tunisia, Algeria and Libya, an area

15

referred to as the Maghreb. The Maghrebi in Torino were concentrated in the northwest corner of the city in and around the Cottolengo district and, being almost exclusively Muslim, their lives were centered around the Cottolengo Mosque. And, while the Maghrebi were by no means the sole residents of the Cottolengo area, it was noteworthy for non-Maghrebi to be associated with the Cottolengo Mosque, and with Farid Bagy, its Imam.

Even so, the man shrugged his shoulders and turned his palms upward. "But, for sure, all we have right now are the rumors on the street about a gathering of martyrs. The rumors are strong. But, in the end, it may be nothing."

"And even if it is something, we can do nothing to prevent it," the Chief Inspector grumbled bitterly. The two men nodded somberly.

It was not entirely true that the Italian authorities could do "nothing" but Mastrota, and the rest of the Italian police as well as the counter-intelligence services were still smarting from being slapped down by the courts in their efforts to address a rising tide of radical Islamism in Northern Italy. For almost two years, the Torino Questura, the local police station, had worked closely with the counter-intelligence unit of the Divisione Investigazioni Generali e Operazioni Speciali (DIGOS) to monitor a suspected Al Qaeda cell in Torino. Ultimately they succeeded in identifying the cell members and connected them to recruitment of mujahadeen for Bosnia and Chechnya as well as support and gun smuggling for Maghrebi groups such as the Islamic Armed Group (GIA), Islamic Moroccan Combat Group (GICM), and the Salafist Group for Call and Combat (GSPC), the last now calling itself the al-Qaeda Organization in the Islamic Maghreb.

But when they arrested the known members and sought to have them charged for their activities, they slammed into a judicial stone wall in the form of the personal biases of one Angelo Portolotti. In the Italian system, the police can arrest and question suspects for up to 48 hours without charging them. At that point, a Public Prosecutor, who is a member of the judiciary decides whether to initiate an investigation and bring charges. Public Prosecutor Angelo Portolotti had made a career in politics before he was appointed as a Public Prosecutor. His district had been Cottolengo and when the

Maghrebi influx changed the demographics of his constituency, he curried their favor in every way he could in an effort to hold on to his seat. It didn't work but even after he'd been voted out, he found it impossible to change his sycophantic ways and persisted in a futile attempt to someday make the voters see their mistake.

So when Mastrota and his team presented Portolotti with the seventeen suspects and voluminous evidence of their plans, Portolotti refused to charge any of them, including the infamous Farid Bagy, Imam of the Cottolengo Mosque. All were given their immediate and unconditional release. Worse, Inspector Mastrota was very publicly castigated by Portolotti for "violating the civil rights of innocent persons who had not yet committed any overt offense in Italy" and of "trying to manufacture offenses based on his own racist leanings." The Chief Inspector had not made things any better by not accepting the criticism quietly. He berated the prosecutor for turning a blind eye to evidence of terror connections and challenged him to be sure he took a very close look at the consequences of his actions when, not if, the inevitable violence came to Torino.

Even though they felt handcuffed, the Italian authorities continued their surveillance and information gathering and shared what they found with other forces and other intelligence services both inside and outside Italy who had a freer hand in acting on what they'd learned. But they chafed at the restrictions and the sense of impotence that arose from them.

Mastrota looked up as a uniformed officer pushed open the door and pointed toward the Chief Inspector's computer screen. "Another one. I downloaded the image to the page."

Mastrota swiveled his chair around and typed on the keyboard. In a matter of seconds, three images appeared on the screen in front of him, the first was of a Caucasian male, dark thin hair, glasses, forties or so. The middle photo was of a young woman, late twenties, light brown hair, angular face. The third image on the right side of the screen was the young Bosnian who'd just arrived.

"Where did we get this one?"

"He came to Koude's stall. In a truck delivering leather goods from Bosnia. *Taglierina* caught his image and sent it over," the officer said, using the flower vendor's nickname.

Mastrota nodded and then spoke without taking his eyes off the screen. "So, what is happening here?" he asked aloud. "Is this even anything?" No one answered. "But it must be something, no?" he went on. "Or else why are they being called martyrs?"

He turned to the men seated opposite him. "The talk is of several 'outsiders'." He looked at the man who had used the term earlier. "Circulate these three photos among all officers and the *Citta Polizia* as well. Have them be on the lookout for any of them." He expelled a sudden burst of air through his lips. *"Che cazzo fanno?"* he spat out. "We need to know more. What is happening? Or is going to happen? And what will be the cost of not knowing?"

5

Via Cottolengo
Torino

Khalida Tahri was slumped forward in a straight-backed chair, the top of her head pointing toward Farid Bagy, Imam of the Cottolengo mosque. From time to time, her head would move slightly but she hadn't looked up at her interrogators for several minutes.

Rashid al-Nassef stood behind Tahri looking down then grabbed her hair and pulled her head up. The woman's face was a mass of bruises and was smeared with blood some of which continued to run out of the sides of her mouth. Al-Nassef looked across the room at Bagy. "I think she still knows more. I need to know if any of the others have been discovered."

"Yes, but your methods have reached their limits of effectiveness, I think."

"Then I shall use different methods," al-Nassef said annoyed at the perceived criticism. He stepped around to the front of the chair and reached down and grabbed the front of Tahri's blouse. With a sharp yank, he ripped the garment from her chest exposing her breasts.

"No," Bagy shouted angrily. He crossed the room quickly and covered Tahri with the torn shirt. "This is not seemly. I will not allow it."

"I must know all the information she has. So far she has said that she only photographed the Bosnian. If any of the others have been identified, I must know that as well." He gestured toward Tahri's now covered breasts. "And shame is a powerful weapon."

"She is not even aware of it, abu Ghadab." The Imam knew al-Nassef only by his chosen nom de guerre. "And even if she were, I will not allow you to do this. Not in my house. The shame would be mine."

"The entire operation may fail if she has more information. That shame, then, would be yours."

Bagy shook his head. He didn't know the details of the operation — or the magnitude of it. Even the Imam might have hesitated had he known. But he had been advised only that it would cause great pain and embarrassment to France, always a consideration for the Maghrebi. "We will learn what she knows, be assured of that. But you — or any other man — will not take this further." He pointed toward the door. "We will let the women have her."

"The women" were an Afghani and a Bedouin conditioned by culture, and in their particular cases, inclination to enjoy the process as well as the fruits of their interrogations. Afghan women in particular were legendary among their enemies for their cruelty as Rudyard Kipling warned "The Young British Soldier" in 1892:

> *When you're wounded and left on Afghanistan's plains,*
> *And the women come out to cut up what remains,*
> *Jest roll to your rifle and blow out your brains,*
> *An' go to your Gawd like a soldier."*

But Khalida Tahri — *Taglierina* — had no rifle to roll to nor any other way to end her ordeal. And the two women were competent and thorough and creative in devising and implementing ways to get Tahri to *want* to tell them everything she knew. Ironically, tragically, she really didn't have any more information than she'd already given al-Nassef. The young man from Bosnia was the only photo she had provided to the police and really didn't know about the other two images in the police computer. And so it was for nothing that she was forced to suffer several hours of prolonged agony before she succumbed.

6

Grosvenor House Hotel
Park Lane
London

"Your car is waiting downstairs, Ms. Price," the hotel concierge advised over the phone.

John had insisted there was no need for her to come out to the airport and hang around the rather grungy Heathrow to meet his plane; he could make his way into London and meet her at the hotel. Of course, both of them knew Katherine had no intention of complying with the request. There was an Aston-Martin dealership just up Park Lane from the entrance to the Grosvenor House and she'd hired a car and driver for the trip to and from the airport.

As always, Katherine turned heads as she walked through the sumptuous Grosvenor House lobby. She was aware of it and comfortable with it without being conceited. It was, she'd long ago decided, better than having people run screaming away from her in horror. But the admiring observer often didn't know why there seemed to be so much more to her than physical beauty. She had a presence that spoke of strength and self-confidence, a sense that she was comfortable in her own skin and content to be the person she was without being self-satisfied.

An honors graduate of a small private law school, she'd gone directly into the Department of Justice upon graduation. Then there was an interesting lateral into the Drug Enforcement Agency out of Miami that lasted about a year. Then she went off to a stint at the Glynco Federal Law Enforcement Training Center—referred to as "fletsy"—before returning to other assignments at Justice, often in the role of 'legal attaché', the euphemism used for FBI agents on foreign soil. Then another stint, this time at Quantico. Very specialized training. From then on, her assignments usually coincided with events in various parts of the world; crises, coups, assassinations, accidental deaths. Some made the headlines. Most did not.

Like Cann, Price had killed. In her case, it had been reactive rather than proactive involving consummately evil people who, in every case, preferred to initiate deadly action rather than be taken. She didn't enjoy it. But she couldn't find it in her heart to mourn them either. Maybe it helped that the first time, she was fortunate — if one could use that word in such a context — that her first kill had been so unequivocally justified.

She'd been assigned as "legal attaché" to the US Embassy during the Congolese civil war, her actual assignment to ferret out what was happening to all the UN aid that was *not* reaching the people who needed it. She'd been out looking around one of the storage areas one night when she heard a whimpering sound. Peering into one of the distribution tents, she was horrified to see a grown man, an adult African soldier in UN garb about to climb atop a cowering naked girl who couldn't have been more than eleven or twelve. She'd heard the stories of the UN personnel requiring sex in return for releasing supplies but seeing it before her eyes she was enraged. She drew her gun and pushed the flap of the tent aside and went in. The soldier sensed her presence and rolled off the girl and grabbed his rifle. He was bringing the weapon around to bear on her when she shot him, first in the chest immediately followed by a second shot to his face.

Price had then helped the little girl to dress and given her all the supplies she could carry to take back to her family. She knew the rescue would last only until those supplies ran out but she'd done what she had to. Later on, when she thought about it, she'd wondered if she'd have shot the man anyway, without warning, because of what he was doing.

Yes, she finally concluded. She probably would have.

After some years, she had gone over to State. It was her intent and she had been led to believe that she would be attached to the Bureau of Diplomatic Security—the Intelligence and Threat Analysis Office specifically. Counter-terror. A perfect fit.

But in her intake interview with Secretary of State Marilyn Sutton, the Secretary interpreted Katherine's confidence and strength as a lack of proper deference and, for no other reason than to prove that she could, switched her assignment to staff attorney. An utter waste of talent and experience but par for the bureaucratic diplomatic course under Sutton.

It was John Cann who'd initially brought Katherine Price to Arthur Matsen's attention. He'd seen her for the first time at a meeting of legal staff of several agencies and was mightily impressed. More than just appearance, he noted the way she made her presentation at the meeting in the most professional manner of anyone there including himself, he admitted, and did so without notes, without posturing, and without missing a beat. And there was a sense of inner strength. He didn't know about her......other activities.

But there was little Matsen didn't know. Or couldn't find out. So he did some checking as only he could do and he liked what he found—that Katherine Price was *very* good at what she did. And an excellent fit with Loring Matsen.

A phone call. A return call. A meeting. It was done.

State, or Sutton at least, had already recruited Katherine Price for something else. She just didn't know what.

Until Arthur Matsen called.

7

Heathrow Airport
Hounslow, Hillingdon
UK

Most flights from the US to the UK leave in the evening, US time, and race to meet the sun as it rises, arriving early the next morning, Greenwich Mean Time. But British Airways has daily 8:00AM flights out of Boston, New York and Washington which arrive in the UK the same evening. Much better. So early Saturday morning John made his way to Dulles International Airport and boarded BA Flight 458.

His plane touched down at Heathrow about 8:30PM, London time. As he came out of the "Arrivals" area, he shook his head but was smiling when he saw Katherine on the other side of the cordoned-off area wearing the driver's peaked cap and holding a handwritten sign with his name on it and a beaming smile on her face. They walked parallel to each other along the dividing rope until it ended where they came together in a warm embrace. They held on tightly without speaking for a long moment then drew back and just looked at each other. Then Price straightened the cap on her head and they walked hand-in-hand out to the car for the fifty minute drive in to the wonderful Grosvenor House Hotel which sits opposite the eastern edge of Hyde Park in the West End of London.

John was tired from the flight but needed to unwind. He sent his bags up to the room and he and Katherine went into the relaxing Red Room lounge. They settled into a plush bench seat against the wall, ordered glasses of wine and spent the next few minutes looking at each other with affectionate expressions that bordered on the goofy.

The entertainment in the lounge that night was a keyboardist accompanying a male/female duo who at various times in their routines did quite creditable renditions of famous duets, past and present. Toward the end of a set that included a Louis Prima/Keely Smith "Old Black Magic" and a quite creditable Nat King Cole/Natalie Cole "Unforgettable", John went over to the singers. After a brief conversation and a tip commensurate with his appreciation, he walked back over to the table and led Katherine out to the small dance floor. She laughed aloud when she recognized the song John had requested — the slightly risqué Rod Stewart/Cher version of "Bewitched, Bothered and Bewildered". It was a song that others had insisted on playing repeatedly at the engagement party and John and Katherine loved the non-traditional lyrics for not-so-young lovers. Especially the last couple of verses which celebrated the recaptured giddiness of youth.

And when the final line of the song implied that perhaps the passion of youth might be more subdued later in life, Katherine put her mouth close to John's and whispered, "Wanna bet?"

Then she took his hand and led him out of the lounge and up to the room as the sound of the music faded behind them.

It had taken them a long time to get together, both having worked at Loring Matsen for several years. They'd known each other but they'd never worked together on a case. Each had a deep professional respect and high regard for the other. From time to time there would be situations where they did interact — office parties, firm-wide meetings, client dinners — and it was universally agreed that the six foot, salt-and-pepper haired John Cann and the five-nine auburn haired Katherine Price made a stunning couple. Both were aware of an underlying mutual attraction but, much to the dismay of the office matchmakers, they had never gotten together on a personal level.

Then, a couple of years ago Cann had been forced to take a sabbatical after an ethical confrontation with no less a personage than the President of the United States. He'd made a lot of enemies in the past and one had reached the heights of power. It was his principled refusal to engage diplomatically with Yasser Arafat that the President saw as insubordination. And so Cann was sent into exile or, as Matsen had phrased it at the time, "gotten out of Dodge for a while".

He'd accepted a chair at a southern university law school and there met a young freshman, Janie Reston, who'd run afoul of some of the local powers of academia. The fact that Janie's behavior had been completely innocent meant nothing. A point needed to be made and she would be collateral damage. Cann stepped in to help.

But there was another element at the university that was pure evil and related to Cann's past activities. Janie Reston became a victim of the most horrific abuse for no other reason than her perceived connection to Cann. He'd hated that he'd not been there to stop it. But he'd tracked the men down and exacted fearsome retribution.

Some time later, someone had asked him, "They never found the people who did that to Janie, did they?" meaning no one had ever been arrested or convicted.

Cann had simply answered, "No they never found them."

He, of course, meant something entirely different.

Janie had survived but with terrible injuries. Cann and Arthur Matsen took it upon themselves to see that she got the best of everything in an effort to bring her back.

Then, about a year after that, elements of Matsen's past related to his OSS activities in World War II Yugoslavia came back after half a century to haunt him. Cann headed off to Europe to address the problem. In his absence, Janie once again fell into danger. It was senior partner Katherine Price who stepped in and using methods both legal and extralegal freed Janie from the clutches of those who would have done her irreparable harm.

But Price barely had time to take a breath when she and Matsen received a videotape from Europe. Cann had been seized by Arthur Matsen's old enemy and would be beheaded if Matsen didn't come over and surrender himself. The elderly lawyer never considered *not* going. Nor did Price. When it was done, Cann was free, Matsen was safe, and Price and Cann had connected on every level. Ever since, they'd wondered how or why it had taken them so long.

8

Hotel Astoria
Torino, Italy

On Sunday afternoon, John and Katherine flew out of London City Airport to Torino where they checked into the venerable Hotel Astoria on the Via XX Settembre late in the afternoon. That evening, they walked a short distance to the *C'era Una Volta* — which translates idiomatically to "Once Upon a Time" — one of Katherine's favorite Torino restaurants. Cann selected one of his favorite wines, *Brunello di Montalcino*, and having directed the *sommelier* to dispense with the usual cork-sniffing, glass twirling ritual, filled his and Katherine's glass about halfway.

After a sip, Katherine leaned forward and put her hand on John's. "So are you settling into a Europe frame of mind yet?" she asked.

John took her fingers in his and nodded. "I'm not the one who's still working, though," he smiled. "You still have that meeting tomorrow."

"Piece of cake," she said "There are no real issues here as far as I can see; just some stubbornness on the part of some lower level managers. I've dealt with the Chairman, Signore Fagnoli, many times. I'm looking forward to seeing him. He's one of those warm courtly old European gentlemen and a delight to work with."

"Uh-oh, should I be jealous?"

"Well he does kiss my hand when I see him," Katherine teased. "Actually, he's told me I remind him of his wife."

"Is that a compliment?" John asked with a straight face. "She'd be in her eighties, wouldn't she?"

Katherine twisted her mouth into an "oh, that's very funny" expression then answered, "She passed away many years ago. I'd bet he hasn't looked at another woman since."

"Except you."

"Except me as I remind him of her. He's shown me her picture. There is a resemblance, I think."

"Then he was a very lucky man. As am I."

"And don't you forget it," she smiled as they leaned back to allow the server to place the antipasto on the table. The food was almost as magnificent as the wine and after the meal, they took a leisurely stroll back to the hotel where they settled in for the night.

Rising early, they shared *cappuccini* and *crescenti* in the Astoria's cozy breakfast room before Katherine went off for her meeting with the chairman of the Italian telecommunications company. John read the daily papers in the hotel foyer for a while then set out to wander aimlessly around Torino with no particular itinerary. He was struck by the notion that he had absolutely nothing to do. He walked all over the city, had cappuccino and a panini for a late lunch and returned to the hotel later in the afternoon. For him it was a rarity, a thoroughly uneventful day.

Via Cottolengo
Torino

Notwithstanding the vicious interrogation of Khalida Tahri, al-Nassef could not be certain that the Bosnian was the only martyr revealed to the police. And al-Nassef did not like uncertainty. In any case, even if only the one martyr had drawn attention, it was one too many. Torino was just a holding area but perhaps he could make the authorities think otherwise. He would give them some misdirection — a diversion.

He met with each of the martyrs separately, except for the married couple, of course, and gave them the information and papers they would need to move on to their next destination. Reservations had already been made with check-ins originally scheduled for Thursday. But even though he would have them leave a day early, al-Nassef would not consider changing the accommodations. The martyrs would have to pass the intervening hours as best they could. Admonishing them that, in no way were they to bring attention to themselves or leave any additional paper trail, he sent them on their way. All but one.

The lawyer from Glasgow — the dark haired man on the left in the three photo array on the Torino police computer — would leave from the Porto Sosa station and take the first train to Menton, just across the Italian border with France. The second photo the police had was of the teacher from Heerlen in the Netherlands, one of the two women in the Torino group. She would be driven south out of Torino to the bus station at the Autoservizi Novarese in Obbassano from where she, too, would continue on to Menton. As none of the martyrs had met, she and the Scot didn't know each other and would have no contact of any kind in Menton or elsewhere. The couple from Albania — the ones with the small child who was napping while they met with al-Nassef — would drive a rental car to Ventimiglia, Italy. The Pakistani Brit was directed to make his way by bus to Roquebrune-Cap-Martin, which sits on the French Riviera between Menton and Monaco.

The Bosnian newcomer Tahri had photographed was last. He was the only one Al-Nassef knew for sure had been noted by the authorities. Al-Nassef, therefore, had special instructions for him. "Your hour of glory is near, *shahid*. You will have the honor of beginning the operation. As such, you will be first in paradise and will show the others the way."

The young Bosnian nodded gravely.

Al-Nassef dismissed him with a wave of the hand and reviewed the situation. then called two men in and gave them final instructions for Khalida Tahri.

Taglierina would go into the Po.

9

Katherine's meeting with the Orizzonte chairman went through lunch and well into the afternoon. John was already back at the hotel when she returned.

"How'd the meeting go?" he asked as they greeted each other with affection.

"Good. We're all agreed. It went pretty much like I thought it would."

"Did he kiss your hand?"

"Actually, he did."

"Hmmph," he pretended to be jealous.

Katherine stepped to him and put a hand on his cheek. "Oh, stop. He asked me to give you his regards. And told me to tell you that you're a very lucky man." She grinned broadly. "I told him you knew that."

John smiled. "I do. I told you."

"But it is touching how he looks at me every now and then. Sometimes he just gets this look on his face. Like he's remembering." She put her other hand on his face and kissed him. "I want to be more than just a memory to you when you're in your eighties, okay?"

"You will be. I waited too long for you and I'm not letting you get away."

"Same here," she said and they kissed.

After a moment, John said he had to go finalize the car rental arrangements for the drive to Monaco the next day.

"Oh, how could I forget?" Katherine enthused, suddenly remembering. "Signore Fagnoli was so pleased with our talks today that he offered us the use of one of the company helicopters for the trip. How about that?"

"Great," said John. He looked at his watch. "That gives us some time until dinner," he said with a smile. "Any suggestions?"

Katherine closed the distance between them and put her arms around his neck. "Well, I do kind of need to unwind. Care to unwind me?"

John's reply turned into a muffled "Mmm" as their lips met.

That evening, they opted for a small *ristorante* just up the Via XX Settembre for dinner. The food was the equal of the *C'Era Una Volta* and the wine selection almost as good. After dinner, they walked for a while along the Corso Vittorio Emmanuel then went back to the hotel for an early night.

The next morning, they again breakfasted at the Astoria and this time both read the papers in the lobby for a while. The Tell-Orrizonte chairman had arranged for a car to pick them up to take them to Lingotto heliport atop the former Fiat car factory. But that wouldn't be until 1:00 PM so they had a few hours to pass.

Katherine was thumbing through a guide book when she looked up. "Oh, John, did you realize the church with the Shroud of Turin is right up this street? Let's go see it."

They left the hotel and walked up the Via XX Settembre to the Piazza San Giovanni. On their right as they entered the piazza was a large white marble structure, the only example of Renaissance religious architecture in Torino. La Cattedrale di San Giovanni Battista — the Cathedral of St. John the Baptist, home of la Sacra Sindone. The Holy Shroud.

Neither John nor Katherine was deeply religious but both had a strong sense of history and an appreciation for the historical as well as the personal significance the Holy Shroud of Turin held for a great number of people. They climbed the set of stairs and went inside. Immediately to the left of the entrance, a replica of the shroud was displayed horizontally on the wall. In front of it were a series of signs explaining the physical and religious implications of the various features, markings and anomalies. There were several other people standing there, some just staring, some praying. It was a moving experience. On their way out, they stopped at a small stand and Katherine purchased a souvenir postcard and a small medal.

Al-Nassef had considered a number of venues for his "diversion" and found one of particular interest. He wanted to see it firsthand. He left the mosque and crossed the Piazza della Repubblica before turning east on Corso Regina Margherita. It was a cool morning in late May, so he didn't stand out in the hooded sweatshirt and sunglasses he wore to thwart the surveillance cameras now standard in most European cities. Only a block or so down, he turned right onto Via Porta Palatina and continued south past the Roman Gate and the Piazza Cesare Augusto — remnants of ancient city of Augusta Taurinorum. Then he took a left and walked east on Via Quattro Marzo, a narrow street that cut back diagonally toward the Piazza San Giovanni. He stood at the edge of the square and looked around.

There were small fashionable shops on the right side of the street and just to his left, where he was standing, a somewhat plain building housing municipal offices. He'd considered targeting a municipal building under his new, improvised plan. Any municipal building is a good target. Over and above the physical damage and destruction and the usual terrorizing effect of an attack on civilian structures and people — which is after all, by definition, what terrorism is all about — there was an added dimension of insult. It becomes not just an attack on a building but an attack on the heart of the city.

But he had something more in mind. He would not attack the heart. He would attack the soul. It stood directly opposite the *construzione comunale* on the other side of the Piazza San Giovanni.

La Sacra Sindone. The Holy Shroud.

John and Katherine came out of the cathedral and stood at the top of the stairs briefly looking to the right at the remains of the Roman Gate. They walked down the stairs to the piazza level and turned left to head back up the Via XX Settembre. Just as they left the square, John's mind registered the image of a man standing off to his right at the corner of the building opposite the cathedral. He couldn't see much of the man's face because of the pulled up hood. And there was nothing otherwise remarkable that would seize his attention. But there was something… some intangible, perhaps even psychic current that passed between them and caused him to turn and look at him again. At that moment, Katherine took his arm and his thoughts went to her. He pulled her closer and they continued down the street.

Al-Nassef watched the attractive couple exit the church and cross the piazza. His attention was principally on the structure and the area around but he was in operational security mode and kept a portion of his consciousness on them as they headed out of the square. For that reason, he noticed when the man glanced his way and then turned back toward him for a longer, but still relatively brief look. Al-Nassef didn't return the stare but was able to get a glimpse of the man's face before he turned back to the woman. Was he imagining there was something familiar about him? There was no actual recognition but… He filed the image close to the surface of his brain and made a mental note to search his memory more closely when he could.

For now, though, he had a "diversion" to put into motion.

10

Fontvieille
Principalité de Monaco

Prince Albert II, Sovereign Prince of Monaco, like his father Prince Rainier III and a long list of other rulers in the Grimaldi line which originated in 1297, is called *Son Altesse Sérénissime*, His Serene Highness. And Monaco is a serene place indeed. Even as the commuter helicopters and mega-yachts come and go and in the midst of multi-million and multi-billion Euro transactions that are the staple and benchmark of its commerce, an air of equanimity prevails. Business and life are conducted in harmony with a pervading sense of quiet satisfaction, a feeling of immunity from the relative hyperactivity of the outside world.

But not this week.

The soon-to-be-teeming masses of Grand Prix fans had already begun to overrun the just under two square kilometer principality that sits on the Mediterranean just south and west of the French-Italian border. And the preparations for the event were already underway. All along the streets that would form the course for the coming weekend's race, grandstands were being constructed at the most favorable viewing points along the track, barricades were being erected to block traffic and guide and control pedestrians, and concrete barriers and chain link fencing were being put into place to enclose the course and protect both the fans and the abutting structures should one of the formidable vehicles go astray.

Monegasques have more than a bit of a love-hate relationship with the Monaco Grand Prix. For the better part of a week, their peace is broken. At first by the hammering and clanking of construction that turns the waterfront section in particular into an unfamiliar maze of inaccessible pathways and temporary dead ends; then, as the Grand Prix weekend nears, by the eclectic swarms that come from around the world to overrun and temporarily overwhelm the principality. To be sure, the citizens and residents of Monaco take it in stride and with good spirits but will often during that week remark among themselves — not to the visitors — that it will be nice to again lunch at their usual café on the Rue Princesse Caroline or buy a glass of beer at their favorite bar for four or five Euros rather than the ten or eleven Euros during Grand Prix week.

But at the end of the day, the Monegasques take enormous pride in the Monaco Grand Prix, the last remaining F1 GP race actually run on public streets — as many of the races used to be. Despite their occasional and gentle resentments, they, like the true F1 aficionados that they are, think of it and speak of it with reverence and warmth and affection, the way a loving family speaks of a favorite aunt, a grande dame whose eccentricities cause the occasional problem from time to time but whom they would not trade for anyone. And Monaco loves and admires its Grand Prix not least because it is the crown jewel in the beyond exclusive club that is the ultimate in motorsport. In a world of Rolex's, it is the Vacheron Constantin.

But, *mon dieu!,* it is disruptive.

The Tele-Orizzonte helicopter landed John and Katherine at the Heli-Air Monaco heliport on the Fontvieille Quay around 3:00 in the afternoon. From there it was the briefest of taxi rides around the Princess Grace Gardens to the luxurious Vespucci Hotel where, at check-in, they were given a note advising them that they would be Sir Robert Foster's guests for dinner that evening in the hotel's five star restaurant.

When they got to their room, they found a large flower arrangement, a bottle of quite good champagne and a basket of fruit and snacks. On the table next to all of it was a card addressed to Mme. Katherine Price containing a handwritten note from Sir Robert congratulating her on conquering what he called John's "chronic confirmed bachelorhood". Katherine smiled and handed the note to John who read it and smiled back at her.

"No card for me?" he asked with a smile.

"I guess not. What would be the comparable term for a woman, anyway?"

" 'Confirmed bachelorette', I suppose."

"A bit juvenile, though, don't you think?"

John thought about it briefly. " 'Confirmed spinster', then?" he said with raised eyebrows and a large grin.

"Don't even....," Katherine mock-glared at him. But she actually enjoyed his amusement at his own humor and shared the chuckle with him.

"Anyway," John finally said, "since it doesn't apply to either of us, let's not worry about it."

Few people knew — John and Katherine had shared their backgrounds with each other, of course — that this would not be the first marriage for either. They'd both married young. And both marriages had been relatively brief. Both had also ended sadly. Not badly. Just sadly.

In John's case, it had been an all-too-common story among special forces personnel — so common it bordered on a stereotype. He'd married his high school girlfriend while home on leave after graduating with his green beret. Then, he was in Vietnam for most of the first year of the marriage. That took its toll. But so did what he was called upon to do in the course of his tour of duty. It was brutal, ruthless work and few men could do what the SOG people did and not carry scars or be besieged by demons risen from the ashes of what they had done. Even the specialized treatments the military developed — a sort of acupuncture to the back of the neck combined with deep hypnosis — couldn't make all the images go away. It suppressed much of the most searing parts but it didn't fully bury the evil phoenixes.

Some of the men couldn't leave the violence behind. That was not what happened with John. When he returned to the US, if anything he seemed quieter. To be sure, the physical absence for so long at the very beginning of the marriage had denied them a foundation to build on. But even after the first tour and times beyond, he was away a lot, sometimes for a few days, often longer. And always when he returned, he was quiet. Distant. That was what ultimately killed the marriage. When it became clear that often, even when he was there, he wasn't there. Soon, neither was she.

Katherine's marriage didn't start till after college but ultimately it had the same ending as John's. All her life, she'd been the achiever; the star athlete, the top student, the homecoming queen, the winner at what she did in everything she tried. Brad was a good person. And a good looking one. Tall, dark and handsome but ultimately insecure in life in general. Introverted. All his energies turned inward to academics. Brad and Katherine were together the last two years of college, their paths having crossed thanks to similar course loads in pre-law. And when they were both accepted at law schools in Boston—although to two different ones—it seemed logical, maybe even a romantic sign that they should marry.

Katherine's school was a small private one while Brad attended a much larger university. But the marriage didn't make it out of law school. Nothing dramatic. The time pressures of first year law are just as intense as they're portrayed. They saw each other first thing in the morning and then late at night, often one being asleep before the other got back to the apartment. It was that simple. It wasn't just that they fell out of love—which they did. They had also lost all their points of contact, their intersections of reference. In the end, all they shared was an apartment. So, when Brad prepared to go off to join the Wall Street firm and Katherine accepted the position at Justice, they simply formalized what already was.

After getting settled in the room, John and Katherine had decided to walk into the center of the principality, the section called La Condamine. The Hotel Vespucci is in the Fontvieille section separated from the center by La Rocher (The Rock) the huge promontory atop which sits the Royal Palace and the section of Monaco called Monaco-ville — the old town. They headed toward the Fontvieille Commercial Center which consists, on the ground level, of shops and a supermarket and a large open air courtyard. Above that, on a second level reached by stairs or by a pair of side-by-side up and down escalators, there are more shops, the Collection de Voitures Anciennes de S.A.S. le Prince de Monaco, the principality's famous collection of antique and classic automobiles, and the Jardin Animalier, Monaco's Zoo. At the top of yet another escalator which runs by the entrance to the zoo, is the Boulevard Charles III where a right turn and a relatively short walk takes one into postcard Monaco, what most people think of as Monte Carlo. In actuality, Monte Carlo is a separate section of the principality on the opposite side from Fontvieille and to the north of La Condamine.

Both John and Katherine had been to Monaco before but not together and neither had been there during the Grand Prix. Even now, with two days to go before the first practices began, the difference from their previous visits was evident. The crowds were already large; the pace palpably more intense.

They got as far as the courtyard in the Commercial Center before deciding they didn't want to face the crowds quite yet and headed back in the direction of the Vespucci Hotel. They took a leisurely walk through the beautiful rose gardens across from the front of the hotel and continued on to the Riviera Marriott in Cap D'Ail where they found a table alongside the Quay. Settling into their seats while they waited for the waiter to bring them their order, they looked out across the Cap D'Ail Marina that abutted the Quay. Closest to where they sat were the relatively smallish vessels — thirty feet or so, then several rows of similarly sized sailboats, and on the far side of the marina were the *real* yachts including a 200 foot plus privately owned ship available for charter and a larger 255 footer owned by an American insurance entrepreneur.

But even those were not the largest yachts in Monaco for the Grand Prix. A short distance to the north of Cap d'Ail is the Port de Fontvieille whose marina held only a single super-yacht (if one could call a mere 193 feet a super-yacht). It was in the main marina, just a bit further north of Fontvieille in the Port Hercule, the famous one shown in all the most well-known photos, where the true mega-yachts were moored. The largest were the 350 foot Lady Nashwa owned by a Bahraini businessman and the 370 and 380 footers owned by two highly competitive Russian businessmen. But even those would be overshadowed by the queen of the mega-yachts owned by — what else — a Middle-Eastern sheik, which was anchored outside the marina in the Mediterranean itself. At 525 feet, it was the largest privately owned vessel in the world. Until, of course, the one being built for one of the Russian oligarchs was launched in a year or so.

They sat in silence for several moments. Then Katherine asked John, "Does your friend Robbie own one of those?" she said indicating the yachts with her chin.

John laughed. "No, he's got money but not that kind as far as I know."

"How exactly do you know him?"

"The first time I met him was when Delta Force did some cross-training with the 22nd SAS Regiment at Stirling Lines way back when." He scratched at his cheek and smiled. "I pretty much thought he was an asshole. With good reason. Most of the SAS guys thought they were the best in the world — also with good reason, I must admit — but Robbie really thought his you-know-what didn't stink. We never came to blows or anything but we did not hit it off.

"The next time we crossed paths is still pretty classified," he looked at Katherine, "but I'll tell you if you like."

"No need," she demurred. Old habits die hard.

"Anyway, after all was said and done on that operation, we'd each kind of pulled the other's fat out of the fire. So…well, let's just say I didn't think he was an asshole anymore." They both smiled.

"We kept in loose touch after that," John continued. "The only other time we actually worked together on something was in 2002. The last several years of his career he'd been more or less permanently seconded to MI6 and got to be considered quite the expert in tracking international monetary transactions. So, when we, the US, got serious about going after terrorist financing following 9/11, I latched on to him and his expertise. We ended up closing down the Bank of Commercial Enterprise — remember that?"

"I do indeed. Good for you."

"As far as I know, Robbie stayed with MI6 until — 2003 or so, I think it was. Then he retired. Full colonel."

"And how does one go from SAS Colonel or even MI6 to running an auto racing team?"

"I don't know exactly. But it's not really such a stretch. It's still a business after all. And what makes a good CEO? Leadership, organization, discipline. He was a hell of an officer." He smiled. "And who better to keep all the prima donnas in line?"

11

Hotel Vespucci
Fontvieille
Monaco

Just after 6:00 PM, John and Katherine re-emerged from the elevator into the glass and chrome, black and white art-deco-ish lobby of the Hotel Vespucci. Dinner would be at 7:00 but they would meet Robbie in the lounge for drinks first. They went past the reception desk and crossed to the open double doors inside which they could see a bar along the left side and tables throughout the rest of the crowded room.

"John!" a fit looking man of average height with brown, thinning hair and a beaming smile shouted from the opposite wall as soon as he saw them enter the lounge. He stood quickly and crossed to them with hand extended. John took it and even before he could begin to introduce Katherine, the man stepped back with a thoroughly admiring look on his face. "And this utterly enchanting person is, of course, your fiancée?" He looked back at Cann expectantly.

"Robbie, meet Katherine Price. Colleague, senior partner at Loring Matsen, and, yes, my fiancée." Fosters eyebrows rose and he nodded over and over, a huge smile on his face. "Katherine," John turned toward her, "Sir Robert Foster."

Katherine extended her hand to Foster and looked directly into his eyes. At an inch or two under six feet, the Brit was only slightly taller than Price herself. "Sir Robert," she greeted him.

"Call me Robbie, please. All my friends do." His lips stretched into a sly smile. "I even allow John to sometimes," he quipped. He threw a grin at Cann then looked back at Price. "And he shall certainly be even more of a friend with such beauty about him now."

"Are you flirting with me, Robbie?" Katherine asked playfully.

"Shamelessly," Foster said still grinning. "To no avail, I suspect, though, eh?"

"I'm afraid not," she replied. She put her arm through Cann's and gave it a squeeze. "My heart is well and truly taken."

Foster turned to Cann and said with sincerity, "Splendid, John. Splendid. Congratulations. I'm delighted for you." Then, once again, he turned to Price. "Though I'm a bit concerned for you, Katherine," he intoned with mock concern. "You do know what you've gotten yourself into with this one, don't you?"

"Nothing I can't handle," Katherine said with a warm smile.

"Ha-haaa," Foster's voice exulted in a rising crescendo of glee. "I do believe she has your measure, then, doesn't she?" he said pointing a finger in John's direction. "Lovely, intelligent, and tough, eh?"

"You have no idea," John said directing a warm admiring smile at Katherine. The look was returned in kind.

Foster turned back into the lounge and extended an arm toward his table to lead them over. Then he stopped suddenly and waved to a distinguished silver-haired older man in a blue blazer wearing a patch over one eye who was entering the room from a small door just at the end of the bar. "Stanley," he called out and then ushered Cann and Price in that direction. "Katherine, John, I'd like you to meet Stanley Appel, managing partner of the hotel and a very good friend."

Appel smiled as he approached them and took Price's extended hand. "Delighted to meet you, Katherine," he said in a somewhat gravelly voice that revealed a hint of a New York City accent. "John," Appel greeted Cann. "A pleasure."

"Join us, Stanley. I have a table just here." Foster said with a gesture. Appel nodded.

The four seated themselves around the table, Foster with his back to the wall, Cann to his left, then Price, then Appel. "This is a truly wonderful hotel, Mr. Appel," Katherine said. "You must be very proud of it."

"I am, indeed, my dear. I consider it the crowning achievement of my career as a hotelier. I'm very proud of the Vespucci."

"Stanley has owned or managed a number of very high quality hotels over the years," Foster commented.

"Really?" she inquired. "Is this one your favorite?"

"Yes," Appel thought about it for a moment. "Well, this and my first. That was in Geneva. The Huntly in Aberdeen was very special to me as well. I have a particular affinity for Scotland having spent so much time there."

"You know, I've often wondered why there's never been a Scottish Grand Prix." John said.

"Oh, but there has been," Appel corrected him. "1951. It didn't count toward the championship points but it was an official Grand Prix nonetheless. There used to be numerous races throughout the year but only eight or ten of them counted toward the World Championship." He looked at John and Katherine. "You're fans?" he asked.

Katherine pointed a thumb toward John. "I'm excited about being here but he's the real fan."

"Since the days of Jim Clark." John looked at Katherine and explained. "Twice world Champion back in the sixties. The most successful Scottish driver until Sir Jackie Stewart in the seventies. Sir Jackie had three championships. So he's the most successful Scot so far."

"And the most successful Stewart," Appel said showing off.

"I didn't know there was more than one."

"Interesting bit of trivia for you. The 1953 British Grand Prix had two Stewarts in it — Jimmy, Sir Jackie's older brother and Ian Stewart. And for both, it was the only official Grand Prix they ever drove in. And there was Johnnie Dumfries?" The others looked questioningly at him. "His proper name is John Colum Crichton-Stuart, 7th Marquess of Bute, Earl of Dumfries. Hence the name he went by. Preferred to be one of the fellows, though. Good man. Down to earth. Very good driver, too."

"Stanley could be official historian for the sport, as you can see," Foster said.

"Hardly," Appel demurred, "but I've been around it since the beginning. Before, actually."

"Did you know Fangio?" John asked. Katherine smiled at his almost boyish enthusiasm.

"Slightly. Quiet man. Surprisingly placid for such a competitor on the track. I knew Mike Hawthorne fairly well. Others over the years." He smiled. "Good memories, mostly. Like everything."

A member of the hotel staff came up behind Appel and leaned over and whispered something to him. Appel nodded and stood. "I'm afraid you'll have to excuse me." He gestured at the door through which he'd entered. "Duty calls, I'm afraid." He gave a small bow to Katherine, and nodded to John. "Delighted to meet you, my boy. Please enjoy your drinks. Compliments of the Vespucci."

"What a charming man," Katherine said as Appel walked away. "And interesting."

"Indeed. And more," Foster offered. "He was on a B-29 crew in the Pacific in World War II. 20th Air Force. From the Marianas to Okinawa and the home islands, I understand. Several decorations. And, I might add, he's continued to be of service over the years from time to time. To Her Majesty as well as your Uncle Sam. He also received the Legion d'Honneur from France for 'unspecified services'." Foster said the last part with crooked fingers to indicate quotes. "Prince Rainier was also a recipient of the Legion d'Honneur. He and Stanley had that in common and would get together from time to time. Not close friends, exactly. Kindred spirits, though."

"How fascinating," Katherine observed. "And it doesn't surprise me. He has that...that...."

"*Je ne sais quoi?*" John asked with a smirk.

She looked at him over her nose and with an amused smirk of her own. "Obviously, *je ne sais quoi*, John," she quipped, "or I'd have finished my own sentence." They shared a warm laugh and Sir Robert joined in.

"Now," the Sunbritech team principal said, "let me tell you what's in store for the next several days. We're essentially finished setting up shop over on the quay and practice isn't until Thursday so tomorrow will be the best day for me to show you how the team works. We'll be working on the cars throughout the day, as always, and you can meet Derek and Jukka, our drivers."

"This is going to be fun," Katherine enthused. "I'm really looking forward to it."

"Then we'll lunch at La Rascasse," Foster said referring to the restaurant that sat directly on the race course corner that bore its name. "And in the afternoon, when I'm not managing some inevitable crisis, I'll take you down through the rest of the pits to see who's around. No one misses this race, John, and I suspect we have a good chance of running into Schumacher, Mansell, Hill and who knows who else.

"Then," Foster rubbed his hands together in exaggerated anticipation, "for the *pièce de resistance*, I will be pleased to escort you to the Prince's Grand Prix Ball in the palace tonight."

"Wow! Thank you, Sir Robert," Katherine enthused. John was equally impressed.

"Do you have a tuxedo, John," Foster asked."

"I do but I didn't bring it with me. I didn't know I'd need one."

"It's not specifically required but is expected. No matter, though. We'll get you one." He turned to Price. "Would you need anything, Katherine?"

"No," she answered. "I brought something suitable, I think."

"You did?" John asked sounding surprised.

"Yes, I did," she said rolling her eyes. "Just a little something, as they say."

"Wonderful then," Sir Robert said. "Be prepared to meet the people who consider themselves the movers and shakers of high society. Some of them are actually quite nice, though. As are the members of the royal family."

"I've seen film of the Prince," Katherine said. "He does seem nice. And he speaks English with a flawless American accent."

"I'm afraid some of us would consider that an oxymoron, Katherine," Foster said.

"What?"

"Flawless American accent," Foster quipped.

12

Wednesday Morning
Via Cottolengo
Torino

The young Bosnian was named Mirko Zubak. He rose at sunrise and performed Fajr, his morning prayers, with particular intensity. The "keeper" assigned to him prayed with him. While close tabs were kept on all the martyrs, from the moment that al-Nassef had told Zubak he would be "first in paradise", he was not left alone. The only time the keeper was not by his side was when the Bosnian had asked the Imam, Bagy, the night before to come and help prepare him for his martyrdom. The two had discussed Islam at length and what was to come for Zubak. That his act of jihad would wash away his sins and he would face no reckoning on the Day of Judgment and would be able to intercede for 70 relatives to enter Heaven, that he would see the face of Allah and, yes, have his 72 *houris*. When they were done, Zubak and the Imam knelt and placed their right hands on the Koran. Bagy ended the dialogue by saying, "Are you ready? Tomorrow you will be in Paradise."

Zubak had had not been told what the target was to be but he did know his act of martyrdom would be by "sacred explosion". He'd done what preparation he could before leaving Bosnia such as paying off his debts and forgiving others their transgressions against him. But the suddenness of his call was disconcerting. He'd expected, as was the norm, to have days, perhaps more, prior to his act to prepare himself. He'd put aside his cigarettes only the night before and had declined to eat anything then and this morning to purify himself as best he could under this accelerated plan. But the

Imam had assured him that the circumstances would be known to Allah and his sacrifice accepted.

The word "Islam" means "submission" and Zubak was determined to quietly and stoically accept the orders of his leader and the guidance of the Imam. But even in the face of al-Nassef's undisguised annoyance, the young Bosnian stubbornly insisted that he be allowed to make his videotape testament. The camera was set up and Zubak recited verses from the Koran, spoke of the voluntary nature of his act, extolled the virtues and necessity of *jihad* and exhorted others to follow his example. When he was finished, he went to be fitted with the instrument of his "sacred explosion".

Given the asymmetric nature of terrorism, most "suicide vests" are simple devices made from readily available materials. A common explosive combination is hydrogen peroxide, often used as a disinfectant or to bleach hair, for example, and acetone, used in various products, nail polish, for one. Together they form an explosive compound called acetone peroxide. While its availability and economy are a positive, it is an unstable compound which can and often does explode while being compressed or plasticized.

Less unstable and also widely used is a compound called ammonal — ammonia nitrate and coal or aluminum powder. It will not detonate of its own accord and needs an initiator (often a small quantity of acetone peroxide) but it too fits the needs and limitations of terrorist cells lacking the resources to obtain stronger, more sophisticated explosives.

For this project, though, al-Nassef had virtually unlimited resources and so the vest prepared for Mirko Zubak contained the much less readily available but far more sophisticated C4, a relatively stable plastic explosive with the consistency of modeling clay which allows it to be shaped as desired. In this case, it was packed in rectangular shaped pockets inside a thin nylon vest. Five kilograms of it. Approximately 11 pounds. A large load.

C4 also requires an initiator and in that respect as well al-Nassef went top shelf using a Belarus-made IED — not the "improvised explosive device" referred to so often in the present day but rather an "instantaneous electrical detonator" that initiates the C4 within milliseconds of being activated. When that happens, the C4 decomposes into gasses which expand at over 25,000 feet per second and reach temperatures in excess of 1,000 degrees. Normal atmospheric pressure on the human body is approximately 15 pounds per square inch. The force of this blast in the immediate vicinity would be 1.5 *tons* per square inch.

Just after 10:00 AM, al-Nassef led Zubak to the target along a slightly different route than the one he had taken the day before. As they came out of the Quattro Marzo opposite the Piazza San Giovanni and the cathedral, Zubak hesitated at the sight of two yellow school buses parked along the Via XX Settembre just in front of the church. The buses were empty. That meant the children were inside.

Al-Nassef had explained the plan to Zubak only minutes before they left Cottolengo. Zubak was to go up the stairs and into the cathedral and go left to where there was a souvenir shop by the replica of the Holy Shroud. There were frequently visitors standing and watching it but the primary rational al-Nassef had given the young Bosnian for this particular target was that it struck a blow at what was essentially the soul of Torino. Zubak had questioned the propriety of an attack on Jesus whom Islam revered as a prophet if not as the Messiah. But al-Nassef had rejected the concern by recalling to him the Hadith prohibition on depictions of the major prophets and explaining that they were not striking the actual Jesus, only an image — one which was a replica in any event.

Looking across the piazza, Zubak shook his head. "Not the children. I will not meet Allah with that shame on me."

Al-Nassef wondered if these objections were a sign that the boy was losing his nerve. He started to order the young man to proceed but thought better of it. He did not need to bring any attention to them and a few more moments would not matter. He nodded his assent.

After about ten minutes, the center doors at the top of the stairs opened and a procession of about eighty children accompanied by teachers and aides emerged. The adults herded the children together and began to count and arrange them prior to reboarding the buses.

Al-Nassef put his hand on Zubak's shoulder and the young man looked at him. Al-Nassef nodded. The Bosnian returned the gesture, then put his hand into the pocket that contained the detonator and stepped off. Al-Nassef retreated a little way back up the Quattro

Marzo and around a corner of the municipal building and watched as Zubak crossed the piazza to the church.

The teachers had the children fairly well assembled, crowded together in pairs, holding hands, about to get on the buses. The squeaks and squeals of their young voices drowned out the other sounds in the area.

Zubak was still about ten meters from the bottom of the steps to the cathedral and right alongside the children when al-Nassef pressed the duplicate detonator he had in his own pocket.

13

People in the vicinity of the explosion — not the immediate vicinity, of course; none of them survived the blast — reported a sharp cracking, ear piercing sound at the instant of the explosion. Then for several moments, there were no sounds, no movement except for the hovering thick dark, grayish cloud of smoke eddying out slowly from the spot where Mirko Zubak had only a nanosecond before existed. He was no more.

Then, slowly, from here and there faint sounds began. Moans. Crying. Not many.

People began to emerge from the Public Works building opposite the church, the façade of which had chunks missing and jagged holes where windows used to be. The sounds of sirens began to be heard in the distance. The first firefighters to arrive leaped off their trucks and stopped, frozen by the carnage before them.

Zubak had been only a couple of meters away from the children lined up along the near side of the buses. Like him, they were all gone. Blasted into non-existence. Disintegrated.

In contrast, something remained of the adults and children who'd been on the far side of the bus. The vehicle itself has absorbed a good deal of the outward and upward energy of the blast but where the side doors had been lowered to accept storage of equipment, including wheelchairs, the force of the explosion had been funneled and directed underneath where it was intensified by the compression. The result was the people standing on the other side had their lower parts cleanly severed with little visible damage to their upper bodies.

Limbs and other body parts were scattered about. Little legs, hands, smaller pieces of what used to be a living child were everywhere. The scene looked like a madman had gone berserk in a doll factory. Still further out were bigger pieces. Torsos. Heads. The toughest of the firefighters got to work, even as they choked on their own tears.

Mastrota's office on the Via Pietro Egidi was only a block west of the Porta Palatina and close enough so that he heard and felt the blast. He jumped up and made his way out of the building and looked around. Smoke from the burning buses was visible to the east indicating the direction of the explosion. He charged down Pietro Egidi then turned left and ran down the Via della Basilica and across a field. He lurched to a stop when he saw the scene before him.

Like the firefighters, even with all his experiences and all he had seen, he too was unprepared for the magnitude of the slaughter. He stood rigidly, his head bobbing intermittently as his brain struggled to place the scene before him into some context he could comprehend. It couldn't do it. After a moment, he shuffled forward, moving slowly as if in a trance. His foot kicked something on the ground. He looked down and saw a tiny sneaker. The sight of the little shoe somehow personalized the incomprehensible scene before him and magnified and concentrated the horror of what had occurred and the innocence of what had been lost. Mastrota just stood staring straight down until suddenly all the air was sucked out of his lungs as he realized the sneaker still contained a tiny foot.

Public prosecutor Angelo Portolotti was seated at his desk in his office a mere five or so blocks away from the cathedral when he too heard and felt the blast. He jumped up and went to his window but it faced east and south and the cathedral was to the north, so he saw nothing. He picked up the phone and called down to security at the front door but they didn't have any information yet. It was coming in even as they spoke, Portolotti was assured. He ordered them to advise as soon as they had any information and went back to his desk.

Several moments passed before his curiosity got the better of him. He put away the papers he was working on and left his office and headed for the stairs. He walked past the security in the main foyer and out the main entrance on Via Antonio Giuseppe Bertola and turned left toward XX Settembre. Looking north from where the two streets intersected, Portolotti could see the activity in the Plaza di San Giovanni. Between where he stood and the scene of the blast, there was evidence of peripheral damage from the force of the explosion that had been channeled down the relative narrow XX Settembre. More curious than concerned, he began walking north on the Via XX Settembre toward the Piazza San Giovanni.

It took a moment for Mastrota to regain a semblance of his professional demeanor and even then a seething rage simmered underneath. To the south of XX Settembre, at the end of the piazza, he saw the first police arriving. Two Istruttori, city officers, and a single patrol car. The two officers on foot were standing at the edge of the carnage looking around but doing nothing. Similarly, no one had gotten out of the patrol car. Mastrota stepped off quickly and walked toward them. Even before he got to the first officers, more were arriving. Though these were not State Police, Mastrota was well-known and respected and his rank of Chief Inspector was recognized. Mastrota ordered the first patrol car and another that had just pulled up to seal off the Via Quattro Marzo and XX Settembre at the south end and issued orders by radio for another car to seal the piazza at the north. He then instructed the officers on foot to secure the area, particularly where the cathedral backed up against the Royal Palace, and then to assist the firefighters, rescue, and medical personnel on the scene.

An Inspector of the city police arrived and Mastrota informed him of the actions already taken. The Citta Polizia Ispettore concurred. Mastrota then asked the Inspector if the photos of the three individuals which had been sent over the previous day had been circulated among the city police. For the most part they had, the Inspector had replied. Mastrota then asked that some Istruttore circulate the photographs immediately among the bystanders and victims who could and would talk to them before a perhaps important witness wandered or was carried off. In less than ten minutes, one Istruttore found a shopkeeper on the Quattro Marzo who had seen the Bosnian standing opposite her shop with another man. She had noticed them, she said, because they just stood still without speaking for several minutes staring toward the *cattedrale*. The man in the photo had been dressed in a quilted jacket and looked a bit over stuffed, she'd said. But she didn't think it terribly unusual since the weather was still a bit chilly. She'd not been able to identify the other man because he'd worn a hooded sweatshirt with the hood pulled up at all times. She'd looked out at them several times and then noticed finally that the man in the photo was no longer there. She was not looking out when the explosion went off.

A second witness inside the municipal building had been crossing past a window that looked out over the piazza and had noticed — for no specific reason he could recall — the Bosnian walking across the piazza toward the *cattedrale* just before the explosion. Fortunately for the witness, he had passed just beyond the window when the blast went off or he almost certainly would have been sliced to ribbons by the imploding glass. He'd not seen the other man at all. The *Istrutorre* took his information to the city police inspector who called Mastrota over and advised him of what had been learned. The connection made, Mastrota looked at the photo of the young Bosnian for a long moment then stared at the results of the butchery before him. A sound that was something between a moan and a growl escaped from his throat.

At that moment, Portolotti came out of the Via XX Settembre where it opened into the Piazza San Giovanni. He surveyed the scene before him and then his eyes met Mastrota's. The Chief Inspector strode at a measured pace up to the prosecutor. For a moment the two men stared at each other. Then Mastrota reached out and grabbed Portolotti by the front of his shirt and pulled him further into the piazza. Portolotti reacted with surprise and tried to pull back. "What the hell do you think you are doing, Mastrota?" The prosecutor pulled at Mastrota's grip but couldn't free himself as the Chief Inspector dragged him forcefully into the heart of the bloodbath. "I'll have your badge for this," Portolotti threatened but Mastrota didn't release his grip and dragged Portolotti over to what was left of what had most likely been a seven or eight year old little girl. The body lay just beneath the nearest bus, her clothing blown completely away exposing a blackened torso; one leg and one arm was gone, and the face was unrecognizable. At least the head was still attached. Mostly.

Mastrota switched his grip to the back of Portolotti's neck and stepped behind him. With his foot, he jammed the back of the prosecutor's knees causing him to drop to the ground. Then Mastrota pushed Portolotti's face down closer to the remains of the little girl.

"Where are this little one's civil rights, Signore Procuratore? Did she not have a civil right to go to school and be safe? Did she not have a civil right to visit a holy place and feel we would take care of her?" Mastrota placed a knee into Portolotti's back and put his weight onto it, forcing the prosecutor's face even closer to the dead child. Portolotti tried to turn his head away. "Did her parents have a civil right to expect their child to come home from school, Signore Procuratore? Or do they have merely a civil right to identify what's left of their bambina?" Mastrota leaned two-handed on the back of Portolotti's shoulders and spat the words at the back of the prosecutor's head. "What will it take to make you understand, Portolotti? If not this, then what? In God's name, Portolotti, what?" With a final shove, Mastrota stood and looked down at the man. "You want my badge? You come and take it any time you want to try." He walked away.

14

Sunbritech Pit Area
Quay Albert
Monte Carlo

After a continental breakfast at their hotel, John and Katherine decided to walk the distance to the Grand Prix pit area following the same route they'd begun the day before. The streets were already beginning to fill but were not yet as crowded as they'd been the afternoon before. They continued all the way through the Fontvieille Commercial Center, turned right and took the Boulevard Charles III to the Place d'Armes, normally an open plaza bordered by shops and cafés but this day packed shoulder to shoulder with vendors of Grand Prix related merchandise. There they turned right onto the Avenue du Port which brought them to the Boulevard Albert I and the center of the race activity.

The race facilities for the teams were situated along the east side of the Boulevard Albert I which is a curved avenue that sweeps along the harbor of Port Hercule and functions as the closest thing to a "straight" in the layout of the race course. As with all Grands Prix, the teams were positioned in the pits in order of their finish in the previous year's Constructor's championship. The winning team — Ferrari — had finished first and was thus right at the entrance to the pits which was situated just after the La Rascasse turn and just before the Anthony Noghes right turn into the "straight". Sunbritech's facilities were about halfway down, just opposite the municipal swimming pool, La Piscine.

Robbie Foster was waiting for them when they got to the gated and guarded entrance into the teams' secured areas and quickly took them to the Sunbritech facilities and showed them around. Like all the teams, each of the two drivers and their cars on the Sunbritech team had its own set of mechanics and pit crew. John and Katherine had hoped to meet the Sunbritech drivers Derek Morton and Jukka Palonen but that would have to come later. Wednesday of Monaco race week was a day of press conferences and sponsor events and the drivers were off performing some of their non-driving duties.

On one side of the garage a mechanic sat in Morton's car looking at the computer screen set directly in front of him examining the data being transmitted from the components being analyzed at the moment. On the other side of the garage area, mechanics working on the race car of Palonen, the young Finn, were preparing to throttle up the engine — often called the "lump" — to try to duplicate certain stresses encountered under race conditions. They would have preferred the real thing; securing the driver into the car and sending him out on the course but that wasn't possible as the streets that would form the race course were still open to traffic. Only at 7:00 the next morning would the streets be closed off and turned over to the race cars for the Thursday practice. At 18:30 that evening, the streets would be re-opened to traffic and not re-closed again until 7:00 on Saturday morning for morning and afternoon practice sessions followed by qualifying. They would open again Saturday evening and then be closed all day Sunday until after the Grand Prix was completed.

Katherine found herself enjoying John's "kid in a candy store" reactions to their experiences. And the highlight of his morning was when Robbie strapped him into the simulator the drivers themselves used to duplicate race conditions when they couldn't actually take the car out onto the course. But this was no mere video game. As with everything at the highest level of formula racing, the concept was taken and refined and developed without regard to cost until the drivers who actually take the cars out and race them declared the simulators to be as close to the real thing as possible. Even the g-forces — roughly 2.5g as the car accelerates from 0 to 100 km/h in just 2 seconds and 0 to 300 km/h in 8, as high as 6g under braking from high speeds, and 5g or more in lateral load during turns — were replicated into the experience.

After a shaky start involving much forward lurching as he tried to get used to the brakes followed by several "shunts" for a variety of reasons, John got the hang of it — sort of. He never got to race driver level with regard to the optimal "lines" to take through the different stages of the course and didn't match the top speeds of professionals who would reach about 290 km/h coming out of the tunnel. But he did take some of the turns at sufficiently high speed to feel the strain in his neck muscles and he got close to 240 km/h in the tunnel after which, unfortunately, he didn't brake soon enough and "crashed" in the chicane.

John couldn't stop grinning as he climbed out of the simulator and didn't stop even as Robbie handed him a piece of paper purporting to be the bill for the cars he "wrecked" that day. "I make it four significant shunts for the day not counting the chicane, John," Sir Robert Foster said with a sly smile. "With each car costing about $750,000, that would be $3,000,000 there. But then the lump and the gearbox and some other bits are most likely salvageable. So we can take about half off for that. Maybe a bit more out of friendship. Leaving, oh, let's say $1,200,000. And of course that major drama at the chicane at the end there was a total loss. So," Foster mischievously licked the end of his pencil and announced, "I reckon the total at just under $2,000,000 for the day. Fair enough?"

"Sure," John said without missing a beat. "How 'bout I buy the drinks later and we'll call it even."

"Done," Robbie grinned. "Always liked a man who doesn't quibble."

Katherine had also tried the simulator and done quite well but wasn't as enamored of the experience as John had been. Still, she'd done enough to get a sense of the conditions and particularly the g-forces. She started to ask Foster a question. "But how do these.....?" her lips continued to move but all sound was drowned out by the incredible whine of the ultra high performance engine in Palonen's car revving its way up toward 18,000 RPM and back down again several times. At 140 decibels, it could do severe and permanent damage to the human ear in a very short time so Katherine, John and Sir Robert all scrambled to secure the earplugs they'd been issued when they entered the Sunbritech pits.

They exited the rear of the garage where they could speak and hear and Katherine asked her question again. "I was just going to say, how can these cars stay on the track taking the turns at such high speed? Why don't they spin out or fly off?"

"Well, there's what we call mechanical grip; that's basically the adhesion between the tires and the track surface." Foster replied. "But overwhelmingly, it's downforce that keeps them on the road at unusually high speeds. It's all about the aerodynamic package we spend a lot of time and money on developing and..." He stopped as a young dark-skinned man who appeared to be in his mid-twenties rounded a corner and headed for rear entrance to the garage area. "Ah, the horse's mouth, so to speak," he said then called out, "Gamil." He gestured to the younger man to come over.

"Katherine, John, I'd like you to meet Gamil Mukhtar, our boy wonder of aerodynamics," Foster smiled. "Gamil, this is John Cann, a very old and dear friend and his fiancée, Katherine Price."

Mukhtar extended his hand to one then the other and said, "Nice to meet you," to each in turn.

"Katherine just asked me what gives the cars their grip, "Foster related, "and I was about to explain 'downforce" to her but you're the expert so, in a few words, can you help out?"

"In a few words, probably not," the younger man said. He spoke in something reminiscent of a Midlands accent but with a bit more refinement. He smiled at Katherine. "Sir Robert does this all the time. Pretends he thinks the concepts are simple. And actually they are. It's the applications that are complex."

"Well, the simpler you can make them for me, the better," she said. "But I'm just amazed at how fast they go, especially the turns."

"Well, briefly," Mukhtar grinned at Foster, "the idea is that we design the car so that the atmospheric pressure on top of the car is greater than the pressure underneath. We..." he interrupted himself to ask Katherine, "Are you familiar with the Bernoulli effect?"

Katherine shook her head. "Afraid not. Sorry."

"Not at all," Mukhtar said politely. "The Bernoulli effect is simply when air is forced through a smaller space it accelerates and the atmospheric pressure it exerts diminishes. So we design the underside of the car as well as wings and other elements to try to maximize that difference so that under speed, the pressure above is greater and presses down on the car to keep it adhered to the surface. The higher the speed, the greater the pressure. The drivers accelerate into the turns not just to keep up their speed but also to enhance their non-mechanical, that is, aerodynamic grip." He looked at Foster again. "See, simple."

"Sounds like the same concept as lift in an airplane," John chimed in. "Upside down, though."

"Very much so. It's not a precise comparison, but…"

"So if you turned the cars upside down, would they fly?" Katherine asked.

"No, there's more to flying than just lift and the cars are certainly not designed for operating upside down. But, you might be interested to know that, while no one's every tried it as far as I know, in theory, once the cars reach a speed of 80 or 90 mph, they could drive on the ceiling without dropping off."

"Fascinating," she said.

"I always thought so," Mukhtar said with a smile as he turned and entered the now relatively quiet garage. Foster, Price and Cann went back inside as well and, as they entered, they saw that much of the previous activity had stopped. Most of the crew members were gathered at a television set hung high in a corner and were watching the scene of the bombing in Torino.

"Oh, John," Katherine said as she put one hand on his arm. The other hand went to her mouth but her eyes stayed on the screen. Much of the coverage was raw footage and the carnage and devastation was everywhere. "Jesus," John muttered as he absorbed the scene. "Jesus," he repeated. Unconsciously, he and Katherine moved together until their shoulders were pressing against each other. An image of the two of them being in that very place less than twenty-four hours earlier came into his mind and his stomach lurched with the imagining of her loss. He looked at her and saw she was looking at him with the same expression on her face. She put her arm through his and squeezed. He returned the pressure. After a moment, they looked back up at the screen.

Though it had only been a couple of hours since the blast, the Torino television feed to the French network they were watching already had the surveillance photo of the young Bosnian boxed in the lower right corner of the screen. That image meant nothing to Cann. But as the broadcast ran the herky-jerky raw footage of street surveillance cameras in the area depicting the events of the morning, Cann suddenly grabbed Robbie's arm. "Is that digital, Robbie?" he asked pointing at the television. "Can you pause and go back?"

"Yes. Why?" he asked but even as he did so he went over and picked up the remote for the set they were watching and pointed it at the television. "What exactly did you want."

John had moved closer to the screen. "Just go back a little." Foster hit the rewind command. "There. Just there," John said holding up his hand. "Hold it there, will you?" He moved closer still and stared but said nothing. "Can we zoom in?" he asked."

"Not on this set," Foster replied "but…" He quickly had one of the techs make a DVD of the newscast and they took it into the back of the garage where there was a wall of screens and monitors. Foster popped the DVD into one of them and returned to the scene John had asked for.

"There," John pointed at the screen. "See the man at the corner of that building? With the hooded sweatshirt?" Their eyes focused on the image. The frame apparently had been snapped at the precise moment of detonation and the force of the blast had, just for a moment before the man turned away, blown the hood back on the man's head revealing his face.

"Can we zoom in on him?" John asked. Foster did so and the face, while not entirely clear was sufficiently identifiable — at least to Cann — for him to mutter. "Son of a bitch. I don't believe it." Then after a moment, "Yeah, I do believe it. The bastards."

"You know him?" Katherine asked.

John nodded slowly.

"Who is it?"

He didn't answer right away, then said slowly, "Rashid al-Nassef."

"Al-Nassef?" Foster interjected. "I thought he was dead."

John didn't answer for a long moment as he continued to stare at the screen. Then finally he said, "So did I, Robbie. So did I."

15

"I've come across al-Nassef twice," John began after they had all moved to Sir Robert's office. "The first time was in April 1979. I was doing another secondment to Sayeret Matkal at a base a couple of miles south of Nahariya."

Because of their backgrounds, Katherine and Robbie both knew that Sayeret Matkal was an elite Special Forces unit of the Israeli Defense Forces (IDF). For her part, Katherine had learned a lot about Cann's background in the course of being a senior partner at Loring, Matsen and Gould and had learned even more since she and John had gotten together. As an engaged couple with the added dimension of being fellow warriors— not to mention they both had astronomically high security clearances — they felt no need to hold anything back. They didn't "swap war stories" on a regular basis but when a subject came up, they spoke freely.

Sir Robert, as a friend and professional colleague, knew some of it but not everything that Katherine knew. For example, they both knew that Sayeret Matkal's best known operation was Operation Thunderbolt, the long distance rescue of over 100 hostages being held at Entebbe, Uganda airport after the hijacking of Air France flight 139 by the PLO in 1976. Katherine knew — Foster didn't — that John had been there.

"On April 22, 1979," John continued, "four terrorists including Rashid al-Nassef set out in a fast inflatable boat from Tyre, that's about 12 miles or so north of the Israel-Lebanese border and headed south." He stopped and there was contempt and anger in his voice. "If you listen to the terrorist version of things, they'll tell you the mission objective was to strike at the military base we were operating out of." He gave a derisive snort. "Bull. No way would they come at us. We could fight back. As always, they were after the innocent and undefended.

"They came ashore in Nahariya. That's about six miles south of the border and a couple of miles north of where we were. But keep in mind Nahariya also had a police military academy, a coast guard installation, a naval intelligence presence, and was HQ for a warship group. There was no shortage of military targets. But these "heroes" headed directly from where they landed on the beach to an apartment complex across the road. On the way, they ran across and murdered a single isolated patrolman whom the pro-terrorist press, of course, described as a pitched battle with an entire patrol.

"Anyway, the four got into the apartment building and began shooting it up. In one of the apartments was a family of four, parents and two kids, girls, two years old and four years old. The mother managed to hide in a crawl space with the two year old while the father tried to reach an underground shelter with the four year old. Al-Nassef and his thugs grabbed them at the door to the apartment and shoved them back inside. They figured there had to be others in the apartment and ransacked it and shot everything up searching for the rest of the family. In the crawl space, the mother could hear everything going on in the apartment. When the two year old started to cry, the mother had to put her hand over her mouth so they wouldn't be heard. After a while, the terrorists took the father and the four year old down to the beach. Al-Nassef shot the father in the back and then made the four year old watch as he held him down in the water to make sure he was dead. Witnesses said — and al-Nassef himself has bragged about it — that he wanted the sight of her father dying to be the last thing she ever saw."

"God, the blind hatred…" Katherine said in disbelief.

"Yeah," John went on. "And then he made sure it was the last thing the little girl saw. He shoved her down onto the rocks and bashed her skull in with the butt of his rifle. Over and over."

No one said anything for a long moment.

"Then," he continued, "as if that's not bad enough, once the mother was sure the terrorists had left and went to get out of the crawl space, she realized her little two year old was dead. She'd accidentally suffocated her trying to keep her quiet."

The three remained silent, emotions roiling; sadness, rage, disgust. And an infuriating sense of helplessness.

"The local forces reacted quickly. We headed out, too, but it was over by the time we got there. I saw the scene for myself, though." His look grew distant for a moment as he remembered. "The father was right on the edge of the water. The little girl was…" He made a gesture that said, "well, you know".

"Two of the terrorists were dead. Al-Nassef and one other were captured. I remember looking at the Israeli captain and asking why these guys shouldn't just have an accident. Or die trying to escape. He looked at me and it was the saddest look I have ever seen. I don't know whether he was sad for what had happened or sad because he couldn't execute them on the spot. But finally, he said, 'That would make us like them.' " John grimaced and shook his head. "I've never bought into that. Never understood that. I don't know that he believed it. I think he was just echoing the party line. But…

"Anyway, they were tried and convicted. Israel doesn't have the death penalty — though there was talk of passing a special bill for this case — and Al-Nassef ended up receiving five consecutive life sentences plus 47 years — a total of 542 years." He looked at Katherine. "End of story, right?" In response, she raised her eyebrows as a question.

"Wrong," he answered his own query. "Five years later, Israel released him in a prisoner exchange."

"Incomprehensible," Sir Robert said shaking his head. Katherine was doing the same.

"Five years. And the first thing he did was hold a press conference in which he bragged about killing the little girl. Called himself a hero for it." He looked at Foster. "Incomprehensible indeed.

"The list of his atrocities goes on and on. He was involved in the *Achille Lauro* hijacking." Cann didn't have to remind the others. In October 1985, in concert and with the full support of Yasser Arafat's Palestine Liberation Organization (PLO), a pack of terrorists led by al-Nassef hijacked the Italian cruise ship *Achille Lauro* off the coast of Egypt. In the course of the hijacking, al-Nassef personally shot a 69 year old, wheelchair bound American and pushed him and his wheelchair into the Mediterranean. Why? Because, he said, the old man was inciting the other passengers to resist. So they killed him and threw him into the sea.

It was a standoff for a couple of days. Both Delta Force and SEAL Team Six were on the scene and prepared to launch an assault when the Egyptians struck a deal with Arafat — who'd been allowed to posture as a peacemaker on the networks — to give the terrorists safe passage in return for the release of the ship and the hostages. As they were being transferred from the cruise ship to the shore, in keeping with the blustering arrogance of terrorists once they feel safe, al-Nassef had insisted on a "victory lap" around the Port Said harbor before being taken to the airport and boarded onto an Egypt Air 737 for a flight to Tunisia.

To his credit, President Ronald Reagan would have none of it and ordered the Sixth Fleet in the Mediterranean to prevent the terrorists escape. The USS Saratoga launched its F-14 Tomcats, along with a number of support aircraft which eventually found the 737 off the Libyan coast. The fighter jets moved into position in total radio silence and with no lights whatsoever, taking positions in front, behind, and to the sides of the Egyptian airliner. Then, they switched on the lights and hailed the 737, directing it to follow them without hesitation or deviation. The Tomcat pilots made it clear to the Egyptian pilot that he could bring the plane down safely as directed, or they would bring the plane down for him. He complied.

In a statement that belongs in the *chutzpah* hall of fame, Arafat called America's actions "an act of piracy".

The F-14's forced the Egypt Air 737 to land at Sigonella Airbase in Sicily. On the ground, the Prime Minister in the Italian coalition government, the pro-Arab head of the Italian Socialist Party, Benito Craxi, refused to allow the Americans to take the terrorists to the United States and called out the Italian military to prevent the transfer. To avoid the dreaded "international incident", Craxi was allowed to take custody of the terrorists on the condition they be held for trial.

Infuriatingly, however, Craxi, or officials in his government, blindly, blithely, proceeded to accept al-Nassef's ridiculous assertion that he'd not been on the cruise ship at all during the hijacking and murder of the disabled American but had only joined the party at the airport as a "facilitator".

They released him. Outright. Unconditionally. Then and there.

It was little consolation to anyone that the Craxi led government collapsed six days later in direct response to the manner in which the Achille Lauro hijacking and the terrorists had been handled. Al-Nassef remained free to continue his murderous ways.

"From Italy, he went to Yugoslavia. Then Libya, Tunisia, Morocco. He moved around a lot. And while he kept his profile low, his signature was on a number of attacks over the years. Finally, after wearing out his welcome in a lot of places, in the mid-nineties, he turned up in Baghdad under the protection of Saddam Hussein."

"Ah, that must be the Saddam Hussein who never had any ties to terrorism, right?" Katherine asked sarcastically.

"The very one," John said wryly. "No ties at all. Unless you count Abu Abbas, Abu Nidal, Hamas, the PLF, the guy who designed the bomb that brought down Pan Am 103 over Lockerbie and a lot of others including plenty of al-Qaeda. And don't forget the terrorist training camps at Salman Pak complete with mock-up airliners to practice hijackings on." He shook his head. "Anyway, there al-Nassef stayed. At least I'm not aware of him being spotted anywhere else. But over the years, there were any number of terrorist attacks that had his fingerprints all over them. And he played a central role in Saddam's blood payments of $25,000 to the families of homicide bombers. Reputed to have his fingers in the oil-for-food business, too.

"The second time I came across al-Nassef was in 2003, right after we went into Iraq. I was over there working with the Coalition Provisional Authority (CPA) on the judicial system that was going to be put into place. In March 2003, right at the beginning of the invasion, our Special Forces guys had nabbed him in the desert west of Baghdad." John frowned. "Heading toward Baghdad, not away." He shrugged. "Good get, though. I sat in on some of the initial interrogations."

"Did he remember you from Nahariya?"

"He didn't appear to. It's not like I was participating directly in the interrogations. I was just an observer. One of several and usually from a distance. Or reading transcripts." He grew pensive for a moment. "I thought about going up to him and saying, 'Remember me?' But since I couldn't do what I really wanted to do to him, I gave my information to the interrogation team to use against him. We had him for the *Achille Lauro* and were going to charge him with anything else we could find where we had even a hint of jurisdiction over him. Though he didn't care. Was as arrogant as ever. Bragged that we'd never keep him. "Turns out he had a point." He gave a humorless laugh. "Or thought he did, anyway. It seems as soon as the Palestinian Authority (PA) learned we had him, they raised holy hell. Said we had no right to hold him and demanded we release him, turn him over to them."

"On what grounds?" Katherine asked.

"Oslo Accords. 1993. Part of the deal reached between Arafat and Peres was amnesty for all acts committed prior to 1993. The fact that the US wasn't a party to the Accords — just a witness to the signing — didn't bother them. They wanted their hero. That's how they refer to al-Nassef to this day, as a hero, even with what he did to that little girl. And all the others."

"But you didn't give him up," Foster said.

He shook his head in the negative and then cast a sidelong look at Katherine. "Not that your boys and girls at the State Department didn't want to."

"They're not my boys and girls," Katherine responded sharply. "Never were."

"I know," John acknowledged. "But State was adamant about handing al-Nassef over. Argued hard for it. Said, well, okay, technically we weren't a party to the Oslo Accords but, in the interests of peace, why don't we release him in the spirit of it. Let bygones be bygones. Little four year old girls with their heads bashed in are just old news and shouldn't stand in the way of peace. I made sure Garner and later Bremer both knew all the details about Nahariya and the little girl. I'd like to think that helped the Coalition Provisional Authority (CPA) and DOD stand their ground against State. Nothing happened either way. It was a stalemate until the following March." He looked at Katherine then at Sir Robert. "Then all of a sudden it was announced that al-Nassef had died. In custody. Of natural causes." He made a face.

"What did you think?" Foster asked.

"That it was about time. Good riddance. He got off too easy. All of the above."

"But did you believe it at the time?"

He shrugged. "I suppose it struck me as a little odd. There'd been no talk of his being sick or anything. But stuff happens. I wondered if maybe an interrogator had gotten a little too enthusiastic. But that didn't bother me. More like wishful thinking. But, no, I didn't really question it. Until now."

"How sure of the ID are you, John?" Katherine asked him.

"Very. You don't forget a man like that. I…" Suddenly Cann's face drained almost completely and a stunned expression appeared on it. "Oh shit," he said in a quietly desperate voice. "Oh, shit. Oh, no."

Katherine looked at John with concern. She'd seen him in tough situations and under a lot of stress but she'd never seen him look like this. "What is it?" she asked reaching a hand out toward him.

John said nothing and continued to stare straight ahead as if looking at something in the distance. Katherine put her hand over his and squeezed.

"John," she repeated. Then again. "John." She gave his hand a sharp tug. Finally he looked at her and spoke. "Yesterday," he said slowly. "As we were leaving the square. Outside the cathedral. There was this guy standing on a corner. Hooded sweatshirt. Just like the one al-Nassef was wearing in the surveillance tape. I couldn't see his face but...there was something about him."

"You didn't say anything."

"I really didn't home in on it. It was just a feeling. Barely that. Sort of like a *déjà vu* kind of thing. But not *déjà vu*. I can't explain it."

"You think it was al-Nassef?"

"Yeah. I don't know. But…same sweatshirt, hood up so his face was hard to see… And he was in the square where the bombing took place this morning." He looked at Katherine with an agonized expression. "What if it *was* him? I sensed something but I ignored it. I should have trusted my instincts. Those kids might still be alive."

Katherine moved her hand up to his forearm and rubbed slowly as she spoke. "No, you can't take that on yourself. You can't. "

Cann didn't respond right away but eventually put his own hand on top of Katherine's and nodded.

"She's right, of course, John, absolutely," Foster said. He reached for the phone. "In any event, I think we need to let our Italian friends know who they're dealing with."

16

Polizia di Stato Questura
Via Egidi Pietro
Torino, Italy

Ispettore Pietro Mastrota sat staring at the photographs spread before him on his desk. Several were stills taken from the same surveillance tapes that Cann and the others had watched on television. Like Cann, Mastrota focused on the man in the hooded sweatshirt knowing instinctively that this man was at the center of the morning's atrocity. Unlike Cann, he didn't recognize him. And, unfortunately, since, like Cann and Foster, most of the world thought that al-Nassef was dead, Mastrota found no match or reference in the active terrorist database.

He did, however, see the resemblance between the man in the surveillance photo and the man captured on a security camera inside a small gift shop that sat just down the road from the guard shack that straddled the Italian-Swiss border at Lavena Ponte Tresa. The gift shop happened to be owned by the *sindaco* (mayor) of the *comune* of Lavena Ponte Tresa and, as such, was the center of municipal business in the town. And, because of its *comunale* function, its security images were automatically transferred into a nationwide intelligence database. Which meant that the images taken in Lavena Ponte Tresa were available to and part of the FERET (Face Recognition Technology) database into which the surveillance images of the Torino blast had been quickly entered after retrieval. The Bochum-based software program performed its function and immediately called a match.

While at first glance, the tragic and violent scene at the Ponte Tresa border crossing had looked like the aftermath of a violent sexual attack and an attempt at self-defense just as al-Nassef had intended, it was a difficult interpretation for the townspeople and investigators to accept. The Italian guard's lecherousness had been well known but nowhere in his demeanor or background had there been a history or any indication of violence. His relatives, while distraught at his death and equally bereft at the loss of the nice young Swiss girl, angrily maintained that the obvious scenario was just not possible and, yet again, castigated both the local and regional authorities for the oft-complained of lack of security cameras at the outpost. The camera inside the gift shop was there to deter shoplifting and, in its municipal capacity to record citizen behavior at meetings but no one had ever really noticed the clear shot in the background of the road running past the security structure. Until now.

Mastrota studied the series of frames that showed a black sedan stopped at the crossing, the Italian guard behind the vehicle, the man then outside of the car. No gun was visible in the images but body language indicated duress as the two guards were herded toward the shack. There followed two images of the man as he returned to the car which was facing south toward the gift shop—and the camera. It was the full face capture as the man left the shack that had triggered the FERET match.

The phone on Mastrota's desk buzzed once. He picked it up and heard the voice of Vice Commissario Giorgio Catrone. "My office, Pietro. Now, please."

He went up one flight and half way down the hall. When he entered Catrone's office, he saw the Assistant Commissioner toss the sheaf of papers he was holding in his hand onto the desk. "What were you thinking, Pietro?"

"About the bombing?"

Catrone peered over his glasses at the Chief Inspector. "About Portolotti."

Mastrota shrugged. "I wouldn't say a lot of thinking was involved. I..." He spread his hands wide.

"Assaulting a prosecutor? He has initiated a complaint. If he has his way, you will be disciplined."

"If he has his way, I will probably be shot."

"True. But, fortunately for you, we took that out of the disciplinary code some time ago." Catrone smirked. "He wants you suspended. Immediately, pending an inquiry."

Mastrota sat forward. "You can't take me off this," he said pointing generally in the direction of the Piazza San Giovanni. "I've already got a lead on the man who I think was the bomber's minder. At the least.

"Explain."

Mastrota brought out the images of the man in the hooded sweatshirt and the man on the video from the Ponte Tresa border crossing. "Assuming the computer match is correct, and I do, at this point, what we have is that this man," he tapped a forefinger on the border crossing image, "entered Italy at the Ponte Tresa checkpoint and," he moved the finger to the Piazza Giovanni surveillance photos, "was also at the bombing this morning. My theory, and I'm only just beginning to form a working theory, is that this man brought something in through Ponte Tresa — the explosives, presumably? — and when it looked like his cargo might be discovered, killed those two guards and made it look like an assault and self-defense." He spread out a series of images. "See the sequence, where everything seems to be calm until the guard moves to the rear of the vehicle." He looked up from the image at Catrone who nodded his agreement.

"So we have him here and here," the Vice Commissario nodded at the two sets of photos. "If it's the same man."

"Of course it may not be," Mastrota said defensively, "but the FERET system is very good and I concur with the match." He spread his palms. "It's a start anyway. Something to build on." Mastrota knew that, from the start of an investigation, you had to have a coherent theoretical whole to test even seemingly isolated bits of information against. To be sure, a working theory would need constant adjustment and reevaluation as the bits came in — and often the theory would have to be chucked and a new one constructed — but a scattershot unorganized approach was far worse.

"So now all we need to do is fill in a beginning, a middle, and an end."

Mastrota saw the irony. "Exactly. The rest is all questions. Where was he before Ponte Tresa? Where did he come from? What has he done while in Torino? Was today's bombing the entire plan? If so, what was the motivation?"

"For terrorists, many times the motivation is the carnage itself." Catrone shook his head.

"Or is it possible that today's work was just a diversion?"

"A diversion," Catrone repeated, the images of the massacre still fresh in his mind. "Good God."

"I mean why the others? There are supposedly several of these so-called martyrs?"

"Do we know how many?"

"We have photos of three. We know where one is," Mastrota said, referring to the young Bosnian. "Or was. And we have photos of two others. We have heard talk of more. A couple perhaps. But we have no further information on that."

"So five in all."

"Perhaps. We can't be sure."

"So, what's next as far as your investigation goes?"

"I'm not suspended?"

"I'll never repeat it but I'd like to do the same thing to Portolotti myself," Catrone smiled. "Keep a low profile. Stay out of his way." He folded his hands in front of him. "Where are you going to start?"

"Lugano. Our guy was coming south and Lugano is the first major city north of Ponte Tresa, less than 15 kilometers on the route 398." Mastrota shrugged. "It's a reasonable first guess. And it's all I have right now. Plus Lugano's not exactly clean when it comes to terrorism."

Catrone knew exactly what Mastrota was talking about. Even with the changes in Switzerland's banking laws, particularly after 9/11, it still remained a bastion of secrecy. And Lugano had been and remained a center for money laundering and fundraising for al-Qaeda, the Muslim Brotherhood and other terrorist organizations. As such, it made Lugano that much more viable a supposition as a starting point.

"I concur with that," Catrone said. "It's the best we have right now. Go with it. What about here in Torino."

"We're focusing on Cottolengo. All our informants are being pressed to find out everything they can. We hear that the arrivals —

the martyrs — have been taken initially, at least, to a residence behind the mosque. But we've not been able to confirm that as yet for ourselves. We're trying to do that without attracting a lot of attention."

"Yes," Catrone agreed. "Try to stay under Portolotti's radar, for the moment at least."

"That's fine with me," Mastrota concurred.

"Are we looking beyond Cottolengo? Or beyond Torino? Do we even know if they're still here?"

Mastrota shook his head in the negative. "No we don't. We're circulating the photos we've got. This one," he pointed at the surveillance photos of the man in the hooded sweatshirt then redirected his finger to the array of the others, "and the three 'martyrs' we knew of. Two now, minus the bomber. The photos are going out nationally. Interpol, too. Television and other media. And we're calling in all the surveillance footage from airports, railway stations, toll booths. The odds are that someone will see something but, right now, we need that break."

"Well, let's get on it. Keep me posted."

Mastrota stood and turned to leave.

"You mentioned your informants before, Pietro," Catrone said. "You had an informant you called Taglierina, no?"

Mastrota caught the past tense and nodded warily. "Yes. She was the one who snapped the photo of the bomber. If we'd had more time, we might have put it to good use."

Catrone nodded slowly. "She was fished out of the Po a little while ago. She'd been tortured."

Mastrota cursed, then crossed himself. "She just wanted to help," he said with a weary sadness. "She came to us. Said she didn't like what was happening in the mosque and didn't want the world to think all Maghrebi were extremists." He looked at Catrone. "I want this man. These people, Vice Commissario. I want them in my grasp." He held up his hands in front of them, curved as if wrapped around someone's neck.

"Then let's find them, Pietro. Anything you need to do it, let me know."

17

Immediately after the explosion, al-Nassef had pulled back into a doorway on the side of the municipal building opposite the cathedral and taken a black golf-style cap from inside his sweatshirt, placed it on his head and pulled it down low over his eyes. He also reversed the sweatshirt itself leaving the hood on the inside so it looked like a patterned windbreaker. Then he walked calmly back up the Via Quattro Marzo to the Via Milano and down to the parking garage on Via Guiseppe Garibaldi to which he'd moved the black sedan earlier that morning. He paid the charges and drove the car out of the garage, turned right then left and then left again on the Corsa Vittorio Emmanuel which he followed in an easterly direction until he crossed the Po. Then he turned right to connect to Highway 20 which took him south out of Torino.

As he had done on the drive from Lugano to Ponte Tresa and then on to Torino, al-Nassef avoided the major throughways. Rather than taking the Autostrada A6 south and then A10 west, he opted for the smaller rural Highway 20 which ran south through the Piedmont, cut through the northernmost corner of France, and then reentered Italy and continued on to Ventimiglia on the Mediterranean coast.

The trip was uneventful until the roadblock. The *Colle de Tenda* — *Col de Tende* in France — is the high mountain pass that runs from Cuneo in the Italian Piedmont to Tende in France and separates the Ligurian Alps from the Maritime Alps. A tunnel of more than three kilometers was dug under the pass in the late 1800's but al-Nassef eschewed that "shortcut" and stuck to the windy and tortuous surface road. He didn't like the confinement of tunnels. Not because of claustrophobia but simply because they eliminated options. Once in, one was in until it ended. Like bridges. Which was another reason he had not wanted to take the east-west A10 which ran along the coast and was cut out of the side of the steep cliffs that plunged to the Mediterranean. The A10 consisted of tunnel after tunnel cut through the rock separated by bridge after bridge all the way to the French border at Menton.

Al-Nassef had passed Limone Piemonte in Italy and was approaching the French border with Tende on the other side. The road was particularly serpentine at an elevation of over 1000 meters when he rounded a sharp bend and came upon a long line of cars stopped in the roadway. That was unusual. Unlike the situation at the Swiss-Italian border, France and Italy were both members of the European Union and there should have been no border checks or formalities of any kind. Looking along the line of cars in front of him, al-Nassef could see no uniforms or official looking vehicles but the road curved sharply again only a hundred meters or so ahead. He couldn't know what lay beyond. His hand drifted down the right side of the seat and touched the Sig P229 that was just under it but the situation didn't call for it — yet. He made the decision to leave the weapon there — for now — as he climbed out of the car and walked toward the spot where the line of vehicles disappeared around the bend.

He'd passed about a dozen cars when he heard the sound of a motorcycle coming up behind him. He immediately regretted his decision regarding the Sig but there was nothing to be done for it now. He turned to look back and saw the two-wheeled vehicle, green with a white stripe down the fender, coming down the wrong side of the road. It neared and then stopped beside him.

"*Dov'e il vostro veicolo, signore?*" the officer asked, scanning up and down the line of cars.

Al-Nassef pointed back to where his vehicle was in the line of stopped cars.

"*Dovete rimanere a vostro veicolo, signore.*"

Al-Nassef explained that he didn't know he had to stay in his car. Before walking back, he asked the officer what was going on ahead.

The officer, a member of the *Corpo Forestale dello Stato* — Forestry Police — gave al-Nassef a long cold look before he deigned to offer a brief explanation that there was a work crew ahead clearing trees and limbs from the steep embankments running up and above the roadway. Then he simply pointed a finger at al-Nassef's rental car and flipped his head in that direction. *"Va, signore. Immediamente, per favore."*

Al-Nassef was back in his car for only a few moments when first one vehicle and then others began to appear in the opposite lane heading toward him. After more time passed, the line of cars on his side of the road began to move. Moments later, he finally crept around the bend that had hidden his view of what was happening and saw the crews above him doing just as the Forestry officer had said. As he passed the work area, he saw the officer astride his motorcycle chatting with some of the road crew.

Al-Nassef crossed into France and then again into Italy and continued without further incident to Ventimiglia on the Liguria, the Italian Riviera. At Ventimiglia, he got on to the A10 highway heading west which became the A8 when it crossed into France. Al-Nassef stayed on the A8 until he was just past Monaco then exited and drove toward the village of Col le Bermasse. There, rather than driving straight to the Hotel Palais de Revere, he drove to a free-standing wooden building on a side street just up from the village center that had been retained some time earlier for use in the operation. It was an out-of-use service station with a large bay for vehicles in the middle and small rooms on both sides.

The large windowless overhead door in the center was secured by a padlock for which al-Nassef had the combination. He released the lock, raised the door and drove the black BMW sedan in. The area was large enough to hold several vehicles but the only other thing inside was an ambulance. Al-Nassef parked the car next to the ambulance and got out. Off toward one side of the large open area at the rear there was a square piece of metal set into the floor with an iron ring on one end. Al-Nassef lifted the trapdoor and looked inside at what was essentially a steep earthen ramp leading down into a long rectangular space, now covered, formerly used by mechanics to work on the underside of cars.

He went back to the BMW, opened the trunk and, with some difficulty lifted the container out. Using a hand truck left for the purpose, he wheeled the container down the ramp and to the far end of the covered space. Then he turned and quickly exited up the ramp and closed the trap door. He stood for a moment mentally examining his body for any unusual sensations. He had been assured that the brief proximity to the container would do no harm but he still wondered. Finally, feeling nothing out of the ordinary, he locked the building and left.

It was a short walk to the Hotel Palais de Revère which despite its name, was anything but a palace and barely warranted its two-star rating. But luxury and ostentation were not a priority and al-Nassef had chosen it precisely because it was so nondescript.

As soon as he was settled in, he set up his laptop. The hotel, not surprisingly, didn't have wireless access but al-Nassef wouldn't have used it if it did. Even with the elaborate system of chat rooms and email drops at his disposal, he still relied on the modem-enabled encrypted satellite phone for optimal security.

Mastrota and Catrone had been off by one in their estimate of how many "martyrs" had originally come to Torino. There had been six, not five, to begin with — the Pakistani Brit had gone unnoticed. With the demise of the young Bosnian in Torino, there were now in fact five "martyrs" left not counting al-Nassef himself — who had no intention of becoming a martyr in any event.

Now, al-Nassef set out to check that the others were where they should be. Months before, as the operational team members had been recruited, vetted, preliminarily trained, and finally made an irrevocable member of the mission team, each had been provided with a laptop computer and trained in the use and access of a secured manner of contact. Al-Nassef turned on his own computer and, one-by-one, canvassed the martyrs to see that everyone was where they should be.

Xhelal Chani and Rozafa Chani, the Albanian husband and wife, and their 18 month old son, Luan, were in Ventimiglia. Their reservations were at the Villa Colline Pedemontana an upscale five star hotel with a view from its southeast-facing rooms of not just the Mediterranean but also of Monaco in the distance.

Neither of them liked being at the villa. For Xhelal Chani, it reminded him of the self-indulgent and dissolute environment he had experienced in his years in Tirana, the capitol of Albania. A highly intelligent boy, his potential had been recognized at an early age by the Stalinist Albanian authorities and he was taken from his rural roots and sent to the best government schools in Tirana.

After the repressive dictator Enver Hoxha died in 1985, there was a slight lessening of the oppressive restrictions with which Albanians had lived for so long but the communists retained a strong hold on the country. Over the ensuing years as the liberalization of Albanian society continued, Chani remained on the fast track initially within the regimented bureaucracy but later in privatized, semi-capitalist business.

But he was never happy about it. He watched in disgust as Albanian society, at least in Tirana and the other large cities, reacted to the removal of what had been universally considered the most repressive regime in the west, if not the world, with an absence of restraint that crossed over into the wanton. Alcohol flowed more than freely, women paraded around in mini-skirts and other indecent attire and sex was as common as a handshake in some circles as far as he could see. As a devout Muslim, Xhelal looked at these behaviors as not just ill-advised or immoral, but as blasphemous. Ultimately, when he was in his early thirties, he could take no more and he made the decision to return to his roots and the ways of his forebears. A marriage was arranged for him and he returned to the mountains of northeast Albania and took Rozafa as his bride. He knew she was young and he was very pleasantly surprised to see she was quite pretty. Soon she gave him a son.

But it was still not enough. Over time, his view of the world went from dissatisfaction to loathing which eventually became self-loathing based on the fact that he continued to be a part of it. That perception evolved into a decision to move on to the better place that was paradise. And the quickest way to paradise, he knew, was *jihad.* It was, in his mind, a blessing to his wife and son that they would be allowed to accompany him. He didn't ask. There was no need. Unlike the whores in Tirana, Rozafa knew the place of a woman.

From birth to the present, Rozafa's life had been determined, manipulated and strictly controlled by the absolute patriarchal dictatorship that constituted the fundamentalist Albanian family. Everything she did — and did not do, like go to school — was intended and calculated to ingrain in her that her sole purpose in life was to serve and obey the men. Her father was, of course, paramount but only slightly subordinate to him were uncles and other males of the extended almost tribal structure of rural Albanian society.

Then at the age of 16, she was married to Xhelal. That was two years ago. She'd had no say in the matter, of course, and in fact hadn't even known she was to be wed until shortly before the ceremony. To the observer, she'd appeared pleased and excited. Because that was what was expected of her. And she had, to the best of her ability, always done what was expected of her.

Martyrdom was expected of her now. She accepted it. More accurately, it would never have occurred to her to question it. She would go where her husband led her and right now, that was the Villa Colline Pedemontana in Ventimiglia which Rozafa didn't like either. Her rural roots and severe upbringing made her uncomfortable with the attentions and ministrations of the staff and her ingrained reticence made her perfectly willing to keep to herself for the duration of the visit. Even so, and despite al-Nassef's admonitions to *not* draw attention to themselves, they had done precisely that within hours of checking in.

The Villa Colline Pedemontana had an Olympic-sized swimming pool. Xhelal went down and saw there were no guests using it so he went back up, dressed himself and the boy, Luan, in speedo-type bathing trunks and went down for a swim. Rozafa was allowed to accompany them but she sat well back from the sides of the pool dressed head to toe in a long skirt, a jacket and headscarf which was also wrapped across the lower half of her face.

For a time, they remained the only ones at the pool but eventually another couple came down and settled into lounge chairs on the other side. When the newly arrived woman removed her bikini top and lay back in the chair, Xhelal stared and, despite his resentment, felt a tinge of arousal. Worse, the man, also dressed in a brief speedo, got up from his chair and walked around the pool toward the diving board. To get there, he had to pass right in front of Rozafa who dutifully turned her eyes downward. As he passed, the man politely said, "Madame" which caused Rozafa to reflexively glance up. She immediately realized her mistake and fearfully looked over at Xhelal to see if he had noticed.

He had.

Xhelal Chani suppressed the impulse to loudly order his wife back to the room. He picked up Luan and carried him out of the pool as he gestured with his head for Rozafa to come at once. As he waited at the entrance to the pool area for his wife to join him, he glared at the figure of the other man calmly swimming laps in the pool. When Rozafa got to where he was, he grabbed her arm tightly and roughly shoved her ahead of him and the boy. He despised this place and the people in it. They would stay in the room until it was time to move.

In the adjoining dining room, two female staff members who had watched the scene unfold looked at each other and shook their heads in disgust.

William Gallacher, the Scots lawyer, was also where he was supposed to be. Mostly. He was in Menton, another Riviera resort city, this one just over the border inside France. And, while he could well have been taking some sun in the seaside café attached to his hotel on the Promenade Du Soleil, he was not. Instead, he found his way to the rougher side of town for a few beers with the type of crowd he had never stopped preferring. Indeed, even though he was an otherwise devout Muslim except for the lagers, he was a walking example of the fact that while you could take the boy out of Possilpark, you couldn't take the Possilpark out of the boy.

Gallacher had been born and raised in Possilpark, a section of Glasgow that sits north of the River Clyde. It is one of the poorest areas in the entire United Kingdom and has one of the highest crime rates in all of the UK. His father, whoever he was, was never around and his mother meant well and tried but had no idea how to control the boy she'd been left to raise alone. As a result, Gallacher's early upbringing was an Oliver Twist sort of tale though Gallacher himself was more of a cross between Jack Dawkins and Noah Claypole. Extremely bright with a capacity to be thoroughly engaging when he wished and possessed of a compulsion to bully, he ultimately ended up in the profession for which he was best suited. The law.

That unlikely eventuality came about despite his less than humble origins when his mother became involved with Anwar Riad, a lawyer who often defended Muslims accused of charges related to terrorism. Indeed, hiding behind a slavishness on the part of authorities to political correctness, Riad was famous for confronting, even berating the judges before whom he appeared and condemning trials he lost as farcical and a tragedy for justice and freedom of speech. Gallacher, who was seventeen by then, already had a deep-seated distaste for judges which meant that his admiration for the man who would do such a thing was immediate and intense.

Riad did not treat Gallacher's mother all that well but then neither did Gallacher. But the older man, recognizing the teen's potential as well as his fundamental disaffection with the society into which he'd been born, cultivated him in the ways of the world and of Islam. And even though Gallacher's initial involvement in Muslim life was superficial and even cynical, over time the beliefs and concepts, including the concept of jihad had internalized. He was truly a *shahid*. He did hope, however, that, in addition to the more well known rewards promised to the martyrs, paradise might have a publick house or two.

Karlijn Bleeker, the Dutch teacher, had been born into a devout Catholic family in the city of Heerlen, a community of over 200,000 inhabitants located in the southeast corner of the Netherlands where Holland, Belgium and Germany come together. From her earliest years, Karlijn was obsessed with the religion into which she had been born to the point that even the parish priest expressed concern with her parents that the child should have broader interests in life. But nothing dissuaded the young girl from her consuming preoccupation with the idea of someday becoming the bride of Christ.

It was in her teens when the idea that the "wedding" might be more symbolic than real caused her to rethink the depth of her commitment. Or rather, to begin to consider that there might be another object for it. She found Islam. And threw herself into it as much if not more than she had her Catholicism.

Like Gallacher, Bleeker was in Menton. Unlike Gallacher, she was adhering strictly to every tenet of Islam and was staying in a rented apartment just off the main thoroughfare of Avenue de Sospel leading into the center of the city. Al-Nassef's GPS confirmed she was where she was supposed to be.

Rafiq Mukhtar was in Roquebrune-Cap-Martin which sits on the last promontory heading south along the French Riviera just four kilometers away from Monte Carlo. Gamil Mukhtar's older brother was no convert to Islam. He had been born into it as a third generation Pakistani citizen of Britain and had embraced it as obsessively as Bleeker had initially embraced her Catholicism. For their part, Mukhtar's family considered themselves to be good Muslims and faithfully observed the tenets and obligations of their religion but that was not enough for Rafiq. He breathed, ate, and slept every aspect of Islam and would not allow himself or others the slightest deviation. It was this unassailable intransigence which led him at the age of eighteen to request — no, demand — he be sent to one of the strictest *madrassas* in Pakistan. His family had heard nothing from him since. Which was how he preferred it. He lived by Islam and would, very soon he prayed, die by it.

All appeared to be in order. Al-Nassef closed out the secure computer program and went to a website that purported to sell used goods on consignment by auction. He had a list of items, different for each day, on which he would enter a bid. The amount of the bid would be seen by those for whom it was intended. And they would know what message the amount conveyed. This day's item was a rather drab furniture suite for which Al-Nassef bid 470 Euros.

In Tehran, the aide monitoring the online auction site saw the offering made on the specific item in the specific amount by bidder AG. He brought the message into the office of the Revolutionary Guard General who read it in silence. After a moment, his lips tightened in what might have been a smile.
"Excellent," he said mostly to himself. "Everyone — and everything — is in place."

18

Several years earlier
A clandestine location
Somewhere in Iraq

Rashid al-Nassef had had no objection in principal to the trade.

He'd been held at the secure detention facility at Baghdad Airport for almost a year since the invasion but that wasn't going to last forever. He knew the US soldiers had begun holding prisoners at the abu Ghraib facility and he wouldn't particularly care to go there, even though there was no question the soft Americans would never approach the degree of inhumanity that was reached on a daily basis under Saddam Hussein. And on a couple of occasions, his interrogators had hinted at his being transferred to the facility at Guantanamo Bay in Cuba. That was possible, he supposed. Neither was a desirable option — not that it was up to him — but either one would be better than what he would have done to prisoners in his custody.

But the crimes for which the Americans were holding him had taken place years before. He was, he knew, not being held as a prisoner of war but as a criminal. Indeed, he stood indicted and would be tried for the killing of the foolish old man in the wheelchair who'd tried to incite the other passengers on the cruise ship to rise up against him and his men — and, al-Nassef had been warned and threatened on many occasions by his so-called interrogators, on as many other charges as his captors could come up with.

He sneered at the prospect knowing he would be turned over to the civilian authorities in the United States where he would go into the American judicial system with its laughably slavish devotion to their quaint concepts of civil rights and due process. Where he'd be treated as innocent until proven guilty even though he had bragged on numerous public occasions about his heroic actions and his pride in what he had done. He had examined the American system and knew he would be provided with a legal team which would consider it their ethical duty — the irony was inescapable — to do everything in their power, legally or, in some cases illegally, to help him escape the charges. So that, no matter what, the process would go on for years. And, he laughed again to himself, it was the American people, whom he had sworn a blood oath to destroy, who would be paying for all of it. Amazing, he thought to himself. How did such a people ever gain the prominence they had? No matter, he thought eventually. It would end.

But as it turned out, none of that happened. He'd been made aware by the contact from the US State Department that his release had been sought from the beginning of his captivity by the Palestinian National Authority and others and he had also been made aware by the same contact that the US State Department favored his release. It was, and he said so frequently, a laughably transparent attempt to gain his trust. But he would play out the string and show the invaders his strength.

He was a hero. He knew he was. And was gratified that his people knew he was. But the Palestinians, in the world order of things, had nothing to offer to the United States to trade.

Iran, however, did have something to trade and they made the State Department an offer it couldn't refuse. Or at least one that it didn't want to refuse.

Iran has had a nuclear program of sorts since the Atoms for Peace program of the fifties but after the Iranian revolution in 1979, contracts with Western Europe, notably France and Germany were abrogated and monies on hand were seized. Further development of Iran's nuclear program foundered until Russia stepped in to help in the nineties and the early 2000's. Then in 2002, evidence was unearthed of previously unknown facilities in Natanz and Arak which appeared to be dedicated to processes not related to peaceful nuclear use. Ever since, the US, Western Europe, and the UN had sought unsuccessfully to gain access for the International Atomic Energy Agency.

So what would Iran trade for al-Nassef? Simple. The desired access. Or more accurately, the West's ability to announce it had achieved such access without contradiction from Iran.

In the world of diplomacy, words speak far more loudly than actions. And for the US to get a public assurance that the IAEA would be allowed to inspect Iran's enrichment and heavy water facilities, was the kind of preening moment for which Foggy Bottom lives and breathes. The fact that many of the striped trousers set knew full well that the inspectors would see only what the Iranians wanted them to see was irrelevant. That's how the game is played. Diplomacy did exactly what it was expected to do.

But it wasn't an entirely one-sided bargain, of course. The State Department decided it was to be no mere pushover, insisting that the release of al-Nassef be hidden from the world. The Iranians said, in effect, "sure, whatever". And in this regard as well, there was no great illusion that the secret would be kept forever. But State had its moment of glory.

Initially, the leadership of Iran actually kept the secrecy part of the agreement. Iran is good at such things. The world knows that the Islamic Republic is the largest state sponsor of terror in the world. Iran knows that the world knows and, indeed, takes pride in the designation. But to publicly revel in the title, as it did so privately, or even to acknowledge it, was not the way the game was played either. Deniability. It allowed Iran to publicly express outrage over the designation all the while laughing up its sleeve at the West's pathetic unwillingness to do anything about it.

Another thing that everybody knows and no one does anything about is that Iran operates a virtual relocation program for fugitive terrorists in the name of Muslim brotherhood. Shia. Sunni. It doesn't matter. In its virulent antipathy towards the West, Iran vigorously subscribes to the principle that "the enemy of my enemy is my friend". In this aspect as well, for the dual purposes of tweaking the West as well as forestalling consequence, Iran keeps its harboring of terrorist luminaries under the radar. It was thus with Rashid al-Nassef.

Like the others, he was kept under close tabs, almost akin to house arrest. A sort of velvet prison, but it was a prison nonetheless. And he chafed under the restraints and the lack of activity and purpose. But most of all, he hated the lack of attention. The cessation of his celebrity. The world no longer knew of him even as he knew what was happening in the world. And every time he read or heard of an action — the London subway bombings, the train bombings in Mumbai and Madrid; as relatively simple as they were, he particularly liked the kidnappings of Gilad Shalit and then Goldwasser and Regev which led Israel and Hezbollah into all out war — it rankled.

Al-Nassef missed the action. Wanted a piece of it. Time after time, he devised and submitted action plans to his minders to be sent up the chain of command. But he never heard back on them. In truth, most never got very far up the chain. The plans were always well thought out, usually complex, and al-Nassef knew they were more than feasible. But among the lower ranks especially, through whose hands the schemes had to be passed, there was often a substantially limited level of imagination accompanied by a justifiable fear of having one's fingerprints on a plan too grandiose to be accepted.

Then two things happened in rapid succession. The French ambassador to Syria was assassinated by Hezbollah while on a trip to Beirut. The leader of the Lebanese parliament was also killed in the car bombing and may have actually been the primary target. But, to France, the assassination even if a mistake was inexcusable. The French protested to Syria and Iran. Syria, the dominant force in Lebanon for years, denied all involvement. Iran, the creator, supplier and banker to Hezbollah rejected the protest outright, in somewhat less than diplomatic terms essentially telling the French to "piss off".

In the past, political and economic considerations may have caused France to leave it at that but the recently elected new French government was determined to make it clear there was a new *shérif* in town, so to speak. The matter was turned over to the Action Division of the Direction Générale de la Sécurité Extérieure, DGSE. Jokes and snide comments about France and French combativeness aside, make no mistake, DGSE is not an organization to be taken lightly. And its Action Division, which plans and carries out clandestine operations, is to be flat out feared.

That part of the Middle East containing Syria and Lebanon had, in colonial times been in the French sphere of influence and France still considered itself a major player. Its intelligence services, including the DGSE, were active in the region and quickly confirmed to the French government's satisfaction that the killing of the Ambassador had in fact been planned and executed by Hezbollah. The world had known for years that Azzad Musleh, a legendary and revered Hezbollah leader, was living under Syrian protection somewhere in Damascus but, given its contacts and agents, DGSE knew precisely where. As Musleh was getting into his car one morning not long after the Beirut assassination, a bomb obliterated man and vehicle.

Hezbollah was stunned and outraged. Not just at the death of their leader but at the sheer effrontery of the West replying in kind to one of their terrorist atrocities. Hezbollah suspected and Iranian intelligence confirmed the French were behind it.

Then concurrent with the Musleh operation, DSGE provided firm intelligence to Israel which confirmed what the Jewish state's own intelligence had suspected but was not certain of. That a nuclear facility was being secretly developed with Iranian help in northeastern Syria and, far more significant, was about to begin the fueling process. Within forty-eight hours of receiving the French intelligence, before the nuclear materials could be introduced on to the site, Israel bombed it out of existence. Strangely but tellingly, there was little reaction from any of the countries involved. Israel said nothing unlike in 1981 when they destroyed the Iraqi Osirik reactor south of Baghdad. Even the Syrians said nothing which was a pretty clear indication that what had been taken out in the attack was something the players didn't want the world to know existed. Word leaked out that numerous Syrians had been killed in the raid along with a number of North Koreans. But it was not, as might be believed, a North Korean operation. It was an Iranian project farmed out to Syria as much for diversionary reasons as for security. The world may not have known what had happened but Kim Jong-Il did and he was livid. The dead North Koreans had been sent to Iran, not Syria. And Iran had sent them on, lent them to Syria without the knowledge or assent of the North Koreans. It was a profound embarrassment and created a rift that threatened significant elements of Iran's own nuclear development program.

Now the mullahs as well as Hezbollah were incandescent with rage. A call went out for plans of response. It didn't matter how complex, how difficult, even how outrageous they might appear on paper. A mighty blow had to be struck against the West and especially the *kafir* who had had the audacity and insolence to strike back.

The call trickled down and now, those who had previously been reluctant to appear to foster ideas and concepts that might be seen as outlandish, felt free to pass on several of al-Nassef's plans. One of those in particular stood out among the rest. It had everything that was desired. Imagination. Boldness. Inhumanity. It would strike fear into the West in ways not yet seen. Mass casualties. Cruel death. For the world to see. And enormous economic damage and the destruction of one of the West's foremost examples of decadence.

And so it was that Rashid al-Nassef was summoned from his velvet prison to Tehran to meet with very high ranking officials of the Islamic Republic of Iran and Hezbollah. And from there he went to Doha. And on to Zurich and Lugano and Torino. And Monaco.

19

Mastrota had contacts in police organizations around Italy, Europe and, in some cases the world. As far as Lugano was concerned, he had worked with elements of the Ticino Cantonal police on a number of criminal cases. More importantly right now, he had also worked with the Federal Security Service (FSS) on several occasions including aspects of the international investigation into money laundering and terrorism following the 9/11 attacks in New York City.

He placed a call to Gioele Nef, an investigator on the staff of the Swiss FSS Unit for Protective Intelligence and Evaluation. After accepting Nef's condolences on the tragedy of the morning, Mastrota gave the Swiss officer the information he had on the bombing that morning as well as the murders of the border guards at Ponte Tresa. As he spoke, he emailed the surveillance photos of the man in the hooded sweatshirt and at the border crossing. He also emailed the photos of the three "martyrs", adding that the youngest one, the Bosnian, was the apparent bomber. The Italian acknowledged it wasn't much and explained why he was looking to Lugano as a starting point, which, other than the geographical proximity, was essentially that he needed to start somewhere. Nef solemnly promised he would give this search the highest priority and get back to Mastrota as soon as possible. As soon as he hung up the phone, the Swiss turned back to his desk and began punching keys. There is a popular conception that computers have substantially changed the investigative process. They haven't. But they have surely speeded it up.

Nef. like Mastrota, ran the photographs through an active terrorism database and came up empty. Al-Nassef was considered dead and the others had been chosen in part precisely because they had no previous exposure on operations of any sort. Obviously, there were few repeat performances for "martyrs".

Then Nef ran the photos through a more generalized database which also ran the same FERET technology as Italy used. For the moment, he limited the search to Lugano and its canton, Ticino. But he got a hit. A traffic camera on the southeast corner of the intersection of Via Ginevra and Corso Elvezia caught the subject's face as he had leaned forward looking up and out through the windshield apparently checking the street signs. Then the subject made a right turn onto Corso Elvezia. Nef checked the date and time stamp of the first traffic photo and then brought up on the computer the images snapped by a sister camera on the northwest corner of the same intersection at the same time and several seconds beyond. Just as he'd thought, that camera caught the image of the car, a silver Renault Laguna, as it headed in a southerly direction away from the intersection. In so doing, it captured the car's license plate.

Nef immediately punched the license number into another database and quickly learned that the vehicle was a Eurohire rental car. He knew that, in this instance at least, a phone call to the car rental company would yield more information than the computer and learned within minutes that the car in question was based at the Zurich Airport location. He was also told that the car had been hired beginning 2:17 PM the previous Wednesday under the name Hafez Samrallah and had been dropped off in Milan at 12:26 PM the following day. That part didn't seem to fit but Nef moved on. Was there airport arrival information on the car rental contract? After a brief pause, the rental company advised that, according to the contract, Mr. Samrallah had arrived on Qatar Airways Flight 063 out of Doha at 1:46 PM that same day.

Nef returned his efforts to the Lugano/Ticino area and entered the license number of the car into the traffic database looking for other matches for the number on other traffic cameras. He came up with several which effectively tracked the car's progress to the northeast of Lugano. The last image was one of the car turning onto a steeply sloped road that had a prominent sign at its base that read "Private!"

Nef took the GPS coordinates from the traffic camera image and entered them into Google Earth. In a moment, the image from space appeared on the screen and Nef zoomed in on the location. As it became clear what he was seeing, his fingers pulled back from the keyboard as if it had become hot and his hands hovered motionless for a long moment. He was looking at the villa of Ottah Younis. He knew it well. And he knew that Ottah Younis was off-limits.

In 1988, Ottah Younis was one of the founders of the Al-Istilah bank which placed its headquarters in Lugano but from its inception had branches around the world. All of the principals of the Al-Istilah Bank were members of the Muslim Brotherhood, founded in Egypt in the 1920's and out of which had grown numerous other organizations like Salafist Group for Call and Combat (GSPC) and al Qaeda. Indeed, the motto of the Muslim Brotherhood is *"Allah is our objective. The Prophet is our leader. Qur'an is our law. Jihad is our way. Dying in the way of Allah is our highest hope."* Nonetheless, Younis and the others always maintained that their endeavor with Al-Istilah had nothing to do with terrorism and everything to do with service. The bank operated as a normal banking institution but also as one with the stated purpose of providing Islamic banking services in accordance with Sharia law, the principal stricture of which was its prohibition of *riba* or interest.

Al-Istilah also conducted business involving the money transfer process called *hawala*. By its very nature, *hawala* allowed an individual or entity to transfer money to someone else whether as a medium of exchange in a commercial transaction or as the provision of funds by one party to another for whatever purpose without leaving a paper trail of any kind. Such a transaction takes place between intermediaries called *hawaladar*. Initially, someone approaches a *hawaladar* and advises he wants to send a sum of money to someone else in another part of the world. The first *hawaladar* contacts a second *hawaladar* in the receiving location and between the two they arrange for the second *hawaladar* to disburse the desired amount to the ultimate recipient. The first *hawaladar* is, as a result of the disbursement, indebted to the second in the amount of the sum disbursed plus any agreed upon fees. But, and this is essential to understand, no money has changed hands between the actual parties and no money has crossed international borders. The two *hawaladar,* who have an ongoing relationship, keep their accounts between them and will settle up in their own time and in their own way, perhaps by a purchase of goods or, frequently, by the first *hawaladar* simply performing a like service for the second *hawaladar* at some point in the future.

Hawala is prohibited in some countries, including, ironically, India where it originated. But it is not illegal in most countries in the West and was not illegal in Switzerland. This was so even though the possibilities for mischief under the *hawala* system were legion and obvious. And, in spite of its assertions that its activities were universally benign, Al-Istilah was in fact engaged in mischief in a very big way as a conduit of funds from numerous sources around the world to terrorist organizations — including Al Qaeda.

Even so, Switzerland has always been proud and protective of its banking laws and system and the putatively impenetrable secrecy that is its hallmark. Switzerland also has a deep-seated and well-cultivated ability to turn a blind eye to the consequences of its commitment to such secrecy. So the Swiss authorities turned a consistently deaf ear to the concerns of other western countries who feared and suspected but could not prove conclusively that the funding for atrocity after atrocity may have been going through Al-Istilah.

Then came 9/11. The United States turned up the heat by, unilaterally if need be, freezing funds of entities it determined to have sufficient contact to terrorist activities and that included Al-Istilah. The U.S. and it allies also exerted heavy diplomatic and financial pressure on other countries to the extent that even the Swiss, reluctantly, had to make accommodations to it.

Al-Istilah was shut down and its assets frozen. A full-scale federal investigation was initiated but went nowhere. The professionals in the Federal Security Service were prepared to pursue the evidence diligently but the politicians and bankers threw up every roadblock they could and the investigation floundered. Then, after some five years of investigation, the Swiss Federal Criminal Court stepped in and roundly criticized, not the government, but the Federal Security Service for "persecuting" Younis and other principals in Al-Istilah without bringing charges. Not only were the freezes on funds lifted — the ones held in

Switzerland, anyway — but the Court ordered the Swiss government, particularly the FSS, to leave Younis alone.

Gioele Nef had worked on the task force investigating Younis and Al-Istilah and was convinced they were as guilty as sin. But the FSS couldn't touch him. For now, anyway. And he knew it was at least arguable that bringing Younis to the attention of another investigative force — even one of another country — could be a technical violation of the order of the Federal Criminal Court.

But then the images of the tiny body parts he had seen on the television screen that morning crept into his mind and wouldn't leave. He turned and picked up the phone.

Ispettore Pietro Mastrota also knew who Ottah Younis was. And knew that such a connection raised the stakes as well as the parameters of the situation. The morning's blast in the Piazza San Giovanni was horrible enough on its own but the addition of participants at the level at which Younis and his peers acted raised a frightening specter indeed.

At this point. they knew the man in the hooded sweatshirt had flown into Zurich from Doha, Qatar last Wednesday, rented a car upon arrival and driven straight to Ottah Younis' villa in Lugano. Nef advised Mastrota that, according to the rental company, the car rented in Zurich had been turned in at 12:26 PM the next day in Milan, as per the contract. The Swiss commented that this seemed not to fit but Mastrota disagreed, pointing out that the car in the Ponte Tresa photos was not a silver Laguna but rather a black sedan, perhaps a BMW. Also, it couldn't have been the man they were looking for that dropped the car off in Milano if at roughly the same time on the same day, Monday, he was at the Ponte Tresa border crossing busily committing a double murder. The Italian, however, would have the Milan car impounded immediately — he prayed it hadn't been rented out in the interim — and gone over closely for any clues or further information.

So, the two men continued to theorize, it would appear that their suspect switched cars at the villa, leaving in a different vehicle than the one he arrived in. Nef related that the traffic camera at the foot of the road leading to Younis' villa caught three vehicles leaving the estate on that Thursday morning. Though the angle of the camera didn't photograph the license plates, one of the three was a silver

Laguna, likely the one dropped off in Milan. Of the other two, one was a blue, late model Peugeot 607 and one was a black BMW 3 Series sedan, very much like the car in the Ponte Tresa surveillance photographs. Definitive? No. But another connection.

"So." Mastrota recapped, "our subject leaves Lugano and less than an hour later kills the two guards at Ponte Tresa." He explained to Nef his theory that the killings had to do with something the man was transporting in the trunk of the car. "And." The Inspector went on, "we have nothing that would rebut the reasonable presumption that he continued directly on to Torino which would have put him here by Thursday afternoon." Both men knew there was as yet no specific information at this point as to what the man would have been doing in Torino between last Thursday afternoon and this Wednesday morning. But the time frame fit with the arrivals of the martyrs and led up to the bombing which also fit his theory.

Mastrota thanked Nef for his efforts. "You've given me some good information here that I can work with. I'll keep you posted."

"Well, if you do, please do so quietly, Pietro," the Swiss cautioned. "I broke a few rules here and would rather not have that fact too widely known."

Mastrota nodded. "And for that I thank you even more, my friend."

20

Marco Tridente was now *Capo della Polizia di Stato*, Chief of the Italian State Police. That made him Mastrota's boss, Catrone's boss, everyone's boss as far as the State Police were concerned. But in December 1983, he was a mere Captain, in charge of an elite unit of the Italian Special Forces known as NOCS, the *Nucleo Operative Central Securezza* (Central Operations Security Service) which rescued a British General who had been kidnapped by the *Brigate Rosse*, the Red Brigades while on a visit to the US Army Installation at Vicenza, Italy. Accompanying the 12 man rescue part was a British Special Air Services Captain named Robert Foster.

In the course of the rescue, the unarmed Captain Foster happened to be standing next to Captain Tridente when one of the Red Brigades terrorists pulled a hand grenade out of his shirt and went to pull the pin. Foster grabbed the terrorist's hands and held them immobile, pressed against his own body, until the NOCS force could subdue the man and get the grenade free. Captain Tridente was understandably grateful and had remained friends with Foster over the ensuing years. So, now, decades later, when Sir Robert Foster called, *Capo della Polizia di Stato* Marco Tridente took the call at once.

Polizia di Stato Questura
Torino

In his office, Mastrota was still in the process of integrating the information he'd gotten from Nef into his own increasingly voluminous notes when the phone on his desk rang. He looked at the caller ID and saw it was Vice Commissioner Catrone on the line. He quickly punched up the call.

"Ispettore Mastrota," Catrone began unusually formally, "I am on the line with Capo della Polizia di Stato Tridente."

Mastrota unconsciously sat up a bit straighter and lifted his chin.

"Buon giorno, Ispettore Mastrota," Tridente said assuming the lead in the conversation. "Before we begin, let me advise you that this is a conference call. On the line with me is Sir Robert Foster, formerly of the British SAS," he said pointedly. "He and I have worked together in the past and I consider him a good friend."

"Si, Signore."

"Also with Sir Robert on the line is an American, John Cann. I do not know Signore Cann myself but Sir Robert does and he vouches for him as a man to be respected and trusted. We will speak freely with them. *Capisci, Mastrota? Catrone?"*

Both men acknowledged they understood.

"Commissario Catrone has brought me up to date on what you have learned about this morning's terrible event, Mastrota, and what you are doing. You have done well in a very short time."

"Grazie, Signore. And I have more."

"Go ahead."

Mastrota related in detail what he'd learned from Nef. When he was done, Tridente exhaled audibly. "Disturbing," he commented after a while. "To say the least. This matter appears to be far broader than we thought. Good work, Mastrota. And Signore Cann has valuable information for us as well. Including an ID on the man in the hooded sweatshirt. Mr. Cann?"

Mastrota gripped the phone tighter and leaned forward.

"Rashid al-Nassef," Cann said. "Also known as Abu Ghadab."

Mastrota knew the name but… "Al-Nassef?" he questioned. "The *Achille Lauro*?

"Yes," Cann said firmly. "But he has a lot more than the Achille Lauro on his hands."

"Wasn't he supposed to have died several years ago?" Catrone asked.

"That's what was reported. But I'm certain the man in the surveillance photos is al-Nassef."

"How can you be sure?" Mastrota asked bluntly.

Cann related the details of his past dealings with al-Nassef. "I've been face to face with him," he concluded "Seen him up close and seen him in action. It's al-Nassef." He also described his possible encounter on Tuesday evening in the cathedral square.

"But you are not as certain the man in the piazza was al-Nassef, yes?" Mastrota asked.

"No I'm not. It's partly instinct. Gut feeling. But I can't help wondering if I'd checked it out, looked harder, maybe it would have made a difference."

"We can understand that feeling, Signorc Cann," Tridente said. "But as you said, you didn't see his face. And he was supposed to be dead."

"I know," Cann answered. "But still…"

"Let's concentrate on what we have," Tridente went on. "Do we have any idea where al-Nassef is right now, Mastrota?"

"No, Signore. There is even some talk on the street that the 'martyrs' have left Torino. But we just don't know."

"Martyrs?" Cann asked. "Plural?"

Tridente gave Cann and Foster a rundown on what Mastrota was referring to. "This bomber," the Capo continued, "the one whose picture was also on the television, was the last to arrive. Only yesterday, one of our informants photographed him being received at a leather goods stand in the Porta Pallazzo."

"Si, signore," Mastrota said stiffly. "And it appears that she has paid for it with her life."

"Yes," Tridente said angrily. "Catrone has advised me of this. "We cannot allow such a thing to stand," the Capo said firmly. "What specifically are you doing?"

"We have increased the pressure on the street, Signore," Catrone replied, "and I was briefed on our progress just before your call. Word is that two men were seen escorting a man who fits the bomber's description away from the Porta Pallazzo yesterday. As far as we can determine, that occurred about the time *Taglierina* sent us the photograph of the bomber. Then, according the witness statements, the same two men returned shortly thereafter and led *Taglierina* herself away. That was the last time she was seen alive."

"Do we know who the two men are?"

"The descriptions fit two men known to us and photo ID confirmed it. They are two of Imam Bagy's henchmen."

No one spoke as they absorbed the information. Tridente broke the silence. "So, we have Al-Nassef, one of the world's worst terrorists and we know he was on the scene when the *bambini* were slaughtered. And now we know the bomber was met by Bagy's thugs. Who returned to take our informant away. Who later ended up in the Po. It's time to sweep Cottolengo. The mosque included. Bring in Bagy and his men, Mastrota. On my authority." He hesitated only briefly. "And I am bringing in NOCS." They all knew of Tridente's past with the Special Forces Unit of the Italian State Police. "But you will remain in charge of the investigation, Mastrota. Use them wisely. Starting with Cottolengo."

"Si, signore," Mastrota responded, "but Portolotti will likely interfere as he has done in the past."

Tridente was quite familiar with what Mastrota was referring to. And not in the mood to have it interfere with what had to be done.

"Conduct the sweep, Mastrota." The Capo della Polizia di Stato said brusquely. "I will deal with *Procuratore* Portolotti."

21

Wednesday Evening
Royal Palace
La Rocher
Monaco

"Wow!" John said as Katherine twirled gracefully showing off the clingy floor-length low cut sleeveless gown of dark green that she would wear to the Prince's ball.

"You like?" she asked playfully.

"I do," he said sincerely. "And the way the gold jewelry sets off the green. What's that color called?"

Katherine looked down. "I don't really know. Forest green maybe?"

"I'd call it British Racing Green," John deadpanned.

Katherine just looked at him for a moment. "Yes, you would, wouldn't you," she replied dryly. But then she laughed and turned her back to him. "Zip me up?"

"Do I have to?"

"Yes you do. It's not good form to keep royalty waiting." John did as he was asked and when he was done Katherine turned back and looked him up and down. "And you, sir, look awfully dashing, may I say."

"You may," he replied as she slipped her arm through his and they headed for the door.

The parade of limousines moved slowly in an arc from right to left in front of the guard houses and double entrances to the royal residence officially called the Prince's Palace of Monaco. There were more Mercedes than anything else and a large number of Jaguar and BMW limousines, many of stretch configuration. Even those were overshadowed in many instances by the Maseratis, Aston Martins, Rolls Royces and even one huge stretch Bentley. The distinction for the biggest vehicle went to an enormous stretch Hummer, owned by a Russian billionaire, which barely negotiated the narrow streets of Monaco-ville. While its owner was proud of the statement it made, it was considered quite gauche by many of the guests at the Prince's Grand Prix Ball.

John and Katherine arrived in Sir Robert's relatively normal sized Jaguar XJ8 and were quickly and graciously ushered through the outer entrance and up the external horseshoe-shaped staircase to the reception area in the Mirror Gallery. Sir Robert clearly knew an extraordinary number of the guests and introduced them to luminaries of government and stage and screen in addition to the larger lights of motorsport. Staff circulated around the guests balancing flutes of champagne and hors d'oeuvre on trays.

Even with the glamorous and festive veneer, the morning's bombing in Torino was a recurring subject of discussion and Katherine was in the process of extricating herself from a conversation with a bejeweled woman who was insisting that, "We need to understand what it is that makes these people hate us so."

"No, it doesn't matter what reason they *think* they have," Katherine countered. "No one has a right to do what they've done." Without waiting for anything further she turned away and saw John a few feet from her, also apparently engaged in a conversation he didn't want to be in. She stared at him for a moment before he turned and saw her looking at him. He smiled back and gave a rueful twist to his mouth when the man he was talking fervently tried to drag him back into the discussion. Katherine was still watching him, a bit of a loopy grin on her face, when she realized Stanley Appel had been standing in front of her for several moments trying to introduce a tall, balding, athletic looking man in his forties who happened to be His Serene Highness Prince Albert of Monaco.

"Oh," Katherine started, "I'm so sorry, Your Highness," she said as she took the outstretched hand. "I was just…" She waved her other hand generally and didn't finish the sentence. The Prince smiled at her and glanced over at Cann. Appel explained into the Prince's ear, "That gentleman is Ms. Price's fiancé."

"Ah," the Prince said slowly raising his chin in understanding. He looked back at Price and said, "Well, he's a very lucky man."

Katherine suppressed a chuckle as it occurred to her that she'd been hearing that a lot lately. "I think I'm very lucky as well, Your Highness," she replied simply. More pleasantries were exchanged and then the Prince moved on.

A moment later, Stanley introduced the Prince to John. They, too, exchanged pleasantries and made some small talk before the Prince commented that he'd met Ms. Price a moment before. "You're a very lucky man, Mr. Cann, if I may say so." John looked over and saw Katherine watching with a broad smile on her face as if she knew what the Prince had just said. Cann toyed with the idea of saying "I know, I know," in mock exasperation but didn't. Instead, he merely replied, "Yes, I am, Your Highness." When the Prince walked away, John looked over and sent a wink Katherine's way. She winked back.

The rest of the night was memorable and the ball went well past midnight not including the after-parties in the hotels, homes, and, of course, the yachts. In the course of the evening, Price had had to fend off several invitations from men who all claimed to own the largest yacht in the harbor and, in a testament to gender equality, Cann found himself having to fend off advances from one woman who was less than half his age and later another who could have been his mother. But they had arrived together and would leave together and by the time they got back to the hotel, it was just after 2:00 AM.

Cottolengo District
Torino

The sweep began at 4:00 AM when people are usually at their least alert and most compliant. The force consisting of the municipal police, state police, and several NOCS teams entered the Cottolengo area and secured a multi-block radius surrounding the mosque. The net turned up several fugitives but no one whom they could identify as one of the martyrs. The police took Imam Bagy into custody as well as the two men who had met the martyrs and had taken the flower vendor away. The Code of Criminal Procedures allowed for them to be held for 48 hours for questioning. The law obligated the police to notify defense counsel and the judicial authority within that period — but Mastrota saw no reason to do so right at the beginning. Portolotti did not intervene. He had been called at home the evening before and ordered to make his way at once to Rome for a conference first thing in the morning.

22

Breakfast Room
Hotel Vespucci
Fontvieille
Monaco

In their younger, operational, lives, both Cann and Price had been called upon to be up at any and all hours of the day and there were numerous occasions when they'd gone days without any real sleep at all. But that was then and this is now. And now, neither of them were what you'd consider morning people if they didn't have to be. Add in the late hour at which they'd gotten to bed the night before and the reality was they both had difficulty rousing themselves for the day ahead.

But it was Thursday of Monaco Grand Prix week, the first day of practice and, while the first practice wouldn't begin until 11:00, Sir Robert had plans for their presence in the pits. They ordered a quick pot of coffee from room service to get them up and going and then went down to the restaurant arriving just before the hotel breakfast buffet was broken down. Without discussion, they each headed in a different direction, John for the coffee bar where he picked up two cappuccini while Katherine went to the pastry table and brought back a small plate of croissants, pastries, and butter.

As they settled into their table, Stanley Appel crossed over to greet them. "Is everything satisfactory for your stay?" he asked.

"Perfect," Price replied. "Your hotel is wonderful. Please join us." Cann, mouth full of buttered croissant, nodded his agreement.

"Thank you, I will." Appel called one of the staff over and ordered his second cappuccino of the morning. "If there's anything you need or want, please don't hesitate to ask."

"Thank you, Stanley. Everything's fine."

Appel's espresso arrived and for a moment they were all quiet as they sipped and/or ate. Then Appel said, "Did you enjoy the Prince's Ball last night?"

"Very much," John replied. "It was wonderful," Katherine added.

"Do you know the Prince well?" John asked remembering Appel had made the introductions.

"Yes. I've watched him grow up. I knew his father for a very long time."

"So Robbie said."

Appel raised a single brow and changed the subject. "Speaking of Sir Robert, you'll be watching the practice from the pits, I understand?"

"Mm-hmm," John said swallowing. "I hope I don't break anything.'

"You'll be fine, I'm sure," the hotelier assured him with a smile. "It will be an unforgettable experience for both of you."

"Although what happened in Torino yesterday certainly puts a damper on things," Katherine said.

"It does," Appel agreed, "but, sadly, these things happen with such frequency that we have no choice but to carry on. I can assure you the Grand Prix will recognize the tragedy. A moment of silence and more. But just because we move on doesn't mean we forget."

"Or forgive," John agreed. "and Rashid Al-Nassef's involvement — and Ottah Younis' — certainly raise the ante."

Appel leaned forward. "Al-Nassef and Ottah Younis?"

"You know them?" Katherine asked.

"Al-Nassef, no. I know of him, however." He looked back and forth at Cann and Price. "I have met Younis, though, on a couple of occasions. A rather personable man, actually, considering his activities. How are he and al-Nassef involved?"

John explained how he'd recognized Al-Nassef from the surveillance tape and how good detective work had revealed a connection to Younis. "It's still not clear that Younis played a role in the Torino bombing or that he even knew what Al-Nassef was doing but…"

"But al-Nassef was supposed to have died in US custody, I believe. In Iraq. No? How is it that he's even alive?"

"Good question," John replied. "I suppose the 'how' ultimately really doesn't matter at this point. He is and we see the result." He looked at Katherine. "But I have some strong suspicions and I'd like my curiosity to be satisfied, Kath. You still have friends in high places over at State?"

"I never had friends in high places at State, John. That was the problem. But there are a few people I could talk to. Let me make some calls. You never know."

Hotel Palais de Revère
Col le Bermasse

The complimentary continental breakfast at the Hotel Palais de Revère in Col le Bermasse was significantly less than what the Vespucci in Monaco had to offer, consisting of a table that held a large metal coffee urn, some cups, and a tray of assorted bread and supermarket pastries. Al-Nassef stood by a window in the small room sipping the bitter coffee and glancing from time to time at the small black and white television set that hung on a bracket set high in a corner.

The news program being broadcast got his attention when images appeared on the television screen which he recognized as being the Cottolengo area of Torino. He watched with amusement and gratification as the reporter told of the all out efforts by the authorities related to the blast of the day before — which was now being unabashedly referred to as a terrorist attack. The scenes on the television shifted to images of crowds of people marching in the streets of Cottolengo protesting, according to the news reporter, the bias and prejudice of the authorities for concentrating their search for the perpetrators of the terrorist attack in the Muslim community of Cottolengo.

Then the newscaster continued on that the authorities were particularly looking for "this man" and the two images of him came up on the screen, one of his face being revealed by the blast and the other of him at the Ponte Tresa border crossing. Al-Nassef quickly scanned the room to make sure he was still alone then looked back at the screen with a frown. He could tell how the photo at the site of the explosion had been obtained. But he looked closely at the border crossing image. Where had that camera been? Down the road from the look of it. Inside somewhere. That explained how he'd missed it. He hadn't expected to see his face, not so soon anyway. But he wasn't surprised. Or even upset. Ultimately, he wanted the world to know. And he knew how to deal with it.

When it was first developed, facial recognition systems were more a matter of simple look-alike technology that wasn't much more sophisticated than a computerized identi-kit comparison that matched noses and eyes and mouths. Not so any more. The technology has progressed to a more biometric standard that relies on a comprehensive matrix of the subject face and precise measurements of contours and distances between individual components within the matrix — the distance between the eyes, the shape of the jaw, the width of the nose, etc. As a result, makeup and fake wigs and mustaches simply don't do the trick anymore since the basic features of the face remain constant underneath the attempts to cover them.

As with all developing technologies, as the systems got better, those who wished to defeat them worked harder. Thus the good guys who didn't want to be caught by the bad guys and the bad guys who didn't want to be caught by the good guys had a common goal. Fool the computers. And, with a little thought, it wasn't all that hard. Given sufficient time and motivation, plastic surgery would do it. If at least few days were available to wait for the effects, they also could inject Botox to sag the eyes or alter the jowl line or inject a filler of collagen or some other product to fill out lips or other areas.

For the short term, there were less invasive, less permanent tactics which would operate to throw off the precise measurements of their natural faces sufficiently to deny identification. In time pressed situations such as these, Al-Nassef would use nose plugs to distend the nostrils, athletic mouthpieces to stretch the lips and disrupt the differences between mouth and chin, or the bottom half of a mouthpiece to create an underbite, even sunglasses to prevent measurements in the eye area. He was confident he could move about so long as he took proper care.

Then the images of Gallacher and Bleeker appeared on the television screen. Al-Nassef didn't accept that development with the same equanimity he'd felt seeing his own face. *La'anatullah!* May Bagy be deprived of the blessings of Allah, he thought. And those women who had clearly failed to get this information from the accursed flower vendor. He hoped she truly had suffered before she died.

Al-Nassef brought his coffee back to the room and sat down at the computer. The secure contact system involved each of the martyrs being given a specific URL to access on the web. From the initial website, they could link to a secured site which contained separate hidden links for each of them to access a password protected message board which the martyrs had been directed to check frequently. These were not technically cyber "dead-drops" because the martyrs had the ability to reply but that was to be reserved for extraordinary circumstances. Once a message was received and read, their instructions were to commit the contents to memory and then erase it at once.

Al-Nassef posted messages to all the martyrs, not just Gallacher and Bleeker. They had all received instruction on how to beat the surveillance cameras and the facial recognition software but he knew they didn't have his experience or confidence. So he ordered them to limit their movements to the greatest degree possible, exhorting them to be discreet and patient. And to purify themselves and prepare to be *shuhada*. Their time of glory was near.

23

Commission des Institutions Bancaires Monegasques
Rue des Orangers
Monaco

The streets of Monte Carlo that form the actual race course were closed off for the Thursday practice and vehicle traffic for the rest of the principality was, in a word, impossible. For that reason, most of the businesses in Monte Carlo made the day a holiday for their employees.

On the Rue des Orangers, the offices of the *Commission des Institutions Bancaires Monegasques* were on skeleton staff, one telephone operator, one clerical assistant and one manager and, despite the fact that the rest of the world's banking systems were fully active on this Thursday of the work week, the phones were relatively quiet and the clerical assistant and the manager both found themselves with time to catch up on old business.

The email came in just before 11:00 AM. It had originated in Tehran but there was no way to tell that from the headers and originating information since it went through a series of remailers and mixmasters that stripped the post of all identifying information. It arrived at the computer of the clerical assistant in the office of the Monaco Banking Association just before she left for an early lunch. After her return, she'd worked on a couple of other things before checking the email again. When she did, she saw the entry on the list and the title "Urgent Message" which was entirely self-defeating since almost every bit of spam that came in had something like that in it. But every now and then, such a post was actually important so nothing was ever deleted unread. At first, the assistant didn't catch the import of the post but it soon became clear in spite of the flowery language. She re-read it again, slowly and carefully, a sense of foreboding rising in her with each sentence. She printed it out and took it at once to the manager on duty. He read it:

In the name of God the Most Beneficent the Most Merciful, harken to the words of the Patriotic, the National and the Islamic Resistance of the people of the countries of Arabity who will achieve the greatest victories in history in the name of Allah because our cause is just and our resolve is strong. To the infidel banking institutions of Monaco, lackeys of the continuing imperialist France, and the other slaves of the Great Satan: You hold, against the will of Allah, funds belonging to and committed to the cause of Islam that have been seized unlawfully by the order of the infidels — al-kafir — the bloodthirsty, the tyrant, the despotic, the usurper occupier who is still destroying, mass murdering and displacing millions of the sons and daughters of Arabity. We demand these funds be released within twenty-four hours to the following account: SADEIRTE413/093126-30741. If, upon receiving this demand, you the infidels, the kafir, do not comply and if you continue to act in defiance of the word and the rule of Allah, just as it is incumbent on the faithful of Islam to call upon God for assistance and to make war upon them, so shall we wreak vengeance and death.

Our will is strong and the price will be great if you resist. Do so at your peril.

Commander,
Warriors of Jihad
International Islamic Resistance

The CIBM manager took the email seriously. Even if it were a hoax — and he fervently hoped it was — the rule was that any and every such situation called for immediate and vigorous attention. While a hoax could leave them with egg on their faces, ignoring a real threat could...well, no one wished to have that on their record or their conscience.

Initially the manager couldn't locate his superior who had taken the opportunity to travel to Nice to get away from the crowds and the noise of the Thursday practice. Against protocol, the assistant director had switched his cell phone to 'silent' for his lunch at a small seaside café with his mistress and so did not know of the attempts to reach him until mid-afternoon when he finally checked it.

The manager's stress level rose as time continued to pass without a response from his director and, when he heard the scream of the racing car engines as they burst out of the pits for the afternoon practice session he decided, on his own initiative, to place a call to the Department of Public Security which oversees the law enforcement and security of the principality. Similar to many other examples of the close integration of Monaco and France, the head of the Department is traditionally a senior officer on secondment from the French National Police. The content of the CIBM manager's phone call and a copy of the email worked its way quickly to the desk of Director Girard Bazinet who immediately brought in his head of the Criminal Identity Division which generally operated as the department's liaison with Interpol. By the time Bazinet returned the call to the on-duty manager at the CIBM, the Assistant Director, Sebastien Fouquet, was back at the office and eternally grateful to his manager under the circumstances for his initiative in not delaying the call to the authorities.

"There isn't much specificity here, Monsieur Fouquet," Bazinet began. "What funds are they referring to?"

"It is certainly unclear." the CIBM Assistant Director concurred. "Given the reference to France and to the 'occupier', it may refer to the freezing of specific funds in which those countries played a role or it may well refer to all funds frozen in compliance with the Sovereign Orders. There are many such accounts in many of our member banks."

To its credit, the Principality of Monaco had joined the battle against money laundering and the financing of terrorist activities as far back as April 8, 2002 when, by Sovereign Order 15.319 of His Serene Highness Prince Rainier III By the Grace of God Sovereign Prince of Monaco, it implemented the International Convention for the Suppression of the Financing of Terrorism. Going even further, SAS Prince Rainier III by Sovereign Order 15.321 issued Monaco's own order requiring all of its financial institutions to freeze funds of any person or entity that by any means, directly or indirectly, unlawfully or willfully, provides or collects funds with the intention that they should be used or in the knowledge that they are to be used in full or in part to carry out acts of terrorism as defined in the International Convention.

"We are talking about millions of Euros no matter what, Monsieur Bazinet," the CIBM director continued. "But, as you see, we have no way of knowing exactly what accounts they are referring to."

"What about the account in the message where the funds are to be transferred? Does that tell us anything?"

"The first set of characters tells us the account is in a Tehran branch of the Bank Saderat in Iran. The "SADE" in the bank identifier code tells us it is Saderat, the "IR", tells us Iran, the "TE" tells us Tehran and the "413" simply designates a particular branch. The numbers after the forward slash are the specific account number. By themselves, those numbers don't tell us anything about the account holder. And you can be sure Bank Saderat won't be inclined to be helpful."

"Tehran," Bazinet repeated. He knew that the Bank Saderat — the Export Bank of Iran — had been blacklisted by the United States and a number of other countries on the grounds that it was a major conduit for the transfer of funds to terrorist organizations throughout the world. "Once again, perhaps we must look to Iran."

"Bank Saderat is a very large bank," Fouquet cautioned. "With clients worldwide. The account could belong to anyone."

"Yes. I realize that," Bazinet said, frustration evident in his voice. "But we must start somewhere. In the meantime, how long will it take to compile a list of frozen accounts?"

Fouquet pursed his lips and shrugged. "It should not be difficult. Not normally. The Grand Prix leaves us with short staff today and also tomorrow in many cases but I've already drafted confidential memoranda to the directors of all our member banks and requested the Director of the Budget and the Treasury to add his signature."

Sovereign Order 15.321 specifically required institutions to release their information under circumstances such as these "notwithstanding the rules of professional secrecy" but the banks, in an excess of caution, never failed to require the "I"s be dotted and the "T"s crossed. "We may be able to have specific accounts and the amounts involved later today. By the morning, surely, I should think. Even with skeleton staffs."

"And to make an actual transfer?"

"Virtually instantaneous. A simple matter of a few keystrokes."

"When exactly did the email come in?"

Fouquet looked at the paper in front of him. "We have it logged in at 10:58."

"So presumably we have until 10:58 tomorrow."

"So it would seem."

"Very well," Bazinet said, "please expedite your efforts. I have meetings scheduled with several ministers and also with His Serene Highness later this evening and again in the morning. We must have your information as soon as possible."

"Will we transfer the funds?"

"That is not my decision, of course," Bazinet replied, "but whoever is behind this, has certainly chosen a good week. Good from his perspective, of course. Bad for Monaco."

24

Hotel Palais de Revère
Col le Bermasse

Al-Nassef relished a plan that went smoothly from start to finish but it was exceedingly rare that one did. That was fine. He also rather enjoyed making adjustments on the fly. Having seen his and Bleeker's and Gallacher's images on the television and knowing they'd been spotted, if not identified, he'd considered whether he should make changes to the plan. For the most part, no, he decided. But he savored the very process of running an operation. It was good to be back in action.

The plan called for Bleeker to perform the initial act of terror in Monaco. It would be the first of three distinct separate attacks, four if you counted the Chanis' directional action separately. But the young Dutch woman's strike would not involve explosives and so she would be quite recognizable after it. For that reason, since it was clear from the images he had seen on television that she had been spotted, he briefly considered reassigning the task. But his options were limited. There was Gallacher but he, too, had apparently been spotted. Mukhtar was needed specifically for his expertise with the *hadduta* — the final act. That left the Chanis. But their assigned mission and the amount of materials involved required more than one person.

He would stick with Bleeker for that first blow even knowing they would recognize her and make the connection to him. Moreover, they would likely suspect that there was more to come. And logic would dictate to them that whatever it was, it would happen in Monaco. The search would thereafter be far more localized and the pressure more intense. So be it. He had been silent for far too long. He wanted to engender fear and wanted the world to know that Abu Ghadab was still to be feared. That was *why* he was here.

Avenue de Sospel
Menton, France

Karlijn Bleeker was a singularly incurious individual. Throughout her entire life, she had wrapped herself inside her religious fixation and actually took great pride in how little of the outside world she'd ever allowed to penetrate her consciousness.

When she'd checked into the pre-arranged furnished rental apartment on the Avenue de Sospel in Menton the previous day, she hadn't even looked around. She'd noted superficially that the apartment had two bedrooms, a bath, and a small kitchen separated by a four-foot counter from a small living room. She'd taken the small packet of belongings she had with her and put it into one of the bedrooms and immediately done *Asr,* her afternoon prayers.

Afterwards, she'd made a short trip to a nearby *bazarette* where she picked some simple food and juices for her meals. She'd spent the rest of the evening meditating on her faith and her upcoming martyrdom and fell asleep with dreams of her reward in paradise. It differed from what a Muslim man would get. For a Muslim woman, if she was married, when she reaches paradise she will be more beautiful than the angels and will serve her husband who will admire her and want her more than the angels and virgins. If she was not married on earth, then the Muslim woman will have a male angel waiting to serve her. For Bleeker, in her dreams, her male angel bore a striking resemblance to the images she'd seen of Christ.

She'd awakened early, did Fajr, then ate sparingly. The apartment had a small balcony with a view of a small waterway in the distance and she spent an hour just sipping juice and thinking of nothing. When that was done, she checked the password-protected website for messages and found al-Nassef's post cautioning her to use care when going outside. He hadn't said exactly what prompted his concern but the reference to surveillance and facial recognition made her review her short trip of the previous evening. She had encountered only the sales clerk, a young girl who had been far more intent on her cell phone conversation than on Bleeker as a customer.

Reasonably secure that she had not been unduly noticed, Bleeker spent the rest of the morning in meditation and reading the Koran. She ate a small meal around 1:00 PM. Later, after *Zuhr* but before *Asr,* Bleeker checked the hidden website for any new messages. There was a new post. She read it several times to commit its contents to memory, particularly the very precise directions to a very precise location. Then she erased it.

She hadn't looked in the second bedroom since she'd arrived and did so now as directed. In the middle of the unfurnished room was a Campagnolo Mirage bicycle and in a neat pile on the floor beside it a full outfit of bicycle clothing. Bleeker picked up the clothing and noted with approval the absence of Lycra or Spandex which would have offended her modesty. Instead, the outfit consisted of loose-fitting full length patrol pants, jersey, jacket, goggles and a full-face helmet which would totally conceal her features. There was also a hydration pack, a backpack-type accessory which held two plastic containers for fluids the rider could drink through a hose that ran from the pack to the mouth. The young Dutch woman, like so many residents of the Netherlands, had spent much of her life on a bicycle and didn't think there'd be much need for hydration on the trip she would take tomorrow. The ten kilometer ride from Menton to Monte Carlo would pose no difficulty.

Promenade du Soleil
Menton, France

Like Bleeker and the other martyrs, William Gallacher wasn't privy to the plan so when he opened and read the email from al-Nassef, he had no reason to know the instructions were, in fact, an adjustment, the one adjustment al-Nassef had decided to make. The message was brief and to the point. He would make his way the next morning, Friday, from Menton to Monte Carlo — originally, he was to remain in Menton until late Saturday. With his face known, it would be better to get him in position before the heightened security that would follow Bleeker's action. Gallacher received very precise directions to the same location that Bleeker had been directed to. But the message also sternly admonished him to arrive before 11:00 AM.

No later. Finally, the post reminded Gallacher that his photograph was in circulation and he was strongly cautioned to be aware of active and passive surveillance. He was also told to bring food and drink for more than a day with him.

Villa Colline Pedemontana
Ventimiglia, Italy

The Chanis had not been spotted or photographed and, in that sense were not on the authorities' radar. But, in spite of their best intentions, for the second day in a row, they came to the attention of others. And this time the police became involved.

Some of the hotel staff, including the women who had watched the scene at the pool the previous day, had noted the absence of the Chani family from any further public view including dinner on Wednesday and, now, breakfast on Thursday. Nor was there any record of room service having been ordered to their room. The Villa Colline Pedemontana was a five-star establishment and proud of its discretion with regard to its guests' foibles and eccentricities. But there was a growing concern that there was something more than a bit odd about the Albanian man. And the situation.

The maitre d' spoke with the day manager who had a word with the head of housekeeping. The two of them took a cart of towels and cleaning materials up to the second floor and down to the room occupied by the Chani family. There was a "Non Disturbare" sign hanging on the door handle but they announced themselves anyway. After three knocks accompanied by the universal announcement of "Housekeeping!" elicited no response, the manager inserted his pass card and tried to open the door. It opened just a few inches, stopped by the security chain. But it was enough for the manager to be able to see Rozafa Chani turn toward him and then turn sharply away. And it was enough for him to see her bruised face and cut lip.

Xhelal Chani stepped to the opening blocking the manager's view.

"We don't require housekeeping," the Albanian said in reasonably fluent Italian. "Thank you." He closed the door.

The manager stepped back and looked at the head of housekeeping. He shook his head and they retreated to the elevator. Back in his office, he picked up the phone and dialed the police. To do otherwise, was not an option for him. He would not tolerate such as this in his hotel.

The police arrived twenty minutes later and the manager took them straight up to the Chani's room. Again, the knocks went initially unanswered and, again, the manager used his card and opened the door to the limit of the security chain. This time, Chani was already standing at the opening. The lead police officer put his arm into the room and showed his identification. Chani examined the document, his jaw muscles visibly clenching, then he nodded and closed the door just enough to remove the chain. The male police officer came in first and stood aside to let the female officer cross the room to Rozafa who was standing looking through the doors to the balcony holding her son. The woman officer went up to her and gently turned Rozafa toward her and looked at her face. First, she shook her head in the negative and then turned back to the lead officer and nodded. The male officer reached out and took hold of Chani's elbow.

"What is happening?" Chani questioned. "I don't understand."

"I believe you do understand, Signore," the officer responded coldly. "How did your wife's face get bruised?"

Chani hesitated, then said, "A fall. An accident."

The officer looked at Rozafa. "What happened to your face, Signora?"

Rozafa didn't understand any Italian and just looked blankly at the officer.

"Say nothing, Rozafa," Chani ordered in Albanian.

The Italian police officer didn't understand the words but the sense was clear. He tightened his grip and pulled Chani from the room. As the men went out the door, the Albanian spoke to his wife again in their native language and told her to stay in the room. "Do not leave the room. I will be back. When they ask about your face, tell them you had an accident." Rozafa watched the men go out the door and said nothing.

Xhelal Chani was in a holding cell for over an hour before the female officer arrived at the police station — without Rozafa.

"She wouldn't leave. She's afraid. Obviously."

"Could she understand you? Did she know what you were saying?" the sergeant at the station asked.

"Two of the housekeeping staff spoke Albanian and translated for me. She was adamant that she would not leave. And will not press charges."

The sergeant shook his head. "Well, we don't need her to press charges. We can do it ourselves. The law allows that."

"Yes. But she says she fell. And that she is susceptible to bruising." The woman officer was clearly frustrated. "And she absolutely will not testify. Since the hotel people can only testify that she is bruised, not how it happened, we really have no case to present to the procuratore." She shook her head yet again.

"Well, we can still hold him overnight. Let him cool his heels in a cell for a while. I have no illusion that it will change him but...," the sergeant, too, shook his head. "At least it will give him some time to think."

Roquebrune-Cap-Martin
France

Al-Nassef made no adjustment to the plan with regard to Rafiq Mukhtar. There was no photograph of the young Asian Brit in circulation although al-Nassef knew that didn't mean there wasn't one. He was fully aware the authorities rarely released all that they had and often held back bits of information for their own use. But Mukhtar was outside the principality and would remain so until Saturday. Moreover, al-Nassef had been most impressed with the young man who had seemed the quietest and most devout of the martyrs and would thus be the least likely to move about or otherwise deviate from the plan. He would be correct in that assessment. Mostly.

25

Limonetto,
Piemonte
Italia

Appuntato Tomaso Cocuzza of the *Corpo Forestale dello Stato* rolled his green and white motorcycle down the main street in small village of Limonetto in the Piedmont region of Italy just to the north of the French-Italian border. It had been a long, grueling twenty-four hours with no sleep and had been topped off with his having run out of fuel a kilometer and a half from home. Not surprising since he had spent much of the last day and night riding the obscure roads and trails of the foothills of the Italian Alps looking for the lost child and her dog. But his mood was good since the search had ended with the safe return of the child to her family. Too often, the result was far more tragic. So he muttered to himself as he plodded down the last stretch of road before he got home, but only a little.

Cocuzza rolled the motorcycle into the small shed that served as a garage and went inside. Cocuzza's wife worked in the physician's office in Limone Peimonte so he knew she wouldn't be home when he got there. He went into the kitchen and found some coffee still in the pot. It would probably be bitter from sitting but he was grateful to be spared the effort of making some himself. He poured a cup and took some biscotti to nibble on before going to bed. He went into the living room and turned on the television and sat down in his comfortable easy chair knowing he probably wouldn't make it into the bedroom. He was that tired.

His head was nodding within minutes but the words of a television newscaster penetrated his consciousness. "The authorities are looking for this man in connection with the terrorist bombing in Torino yesterday morning." Cocuzza had been out of touch and knew nothing of it. His eyes blinked as he looked up at the screen and tried to focus. There was something familiar…

But then the image switched to the devastation wreaked by the bombing. The Forestry police officer, his emotions closer to the surface than usual because of his exhaustion but also because of the nature of his efforts of the last day or so, choked up. One saved. So many lost. He felt profound sadness and real anger at the same time. He closed his eyes to stop the burning but the images stayed vivid until he finally began to drift off.

Polizia di Stato Questura
Torino

In his Torino office, Mastrota reflected on the days events. After hours of interrogation, Bagy had revealed nothing, his responses to questions switching from outright refusals to answer and demands for his attorneys to cryptic and esoteric recitations of Koranic verses. Mastrota had a growing sense that even the Imam had been kept ignorant of the specifics of the attack or any overall plan. That wouldn't preclude his being involved in a conspiracy but there needed to be something more to support such a charge.

The two men who'd been identified as receiving the martyrs on arrival and taking them to the Cottolengo mosque started out as obdurate as the Imam. Then Mastrota used the time-tested tactic of isolating the two and confronting them separately. He showed them pictures of the flower vendor's body which initially elicited no reaction. But when he related the eyewitness accounts of them taking the flower vendor away and advised each one that the other had implicated him in the murder, they broke. Both of them gave up the two women — the Afghani and the Berber — who'd tortured the informant known as Taglierina. Those women in turn were quickly arrested and brought in, all the while screaming about the affront to their modesty to be in the presence of men. For their part, the women, too, held out for a while but then confessed to what they had done and to Bagy's knowledge and involvement. Indeed, they'd stated for the record, he had sought them out and directed them to do it. Mastrota paid a silent homage to the young informant and immediately began to process the charge against Bagy of being an accessory to her murder. He would add a variety of related offenses. Let him call his lawyers now, the *Ispettore* thought. Or Portolotti.

But they received no useful information on al-Nassef. Indeed, except for Bagy, those questioned didn't seem to even react to the name. And Bagy, who had known him only as abu Ghadab, the warrior, had responded with surprise followed by a smirking satisfaction at the caliber of man he'd been privileged to assist.

Mastrota had a beginning. He even had some of a middle. But was the middle the end? Or was there more? He needed a breakthrough.

Cocuzza Household
Limonetto

Forestry Officer Cocuzza slept in the armchair in the living room until the sound of the television re-entered his consciousness and roused him. Half-awake, he clicked the set off and stumbled to his bedroom where he fell into a deep sleep. His wife returned from her job in Limone around six PM and looked in on him before quietly making dinner for herself.

After a time, Cocuzza began to stir. The image of the man he'd seen on the television screen had crept into his dreams and would not leave even as his body tried to shut it and the rest of the world out. But Cocuzza was a good man and a conscientious professional who cared deeply about the public he served and protected and his dedication won out over his exhaustion. He rolled on to his back, his eyes still closed and focused on the face in his mind's eye. Suddenly, his eyes flew open. That was the man he'd spoken to the day before on the Highway 20! The man who'd gotten out of his car just before the traffic began to move. And this man was being sought in connection with that awful Torino bombing. He turned in the bed and reached for the telephone.

Polizia di Stato Questura
Torino

Mastrota would have stayed as late as need be at his office if he had any reason to. But he didn't. He realized with frustration that he could do at home exactly what he was doing at the office. Which was nothing. Or to be more precise, nothing new. He knew he was just going over and over the same sparse information he had without discovering any new information or reaching any new conclusions. He was gathering his things to leave when Catrone called with the information that had been provided by Appuntato Tomaso Cocuzza.

The ID seemed strong and placed al-Nassef on Highway 20 well to the south, just this side of France. Where was he going? Mastrota could think of nothing on the actual route that would be of value or importance to a terrorist. It was very rural. Small villages. Foothills. Only two cities of any size along the route. Cuneo and Ventimiglia. Of course, he still didn't know if there even was another target. Al-Nassef could be in the process of simply disappearing. If not, and al-Nassef continued on to the A10, Genova was only 160 kilometers to the east and Monaco a mere 25 kilometers to the west. Mastrota considered. Genova with its important port facilities. A good means of escape perhaps. Or a tempting target.

To the east, Monaco. The Grand Prix weekend. Well over 100,000 people jammed into a square kilometer. A very tempting target indeed.

If Genoa were the object, why would al-Nassef not take the A6 southeast out of Torino and get to the A10 only 50 kilometers east of Genova, not 160. He knew, of course, that the route taken could be a diversion, a mere 110 additional kilometers. But he'd pulled al-Nassef's file since Cann's ID and studied it. It was clear to him that the man didn't go for infrastructural damage in his attacks. Or even military targets. He went after people. Innocent victims. The more the better. Body counts.

Ispettore Mastrota picked up the phone. He would see that this information was passed on to all the appropriate agencies, including Interpol. In addition, he would personally call his colleagues in Genova to be sure they knew of the possibility that al-Nassef was headed their way even though that wasn't his prime guess. And he would especially call Bazinet in Monaco. He couldn't be sure, of course. But, for himself, his working theory was that, if there was to be another target, it would be Monaco.

26

Hotel Vespucci
Fontvieille

About 9:00 PM, Sir Robert joined John and Katherine for dinner in the Vespucci dining room following a successful Thursday practice for the upcoming weekend's Grand Prix. Successful meant no major shunts (accidents), no significant engine or other mechanical issues, times by both drivers within the competitive range of a couple of tenths of a second off the expected leaders, and fuel and tire calculations within predicted and competitive parameters. Tomorrow, Friday, would be a day with no on-track time but it could hardly be called a day off as the teams would adjust and readjust the cars to prepare them for the final practice and then qualifying on Saturday.

While the Torino bombing and Rashid al-Nassef was on everyone's minds, the conversation had not turned to those subjects, not yet anyway, when Stanley Appel led Girard Bazinet over to the table.

"Sir Robert," Appel began, "you know Monsieur Bazinet, of course." Foster nodded first to Appel then to Bazinet. Then Appel introduced the Director of Monaco Public Security to Cann and Price.

"May I join you?" Bazinet asked looking around the table. All three invited him to do so. "Thank you," he said taking the fourth seat at the table while Appel brought a fifth chair over for himself.

"Allow me to get right to the point, Messieurs et Madame. I received a phone call a short time ago," Bazinet began. "From Capo Ispettore Pietro Mastrota of the Italian State Police. I believe you had a conversation with him yesterday?" The others nodded. "Ispettore Mastrota tells me that you, Monsieur Cann, identified one Rashid al-Nassef as being present at the bombing in Torino yesterday morning, yes?"

"Yes," John said.

"Can you tell me how you know this man. This al-Nassef?'

Cann related his history of the man and his own encounters with him.

"I see," Bazinet said slowly. "And you are sure of who he is?"

"I'm sure of who he is, Monsieur Directeur. And of what he has done," he added.

"It is what he may yet do, that concerns me, Monsieur Cann. John." The others waited for Bazinet to go on.

"I'm afraid we have what you would call a 'situation' here at present." Bazinet told them about the email, the frozen funds, the extortion demand.

"International Islamic Resistance?" Cann said. "Never heard of them. Do you know who they are?"

Bazinet shook his head in the negative. "It is not an organization we are familiar with."

"Made up just for this purpose?" Katherine suggested. The others all nodded agreement with that possibility.

"And you think al-Nassef might be involved in this, Girard?" Foster asked.

Bazinet gave a textbook Gallic shrug. "I am certain of very little, Sir Robert, but dare I overlook anything in a matter like this? Ispettore Mastrota's main reason for calling me was to tell me he believes al-Nassef may be coming here. Or that he was headed in this direction anyway." Bazinet described the information Mastrota had provided regarding the forestry officer's ID. "I, of course informed him of our "situation" here and Ispettore Mastrota feels this is not coincidence." He looked around the table. "I doubt that any of us believe in coincidence, do we?" he asked rhetorically. No one disputed him.

"And Ispettore Mastrota also told me about this al-Nassef meeting with Younis in Lugano," Bazinet continued. "Younis' operations have had significant funds frozen on allegations of money laundering. And we know Younis' bank, Al Istilah, and Bank Saderat were both major elements in a *hawala* network very much dedicated to the untraceable funding of terrorist acts." Bazinet looked around the table. "You know what *hawala* is?" All did. "None of this is definitive but..." He shrugged again.

"Well," John threw in, "I can tell you that al-Nassef was definitely involved in money laundering as well as the oil-for-food program in Iraq under the Saddam Hussein regime. So I'd have to think he'd been involved in the *hawala* network. And not just on the receiving end."

Bazinet absorbed that information. After a moment he took a deep breath and expelled it. "All of which," he said, "adds to the possibility he may be involved but, ultimately, does nothing to help us address the immediate problem."

"What are you going to do then?" Katherine asked. "Will you turn the funds over?"

"I have already met with the ministers and His Serene Highness. It is His Highness' position, all of our positions, that we cannot be seen to accede to such demands every time an email is sent from somewhere. His Highness is adamant that we not deal with terrorists and certainly that we not be seen to act in blind fear of them. He has personally directed us to take any and all steps necessary to react to this and deal with it. And he expressly advised all of us that we can act on his personal and governmental authority and on his full responsibility."

"Will he stand behind that?" Foster asked thinking of the vacillation of many political leaders under pressure.

Bazinet nodded. "He will. Indeed, His Highness' exact words were, '*Any* measures, Bazinet. *Any.*' And the Prince also added, 'And if there is any reluctance on anyone's part to do so, inform me. I will act personally.' "

"He's his father's son," Appel said with a satisfied smile.

Bazinet nodded agreement, then looked at Cann. "I know you are here for pleasure, Monsieur Cann, and I apologize for seeking to impose upon you, but given your knowledge of this man, may I prevail upon you to be available to assist us in this?"

"Absolutely," John answered immediately.

Bazinet looked at Price. "And I understand you have worked with several of your government agencies including the State Department, Madame?" he asked.

Both John and Katherine raised their eyebrows then looked at Appel who shrugged. "Forgive me but I did give Girard a rundown on your respective resumes. To the extent I know them." The older man smiled at Foster. "Sir Robert will never admit it but he rather brags about you, John. And," Appel said turning to Price, "he is quite impressed by you as well Katherine."

Foster just lifted one shoulder and then dropped it.

Katherine smiled and looked back to Bazinet. "Anything I can do, Monsieur Bazinet. I want to help in any way I can."

"Merci, Madame."

"I as well," Foster chimed in. "Even though I do need to be with the team for the most part. But please, Girard, don't hesitate to call on me in this matter. I'll do everything I can."

"Merci, Sir Robert. That is appreciated."

"One question, though," Katherine said slowly, seemingly forming the question as she spoke. "About al-Nassef's part in this. If there is one," The others gave her their attention. "Why would al-Nassef even need to come here as far as this business with the frozen funds is concerned. The email comes in over the Internet, the funds," she looked at Bazinet, "if they're transferred, would go out the same way. Untouched by human hands as it were. Demand in. Money out. End of story. No need for him to be here."

"Excellent observation," Bazinet replied although the same thought had crossed everyone's mind already. "Perhaps," he said tensely, "because this, whatever this is, is not the end of the story."

27

Friday AM
Hotel Palais de Revère
Col le Bermasse

Al-Nassef rose early with the feelings of tension and anticipation he always felt as he prepared to carry a complex plan into action. He altered his appearance with a half mouthpiece, nose plugs, and sunglasses and pulled a brimmed hat low over his eyes. He packed his laptop into a carryall which also held other items and left the hotel walking through the old village to a local bus stop on the coast road. Col de Bermasse was a regular stop on the SCNF train route from Nice to Monte Carlo but al-Nassef knew that the renovated main station in Monaco had high security, especially this weekend, as well as state of the art surveillance and was to be avoided. After a fifteen-minute ride, he alit from the bus at a local stop in Cap d'Ail and walked through Fontvieille, rode the escalators in the Commercial Center up to the Boulevard Charles III, and turned right toward the center of Monaco. His destination was the top of "the Rock" from where he planned to begin the destruction of an entire country.

Only a small part of central Monaco is at sea level. La Condamine, of course, with its famous harbor packed with yachts large and small opens to the Mediterranean on its eastern side but on the other three sides, the land quickly rises up and away from the water. To the north of the harbor, the slope upon which sits the Casino and private residences reaches a height of about 35 meters. To the west running directly away from the harbor, after the Quai, and Prince Albert Boulevard, the land climbs sharply up through businesses then residences and on up to Mount Agel at 140 meters. And on the south side of the harbor, the land rises 60 meters to the rocky headland upon which sits the Palace de Monte Carlo, the residence of his Serene Highness, the Prince of Monaco. This is called "The Rock".

In front of the palace is an open square appropriately named La Place du Palais which is generally filled with milling tourists and visitors from around the world. Not surprisingly, then, the opposite side of the square across from the palace, with one exception, is lined by bars, cafés, and numerous souvenir shops. The exception is the building which houses the Compagnie des Carabiniers du Prince, the personal guard of His Serene Highness which, every day at 12:00 noon conducts a formal changing of the guard ceremony announced by the blare of eight trumpeters.

Behind the row of shops opposite the palace is Monaco-ville, the old city of Monaco. The narrow streets running directly away from the square are also filled with bars and restaurants and shops for a distance, but then Monaco-ville becomes a residential area of apartments and condominiums and even some single family residences.

To get up to the top of the Rock to Monaco-ville and the palace, one can drive or take a bus from the east along the Avenue de la Porte Nueve and then climb steeply to the top or one can make a somewhat arduous climb up the Rampe Major, a wide pathway which zig-zags back and forth along the steeply sloping northern side of the Rock which faces and looms over Monte Carlo below.

Al-Nassef joined the people making the climb on foot up La Rampe. When he emerged through the last gate at the top, the palace was to his right, the open square in front of him, the shops and Monaco-ville to his left. He turned in the direction of the shops and walked along the Rue des Remparts with the edge of the steep slope on his left and the open square to his right. Just past the shops was an apartment building. He entered and climbed to the second floor flat which had been rented several months ago and which had been empty for most of the time since. Except for the deliveries.

He let himself in with one of the keys he'd picked up at Younis' villa — along with the *hadduta* — and stepped into the apartment.

There was a sparsely furnished living room in the center with a bedroom located on each side. The one on his right was empty. Al-Nassef went into the one on his left which sat at the corner of the building. A window on one side of the room looked out over the roofs of the shops and onto the square. Another window in the room on the side perpendicular to the first looked out over the Rue des Remparts and beyond it the city of Monte Carlo far below. That bedroom had no furniture but did contain several large drums of the sort that held industrial liquids. Sitting on the floor among the drums was a large sealed stainless steel tank with a braided stainless steel line running into it from each if the drums. There was a spigot on each drum just above the braided line running out of it. Turn the spigots and fluid from the drums would combine in the tank. At the base of the stainless steel tank was a nozzle to which a hose much like a fireman's hose could be attached. In the wall, where the installed air conditioner had been, a dummy A/C unit had been substituted. It was a shell, the original components removed and replaced by a commercial vaporizer. On the interior side of the A/C shell, inside the apartment, was another threaded nozzle to which the other end of the hose running from the tank could be connected.

Half the drums held isopropyl alcohol, a readily available alcohol product that was relatively harmless until mixed with what was in the other drums. Weeks ago, it had been purchased over a period of days in a number of stores in different locations so as not to rouse suspicion and stored in the apartment ever since.

The other containers held methylphosphonyl difluoride. It is not so readily available. Indeed, under the Chemical Weapons Convention (CWC) it is a schedule 2 chemical which means its manufacture and storage are highly restricted among the signatories to the CWC.

One country that never signed on to the Chemical Weapons Convention, however, was Iraq under Saddam Hussein. And in the years preceding the Iraq invasion in 2003, that country produced somewhere in the neighborhood of twenty thousand tons of methylphosphonyl difluoride. It has been claimed that all of it was destroyed prior to the invasion. It was not.

Another country that did not sign the CWC was Syria. Traditionally, Iraq and Syria have not been allies. Indeed, Syria backed the coalition that attacked Iraq following its seizure of Kuwait in the early 1990s.

But in the early 2000s, relations between the two countries warmed somewhat so that, as the coalition nations marshaled their forces on the borders of Iraq in 2003, Saddam ordered the transfer of Iraq's stockpile of chemical and nuclear weapons to Syria. Once there, the materials were dispersed among three distinct sites throughout the country.

In the weeks preceding the invasion in March 2003, convoys of vehicles carrying WMD streamed across the borders into Syria. Rashid al-Nassef was by then a trusted ally of the Iraqi regime and played a significant role in the transfer. Indeed, it was while he was returning from Sjinsjar in southern Syria that he was captured in the western desert of Iraq by American Special Forces.

But his participation meant he not only knew of the WMD's existence, he knew where they were. And that knowledge played a significant role in the development of this plan.

Unlike Iraq and Syria, Iran and Syria are long standing allies and proudly share the distinction of being the two largest state sponsors of terrorism. So Syrian cooperation in the present endeavor was readily forthcoming. A quantity of methylphosphonyl difluoride was unearthed from its hiding place under the town of Al-Baida in western Syria and placed into a number of containers the size of five-gallon paint cans. Those cans were then trucked 100 kilometers to the port city of Latakia where they were placed on a small fishing boat. That vessel headed due north where it met with a huge luxury yacht that had started this particular journey in the Black Sea crossing into the Mediterranean through the Bosporus Straits that divide not just Greece and Turkey but Europe and Asia. The cans were quickly transferred to the larger vessel which enjoyed an uneventful 2500-kilometer voyage across the Mediterranean. Some twenty kilometers off the northeast coast of France, the yacht slowed but did not stop completely as it effected a moving transfer of the drums of methylphosphonyl difluoride to a fast-boat with just enough room to carry the clandestine cargo.

Once the transfer was complete, the smaller vessel, which had been selected both for its high speed and low radar profile, raced off toward the coast and a tiny village blessed with innumerable coves and caves which could not possibly be watched all the time by the authorities. At the rocky shore, the two man crew who did not know what they were carrying, loaded the cans of contraband onto a delivery truck, secured the load, ran to their boat, and sped off into the dark sea.

Almost an hour later, a single individual who'd been watching the truck since he'd parked it long before the fast-boat had arrived, finally approached. The vehicle had been rented in Cannes but when the man was done, he would drive it to the Nice airport where he would leave it with the windows open and the keys in the ignition. Inside the airport, he would call the rental company and report the vehicle as stolen. Then he would board a plane for the flight east. Right now, though, he got in and drove to the apartment at the top of the Rock.

This same man had earlier stocked the apartment with the isopropyl alcohol. Now, he carried the cans of methylphosphonyl difluoride inside one at a time and set them down carefully in the corner bedroom. Then, dressed in protective gear, he poured the individual cans into the larger drums and sealed them tightly. He checked the fittings on the assembly and made sure all was in order. Then and only then did the man relax slightly. Unlike the boat crew, he did know what had been in the cans; and that methylphosphonyl difluoride alone is dangerous enough in its own right if inhaled or ingested. But he also knew that those ill effects from the element alone are nothing — literally nothing — compared to what it becomes when it is mixed with isopropyl alcohol. The resulting compound is one of the most lethal of all chemical weapons of mass destruction — Sarin.

Sarin was developed in Germany in the late 1930s, first as a pesticide but later as a chemical weapon — one that was never used in World War II precisely because its effects are so horrific, it was made clear that the use of such a weapon would bring the most devastating in-kind retaliation possible. It has been used, though, along with the other nerve agents Tabun and VX, by Saddam Hussein's regime against the Kurds in 1988. Or perhaps the world best knew of Sarin from the 1995 attack on the Tokyo, Japan subway system by a religious sect, Aum Shinnikyo.

Sarin is a nerve agent. That means it affects the proper functioning of the nervous system. When a person's brain gives an order to the body to engage in a motor activity — any motor activity — a chemical called acetylcholine, referred to as a neurotransmitter, is released to carry the impulse along and between the motor neurons to make the desired act happen. Once the activity is completed, the body creates aceytlcholinesterase, an enzyme which breaks down the acetylcholine and stops the initiated action from continuing. Sarin is a cholinesterase inhibitor which means that it prevents the acetylcholinesterase from doing its job. And it is an *irreversible* cholinesterase inhibitor. The result? Every motor activity in a victim, voluntary and involuntary, once it is initiated will not stop. The neurons keep firing and firing until the victim loses control of all bodily functions. At first there are flu-like symptoms, then respiratory distress and nausea followed by vomiting and then complete loss of excretory functions. Soon the victim begins to spasm and writhe uncontrollably until he or she loses consciousness and, mercifully, soon thereafter dies. The time involved varies slightly from individual to individual but, usually, death comes within a minute of ingestion. It is not pretty to watch. That made it especially attractive to al-Nassef and central to the plan.

What would happen was, on Sunday, race day, in the hours leading up to the Grand Prix, the slope running from the top of the Rock down to the city of Monte Carlo would become jammed with spectators. With reserved seating at the other locations around the track costing hundreds of dollars and more per person, the side of the Rock is the functional equivalent of the cheap seats looming above the La Rascasse turn and affording additional distant views out over several parts of the track. In actuality, there are no seats, no benches, no amenities whatsoever on the side of "The Rock". Just thousands and thousands of people standing, sitting, in the trees, on the walls, on the ground.

Just before the race would be about to begin, al-Nassef's plan was to open the spigots on the drums and start the flow of the chemicals into the stainless steel tank where they would mix to form Sarin. Inside the tank was a device similar to an automobile fuel pump which would eject the binary agent into the hose. The compound would then flow into the vaporizer inside the shell of the A/C unit embedded in the outer wall. The vaporizer would do its job and the Sarin would be pushed out through the grille on the A/C front. It would, at that point, mostly be a mist, a few droplets perhaps. That would be enough. Anyone standing under the emissions when the flow began would be only the first to be doomed. As a liquid, a drop the size of a pinprick on the skin can kill an adult human. Sarin is also the most volatile of the nerve agents and the mist would evaporate readily into a colorless, odorless vapor. Inhaling less than one-half of a milligram of the Sarin will also be fatal.

Sarin is also heavier than air. The mist and the vapor would settle downward seeping invisibly over the Rue de Remparts and then cascading over the edge of the Rock and down the slope like a spectral avalanche enveloping — and killing — everyone in a deadly fog. The Sarin also works quickly. The people at the top would start to feel sick — runny nose, stuffed head — and get worse rapidly. By the time the people a few yards down the slope began to feel the same, the people above them would already be experiencing serious discomfort, difficulty breathing, pains in the chest and elsewhere. By the time more people a bit further down first sensed something was wrong, the people at the top would have lost control of their muscles and their bodily functions. They would be twitching and jerking and writhing and dying. But those below wouldn't see it. They would be experiencing the same discomforts and agonies themselves. And, after the Sarin had covered the slope and was creeping across the streets, even though it would dissipate fairly rapidly, it would remain on the ground below long enough to kill many more at sea level.

There are antidotes to Sarin. Atropine is the most common. Monaco, like most developed countries, maintains a stock of atropine as part of its hazmat programs. But no country, Monaco included, has a supply sufficient to address the thousands of victims that would result from this attack. Moreover, atropine must be injected immediately. A lethal dose of Sarin which enters the body by inhalation kills in a few minutes. A lethal dose on the skin kills in even less time. There would simply not be enough time to save virtually anyone.

With a high profile event like the Monaco Grand Prix, cameras would be everywhere. The world would get to see the gruesome deaths of thousands played out before its very eyes. Al-Nassef smiled as he thought of the fear that would engender. It was, he thought with satisfaction, why they call it "terrorism".

And even that would not be the end. When everyone was at their most vulnerable, he would bring out the "*hadduta*" — the bedtime story. And put Monaco to sleep for a very long time.

But first, the opening act.

28

Avenue de Sospel
Menton

Karlijn Bleeker had also risen early on this Friday knowing it would be the last day of her life on this earth. She took great care in cleaning herself, did Fajr, and ate nothing. She then dressed in the bicycling outfit that had been left for her, including the hydration pack which she didn't feel she needed. But she'd been ordered to wear the complete outfit. Everything in the room. She obeyed.

She had brought little with her to Menton and had been ordered to leave everything except the laptop computer behind when she left. That was because for many soon-to-be martyrs, throwing away their personal belongings, even if there were not many of them, can be a trigger for reservations about what they are doing; a confrontation with the finality of their actions. She was also directed to leave the door unlocked and the key on a kitchen shelf. Someone would come by and remove everything.

She carried the bicycle outside, got on and set off for Monaco at a steady unforced pace. It was a somewhat more difficult ride than she'd anticipated simply because she hadn't given a lot of thought to the terrain involved, the multiple climbs and descents even on the more coastal N7. Still, without really pressing, she covered the distance from Menton to Monaco in well under an hour.

She entered the principality from the northeast on the Avenue Princess Grace which took her along the water and beaches, through the famous tunnel, and on around the Port Hercule and the Quai d'Albert to the foot of "The Rock". She walked the bike up La Rampe and came out into the Place de Palais through the same gate al-Nassef had used not long before. Following the detailed instructions she'd been given, she, too, went to the left and to the apartment building where al-Nassef waited.

He opened the door before she knocked and said nothing as she entered wheeling the bicycle alongside her. Meeting al-Nassef again, Bleeker felt the sense of distance she'd experienced when she'd first met him in Torino and on the few other occasions when she'd been in his company thereafter. In a way, it was a familiar feeling to her. Since converting, her experience with many of the Muslims she'd met who'd been born into Islam was one of having been treated with disdain, an air of superiority as if the religion had come to them, not the other way around; as if those who were forced to seek it by an accident of birth were somehow less "muslim" than they. In fact, al-Nassef hadn't put much energy into the religious aspect of any of this and showed no concern for the depth of his or anyone else's "muslimism". He was businesslike to the point of being hard and cared not a whit for those he was dealing with. Bleeker recognized this and that was fine. She knew al-Nassef saw her as a tool to employ in attaining his goal. Karlijn Bleeker saw him in the very same way.

Department of Finance and Economy
Rue de Gabian
Monaco

To the south and east of the rock in the Fontvieille section of Monaco, not far from the Louis II Stadium, the Ministers of Finance and Interior met with Director of Public Security Girard Bazinet and a representative of the *Service de Information et de Controle Sur Les Circuits Financiers* (SICCFIN) the body specifically charged with monitoring and addressing the issue of money laundering in the Principality of Monaco. Also present was an accountant with the *Commission des Institutions Bancaires Monegasques.* The CIBM had gathered the needed information of accounts and frozen funds and the officials around the table had spent the last several minutes going over it.

Sub-minister of Finance for Banking Jacques Bedard was the first to look up from the documents in front of him. "So it appears we have 23 accounts which hold funds frozen under Sovereign

Orders 15.319 and 15.321 in an aggregate amount of 42.7 million Euros, yes?"

The CIBM accountant nodded. "These are all frozen accounts held in member banks, Monsieur le Ministre. From all sources, not just terrorism."

"So this figure includes…what?"

"Monies seized from criminal activity — drugs, fraud, theft, smuggling, even human trafficking — as well as monies related to civil infractions and pending litigation in which the principality is a party. In addition to terrorism."

"Do we have a breakdown?" Bedard asked.

"Roughly 60% of the funds are related to terrorism or money laundering, Monsieur le Ministre." The CIBM man looked down at his notes. "In all we have identified 11 such accounts that held deposits directly or on a correspondent basis from individuals or other institutions."

"What about funds specifically from Al-Istilah or Bank Saderat?" Bazinet asked.

The woman from SICCFIN, who was also an attorney, answered the inquiry. "Those would in fact be the two largest accounts among the list compiled," Monsieur le Directeur. 8.6 million Euros from Al-Istilah and 6.7 million from Bank Saderat. As I'm sure you know, both banks have pending actions in the courts to recover those funds so permission from the court would be required for us to release them."

"Normally, yes," Bedard responded. "But we have consulted with the Ministry of Justice and they advise us that, in these unusual circumstances, releasing these funds, or their equivalent, to one or more of the very parties who are suing for exactly such a release would not constitute a misapplication. So I don't think that is a factor here."

"In any event, Minister of the Interior Roger Masse pointed out, "His Serene Highness has not authorized a release of any funds and has made it clear that his preference would be to thwart this entire scheme and punish the perpetrators." All eyes went to Bazinet.

"I, along with His Highness, would like nothing better," the Director of Public Security said, "but we have little or no information that would constitute a direct lead. We do have information of people who could be involved but we cannot be certain of even that. Furthermore, we have been unable to obtain any information or assistance from Qatar or Iran. Both are pleading complete ignorance about any of this. Syria denies any knowledge whatsoever. And Iran has taken the position that the account number referenced is not even a valid account of Bank Saderat." He shook his head in disgust and frustration.

Interior Minister Masse was scribbling on a pad before him. "60% of 42.7 million Euros is 25.6 million of which 15.3 million came from Al Istilah and Bank Saderat. What about the remaining 10.3 million Euros?"

"Of the nine account holders, two are banks — Banque Syrie and Bank Negara Kelada, and seven are individuals," the CIBM accountant said.

Bazinet looked at his watch. "It is just after 10:00 AM, Madame at Messieurs. In less than one hour, it will be twenty-four hours since the email was received at CIBM. We are approaching the deadline stated in the post. We will not transfer funds so, barring any further development, I suggest we prepare to hold our breaths. For now, let me check in one more time with my people to see if we have anything new. If not…" He didn't need to finish the sentence.

"What if we released just the 15.3 million Euros, not the 25.6 million, or the entire 42.7?" the CIBM accountant queried. "As a sign of good faith?"

"Good faith, indeed," Bazinet muttered as he clicked off the cell phone and shook his head in the negative to the others around the table. "How do you…why would you attempt to show good faith to such people as these?" The question was clearly rhetorical and he didn't expect or wait for a response. "In any event, that has been discussed and rejected. It would still be surrendering to terror, just for a lesser amount than they may want, and that is surrender nonetheless. As we have discussed over and over, we don't even know if the email is genuine or if they know how much money is involved. And, if they do have a specific figure in mind, sending less could provoke a consequence anyway."

There was another long moment of silence before Masse finally said, "So we just wait then." Around the table everyone looked at their watches. But no one spoke."

The time was 10:09 AM.

Rue des Remparts
The Rock
Monaco

Al-Nassef spread a city map of Monaco on the low table in front of the couch and leaned forward over it. Bleeker stood behind him and to his left looking down over his shoulder. "We are here," he said laying a finger on where the Rock was on the map. "When it is time — it will not be long — you will go back down La Rampe and at the bottom, the street to the right is the Rue Grimaldi. See here." He moved his finger along the map. "It bends around and runs toward le Gare, the main train station. But here," he jabbed again, "on the left of the street before you reach the station is a branch office of La Banque des Maritimes. This is where you will strike your blow for the *jihad*." Bleeker nodded.

"Come," al-Nassef said as he stood and carried the hydration pack into the bedroom over on the corner. Bleeker followed and as she entered the room took in the industrial drums and other equipment with a modicum of interest. She was intelligent enough to get a sense of what it was all about but didn't expend a lot of energy trying to analyze it in any great detail.

Al-Nassef opened the hydration pack and took out the two plastic containers meant to hold water or other fluids for the bicycler to drink. From the floor by the main tank, he picked up two stainless steel containers which were identically sized to the plastic ones and turned each of them upside down. This was to show Bleeker they were empty and also to exhibit a threaded fitting on the bottom of each. Al-Nassef then went to one of the drums and disconnected the hose from the spigot and filled one of the steel containers about half way with methylphosphonyl difluoride. Then he went to a different drum and added the same amount of the isopropyl mixture to the other container. He looked at Bleeker. "Don't worry," he said with what for him was as close to smiling as he got, "they are relatively harmless as long as they are apart."

Bleeker was almost amused at the irony of al-Nassef's exhortation to her not to worry. What was there to be worried about? Dying? That was the point of the exercise, she thought to herself.

Al-Nassef put the containers inside the hydration pack and secured them with their strapping. "Keep them in the pack until you get to bank building. Then," al-Nassef held up a thin foot-long black cylinder that looked like a bicycle pump — which is what it was supposed to look like. "When you arrive, take the pump from the bicycle and go inside — with the hydration pack, of course.

"You will see that the room you are in is not very large. Perhaps 20 meters deep and 10 meters wide. To the right is a counter behind which the tellers sit and at the rear, two offices for the manager and her assistant. Along the left side of the room will be only chairs and tables with magazines and so forth. For customers to wait. There may or may not be customers. No matter." He looked at Bleeker to see if she was paying attention. She was.

"There is a rest room on the left about halfway down, near the waiting area. Go into it and make sure you are alone, of course. Remove the two containers. Then take this," Al-Nassef held up a handful of black tubing.

"Pay close attention," he said. The tubing was "Y" shaped and each of the three ends had a threaded compression fitting. Al-Nassef held up the two "Y" ends of the tube and instructed Bleeker to connect each of those to the fitting he had shown her on the bottom of the two stainless steel containers. It didn't matter which went to which. Then he held up the base of the "Y" shaped tubing in one hand and directed Bleeker to connect it to the fitting on the end of the black cylinder pump.

"Just before you go out into the main area, turn the fittings of the bottom of both containers to allow the fluids to flow into the pump. Then go out into the room and pump in an upwards direction. It will come out as a mist and will settle of its own weight. It will not be necessary," al-Nassef further instructed Bleeker, "to actually get it on the people in the room. The vapor will suffice. But be sure to cover as much of the room as possible. And try to pump all of the contents out before you…finish."

"Do I need to pump it on myself? In my face to breathe it in?" Bleeker asked calmly.

"No, you should continue to pump as long as you can." Al-Nassef was impressed with her calm. "But once you begin, make sure you complete your task quickly."

"How quickly?"

"A minute," al-Nassef said calmly. "Perhaps a bit more."

For a moment Bleeker was quiet. Then, "Will there be pain?"

"No," Al-Nassef assured her firmly. "One moment you will be standing doing Allah's work and the next, you will be in Paradise receiving your eternal reward. It will be beautiful for you."

"How would you know?" Bleeker thought cynically. But she didn't say it. She had no desire, no interest in having such a conversation. Al-Nassef didn't care. Neither did she.

29

After talking to Bazinet the previous evening, Ispettore Pietro Mastrota had decided to take his investigation into the field. He had a good crew here in Torino — even if they didn't always know that he thought so. But he needed to do something. Make something happen. And he didn't feel he could do that behind his desk. So early the next morning, he headed south following the route al-Nassef had taken. He really didn't know what he would see or find but it was not his way to just wait for things to come to him.

He was on his way just after seven AM and out of the urban environs of Torino shortly thereafter heading down the rural two lane road that is Highway 20. There are only two cities of any size on Highway 20 between Torino and the coast, Cuneo and Ventimiglia. He passed through Cuneo about an hour or so after leaving but didn't stop. Al-Nassef had been seen well south of there, past Limone Piemonte in the vicinity of Limonetto on the border with France. He knew Limonetto was the home of the Forestry Officer Cocuzza and someday would commend the officer for his observations but for now, he drove on through.

He did stop in Ventimiglia. He had no specific reason, no information that caused him to do so. Indeed, he couldn't know even whether al-Nassef had stayed on Highway 20 after Limonetto. But he knew the local Ventimiglia chief and inspectors quite well and decided to both brief them and pick their brains in relation to what he did know. It would be a shot in the dark but such inquiries occasionally bore fruit. Also, having been constantly sipping coffee for the last couple of hours as he drove, he needed to stop somewhere.

The Ventimiglia *questura* is located in the center of the city near the Giardini Pubblici. Mastrota came in from the west on the Via Tenda and entered the center of the city on the Lungo Roia Gerolamo Rossi. It was a mistake. In short order, he found himself immobilized in a line of traffic that was motionless as far ahead as he could see. At first, he assumed it was a run-of-the-mill traffic jam but then he suddenly cursed himself as he recalled that on Fridays, many of the streets along the River Roia are completely blocked off and packed solid with stalls and vendors and a significant number of black marketeers and hawkers of counterfeit goods in Ventimiglia's famous street market. He worked his car back and forth until he was able to make a u-turn and retrace his route until he was able to make a right turn and then another to bypass the market congestion. Even on the alternate route the traffic was stop-and-go and it took some time to get to the municipal parking area off the Via Vittorio Veneto. He walked the remaining way to the *Polizia del Stato questura.*

He didn't know the officer on the desk in the open lobby nor did the officer know him. So, when Mastrota asked to be permitted to go up to see the local *Capo Ispettore,* whom he did know, he was required to provide his identification. While his documents were being examined, another officer came out of a hallway on the right holding tightly to the elbow of a man who was apparently being released after a night in one of the cells. "You can go now," the officer said releasing his grip on the man.

"How am I to get back to the hotel?" he asked more harshly than he intended.

The officer just shrugged. "There are buses," he said with more than a hint of satisfaction. "Just out the door and down the street to the right is the nearest stop. You want the number 127." His smile was more of a smirk.

Xhelal Chani stared at the officer for a moment then turned away. As he strode across the lobby to leave, his and Mastrota's eyes locked for several seconds but, as there was no reason for either man to know the other, the mutual gazes were empty. Chani reached the door and pushed his way out, turned right and disappeared from view.

Villa Colline Pedemontana

Ventimiglia, Italy

Rozafa Chani had never before spent a night alone. Growing up under the harsh male-dominated regime of rural Kukes in the northeast corner of Albania, it may very well have cost her life if she had. Even if the males were absent, and they often were, it was incumbent on the females to seek each other out for mutual protection and supervision. A woman alone was a woman without restraint and, well, the worst could be imagined. And that would have been enough. It would not have been necessary for her to have actually *done* something. Simply that she *could* have would have been a lapse in the authority of the males and a stain on the honor of the family.

But she'd always had someone, a father, uncle, brother, husband to provide guidance and limits. Not so now. Since yesterday she'd been alone.

Of course, she was not entirely alone. She had Luan with her. But Luan was only 18 months old and still under the care and control of his mother. In time, he too, would come to dominate but, for now...

Xhelal had ordered her to stay in the room and she had. He'd also said he would be back and she knew he would be angry if she had not obeyed. So she and Luan remained in the room throughout the day. After the incident at the pool, Xhelal Chani had insisted that they fast on the Wednesday evening nor had they eaten on Thursday morning before the police arrived. As a result, neither she nor Luan had eaten since Wednesday afternoon and it was now mid-morning on Friday.

She could deal with her own hunger pangs but Luan's sobs cut right through her. The boy didn't understand, of course, and had cried much of the day yesterday and most of the night as well. She'd even tried breast feeding the boy but she'd only done that for the first eight months or so of his life. So now, when she tried, it was futile.

Still, she kept telling herself, Xhelal would be back at any time. And so they waited. Now, as the sun rose higher and higher over the Mediterranean, Rozafa felt resentment that her baby should be put through this. And, for the first time in her life, she made a decision.

And, even more frightening, it was one that she knew went against what she had been told to do. By her husband.

She wrapped her headscarf carefully around her and left the room, looking for one of the Albanian speaking woman who had translated for her the day before. She took the stairs down to the main floor taking great pains not to make eye contact with any males she might encounter. The hotel manager saw her from the lobby and spoke a greeting but she turned away and walked down the hallway toward the sound of voices and dishes and utensils clinking. The breakfast service had long since ended but many of the smells, particularly the breads and pastries hung in the air making the pangs of hunger even worse. Looking about her carefully, Rozafa didn't see either of the women she sought and she felt the beginnings of tears of frustration.

At the lobby desk, the hotel manager watched Rozafa avoid his gaze and walk away from him. He picked up the phone on the desk and dialed housekeeping. When the head of the department answered, he asked, "Are Nevila or Vesa in today?"

"Vesa is just coming in now. Is something wrong?"

"No. But send her to me right away, would you? I need her language skills again."

The head of housekeeping didn't care for her staff to be diverted from their work but, since it was the manager, she couldn't argue. "I just hope he remembers who called her away if all her work doesn't get done," she thought to herself. Out loud, she said, "Si, Signore Lorenzo."

The woman called Vesa reported to the manager who summoned her to follow him in the direction Rozafa had taken. He spotted her sitting with Luan on her lap at one of the outdoor tables that looked out over the Mediterranean. The manager stopped short and instructed Vesa to go over and engage the young woman in conversation and find out what the situation was. "In particular," he directed, "find out if she and her bambino have had anything to eat. If not, have the kitchen feed them. At once. And tell Cirrillo that I am directing this and, yes, I know, it is out of the schedule."

"Si, Signore Lorenzo," the maid answered. The manager stayed back as Vesa crossed to Rozafa and did as she was instructed. In a moment, the two women and the boy were in the dining room and Rozafa was trying to keep Luan from eating too fast, even though she herself was tempted to do the same thing. As the woman and boy ate, Vesa watched Rozafa closely and drew two impressions. One was that the younger woman didn't appear to be very educated or worldly. Not that there was anything wrong with that but it seemed more than a little out of place in the sophisticated and polished *Colline Pedemontana.* The second thing she noticed was that Rozafa was very afraid.

After a time, Vesa ventured to pry just a little into Rozafa's home and upbringing. The story was quite familiar to her. And disturbing. But it was nothing she hadn't heard before. Vesa's own experience in growing up in super-patriarchal Albania had some similarities to Rozafa's but, at least in Vesa's case, she had been raised in the capital city of Tirana which was a far cry from the almost medieval atmosphere of the rural countryside. Still, most Albanians knew what it was like for women. And most Albanian women who had fled, had at the very least, an abiding empathy with those who had had it the worst.

Rozafa had opened up somewhat and, it seemed to Vesa, had reached a certain level of comfort with her. So she ventured to help. "There are places you can go, Rozafa," the housekeeper said. "Places that can help you."

"Help me for what?" Rozafa asked.

Vesa gathered her thoughts before she spoke. "What it is like for you — what it has been like in your life, it is not like that everywhere. It is not like that here in Italy. You don't have to be afraid all the time. You don't have to obey your husband in everything."

Rozafa looked at Vesa with an expression of genuine confusion on her face. And fear. "I did not say that I am afraid. Why do you...?"

Vesa put her hand out and laid it on top of Rozafa's. "I know you didn't say it. And I would not ever..." She stopped talking when she saw Rozafa look past her over her shoulder and an expression of terror appeared on the young mother's face. Vesa turned to see what Rozafa was looking at and saw Xhelal Chani standing at the far entrance to the dining room staring at his wife and son icily. After a moment, he crossed to the table. "I told you to stay in your room," he said brusquely in Albanian."

He was surprised when Vesa answered him in the same language. "She is just getting something to eat. For herself and your son."

Chani struggled to keep his anger in check. "You could have called room service," he said to his wife.

Rozafa looked down. "I did not know how," she mumbled softly.

"Go up to the room," Chani said forcing himself to sound calm and reasonable.

Rozafa Chani stood slowly and gathered Luan up in her arms. Without a word she walked past Vesa and out of the dining room. Xhelal Chani turned to Vesa who opened her mouth to speak.

He cut her off with a curt, "Thank you for your concern,' and turned away.

30

Rues des Remparts
The Rock
Monaco

Al-Nassef looked at his watch. "It is time, *shahida*."

He asked Bleeker whether she had any possessions on her person and she advised him she had left everything in Sospel except for the computer as she had been directed. He complimented her on her thoroughness and then left her alone in the second, empty bedroom to give her time to herself. As he went out of the room, he turned in the doorway and asked, "Would you like me to pray with you?"

"No," the young woman said without emotion. "I have made my preparations and am ready to perform my holy act." Almost as an afterthought, she mumbled, "Thank you."

After a few moments, Bleeker came back into the living room where al-Nassef waited with the hydration pack. She turned and he stepped forward to help her put it on. There was little likelihood of an accident as long as the binary elements remained separate but they both moved quite carefully nonetheless. Al-Nassef attached the pump to the support piece of the bicycle. Without speaking, Bleeker gripped the middle of the handlebars of the Campagnolo Mirage bicycle and wheeled it out the door held open by al-Nassef. Neither had said a word.

Bleeker carried the lightweight bicycle effortlessly down the stairs and out onto the Rue des Remparts. Turning left, she walked the bike along toward the gate at the top of La Rampe which led down from the Plaza del Palais. La Rampe is part stairs, part slopes but very steep all the way down and Bleeker didn't ride at any point along the way. At the bottom of La Rampe, she gave temporary custody of her bicycle to the attendant in the public women's rest room and went into a stall to relieve herself one last time. She could have done so before leaving the apartment — it had a bathroom, of course — but, for whatever unformed reason, she had not felt comfortable bringing such a need to al-Nassef's attention.

Having rid herself of all material possessions, including, at this point, money, she left the WC without tipping the attendant. She stood at the intersection of Avenue de la Porte Nueve and Rue Grimaldi and waited for the white uniformed Monegasque police officer to signal it was permitted to proceed.

She climbed onto the bicycle and pedaled off down the Rue Grimaldi. After the street took a bend to the right, she began to look on the left side for the *Banque des Maritimes.* The street was most crowded as she passed the building where the Automobile Club de Monaco had set up a ticket distribution office. Her final destination was beyond that point, she noted with some relief. Relief because, unlike al-Nassef, she was not concerned with body counts and indeed regretted somewhat that her martyrdom necessitated the deaths of others. Karlijn Bleeker was not anti-people. She was just pro-shahadat.

The time was 10:47 AM.

Banque des Maritimes
Rue Grimaldi

Helène Levallier unconsciously flipped her hair out of her eyes as she pored over the spreadsheet before her. Time and again she had shown Patrice, the new teller, how to prove her transactions, that is, balance her daily dealings and, yet, once again, here she was, the newly promoted branch manager, doing the job for her. It could not continue. Levallier promised herself, for heaven knows how many days in a row now, that she would make it clear, once and for all, that either Patrice got this vital aspect of her duties right or she could not continue in her position. Levallier could, of course, pass the unpleasant task on to her assistant manager, herself newly promoted from head teller, but decided as a matter of principal that it was unleaderlike to do so.

Out front, Patrice and two other tellers were doing a brisk pre-lunch hour business heavily weighted toward currency exchanges for members of the Grand Prix crowd in addition to the usual personal and business transactions. Each of the three tellers had several customers in line before them and five more people, two couples and a young man, sat in the waiting area. Only the young man paid any particular attention to the slender young bicyclist who crossed directly in front of him on her way to the ladies' room

Minutes before, Bleeker had gotten off the *Mirage* bicycle and guided its front wheel into the rack provided for public use. Out of habit, she began to get out the chain and lock to secure it to the post. Then, remembering her obligation to divest herself of all possessions — the bike wasn't really hers in any event — and realizing with an almost amused reaction that she certainly wasn't going to need it any more, she left it unsecured. The same with the helmet. She took it off and hung it by the opening in the face on the left handlebar. With the hydration pack on her back, she walked to the front entrance of the Rue Grimaldi branch of the Banque des Maritimes. Just before she went in, she noticed a street surveillance camera high on a building opposite the bank. The young Dutch woman paused and looked directly into the lens. And smiled. Somewhere in cyberspace, a FERET's program was taking note and beginning the matching process. It would be far too late to do any good.
It was 10:51 AM.

She moved slowly. At least it seemed to her she was moving slowly and she wondered vaguely if it was just her own perception. No one seemed to be paying particular attention to her and she felt unnoticed as she passed the waiting area and went into the ladies' room. There were three stalls inside and she made sure they were empty. Then she took the hydration pack off her back and stood it on the faux marble counter between the two sinks. She felt disappointment in herself when her hands quivered slightly as she took the two stainless steel containers out. She went to stand them up on the surface but, because of the fittings on the bottom, she couldn't and laid them gently on their sides. Even if they somehow leaked, she counseled herself, there wouldn't be a problem as long as the two chemicals didn't mix. She couldn't tell at this point which container held which chemical but realized it really didn't matter.

She took a deep breath and reached back into the hydration pack for the tubing which she pulled out and attached it to the two containers just as al-Nassef had shown her. Then she brought out the pump and attached the remaining loose end of tubing to it. She had a fanny pack around her waist with holsters of the proper size to hold the containers, one on each side. She opened the threaded fitting on the bottom of each container and fitted each one properly into its holder. Then she picked up the pump and held it in front of her and turned toward the door.

For the first time in all of this, she felt a twinge of hesitation. A little bit of fear and a little bit of doubt. Up till now, this had been a glorious exercise; a religious fantasy focused solely on the glory of martyrdom and the promised rewards of a personal heaven. She'd heard in her mind the voices of the crowds and the exhortations of the imams for others to praise her bravery and follow her on the path of glorious jihad. Now, her thoughts went to this life, the only life she knew and of times and events that had been, well, at times, really quite good, and she doubted, for a brief moment, whether she really wanted to leave it.

In the end it was fear of cowardice that caused her to proceed. That and a self-orchestrated sense of inescapability from what she had promised to do. What would be the consequence of failing to keep that promise she had made to herself, to the world, to Allah, and even her male angel? She opened the door and stepped out into the main room.

It was 10:54 AM.

Bleeker first went directly to the rear of the building and stepped into the office on the left. She held the black cylinder out in front of her pointed upward over the assistant manager's head and pumped it several times. The startled woman behind the desk looked at first confused then frightened as she felt the mist settling on her. By the time the first victim had started to sniffle, Bleeker was already in the manager's office repeating her actions. Her second victim, too, felt the same sense of danger from the odd actions of this person who had just sprayed her with... something. And even as her eyes and nose started to get runny, Helène Levallier was reaching for the phone.

Bleeker stepped back into the main room and walked straight to the front door. There she turned and began to walk steadily back toward the rear of the building holding the pump up at an angle and sweeping it from side to side all the while steadily expelling the deadly mist into the air. By the time she reached the middle of the room, she was already feeling the first symptoms herself. She continued on.

As Bleeker went about her lethal work, there was initially, strangely enough, little overt reaction from the people inside the bank. A couple of customers made mild verbal protests about being sprayed with something but most of the others appeared more confused than angry. That changed very quickly, as the symptoms became evident. Looks of annoyance changed into concern and then fear as it became clear that they were being affected by... something. It is simple human nature to exercise a degree of denial in the face of unknown consequences. And the worst of these consequences are not allowed into the consciousness until the realization that they are inevitable.

That realization came when Helène Levallier staggered out of her office drowning in her own vomit. In the adjoining office, the assistant manager was on the floor next to her desk curled into a writhing fetal position and no longer able to control her motor functions in any way.

Levallier had managed to dial "17" the police emergency number but by the time the call was answered, and there had been no undue delay, she was in respiratory distress and unable to speak. Cars would be dispatched automatically. They would, of course, be too late.

All of the people nearer the front of the bank, tellers and customers alike, were fully incapacitated by then, some of them already dead, but the ones further back who had been sprayed marginally later than the first victims, charged as one for the front door. It was well beyond too late for them but they couldn't know that. Only the young man and a middle-aged woman made it that far. The front door opened more as a result of the man falling on the push bar of the door but it was enough for him to spill into the street. Behind him, the woman was able to take only a step or two before she, too, fell to the ground. A crowd gathered and watched in growing horror as the ghastly symptoms consumed its victims.

Where the young man had fallen, he was barely through the door and his leg now kept it from closing completely. Inside, the mist settled slowly to the floor and would soon dissipate. But a tiny amount of the deadly vapor had made it into the street and when the members of the crowd closest to the door also began to exhibit distress, a small panic ensued which had the fortuitous effect of clearing the street anywhere in the vicinity of the bank.

Inside, almost all the way to the rear of the building, Karlijn Bleeker had sat down with her back to the wall not far from the bleeding, reeking corpse of Helène Levallier. She'd run through the same gamut of effects from the Sarin as had her victims and felt a sense of profound embarrassment, even regret, when she lost control of her bodily functions. After which came the cramps and the excruciating physical and mental torture of nerves and muscles run amok. Somehow, even in the grip of the wrenching paroxysms, she'd felt a brief, grim satisfaction at knowing that al-Nassef had been quite wrong when he'd said there would be no pain. Soon, the muscles became too exhausted to continue their stinging, biting spasms. But that brought no relief. As with all of her systems, her respiratory function failed and she knew she was suffocating. It is a thoroughly unpleasant way to die. It takes a long time as the brain, programmed for survival, screams out for the life-giving oxygen it needs even as it is forced to accept the growing realization that it lacks the neurological ability to make it happen. In time, vitally aware that there is nothing it can make the body do, the brain surrenders and prays for the blessed relief of unconsciousness, even as it knows it is an unconsciousness from which it will not return. The final irony is that the body doesn't even know it when the relief finally comes so that the last thing it experiences on this earth is the pain. For Karlijn Bleeker a further final irony was that it hurt so much, she forgot to pray.

The time was 10:57 AM.

31

The dispatcher who answered the '17' emergency call from the bank manager tried several times to get a response from whomever had made the call. When she received none, she immediately implemented policy by sending out a call for available units in the area as indicated by the caller ID. The first responder to arrive on the scene was a foot patrolman who'd been working crowd control further down Rue Grimaldi and had heard the general call on his shoulder transponder.

The first things he noticed, of course, as he approached the bank were the bodies by the door. The two customers who'd been inside the bank when Bleeker staged the attack had been dead for minutes now and three bystanders soon would be. One had actually put his head inside the bank while the other two had inadvertently ingested tiny, but sufficiently lethal amounts of the Sarin in an attempt to minister to the original victims. The second thing that struck the young officer was the distance of the onlookers from the scene itself. Normally, gawkers would press in as close as possible to the scene of a tragedy but this crowd held back, many with expressions of fear on their face. That he noticed this anomaly may well have saved the young police officer's life.

Instead of rushing into the heart of the scene, the officer opted to ensure that the crowds stayed back from whatever had occurred. This was not cowardice. Securing a scene is always a priority. Moreover, the young man knew that something was seriously out of the ordinary here and, as he ensured the integrity of the area, he sought and received preliminary information on what the observers had witnessed. What he heard caused him to make an immediate call to his superiors to alert them to the possibility that they had a hazmat situation on their hands. He would later receive a commendation for his actions.

Two marked units soon appeared and after a quick consultation with the first officer on the scene, they too made it their priority to keep the scene intact and onlookers away. The crowd was moved even further back in both directions on Rue Grimaldi to widen the sterile area and the two police vehicles were each parked perpendicular to the roadway at opposite ends to further restrict ingress. A supervisor was called for and he arrived several minutes later, concurred with the steps already taken and placed a call to the La Condamine barracks of the Corps des Sapeurs-Pompiers. The Corps is a militarized armed force and not part of the police structure under the Director of Public Safety but is, like the police, under the general supervision of the Minister of the Interior. Most importantly, the Corps de Sapeurs-Pompiers, among its duties, is the force that is trained to handle incidents involving hazardous materials and is equipped with special hazmat incident vehicles and equipment.

The Corps incident team arrived on the scene in a matter of minutes, one of the marked police units being temporarily moved to allow the specially equipped vehicle access to the scene. It stopped about ten meters from the nearest dead body. Two men dressed in sealed hazmat suits climbed out of the back and approached the front of the bank. They examined the bodies as closely as the cumbersome suits allowed. The two men were extremely well-trained and the sergeant, the higher ranking of the two, had almost fourteen years of experience and, more importantly, highly specialized training in this field. Based on his visual observation of the bodies outside, he already suspected a nerve agent as being at work here. But testing would be needed to know for sure. Autopsies would be able to tell, specifically by detecting hydrolysis products in the cerebellum of a victim. But that took time and it was vital to know as soon as possible what exactly had been at work here. Establishing the precise nerve agent used was also important to post-incident considerations like tracing back to the source and clean-up.

In seeking to identify the agent itself from evidence or residue at the scene of the incident, traditionally a determination of the nature of a toxic agent relied on gas chromatography-mass spectrometry. It was an effective method of detection but its drawback was it was best done in a laboratory environment and was a relatively slow process in any event. Fortunately, however, Monaco is a wealthy principality and does not disperse its wealth solely among casinos and Grands Prix. The Corps des Sapeurs-Pompiers is equipped with the newest, highest tech devices and it had recently acquired Quartz Crystal Microbalance sensors that utilized thin quartz crystals sandwiched between electrodes to quickly analyze and detect various chemical agents. Because of his extensive training, the sergeant knew that the QCM technology was particularly efficient at detecting organophosphates, the class to which most nerve agents belong. The QCM sensors were quick, portable, capable of being used on-site, and extremely precise. In short order, it confirmed that the *Banque des Maritimes* had been subjected to a Sarin attack.

Department of Finance and Economy
Rue de Gabian

Bazinet, the ministers and others at the meeting on Rue de Gabian waited for 11:00 AM to arrive. Glancing repeatedly at the clock on the wall, the closer the moment came, the less any of them spoke. The digital readout went to 11:00, then 11:01, then 11:02, then 11:03. The time passed without the chirping of phones, or buzzing of intercoms, or whatever signal each might have entered into the blackberry to announce an incoming voice or text message. But there was no sense of real relief for either the short or long term. They knew full well that, if the email were legitimate, so to speak, and if there were to be repercussions for their failure to transfer funds, such a consequence might not come for an hour, or a day, or a week, or who knows when. Still, as the numbers of the clock ticked on, some of the tension just started to moderate. It would not evaporate, not for a time if at all, but might settle into a somewhat more generalized apprehension about some future act at some undetermined time. That ended when all of their cell phones and Blackberries started to go off simultaneously.

In the minutes that followed, information came in to the assembled officials in a frustratingly incremental manner. At first, they learned only that some sort of attack had occurred and where. They all wanted details as quickly as possible but it was Bazinet who first learned of the suspicion of the patrol officer on the scene that this might be a "hazmat" situation. He repeated the single word "hazmat" loudly enough to penetrate the conversations the others were having and for a brief moment, there was a chilled silence. Each of the attendees had a different sphere of activity and influence and a different role to play as he or she acted to implement the procedures for their respective ministries, bureaus, and offices. And "hazmat" required special handling by all.

Bazinet, as Director of Public Safety, chafed at receiving information second hand and decided his place was at the scene. He quickly took the lift to the basement level and ran to his car. He'd driven to the meeting straight from his home that morning and so had his personal car with him. Private vehicle or not, however, it was equipped with a police radio and, as always, it was open to the main police channel. As soon as he turned the ignition and started the car, the radio came to life and as he drove he listened to the unusually heavy and frenetically intense chatter that caused him to constantly revise his estimation of the severity of what he had referred to the previous evening as a "situation." And although the people he could hear on the radio were being intentionally cryptic, speaking in police jargon and abbreviated sentences, as the details came through, his hands tightened on the steering wheel.

Even without any official, spectator-oriented Grand Prix events scheduled for that day, the streets were still jammed with people, the tens of thousands of fans increasing exponentially the usual complement of Monegasque citizenry attempting to go about their normal business. Bazinet made little progress on the city streets, his passage measured not in kilometers per hour but in meters per minute until he finally reached the Rue Grimaldi. He rolled down his window and stuck his hand out holding his Department of Public Security ID. There were police officers ranged up and down the street on either side and they attempted in vain to get the crowd to part for the Director's vehicle. The utter futility of the effort became apparent and he pulled to the side as best he could. He got out and began to push his way through the milling throngs toward the bank.

He reached the edge of the crowd where it had been set by the police line and bent to go under the yellow tape. An officer saw him and moved quickly to prevent the apparent trespass then held back when he recognized Bazinet. "Monsieur le Directeur," the officer said with a nod and an arm outstretched toward the heart of the scene. Bazinet nodded back almost absently as his attention focused on the sheet-covered bodies at the entrance to the bank. When he was closer but still some distance from the scene, he grabbed an officer by the elbow and inquired as to who was in charge. The officer pointed to Detective Inspector Yves St. Cyr. Bazinet knew and respected the DI.

"What do we have, Yves," the Director asked.

"Nerve agent. The Corps sergeant has confirmed the presence of Sarin."

Sarin!" Bazinet repeated. He couldn't have given a precise chemical analysis of the compounds but he knew what it was and what it could do. "My God!" he said sounding both shocked and angry. "How many victims?"

"Nineteen, it appears. This comes from the Corps people, of course. They are the only ones who've been inside. But they say five appear to be bank employees, ten apparent customers and three additional victims out here on the street just outside the front entrance. And the attacker. A young woman."

"Why do you identify her as the attacker."

The DI raised his brows in an almost imperious manner at the same time going to great pains not to appear patronizing or supercilious to the Director of Public Security. "I am told she is sitting against the rear wall of the bank building holding two canisters of what we assume to be the constituent chemicals of the compound connected by tubing to a hand pump she used to disperse the device." He cleared his throat before continuing. "As I'm sure you know, Monsieur le Directeur, Sarin acts very quickly indeed. There is really no reasonable chance that someone else perpetrated this act and then made it look like an innocent person had done it." The Inspector pursed his lips and shrugged. "Though I suppose it could have been done by someone wearing a mask or protective gear who escaped. But, again, given the speed with which these things kill, these people," he pointed at the victims on the street referring particularly to the two bank customers who had tried to escape, "would likely have been the first, and apparently only ones to try to get out."

"Rear door?" Bazinet asked. But he said it with an expression meant to indicate that he knew full well the DI would have thought of that.

"Still locked from the inside. Again, it could have been someone with a key but…" He shrugged again.

"Yes," Bazinet concurred. "We can consider all sorts of possibilities and we shall keep an open mind but clearly, your assessment is the most likely. Thank you."

The front of the bank was no longer visible as a tent-like structure was being erected to enclose both the scene and any potential residual vapors. Bazinet had seen one of the protective-suited men from the Corps des Sapeurs-Pompiers — it was the sergeant — come out and head for his vehicle. The Director gestured from a distance to get his attention. The Corps sergeant didn't see him but an officer on the other side did and pointed to direct his attention. When he looked at Bazinet, the Director held up his radio and flashed his fingers several times to indicate a frequency he wanted the sergeant to talk to him on. The hooded man nodded that he understood and held up a gloved hand, one finger extended to express that he needed a moment before he could comply. Bazinet nodded he understood.

A short time later, the radio in Bazinet's hand came to life and a voice at the other end identified itself.

Bazinet did the same and asked at once, "How long before we can go in?"

"I'm afraid I will have to say that is indefinite, Monsieur le Directeur. As you may know, Sarin dissipates quickly and our equipment puts the levels at quite low already but, given the nature of the agent, extreme caution is advised."

"Of course, Sergeant, but I would like to examine the scene as soon as possible. You understand."

"Oui, Monsieur, I do understand. My Corporal and I have taken digital video and still photographs of everything. Your man has seen them and they are quite complete. We have done many scene-of-crime operations, Monsieur, I assure you."

Bazinet was not in the Sergeant's chain of command but he knew he could prevail on the Minister of the Interior to gain access if necessary. But he preferred to avoid being overbearing. "Thank you. That will be of great value. But there are things that must be seen and sensed in person. Perhaps if I suited up?"

"Oui, Monsieur. That is possible. I continue to advise against it but, if you wish…"

"I will be right down."

"No, no, Monsieur You cannot come even this close unsuited. There is a second vehicle just down the Rue Florestine behind you. Please go to them. They can outfit you. When you are ready, I will take you inside."

Once Bazinet was hermetically sealed inside the suit, a Sapeurs-Pompiers enlisted man escorted him to edge of the secured scene. Bazinet closed the remaining distance and joined with the sergeant. They pushed through the fabric of the tent enclosure.

What he saw inside was nothing less than macabre. Twisted tortured victims whose last moments were clearly agonizing. Fortunately for Bazinet, thanks to the suit, he was insulated from the foul stench.

He walked slowly but directly to the back of the main room and stood over the body of a young woman who, as the Inspector had said, was leaned against the rear wall holding what certainly appeared to have been the instrument of death. The woman's face, like the others, was twisted in a mask of pain but Bazinet recognized her immediately from the photographs Torino had circulated. The meaning was clear to him. Al-Nassef was indeed here. He sensed — knew — this would not be the end.

32

Rue des Remparts
The Rock

As al-Nassef had planned, Gallacher had arrived at the apartment on the Rue des Remparts before the attack at the bank but after Bleeker had left. The two hadn't crossed paths. Bleeker was actually walking her bicycle down La Rampe as Gallacher was riding a bus up to Monaco-ville from the other side of the promontory. They'd never met, didn't know each other and never would.

It probably wouldn't have created a problem if they had met but throughout the planning of the operation and into its initial stages, al-Nassef had, as a matter of operational security, taken pains to ensure that the martyrs didn't get to know each other or even to meet. For one thing, there was no reason for them to interact. But more importantly, what wasn't needed in this operation was a relationship or connection of any kind among the component elements. He was leader and as such he knew who would do what and where they would do it and when. The individuals didn't need to know anything more than their assigned roles.

Al-Nassef let Gallacher into the apartment and nodded with satisfaction at the cosmetic and other steps the Scots lawyer had taken to address the potential problem presented by the facial recognition technology and other surveillance. The terrorist leader quickly assumed the attitude of briefing officer and showed the Scot around the apartment ending up in the second bedroom on the corner of the building. Gallacher looked around at the drums and tubing and equipment and got a general suspicion of what he was looking at but said nothing. Al-Nassef explained what everything was and how it worked, Gallacher listened closely. The Scot was highly intelligent and grasped the mechanics as well as the methodology in the first instance. For that, al-Nassef was pleased. He was anxious to leave. Now that Bleeker had acted, he knew things would heat up quickly and he wanted to be out of Monaco before the initial emergency responses moved into the next inevitable stage of investigation and pursuit.

Before he left, al-Nassef ran quickly over the essential points of the operation one more time. "Stay inside," he stressed. "That is critical. As I have told you, the authorities have your photograph and have been circulating it. They also had the photograph of another martyr who has just now performed her act of *jihad*. This connects her to me and to you. So they will be looking very intensively. Do not take another chance on the disguises, you understand. Just stay inside." Gallacher nodded.

Al-Nassef then pulled a state-of-the-art gas mask out of his carryall. For the first time, Gallacher looked confused.

"Yes, I know," al-Nassef said holding his hand up. "You are to be a martyr. But this," he held up the gas mask, "is not for you to use on Sunday." In reality, al-Nassef didn't care if the Scot did use it to survive. Once the Sarin was expelled to the outside, it was of no consequence — except to Gallacher himself surely — whether the man lived or died.

"This is for your use if it becomes necessary prior to 13:00 hours on Sunday. If somehow there should be a leak — and remember there would have to be a leak of both elements and they would have to combine for there to be a premature release of Sarin — use this to deal with it. And don't let any get on your skin. But that should not be necessary. The assembly is ready so there is no need to go near it until it is time. But above all, the timing is of the greatest importance.

"Use the sounds of the race cars as your cues," al-Nassef went on. "Just before the race starts, the cars will be set up to drive a formation lap where they will go around the course at relatively slow speed. You will hear the engines as they start off, loud but not the scream of when they are racing. When they return to the start-finish line on the Boulevard Prince Albert, there will be only a brief moment before the race truly starts. You will not miss the sound of that. It is deafening. You will have everything ready at that point and it is at that moment that you start first the pump and then the vaporizer."

While there was no way to make the timing of the sequence of events entirely precise, in all likelihood, by the time the cars made the right-hand Sainte Devote turn and headed up the hill to the Casino, the mist would be dispersing out and settling down on to the Rue des Remparts. As the cars sped past the Casino and into the Mirabeau turn and then downhill to the famous hairpin at the bottom of the Avenue Des Spélugues, the heavier-than-air vapor would be seeping along the surface of the street and over the edge of the Rock. Then, as the race cars came around the Portier corner and headed to the right into the famous tunnel, the first people at the top of the crowd on the side of the hill would probably just be beginning to wonder if they'd not suddenly contracted a cold. The course would be quiet for a moment while the cars were inside the tunnel but then the noise would re-explode as the cars came racing out into the light and through the Chicane with the harbor on their left. Then the racers would turn left at the Tabac and head toward and around the swimming pool and on to the La Rascasse corner at the bottom of the Rock directly beneath the crowd that was just beginning to die. By then some of the people at the top would already be dead, the ones just below them dying, the ones below them choking, some would be falling down the steep slope knocking others before them. By the time the cars turned right again onto the main straight of the Boulevard de Prince Albert and were speeding back toward the start-finish line, the world would be starting to know that something was terribly wrong.

Gallacher didn't know — didn't need to know — but there was more to come at that point. Just about the time the bodies began dropping down the face of the side of the Rock, the Chanis, Xhelal, Rozafa, and Luan, would perform their act of jihad. They would be just outside the barriers surrounding the race course on the opposite side of the harbor from the Rock, near the St. Devote turn. The Chanis would have taken the train in from Ventimiglia the morning of the race and gone to yet another previously rented location where some twenty kilograms of C4 had been left for them. Each of the parents would have strapped five kilos of explosives to themselves and packed the remaining ten in Luan's carriage. The magnitude of their explosion would be something on the scale of four times more destructive that the Torino explosion had been. Many people would be killed in the blast itself but what pleased al-Nassef particularly was the panic that would follow. People, not just on the north side of the course where the explosion would take place but along the main streets as well would, quite naturally, run away from the scene. They would run south. Straight toward the cascading Sarin that would be oozing invisibly out along the surface of the streets to greet them. It wasn't vital to the plan. But it added to the visual image and the body count. It was, al-Nassef thought with satisfaction, a nice touch.

He altered his appearance once again, gathered up his carryall into which he'd stuffed Bleeker's computer and left the apartment. All the way down La Rampe he could hear sounds of a police emergency to the north of where he was. The commotion and activity were to his benefit because right now the attention was on the incident itself but there could be no question that the focus would soon shift into investigative mode and he wanted to be well away when that happened. At the intersection by the Place d'Armes where Bleeker had gone to the right toward the bank, al-Nassef turned left and walked up the Boulevard Charles III toward the Fontvieille Commercial Center. He took the first escalator down from the Boulevard level down to the entrance to the Jardin Animalier. Then he went right and took the second set of escalators which went down to the courtyard. As he began his descent, his gaze fell on a man who just getting on the up escalator that ran alongside. At first, al-Nassef couldn't quite put his finger on why the man caught his attention. Then he realized it was the man he'd seen in Torino Wednesday evening. But he felt certain even then wasn't the first time he'd seen him. Why was he familiar?

The other man wasn't looking at him so al-Nassef continued to examine the man's face as he rose closer and closer and kept his gaze on him even as they slid past each other. It was at that point, that al-Nassef realized that the very beautiful woman directly behind the man was watching him. He immediately looked away and rode the escalator to the bottom. Fighting the urge to look back, he walked quickly to the corner and went to his right. He regretted having brought himself to anyone's attention however briefly and chastised himself for the uncharacteristic lapse.

But as he strode off toward the bus stop in Cap d'Ail, his mind remained on the man on the escalator. What was it about him? Where had he seen him before?

Roseraie Princesse Grace
Fontvieille

With no spectator events on the Friday of Grand Prix week in Monaco, John and Katherine had slept in, breakfasted late, and then spent the remainder of the morning in the Princess Grace Rose Garden which was across the street from the front entrance to the hotel. It is in fact a memorial garden established by a deeply grieving Prince Rainier in memory of his adored Princess Grace following her death in a car accident. It is a warming, caring environment, curving paths meandering among an enormous variety of rose species, all marked and explained on plaques.

They walked hand in hand, mostly in silence, stopping frequently to read the descriptions and information on the various displays. For the moment, the issues of al-Nassef and the email and extortion demand were pushed to the back of their minds as they enjoyed the peace and tranquility of the garden. And, since the rose gardens are separated from the center of Monaco by the marina in the Port de Fontvieille and the imposing mass of the Rock looming above, they didn't hear the sirens and claxons that responded to the Banque des Maritimes.

They left the gardens intending to head into La Condamine for lunch, maybe at La Rascasse which they'd planned to do on Wednesday before the Torino bombing and John's recognition of al-Nassef had diverted them from it. They crossed into the Fontvieille Commercial Center and got on the up escalator. John was looking at nothing in particular but Katherine found herself glancing at the faces of the people on the down escalator to her left. Her attention was struck by one man who appeared to be looking hard at Cann. Price focused in on him and noted that his face looked strange, somehow distorted. As the man slid past on her left, Price leaned forward.

"John."

He turned and looked at her.

"That man in the brimmed hat," she gestured with her left thumb toward the bottom of the escalators. "I think he was staring at you. Hard. Maybe it's just because it's so much on my mind but I saw a resemblance to al-Nassef. His face looked odd, though. Out of proportion."

Cann looked past her and down the escalator at the man who was already across the courtyard and turning right toward Cap d'Ail. From this distance, he saw only his back but he trusted Price's instincts implicitly. He pushed past the people ahead of him on the up escalator and, as soon as they got the top, turned and got on the down escalator, again pushing past the people ahead of him. At the bottom, he ran to the corner but by the time he got around it, there was no sign of the man. He ran down the street as far as the next corner to see if he could spot the hat or anything familiar but there was nothing. He looked around at the crowded streets and noted the large number of shops and offices into which the man could have disappeared. After a few moments, he walked back to Katherine who by now was also back down at the courtyard level. John shook his head. "He's gone. What did he look like?"

"Dark hair, dark complexion. About 5' 10" or so. As I said, kind of like the face in the surveillance photos except the nose was distended, like he had something in it and his jaw jutted out. But it didn't look like your usual underbite." She gestured broadly to the obvious surveillance cameras all around. "Just what you'd do to avoid those."

John nodded agreement as Katherine continued. "I could be wrong but I don't think so. There was just something about him. He had sunglasses on but I'm sure he was staring at you. His head even followed you as we passed, then he saw me looking at him and he looked away. That's when I told you." She shrugged. "Or maybe it's just the power of suggestion. I don't know."

John shook his head. "No. If there was enough to make you think it might be al-Nassef, it needs to be followed up. Let's get hold of Bazinet."

For the second time, they aborted their plan to eat at La Rascasse and headed back to the hotel. On the way, John tried using his cell phone but got only a broken signal at best. Perhaps it was the Rock looming overhead to their left. Back at the hotel, he again tried to call Bazinet's office this time from one of the lobby phones but was advised that the Director of Public Security was out of the office. He left his name and a message asking for a return call as soon as possible and then crossed over to where Katherine was watching a newscast of a "bank robbery" that had just taken place on the Rue Grimaldi.

33

Polizia di Stato Questura
Ventimiglia

Ispettore Pietro Mastrota hadn't given up. Not by a long shot. And wouldn't. But, so far, his visit to Ventimiglia had yielded no information that would bring him any closer to any of the answers he sought.

Once his ID had been verified, he was allowed up to the office of the Capo Ispettore for the Ventimiglia questura. The two men knew each other well enough to engage in the usual faux insulting pleasantries then Capo Ispettore Francesco Bormida leaned back in his chair and asked with a smile, "So what brings you all the way down here to the provinces, Pietro?"

The smile disappeared at the mention of the Torino bombing. Bormida's face hardened into an expression of anger and disgust. "I bambini," he said shaking his head side to side. "I mostri."

Mastrota nodded agreement and then proceeded to relate what he had learned about the martyrs, al-Nassef, Lugano and Younis, finally explaining his presence in Ventimiglia with a reference to the sighting in Limonetto. "I've found nothing along the route that helps in any way and so I decided to come here and pick your brain."

Bormida nodded slowly. "I don't know how I can help. I of course knew about the bombing, Pietro, and I assure you my people have been given copies of the surveillance photographs. You should hear them talking about how they would like to be the one to come across these animals. What they would do to them. Nonetheless, I'm afraid we have not had any contact that I am aware of." The chief inspector interrupted himself and placed a call to the sergeant on duty to confirm there had been no sightings. He shook his head in the negative as he hung up. "As I said. Nothing, I'm afraid."

The two men then chewed over the facts in hand as good police officers will do, knowing that at any time some bit of information might suddenly stand out in a previously unexplored context. Even that process generated nothing useful.

They went to lunch and made a concerted effort to not talk about the matter in the hope that some inkling, some idea would work itself to the fore of its own accord without being labored at. Still nothing.

The break, when it came, almost didn't happen. They'd gone back to Bormida's office and brainstormed a bit more but finally had to acknowledge that what little they knew wasn't enough to build on. The conversation between the two career police officers, as with many if not most professions, turned to shop talk. War stories. Tales of events or incidents or people that stand out for their excitement or humor or pathos. And the latter brought Bormida to mention the man who'd spent the night in the jail after the staff at the Villa Colamine Pedemontana reported suspected abuse of his family. "Apparently, he'd been keeping the wife and child in the room and may not have even been letting them eat. When the hotel went to check on them, there were signs of physical abuse and we responded. But the wife refused to cooperate…"

"But under the 'maltreatment of family law', as you must know, Francesco, charges can be brought by the state. You don't need the wife to press charges."

"Of course I know that, Pietro," Bormida said indignantly, "but as *you* must know, to prove a charge of maltreatment you must establish a pattern, a sequence of repeat events. And without the wife, we do not have the proof. Besides, they are not Italians, they are visitors and have only been here since Wednesday. That in itself would make it difficult to establish a pattern."

"Where are they from?"

"Albania." Bormida pulled a folder on his desk toward him. "I was reviewing the file this morning to see if we could hold him further but I could find nothing so we felt we had to let him go. It was just about the time you arrived here."

Mastrota recalled the man he'd seen that morning. "Black hair, angular face?"

"Yes, that was him. A disturbing situation."

"How so?"

"On the surface he seemed composed but underneath, he was clearly very angry. Just barely holding it in, in my opinion. I worry for his family."

"Did he resist arrest?"

"No. As I said, he was calm. On the outside anyway. After he was in a cell for a while, we could hear him talking. We thought maybe he was talking to himself — going around the bend, maybe. But he was just praying. Then he requested a Koran."

"He is Muslim?"

"My understanding is that many Albanians are."

Mastrota said nothing and Bormida could see the wheels turning in his mind.

"Oh come now, Pietro," Bormida chastised his colleague, "the fact that the man is a Muslim by itself means almost nothing."

"Of course not, Francesco," Mastrota replied. "I suppose I'm desperate." He thought a moment longer then asked, "You said they are only here since Wednesday. Where were they before that?"

Bormida checked the file again and looked up with an upraised eyebrow. "Torino. But still…"

"I know. I know. But let me play with this a bit." Mastrota pointed a finger at the file. "Do we know how long they were in Torino before coming here? Or where they stayed in Torino?"

Bormida shook his head in the negative. "That wasn't relevant to our inquiries."

"Does that say how they came from Torino to here?"

Bormida checked. "Rental car."

"To be dropped off?"

Bormida shook his head. "Returned to Torino."

"Meaning the car was rented in Torino. Does it say where in Torino?"

Bormida read some more. "A location on Corso Giulio Cesare."

"Very near Cottolengo."

Bormida twisted his head as if to say well, okay, but it still isn't anything to act on. Mastrota nodded in agreement with the gesture but held up his right index finger. "Stay with me on this, Francesco." The Torino detective thought some more then said, "They are from Albania you said."

Bormida nodded.

"And Albania is not in the European Union."

Another nod from Bormida.

"So...," Mastrota chewed his lip, "they would need to have entered the EU at some point. And coming from a non-EU country, they would have needed a visa to do so.'

Bormida flipped through the papers in the folder before him. "We photocopied his papers, of course. Here." He read the document. "They entered by train into Slovenia." That was logical. From Albania they would have traveled north through Croatia which is a candidate for EU membership but not yet an EU member. "From that point on they would be able to travel freely to any other EU country."

"Yes but if I remember my EU law correctly, the visa needs to be issued by the final destination country."

Bormida looked at the document again.

"Issued by the Italian Consulate in Tirana."

"Which tell us Italy was their destination before they left Albania. And also if I remember correctly, they needed to have a sponsor and a specific address in the destination country when the visa application was filed in the first place.'

"I believe so, yes," Bormida replied, "but that information wouldn't be on the visa itself. It would be on the application."

"Which is where?"

"I'm not sure. Tirana, perhaps. The consulate? Or perhaps there is a copy here in Italy."

"Let's check."

"Pietro..." Bormida said in a cautioning voice. "This is still a very large stretch."

"I agree but as we have gone from point to point we still haven't come up against an item or a fact that would tell us "no, this cannot be."

"Perhaps but that is certainly not enough to draw any conclusions."

"I have absolutely nothing to work with otherwise, Francesco. Humor me. Please."

Bormida looked at Mastrota for a long moment then picked up the phone. He explained what he wanted and listened to the response. Then he muttered, "Grazie" and hung up.

"It may take some time to track down, they said. An hour. Perhaps more."

Mastrota nodded his thanks. "Where is this Colline Pedemontana where they are staying?"

"At the top of the Colle d'Astria overlooking the sea. Across the bridge, to the right and up a very winding road. Why?"

"I thought I might take a look around while I'm waiting."

"You want to check him out," Bormida said coldly. "Please don't." This time he held up his index finger. "It's your turn to humor me, Pietro. As despicable as I found this man Chani to be, we do not have enough to make him the subject of an official inquiry."

"I understand and I give you my word, I will do nothing to make things awkward." He looked at his watch. "This place has a bar, I assume?"

Bormida nodded.

"Good view?"

"Incredible."

"There," Mastrota opened his hands. "I'll just go up there and relax over a nice glass of wine."

"You're on duty," Bormida said sourly.

"True," Mastrota replied. "But we're always on duty, aren't we."

Bormida didn't smile so Mastrota said, "Okay, so I'll have a Fanta instead." He stood and leaned across the desk offering his hand to Bormida. "Seriously, Francesco, I give you my word I will only make some observations. This is your territory and I will respect it."

Bormida grunted then accepted Mastrota's proffered handshake.

The Torino detective stood then leaned back down and picked up one of several copies of the mug shot of Chani contained in the file. "May I take this?"

"You won't recognize him without it?"

"I'll recognize him. I want this in case I need others to do the same."

Villa Colline Pedemontana
Ventimiglia

Rozafa Chani sat on the bed in the hotel room at the Villa Colline Pedemontana holding little Luan on her lap and humming a lullaby to help him sleep. Xhelal Chani was out on the balcony overlooking the Mediterranean with the laptop computer open on the small table in front of him. He had checked his cyber drop several times for a message from the leader of the operation since coming back from the questura and this time he again found none. He closed the lid of the laptop computer with more force than was necessary and stared out into space.

He was anxious to get going. The leader had promised that their time was near and Chani wanted to get on with it. He looked forward to his martyrdom and was proud that he would bring his wife and son with him. He would, he had promised himself, consider foregoing his virgins if Rozafa performed well. But he was now greatly concerned in that regard. To his anger and shame, she had disobeyed him and left the room when he was not here. That undoubtedly had much to do with this dissolute and soulless place. Still, who knows what she may have done while she was outside his presence and outside his control. In the old country, his honor would have required her death. He cared for her but he would have done what was necessary. Here and now, he would forebear from taking any action. Her death, their deaths were coming soon and he would wait until they were in heaven. There he would know all he needed to know and he could make his decision about eternity at that time.

He opened the computer yet again just as the phone rang inside the room. Rozafa was forbidden to answer it so he stood and slid back the glass door separating the room from the balcony. When he picked it up, he heard the voice of Signore Lorenzo, the hotel manager on the other end.

"Signore Chani," Lorenzo said coldly, "I am calling to ask if your family prefers the early or late sitting for dinner tonight."

At first, Chani had trouble processing the question. Why would this man be asking…? Then it hit him that he was essentially being told to bring his family down for dinner. This was an insult, an affront to his authority within his own family. He started to react angrily but caught himself, realizing he did not need another encounter with the police.

Suppressing his fury, he answered calmly, "The late sitting will be fine, Signore."

"Very well," Lorenzo said. "Do you care to order in advance or…"

"No," Chani replied, "we will order at the time. Grazie, Signore.

"Prego, Signore."

Chani barely managed to refrain from slamming the phone into the cradle. After he put it down, he turned to his wife.

"Pack our things," he ordered. "We are leaving."

34

Bazinet completed his examination of the scene and returned to his office. The first order of business was to dictate an alert to go out to police and Interpol — but not to the public. They didn't need a panic on top of everything else. He had several phone calls he needed to make but when he sat down behind his desk, he put his head in his hands allowing himself just a moment of reflection and a little second-guessing. Could he have stopped this? Would there be more? Knowing there was at least one more of al-Nassef's martyrs out there, it was very likely. He shook his head slowly and took a breath. Enough of this. There was work to do.

He saw Cann's message on his desk and made that call first.

"Monsieur Cann. Girard Bazinet."

"Monsieur Bazinet," John answered. "I called earlier."

"Yes, I see the message. But I was going to call you in any case. You have seen the news? What took place on the Rue Grimaldi?"

"The bank robbery?"

"It was not a bank robbery, I'm afraid."

"It wasn't a bank robbery." John repeated the words for Katherine's benefit. She had been watching him closely and made a grimace when he said that. She had a feeling about what that meant.

John listened in silence for several moments as Bazinet described what had happened. At one point, he repeated the single word, "Sarin" out loud. Katherine, who had not taken her eyes of him, took a sharp breath.

"And," the Monaco Director of Public Security continued, "there is no question that the attacker is the woman in the surveillance photos taken in Torino. So there can also be no question, in my mind at least, that this attack is connected to al-Nassef."

"Who we may have just seen," John said. "That's why I called you."

"Seen him?" Bazinet said instantly. "Where?"

"In the Fontvieille Commercial Center. He was going down the escalators while we were going up. Katherine saw him, not me."

"Are you certain of the ID?"

"Not one hundred percent. It sounds like he'd taken some measures to alter his appearance. I didn't see him myself but I'd count on Katherine's instincts. If she says she's 95% sure, you can be 99.9%."

"Were you able to see where he went?"

"I tried to follow him but he disappeared around a corner. He was heading in the general direction of Cap d'Ail, though. Do you have surveillance cameras out there?"

"Of course. Monaco does. Cap d'Ail not so much." Bazinet was already punching a button to summon an assistant. "Give me a description of what you have."

"I'll put Katherine on. She saw him."

Price picked up the extension in the room's foyer and described the sequence of events in detail as well as what the man was wearing. She put as much detail as she could into the description of the man's face and its anomalies.

"Thank you, Madame. We should have the surveillance images within an hour or so. If you would be willing to look at them, I would be grateful."

"Of course."

"And, John, as I said, I was planning to call you even if you hadn't called me. You are, as far as I know, the only one here who has actually met this man and dealt with him. I would like to ask for your help. Can you come to my office this afternoon? Both of you?"

"Of course," they both said together.

"Bon. Merci. Also let me tell you we are of course still looking for the other man in the Torino surveillance photographs. And will be trying to trace the bank attacker's movements back from the bank. We're canvassing the public now."

"If they're moving around," John said, "there's a chance of spotting them but if they've gone to ground, the chances are probably slim to none."

"Making your possible sighting all the more important."

"But if they've gone to ground," Katherine said slowly, "does that mean that they're done? Or that they're waiting? And for what?"

"Indeed," Bazinet said. "This is not happening the weekend of the Grand Prix by coincidence. There will be over one hundred thousand people here on Sunday. A terrorist attack would be devastating. We must find out what is happening. And quickly."

Villa Colline Pedemontana
Ventimiglia

Bormida was right. The view was indeed incredible. Mastrota sat at the bar sipping his Fanta and looking into the distance where he could just see the entrance to Monaco's harbor.

Lorenzo, the hotel manager, walked over. "You asked to see me, Signore?"

Mastrota turned in his seat and extended his hand. "Yes, Signore…" His face took on an inquiring expression.

"Lorenzo. And your name is?"

"I am Capo Ispettore Pietro Mastrota of the Italian State Police." He pulled out his identification and handed it to the hotel manager to examine. Lorenzo did and handed it back. "Yes, Ispettore, what can I do for you."

"You have a guest by the name of Chani here?"

"I did," Lorenzo replied. "But if you are here to arrest him you are unfortunately too late."

"He's checked out?"

"Abruptly. Just a short time ago."

"This was not scheduled?"

"Not at all, Signore. He was scheduled to check out on Sunday."

"You said abruptly. Do you know what might have caused it?"

"Si. I'm afraid I took it upon myself to see that his wife and child be fed while they are here." He paused. "There was a problem yesterday with…" he began to explain but Mastrota waved him off.

175

"Yes, Capo Bormida has told me about this."

"I am all for respecting others cultures, Ispettore, but I expect mine to be respected as well. And I have an abiding contempt for a man who does not put his family first. So I called him to try to ensure that he bring his family down to dinner or at least order room service."

"He didn't take it well?"

"I sensed he was angry but he reacted calmly. But then they left shortly afterwards. I fear they may be worse off now. Frankly, I wish he'd directed his anger directly at me."

"Si. I understand. Tell me, did he check out without paying?" Mastrota asked.

"No. His stay was paid in full, in advance."

"By whom?"

"It was a tour company voucher." Lorenzo thought hard for a moment. "Para-euro Tours, I think was the name. I had not dealt with them before but the voucher cleared the bank so…"

Mastrota thought for a moment then asked, "Do you know what bank it was drawn on?"

"Not offhand, Ispettore, but I could find that out if you wish."

"Please," Mastrota said. The manager walked back toward his office.

Mastrota was mulling over this information seeking in vain for something to latch on to when his cell phone rang. He clicked it on. "Mastrota," he announced into it. It was his questura in Torino calling.

"Assistente Donato here, Ispettore."

"Si, Donato. What is it?"

"Signore Bazinet from Monaco is trying to reach you, Signore. He would like you to call him."

"Do you know what it's about?"

"Si, Ispettore. The incident in Monaco."

Mastrota tensed. "What incident?"

"Are you near a television, Signore?"

Mastrota looked around and saw one above a corner of the bar. He looked at the bartender and asked him if he could turn it on. The *barista* picked up a remote control and pressed the power button. The television came to life showing a bath soap commercial.

"What am I looking for, Donato?" Mastrota asked.

"Sky Italia is running a story now."

Mastrota repeated the words "Sky Italia" to the bartender who switched to that channel. On the screen appeared a scene of a building with the entrance covered in a tented structure of some sort. The street out front was empty except for an emergency vehicle and two men walking around in what Mastrota knew to be "hazmat" suits. The barman upped the sound and they listened to the reporter relaying the official public story about a "robbery".

"Not a robbery, I assume, Donato?"

"It doesn't appear so. Signore Bazinet was reluctant to give me the details over the phone and he asked me to have you call him as soon as possible."

"Do you have his numbers?"

Donato read them off his notes.

"Does he know I am in Ventimiglia?"

"I told him, Signore. He was pleased by that and asked if it would be possible for you to come to Monaco at once. He said it was urgent."

"I'm leaving now. Anything else, Donato?"

"That was all, Signore."

Mastrota thanked the Assistente and clicked off. He paid for his Fanta and turned to head for his car as the manager returned. "You are leaving, Ispettore?"

"Yes. I have to go to Monaco. Thank you for your help."

"Of course, Signore. But you wanted to know what bank the voucher was drawn on?"

"Oh, yes, of course," Mastrota stopped and waited.

"It was the Bank Saderat. In Tehran."

35

Col le Bermasse
France

As far as he could tell, al-Nassef had managed to leave Monaco without being followed. He hadn't seen Cann come after him but he knew there were surveillance cameras about so he'd ducked into an office building just before crossing out of Fontvieille into Cap d'Ail. Once inside, he went into a lobby rest room where he'd taken a different hat and jacket out of his carryall and switched what he had on. Then he went out a different exit and walked a bit further to a different bus stop than the one he had arrived at that morning. As another precaution, he rode the bus past Col le Bermasse to the next town and then taken another rural jitney back to a kilometer or so from where he was staying. He walked the rest of the way seeing no one on the route.

Once inside his room, he'd lain on the bed clearing his mind except for the image of the man on the escalator. Who was he? Strangely, when he finally remembered, it wasn't the more recent contact in Iraq in 2003 that came to mind. For some reason, when the recognition hit him, he remembered the American who had been with the Sayeret Matkal forces in 1979 following the Nahariya operation.

Al-Nassef remembered more about the man. How in 1979, the man had suggested he and the other surviving terrorist should be killed on the spot. He didn't know as much English then as he did now but he understood enough to know that the man was pressing for his immediate death. Which is what he'd frankly expected to happen. But it didn't. It was the first time he'd realized just how ineffective and weak this enemy was that he was fighting. Indeed, it was a testament to the weakness of his enemies that he was around in 2003 and still around even now. He thought back to that night in Nahariya in 1979. With the roles reversed, he wouldn't have hesitated.

Then with a start, he made the connection between the man who'd been present at his arrest in Nahariya and the attorney that was present at many of his interrogations in Baghdad. Oddly enough, in 2003, he hadn't recognized Cann or made a connection to the earlier time. But memory can be strange and now, for some reason, he did make the connection.

So what did it mean? He had crossed paths with this man, not once or even twice, but now three times. Four if you count Wednesday evening in Turin. Coincidence? Al-Nassef had not survived this long by dismissing anything as coincidence. He thought on it long and hard and still could not come up with a plausible reason why this man would be here now. Of course, sometimes things are unexplainable because there is no explanation. Perhaps he was simply here to see the Grand Prix. Possible. Still…

And what of the woman? She was with the man in Torino and they had traveled to Monaco together. Perhaps they were married. Or partners. There was no question she'd taken notice of him on the escalator and he cursed himself again for falling out of operational mode if even for just a moment. No doubt she'd gotten a very good look. He was disguised, of course. But the steps he'd taken were designed to confuse computer matrices. They were less effective close up and to the human eye. He wondered if she'd called him to the attention of her companion. Probably. But he'd not been followed. Or found, at least. So ultimately the question was what effect had the day's events had on the execution of the overall plan.

He could think of none.

He wasn't entirely happy with the delay from the first strike today to the final blow. He looked at his watch — forty-plus hours in which anything could happen. It is axiomatic that no operation goes exactly as planned and, if his original plan had been followed to the letter, things would have happened much closer together.

But the powers in Tehran had seen an opportunity to add even more insult to injury and in the process extort a great deal of money from the *kafir* and make them pay for their own destruction. Al-

Nassef appreciated the irony and the added indignity and, since Iran was paying the bills, so to speak...

Al-Nassef knew a demand for money would have been made. But he had no idea whether or not it had been met. Indeed, the assumption was that the authorities would probably not meet the demand initially. What the infidels did not know was that it didn't matter. The attack would go forward in any case. If no money had been paid, there would be a second note blaming the westerners for the attack at the bank today and giving them another chance to pay. If, contrary to expectations, monies had been paid, the second note would criticize them for not sending enough and demand more.

Another nice touch, to al-Nassef's way of thinking. Another testament to the weakness and gullibility of the enemy. Now they just needed to wait.

All was proceeding according to plan. As far as he knew, the authorities had no images of the Albanian couple and, in any case, they were still settled in Ventimiglia. There was no need for them to move until Sunday morning when the trains into Monaco would be especially crowded making surveillance difficult. And the apartment in Ste-Dévote where the C4 was stored was only minutes from the Monaco train station. Besides, everyone knows that, except for the Israeli's perhaps, no one attributes violence to a couple with a baby in a carriage.

Gallacher was at the apartment on the Rock with the chemicals in place and ready to go. The only thing remaining in that regard was to implement the dispersal of the Sarin. And the Scot was under strict instructions to stay inside until 13:00 Sunday so there should be nothing between now and then to draw the attention of the authorities.

And the young madrassa-trained Brit was still in Roquebrune-Cap-Martin. He, too, appeared to have escaped notice and since his particular expertise would not be needed until tomorrow, there was no need for him to move about until then. Al-Nassef knew the young *jihadi* was the most serious and most dedicated of the martyrs and for that reason had the most confidence in him. He also knew Mukhtar was the most genuinely anxious to be a *shahid* and would be chomping at the bit to get into action. For that reason, al-Nassef had decided to send the email tonight directing the young *jihadi* to travel the next day, Saturday, to the location in Monaco where he would construct the explosive devices that the Chanis would use at race time on Sunday. Then Rafiq Mukhtar would be ordered to come to the garage in Col de Bermasse where he would be honored, al-Nassef was sure, to assemble the ultimate device which the world of terror had sought for these many years of *jihad*.

Menton,
France

When Xhelal Chani had stormed out of the Villa Colline Pedemontana with his family, he had no clear idea of where he was going. Just away from the interference of the police and the people of Ventimiglia and that cursed hotel in particular. He came down off the hill atop which the hotel was located and headed straight for the A10 where he had a choice to go to the north and east or the south and west. Xhelal Chani may have opted to abandon urban life years ago and return to the mountains but in so doing he had by no means lost his awareness of the world. He knew full well that it was Grand Prix week in Monaco and had already concluded that would be a fine venue for an attack.

So he chose south and west.

The first town he came to was Menton and he got off the highway at that exit and headed for the center of the city. As he drove down the Avenue de Sospel, he was, at one point, not very far from the apartment Karlijn Bleeker had occupied for the last couple of days. He continued down the Avenue until it ended at a "T" intersection with Avenue Carnot. Directly in front of him was Menton's casino, a lovely but considerably less famous gambling establishment than Monaco's. Chani turned left and then took the first street on the right which ran along the side of the casino down to the Promenade du Soleil which ran parallel to the rocky beach and the Mediterranean beyond.

He'd given a good deal of thought to what he should do now that he had, quite uncharacteristically, removed himself from the strict confines of the leader's plan. He had to make contact — something they had all been cautioned against except in the most extraordinary circumstances — and the only way he had to do that was with his computer.

He drove alongside the *plage* which was sparsely populated with bathers, some, to Chani's further chagrin and disgust, topless. He glanced in the rear view mirror at his wife with her eyes properly downcast, holding Luan on her lap. The water was on his right and along the street on his left were a series of cafes and hotels, including the one where Gallacher had been staying. He was searching for a Wi-Fi symbol on one of the cafes so he could park outside and use that portal to access the Internet. He and the others had also been briefed on "warchalking" which was the product of someone "wardriving" around in search of wireless access points which they would then mark with chalk symbols which others in the know would recognize as such. Such a discovery would allow him free — and, far more importantly — relatively anonymous access to the Internet.

He found nothing along the promenade that fronted the beach. He turned left and left again and drove in the opposite direction down the next street over which was a block away from the Mediterranean. Just before reaching the intersection with the Avenue de Sospel again, Chani caught sight of one of the wireless network symbols he sought and looked around for a parking space. There was none. He went further and turned right onto the Avenue de Sospel which had diagonal metered spaces up and down its entire length. He pulled into one, turned the car off, got out and put enough coins into the meter to give him a half hour of time. "Wait here," he said to Rozafa after getting the laptop out of the trunk. Then he walked down the avenue and disappeared around the corner to the left.

There were four tables on the sidewalk in front of the café that had the Wi-Fi symbol and three of them were empty. Chani sat down and ordered a strong coffee then set up the computer. He accessed the site that contained his cyber-drop and saw first that there were no messages to him. He hit "compose" and advised the leader of the situation, swallowing his pride for the sake of the mission and giving a brief but accurate summation of his reasons for leaving the hotel. It was incomprehensible to him that that the leader would not understand and accept that no good Muslim could tolerate the immorality and interference with his family that he had been subjected to. However, he did not see the need to tell the leader about his encounters with the police. When he was done, he hit "send" and settled back to wait for a response.

In the car around the corner, Rozafa Chani cracked open the front and rear doors on one side. It was not an exceptionally warm day but it was sunny and the temperature was becoming uncomfortable inside the parked vehicle. Xhelal had left the power windows closed and taken the keys with him or she would have just cracked open the windows a bit. Slowly, carefully, she raised her eyes and looked back in the direction Xhelal had gone. She didn't see him. She began to look around at her surroundings. Everywhere there were people who seemed, at least, to be having fun or at least doing what they wanted. She looked in fascination at young men, many shirtless, some on bicycles, some on motorbikes and motorcycles all zipping about with an obvious sense of abandon. She suddenly caught herself and quickly looked in the mirror to make sure Xhelal was not coming back. Then she looked around some more.

She was fascinated by the men but couldn't help being dumbfounded by the women she saw — at least the young women. While none of them were entirely shirtless, they walked about freely in clothing and outfits that astonished her. The most covered of the women wore skirts and blouses but many wore considerably less ranging from shorts and halters to a few who roamed the main streets of Menton in bikinis that required far less material than her least modest underwear. She found to her surprise that she was not shocked, but embarrassed.

Her eyes went back to the young men. Not out of lust but out of fascination with their obvious independence. While it was true that men in Albania — her region of it, anyway — had absolute power over their families and villages, in moments of reflection, she'd sometimes thought that even that kind of omnipotence entailed restrictions of its own. Not that she felt badly for the men. She'd often envied them their societal pre-eminence and wondered what it would be like to be in such control. But she'd also sometimes wondered if the men themselves weren't just as bound by the rules they felt required to enforce. And had wondered if there were times, even just once in a while, when they wished for the freedom to be kind. Probably not, she'd usually concluded. It was just the way things were.

She watched the scene with growing sadness. She'd wondered briefly if she could ever learn to be as free as these people she was watching now. In the end she knew that such freedom would never be hers.

Once more, her eyes went to the young men, some still boys really, with their swaggering air and happy faces with cigarettes dangling from their smiling lips and she began to wonder, "But why should not Luan have an opportunity to be so happy. And free."

36

Department of Public Security
Office of the Director
Monaco

Bazinet ushered John and Katherine into a large conference room that was to be used as a command center and think tank. There were several computers around the room. Bazinet led Price to one that was set up on a side table against the rear wall of the room.

"We have loaded the digital surveillance files into this computer, Madame Price. If you would be so kind, you need only choose a camera by location and then click through in sequence according to the time frames involved." He gestured to an assistant standing nearby. "Noelle is available to assist you if need be. Thank you for your help."

"*De rien,*" Katherine said as she pulled the chair back from the table and settled in.

Bazinet crossed back to Cann. "I placed a call to Ispettore Mastrota to advise him of these latest developments. It seems he is in Ventimiglia, just a few kilometers from here. His Assistente told me he had decided to trace the route he thought al-Nassef might have taken to see if he could find anything. I don't know if he has but I feel it is fortunate he is in the area. He returned my call and left a message saying he was on his way."

"Good," John said. "I only spoke with him once but he sounded sharp. And his superiors spoke very highly of him."

"I have worked with him on occasion in the past. He is very good."

"So, can you tell me where things stand right now?"

Bazinet nodded. "We sent several officers out among the crowds with photographs of al-Nassef and the other man. Of course, if the man you saw in Fontvieille was in fact al-Nassef and he has changed his appearance the original photographs will not be so helpful. We have no reported sightings of either man so far. We also gave the officers the photograph of the woman who perpetrated the attack in the bank and photographs of her clothing and a helmet and bicycle left outside the bank building. Two passers-by, a Monegasque and a tourist seem quite certain that they saw her in the moments before the attack. One said he saw her coming north on the Rue Grimaldi from the direction of the Place d'Armes and the other at the bottom of La Rampe outside the restroom. An officer had the presence of mind to question the restroom attendant who was able to confirm not only that the dead woman was in the restroom but that she carried the helmet in the photograph — or one exactly like it."

"So," John said slowly thinking as he went along, "the restroom at the base of La Rampe is at the corner of the Avenue de La Porte Nueve and Boulevard Charles III, yes? Correct me if I'm wrong here. You know this area much better than I. Does that mean she had to be coming either from La Rampe or from Fontvieille?"

Bazinet shook his head in the negative. "I'm afraid not. There is also the Avenue du Port that comes up from the Quay and it is possible she could have come from anywhere along the harbor."

"But if you add in the fact that we saw al-Nassef in Fontvieille — in the Commercial Center *after* the attack, heading *away* from the scene, might we not surmise that he and the woman attacker *came* from that direction. That wherever they staged from is in that general direction?"

Bazinet wasn't convinced. "We might surmise that, perhaps, but we certainly cannot conclude it," he said with a shrug. "Besides, John," the Director said with a rueful smile, "almost all of France is in that general direction."

Katherine was listening in as she scanned the surveillance files and called out a question over her shoulder. "Do we have the surveillance from earlier in the day for this area I'm looking at?" she asked. "If he — or they for that matter — came in from that direction, we might see it. Maybe even wearing the same clothing and hat as he was when I saw him. And the woman did have that distinctive helmet."

Bazinet directed the assistant to make sure they had the files Price referenced and set them up for viewing.

Then John had a thought. "Can your FERET software distinguish colors? And patterns?"

"I believe so."

"Well, the woman's helmet is fairly distinctive. Let's put the photo of the helmet into the FERET then. See if it comes up with anything."

"It is designed for faces." Then he shrugged. "But why not?"

"No harm in trying," John said.

"Of course, we don't know if they even arrived together," Bazinet said to no one in particular. "Operationally, that would not necessarily be the norm." John nodded his agreement.

"Nor do we know if the man you saw was actually al-Nassef. Merde." Bazinet caught himself. "Pardon, Mesdames," he said.

"*Pas du tout, Monsieur*," Katherine dismissed his concern. "*Il n'est rien que je n'ai pas entendu avant. Ou dit.*"

Everyone in the room smiled as she turn back to the monitor. A moment later she shouted, "Bingo!"

"Got him?" Cann and Bazinet crossed to look over her shoulder. Price had a finger touching the screen. Bazinet summoned the assistant who took over and worked to enlarge and enhance the image.

"That's him," Katherine said as the shot became clearer. That's the man I saw."

John peered closely. "It sure looks like him to me," he said. "He's distorted his face to fool the FERET system but what the human eye can do that the computer can't is make judgment calls. And I call it a hit. In my opinion, that's al-Nassef."

"Excellent." Bazinet enthused. "Now let's see how well we can track him." He turned to the assistant. "Follow him in sequence, s'il vous plait."

From the starting point, they were able to click forward frame by frame. They had him initially on the Avenue Albert II which was the street that ran alongside the Commercial Center until it came to a cross street. The next image had Al-Nassef — if the man in the hat was al-Nassef — on the other side of the intersection and the next after that had him nowhere to be seen. The assistant forwarded through several frames and from camera to camera but there was no further shot of him.

"How many entrances to that building?" Katherine asked.

Bazinet thought. "Three. Front, back, and that cross street side. The other side abuts the next building." He knew what she was getting at. "Bring up the Gabian entrance from the minute he disappeared forward," he told the assistant.

They scored. Four and a half minutes after the last frame on Albert II, a man of similar appearance although with a different hat and jacket, came out onto the street. Once again, the assistant enlarged and enhanced and it was clear that it was the same man. They man could be seen walking away and crossing into Cap d'Ail. Bazinet had requested and received Cap d'Ail surveillance and working forward from the time frames and location already established, caught the man again waiting at a small bus stop.

"Only certain buses run from each stop." He called an officer over and pointed at the screen. "Find out what number buses run from there. And their routes." He turned to the assistant, Noelle. "Print out some copies of today's al-Nassef images. And give them to this officer." To the officer, he said. "Take these and canvass the neighborhood of that bus stop. See if anyone saw anything."

"Oui, Monsieur."

"We have a hit on the helmet, Monsieur le Directeur," another assistant called out. "To the north, coming in on the Avenue Princesse Grace this morning."

"So much for my theory that they came together," John said.

"Perhaps. But it shows only that the young woman came in that way." Bazinet spoke to the assistant. "Have you entered this new image of what we just found on al-Nassef into FERET?"

"Just entering it now, Monsieur."

Within moments, the computer scored a hit, displaying a series of images of al-Nassef in the same clothes and hat crossing into Monaco from Cap d'Ail earlier that morning.

"That's not the same bus stop, is it?" John asked.

"No, but it is not far from the other one. And I am quite sure it serves similar routes to the bus stop he left from." Bazinet spoke to the assistant. "Contact the officers I sent to canvass the scene. Be sure they include this area as well."

"Oui, Monsieur."

Bazinet walked to the end of the conference table and sat down gesturing for the others to do the same. When they were all seated, Bazinet folded his hands in front of them. "We are at a point where we need to go over what we have and where we need to go, no?"

John and Katherine were in complete agreement.

Bazinet looked at his watch. "Let us wait a bit more for Inspector Mastrota. All of this began, it would appear, on his territory and there's no sense in starting anywhere but the beginning."

37

Highway D6007
Outside Monaco

For the second time that day, Ispettore Pietro Mastrota was crawling along in traffic. He should have been in Monaco by now. Ventimiglia was less than twenty kilometers from Monaco and most of that was on the multi-laned A10/A8. That part went smoothly enough. Once off the highway, however, the roads are not just narrower. They are winding to the point of being tortuous. Add to that the fact that as one approaches Monaco proper, the roads are cut into the sides of foothills right on the coastline so that when driving in either direction, one has a sharply rising wall of earth on one side and a stomach wrenching drop of several hundred feet on the other. It is a dangerous route and the one that, in fact, claimed the life of Princess Grace in 1982.

Once he'd navigated the roads on the outskirts of the principality, Mastrota found himself tied up in traffic that was part the result of Friday being a quasi-usual business day but mostly because of the Grand Prix and the arrival of the even greater number of fans arriving for the actual race weekend. The pace was particularly frustrating because Mastrota was anxious not only to find out the details of the "bank robbery" that apparently wasn't one but also because he, Mastrota, had gotten some information of his own which might lead to a break.

Bormida had called him on his cell phone not long after Mastrota had left the Villa Colline Pedemontana and while he was driving to Monaco.

"Mastrota here," he answered the phone.

"Tell me, Pietro, are you a psychic or just a lucky guesser," the Ventimiglia inspector said cryptically.

"My experience has been that it usually doesn't matter, Francesco. What are you talking about?"

"Congratulations are in order, Capo Ispettore."

"Thank you, Francesco, but why?" Actually Mastrota had an idea what his colleague was getting at.

"The consular office called and advised me that the visa for the Chani family was applied for in Milan and the address of their sponsor and final destination was…care to guess?"

"Cottolengo?"

"Not just Cottolengo but the Cottolengo Mosque. With Imam Bagy as the sponsor."

Mastrota said nothing for a while and Bormida spoke. "This still may not be definitive, Pietro, but in my opinion this is more than enough to justify the Chanis being brought in for questioning. You told me Capo Tridente placed you in charge of this investigation so, say the word and I will bring them in on your authority."

"You have it but they are not at the Pedemontana anymore. They've gone."

"Gone? Where? When?"

"The 'when' was earlier this afternoon. Apparently the hotel manager was pressing the man on his treatment of his family and he checked out. Taking the wife and son with him. As for the 'where', I have no idea. Call the hotel and get the information on his rental car. That should help you find him. Let me know when you get it, would you? I'm on the road now."

"Where are you?"

"Almost to Monaco."

"Monaco?" Bormida asked. "I thought you were at the Pedemontana."

"I was. But then Bazinet of Monaco Public Security called about what happened in Monaco earlier and asked me to come there. An incident at a bank which is being reported as a robbery but apparently isn't. Do you know anything?"

"I'm not familiar with it." The Interpol report was in the process of being circulated but hadn't reached Bormida's desk quite yet.

"Well, thanks for the information of Chani's visa. Please put out a "be on the lookout" for Chani as soon as you get the information on his rental car. Let me know what happens. If you can't reach me on my cell, contact me through Bazinet's office." He gave Bormida the number.

Mastrota finally got into Monaco and made his way slowly to Bazinet's headquarters. His Italian State Police ID — that and Bazinet's instructions to the guards to expect the Italian at any time — got him into the secure parking lot with not trouble. He rode the elevator to the seventh floor and an officer preceded him into the conference room.

"Inspector Mastrota is here, Monsieur," the officer announced.

Bazinet turned around crossed the room extending his hand to Mastrota. "Inspector, thank you so much for coming. We are fortunate you were nearby. Much has happened. And we can certainly use your help and expertise."

"Thank you, Director Bazinet. I will do what I can. I am at your disposal."

"Allow me introduce Monsieur Cann to you, Inspector. You spoke with him on the phone on Wednesday."

"Of course," Mastrota shook Cann's hand. "Thank you for your ID of this al-Nassef, Signore Cann. It was invaluable. We did not even have a starting point before that."

"Well we have much more now, Inspector, thanks in part to Madame Price." Bazinet pointed at Katherine who turned from the computer and smiled a greeting at Mastrota.

"Signora," Mastrota said with a formal nod of his head.

"Madame Price is a senior partner in the same law firm as Monsieur Cann," Bazinet informed the Italian. "She is also Monsieur Cann's fiancée."

Mastrota turned back to John and nodded his head in acknowledgment. "My congratulations, Signore."

"Thank you," John said. "I'm a very lucky man." He looked at Katherine to see if she'd caught the reference. Her grin told him she had.

"Moreover," Bazinet went on, "Madame Price has spotted al-Nassef for us here in Monaco."

Mastrota was instantly all business. "So he is here."

"He is indeed." Bazinet gave Mastrota the details of both the actual sighting on the escalator and the subsequent confirmation from the surveillance images. "And not only is he here but he has struck again. Let me tell you about this so-called bank robbery."

Mastrota listened as Bazinet described Bleeker's attack on the Bank des Maritimes. Shaking his head, he asked. "And there is no question this is the woman in the photographs we circulated?" Bazinet pushed the still photographs the Sapeurs-Pompier sergeant had given him. Mastrota looked at it for a moment then nodded. "I agree."

"Do you have any idea who she is?" Katherine asked.

Mastrota looked at her. "None, Signora. This started when we began to hear rumblings in the Cottolengo section of Torino about a gathering of what were being called 'martyrs'. The information we received was sparse but over the following days, we were able to get surveillance of three individuals who were reported to be among these 'martyrs'." He looked to Price and then Cann. "You have seen those photographs?"

Both nodded.

"We had the mosque and some people under loose surveillance but didn't have anything that would allow us to move on them." As always when the subject came up, he expressed his resentment. "Had we tried we would have been slapped down. We have had far more on other occasions and have been held back — or worse." Point made, Mastrota returned to his narrative. "Then, in my opinion, something spooked them. I believe perhaps the leader — who certainly appears to be this man you identified as al-Nassef, Signore Cann — got wind that their presence had been noted." He took a deep breath before he went on.

"Then, on Wednesday as you know, we had the bombing at the cathedral. It was a terrible thing. You saw the news?" Again, all at the table nodded. "Then I shall not dwell on the details. We know the bomber was the young blonde man in the photos we have." He looked at Cann. "Then you recognized the other man from the surveillance photos, Signore Cann, but by then, he and the others had disappeared from Torino. We didn't know where. We did a sweep of Cottolengo and made some arrests but came up with very little direct information on the cathedral bombing or the so-called "martyrs".

"How many martyrs were there in total?" John asked.

Mastrota shrugged and made a face. "We never knew for sure. We still don't. Until today we only knew of the three in the surveillance photos."

"Until today?" Bazinet asked.

Mastrota told them about his visit to Bormida of the Ventimiglia police and Xhelal Chani and led them through the chain of observations and links that brought an ID from the realm of wild speculation to a strong possibility. He took the booking photo of Chani that he'd borrowed from the Ventimiglia police and slid it to Bazinet. The Director looked at it then showed it to Cann and Price and then gave it to the assistant to be duplicated.

"We actually know more about this man and his family than we do of any of the others. They are Albanian. They entered the EU through Slovenia by train and apparently continued on to Torino. After the bombing — perhaps even before now that I think about it — they left Torino for Ventimiglia by rental car. We can pin down the exact timing from the rental car and hotel records which Inspector Bormida is gathering even now. The Chanis were staying at the Villa Colline Pedemontana but they left the hotel today rather suddenly after running afoul of just about everyone in Ventimiglia including the police. At least the man did." Mastrota related the tale of Xhelal Chani's run-ins with the guests, staff, and management of the hotel as well as the Ventimiglia police.

"This man has his family with him?" Katherine asked incredulously.

"Si, Signora Price. In Torino, even before the bombing, among the talk on the street, there were rumors that among the martyrs was a family — a couple with a young child — who would commit an act of terror together."

"The child, too?" Price was as outraged as she was incredulous. They all were.

"That was the word on the street," Mastrota replied.

"It's happened before," John said. "It's not even that uncommon. Don't even try to understand it."

"How old is the child?" Katherine asked. "Not that it makes a difference."

"The people at the Villa Colline Pedemontana in Ventimiglia said it appeared to be no more than two years old. Perhaps younger."

Katherine was shaking her head with a pained expression on her face. "How can anyone do that to their own child? A baby. It's beyond my understanding. Unbelievable."

"We lost many *bambini* last Wednesday, Signora Price," Mastrota's voice shook when he said it. "After seeing what these people are capable of it is very easy for me to believe."

Mastrota took a breath and went on. "In any event, Ispettore Bormida will initiate an alert for the Chanis based on the photo and the vehicle information. I am hopeful we will have him in custody soon so we can question him."

"What about photos of the wife and child," Katherine suggested. "Or of the wife at least. Wouldn't the hotel have made copies of her passport?"

"Excellent point, Signora. I believe Bormida will have thought of that but I will call and make sure."

"As for al-Nassef," Bazinet said, "we are canvassing all routes out of Cap d'Ail that run from the two bus stops al-Nassef used. And we are, of course, continuing to circulate the photo of the third man in the original surveillance photos. We will add this Chani's image as well as his wife's if we get it."

"What about the possibility that there isn't going to be more," John asked. "I mean I certainly wouldn't count on that but when we saw al-Nassef, he was heading away from Monaco. And this Chani guy checked out of the hotel in Ventimiglia..."

"I hope there is nothing more," Mastrota said. "But the stay was paid for through Sunday. By a voucher drawn on an Iranian bank, by the way."

"Which bank?" Bazinet asked.

Mastrota consulted his notes. "Bank Saderat."

Price, Cann and Bazinet all looked at one another. "That is the bank to which we were supposed to transfer funds," Bazinet said. "Just another coincidence?"

Bazinet then looked at Cann and answered his earlier question. "In any event, we of course have not discounted the possibility that they could be leaving and have also alerted all the transportation venues — airports, train stations. They will be on the lookout for any of these people. But within the EU, they can move about quite freely so..."

At that moment, another officer entered the room. "Monsieur le Directeur," he said, "you have a call from the Minister on the line." He pointed to the phone on the conference table. One of the lights was blinking.

Bazinet crossed to it and picked it up. "Bazinet," he said into it. He listened for a few moments a hard look emerging on his face. Then, after saying, "Merci, Monsieur le Ministre," he hung up. The Director of Public Security turned and spoke to the others in the room.

"It seems we have received another email from the International Islamic Resistance."

There was silence. Then Mastrota asked the obvious. "What did this one say?"

Bazinet took a deep breath and then exhaled. "That in failing to comply with the previous demand, we are responsible for the deaths of these innocents in the bank today. And that we have another twenty-four hours to transfer fifty million euros to the Bank Saderat account."

"Or what?" John asked. "Any specific threat of what will happen if the money isn't paid?

"No," Bazinet replied. "But undoubtedly we are meant to assume it will be something far worse than what we have already seen."

38

Federal Security Service
Ticino Canton
Switzerland

Gioele Nef of the Swiss Federal Security Service had finally lost his battle with his conscience. Or won it, depending on how he looked at it. He knew he could be placing his career on the line, perhaps throwing it away. But he had to do something.

Two days earlier, he'd pursued Mastrota's inquiries all the way to Ottah Younis. It had started as a favor for a colleague whom he admired and respected but by the time he was done and had relayed the information to Mastrota, it had become something more. If he wanted to play semantics, he hadn't *really* been investigating Younis in violation of the Federal Court's order. He was looking for information on another individual at the request of a sister service and Younis had, well, popped up at the end.

But the 'other individual' — the man who had visited Younis villa — had also apparently murdered a Swiss national, the border guard, albeit on Italian territory. This was not something he felt he should sit on. And yet, the mere involvement of Younis could bring the wrath of the Federal Criminal Court down on him, his superiors, and his beloved FSS. That was bad enough.

Then, to make matters worse, Mastrota had called him back after the conference call with Capo Tridente and the others to tell him that they had an ID on the man who was at Younis' last week. Rashid al-Nassef. One of the world's deadliest terrorists. And he, Nef, had by his own labors established a connection between that man and Ottah Younis.

Nef, like almost everyone had responded to the revelation with surprise and incredulity. Wasn't al-Nassef supposed to be dead?

"Yes," Mastrota had agreed but then explained what he had learned from the American who had met the terrorist twice. "By all accounts, the ID is solid. I felt I owed you a heads up on this one," Mastrota had said.

"Thank you," Nef said. "Now what do I do with it?" he'd asked himself at the time.

Now, having agonized over it ever since, Nef sat in his office with the television set turned to the news report of an incident at a bank in Monaco. The sound was muted but he'd heard what the broadcaster had to say. The official line was that there had been an attempted robbery gone wrong resulting in multiple deaths. But Nef also held the Interpol alert in his hand. It was marked "Confidential — For Official Use Only — Not for Release to the Public" and it told a far different story of the Monaco bank 'robbery'. The alert also contained a photograph of Bleeker, whom Nef recognized immediately from the images Mastrota had sent him, and of al-Nassef, the man, the terrorist who had visited with Younis prior to all of this. Nef knew he could no longer keep quiet no matter what the consequences might be. He had simply too much information that needed to be acted upon. The question remained, then, what indeed should he do with it.

What he did with it was compile what Mastrota had originally sent him along with what he had learned and head straight to the office of Head of the Service for Analysis and Prevention, several levels over his own. It wasn't that he disliked or mistrusted his immediate superiors. They were good men and women. A good part of his motivation was to see that they were not involved in his activities. And they were not at a level that would allow them to act on this information, anyway. Their role in such a situation would be to see that their underlings obeyed a federal court order, not go off on their own initiative. And, as much as they may have wanted to pursue it or even bump it upstairs, to do so could be seen as a tacit assent, an implied sanction of his illicit activity. At the end of the day, they would reason, everything relevant to a crime had taken place on Italian soil, and now Monaco. The only element involving Switzerland directly was the visit to Younis' villa.

And that was a problem.

Manfred Rueger, the Head of the Service for Analysis and Prevention, was an approachable man to an extent but he was also conscious of proper channels and chains of command. He'd granted Nef's request for an urgent meeting but had started it off by asking why Nef had bypassed his superiors. Nef, acutely aware that he was already far out on a limb, saw no value in dissimulation and related his motives exactly as he felt them. Rueger pursed his lips and decided that Nef's reasons, depending on what was to come, were not disloyal and so he gestured for him to begin.

Nef laid it out, literally and figuratively for Rueger, spreading documents and photographs on the desk. He went in chronological sequence: the flight arrival, the drive to Lugano, the visit to Younis' villa — that eliciting a highly arched eyebrow from Rueger but no immediate comment. Then he showed his superior the surveillance photo of Younis' visitor at the border at the time of the murder of the two guards. Then he ran through the surveillance photos of the Torino bombing, specifically pointing out the visitor again — who, Nef advised Rueger, has since been identified as the allegedly dead Rashid al-Nassef. Finally, Nef went over the deadly gas attack in Monaco, pushing the Interpol alert across the desk and tapping his finger on the photograph of al-Nassef. "All connected," he concluded, "and al-Nassef is clearly connected to Younis."

Rueger leaned forward and crossed his forearms on his desk. He took his time reading the alert then sat back and looked at Nef. "I frankly think you may have underestimated your superiors, Nef. This is important information and needs to be acted upon. I think they would have done just that." Nef accepted the chastisement and was relieved when Rueger concluded, "But you are quite correct. This must be addressed. You have done well. I'll take it from here."

Rueger took the matter to the Deputy Director of the Federal Police who carried it forward to the Director who agreed they needed to act but had to tread carefully. Normally, under Swiss law, a search warrant is issued, not by a judicial authority but by a "public official". In this case, however, the existence of the order of the Federal Criminal Court expressly prohibiting the FSS from activities directed at Younis precluded bypassing the court entirely. One of the judges on the court that issued the protective order in the first instance had in fact voted against it. So it was to him that the legal team made their request for a temporary suspension of the order based on the clear nature of the evidence presented, the severity of the acts involved even though committed on foreign territory — acts, it was emphasized, that included the murder of a Swiss national — and the immediate potential danger to the national security of Switzerland and its neighbors and allies. The judge signed off on it. But everyone involved knew there was a very real possibility — Rueger saw it as a virtual certainty — that the other judges on the panel would reinstate the protective order as soon as they became aware of its suspension. So he decided to move quickly.

Hotel Palais de Revere
Col le Bermasse

Al-Nassef's eyes narrowed as he read the email from Xhelal Chani. His initial reaction was one of anger. Anger that his orders had not been followed but more importantly anger that a meticulously planned operation could be put in jeopardy by this fool's deviation from his very precise instructions. And for what reason? Because the man couldn't control his own family? Or his own insecurities?

Chani had ended the message saying he was in a café in Menton and would wait for an answer. Al-Nassef looked at the time the message had been sent and saw it had been over half an hour and that Chani would have been sitting exposed in public. True, there was as yet no indication that Chani had been spotted but one never knew. For that reason, time was of the essence.

Al-Nassef concluded he had two viable options. One was to bring them to Monaco early. Not the location on the Rue des Remparts where Gallacher waited with the Sarin. That was out of the question. There was no need to complicate a situation that was settled and in good order. Another factor was that, given the apparent reasons for Chani's having already breached the plan, al-Nassef had real concerns about the Albanian man's ability to deal with having his wife in the presence of another male in an overnight setting. Most importantly, though, it would be the grossest breach of the highly orchestrated operational security for three more people, two, really, as the child was too young, to learn about what was stored and prepared in the apartment atop the Rock.

He could order them to the other location in Monaco where they were intended to go on Sunday morning anyway, the place where the explosives they would be using were secreted. But he rejected that alternative for several reasons. It had been chosen as a place to deposit the C4 and other materials long before they would be used and was intended to remain empty and unnoticed for as long as possible. In any case, the place was too small. Especially for a family of three. It was not an apartment; more like a bedsit, just a room and a bed without even a private bath or kitchen. That concern was not just a matter of comfort or discomfort. There was the potential psychological issue of having the Chanis spend some thirty-six hours or so sitting in a tiny room — with their baby — and with the instruments of their own deaths sitting beside them.

And to send them there early meant they would be present when Rafiq Mukhtar arrived to assemble their explosive vests, an unnecessary breach of operational security and another potential psychological issue. Even the most dedicated martyr can develop reservations when faced so directly with what he or she is about to do and it is for that reason homicide bombers are kept occupied and distracted in the hours leading up to their 'martyrdom'. It was different for Gallacher whose psychological profile had shown a detachment from self that bordered on schizophrenia. Plus, the Scot knew he had the gas mask and thus knew he could survive if he chose. Al-Nassef had no such confidence in Chani and the Albanian's actions in leaving Ventimiglia against orders did nothing to lessen that his concern.

That left Menton. But before he finalized that decision he considered why Chani had taken his family to Menton and not somewhere else. Was it mere coincidence? It is axiomatic in operational theory that nothing happens by chance. That is, nothing can ever be dismissed outright as coincidence. And a corollary to that is that one automatically looks very closely indeed at anything that appears at first blush to be coincidence as evidence in and of itself that it is not.

There should have been no way that Chani knew Menton had been the staging point for both Bleeker and Gallacher and, al-Nassef concluded, no reason for concern if he had. Unless it was indicative of Chani being something other than what he was supposed to be. Not likely. The pre-operation investigation into the martyrs had been long and thorough and there was no question of Chani's commitment. And there was little —only this move to Menton, actually — that argued for that proposition. It wasn't something to be overlooked and yet, there comes a time in an operation when the need to proceed must take precedence over less than substantially based suspicions. On balance, the weight of the evidence was that Chani's stated reasons for his actions were genuine and so the plan would proceed on the basis that he remained committed to his "sacred explosion".

Al-Nassef typed the email response out quickly. He gave Chani directions to the apartment Bleeker had used and told him to go there immediately. The door would be unlocked and the key on the shelf. When the time came, they were to leave them as they found them. And they were to stay inside. If they needed supplies, get them on the way so there would be no reason to leave until he received his final orders. "You will only need enough food and drink to last until Sunday morning," the terrorist leader advised. "No more deviations," al-Nassef sternly admonished the Albanian. "None."

39

Menton,
France

Chani stopped at a supermarket and purchased some fruit juices, yogurt and goat cheese as well as some rice, chicken livers and lemon for Rozafa to make up some of the traditional soup called *corba.* He found the apartment without difficulty and the three members of the Chani family went quickly inside. Xhelal Chani looked around the apartment while Rozafa settled Luan down on the couch which she could see from the small kitchen. She prepared the soup and left it to simmer then went and sat in a chair opposite her son.

Xhelal came out of the furnished bedroom where he'd put their things and stood looking out the window. The view was of open fields with a small brook running through it. In the distance were some mountains. Alps, he assumed. It looked a bit like his homeland in a way. Just a bit.

He turned when Rozafa spoke his name.

"Xhelal."

"What is it?"

Rozafa's voice was low and hesitant. She wasn't sure how to say what she wanted to say. "This thing that we do, do you know what it is?"

"*Shahadat,*" he said not unkindly. Martyrdom. "You know that."

"Yes," his wife replied. "But how? What is it we will do. What will be the instrument of our martyrdom."

Xhelal Chani shook his head. "I don't know. It doesn't matter." After a moment, he added, "It is not for us to decide."

Rozafa hesitated apprehensive over what she was about to do. This would be as close to defiance as she had ever come and something she would not have thought she would ever do.

"Must Luan die with us?" she asked slowly, her eyes looking downward at her wringing hands.

Xhelal looked at her without expression, not fully grasping what she was asking. Finally he crossed to a second chair and sat down. Rozafa looked at his face and saw that he was not angry. Perhaps she even saw some gentleness and concern in his eyes. She had always felt, even as he conformed to the harsh patriarchal protocols of rural Albanian society, that he did care about her. For her. She knew of many women whose lives were a hell of restriction and beatings. Xhelal had beaten her only a few times. And for that, she was grateful.

When he spoke, Xhelal's voice was equally soft. "You would spend eternity without him?" he asked.

Rozafa continued to look into her husband's eyes as she spoke. "But it would not be eternity. He will come later and join us. But for now…he has lived such a short time."

"Time is nothing compared to eternity. An eternity in paradise. You would deny him that?"

"It is not only *shuhada* that reach paradise, though, Xhelal. All good Muslims will join Allah when their time has come. Can we not allow him to make that choice for himself? After he has seen life for a time?" She couldn't believe she was actually engaging her husband in such a dialogue. Or that he was tolerating it, almost treating her as an equal in this discussion.

Xhelal looked at her for a long time before he answered. "It must be as we have decided. I will go to paradise with my son. Are you saying you do not want to come with us?"

Rozafa lowered her eyes again. She wanted to ask, "But what if paradise is not the reward? What if there is no paradise? What if Luan dies so young for no reason?" But she didn't ask that. Instead she said, "I am your wife. And I will go where you wish me to go."

Xhelal uncharacteristically reached out and placed his hand gently over hers. "Yes. Then it is settled."

Roquebrune-Cap-Martin,
France

Rafiq Mukhtar finished the *Maghrib,* his sunset prayers, and then went to check his email yet again. He felt a surge of anticipation when he saw that he did indeed have a message and again when he opened it and saw that it was from al-Nassef. He read quickly through the post one time then read it a second time more slowly absorbing the details and reveling in the knowledge that he would soon be making his holy act of *jihad.* "Finally," he had muttered as he finished reading the email a third time. "Allah be praised."

In actuality, Mukhtar's final act of *jihad* would not take place until Sunday — after the Chanis' explosion and the release by Gallacher of the Sarin. But he had work to do in the meantime. Al-Nassef's email had directed him to travel to Monaco tomorrow, by bus, not by train. That way he could get off at one of several stops and make his way to the apartment where the bomb making materials were stored. The message also ordered him to time his arrival between 14:00 and 15:00 hours when Monaco's and the world of motorsport's attention would be on the qualifying session scheduled for that period. For that one hour, all of the teams two cars — 22 in all — would take part in a three-tiered elimination format until the fastest lap time won the coveted pole position with the others lined up in pairs in descending order of their own elapsed times. Even for non-fans, if there were any in Monaco on this race weekend, the tension, the excitement, the noise, and the passion of the spectacle would capture and focus everyone's attention on the track and not on a single pedestrian making his way to a location on a hill rising above the St. Devote turn.

Mukhtar had a key, given to him in Torino before he had left. Until now, he hadn't known what it was for. Tomorrow, Saturday, sometime in mid-afternoon he would use it to let himself into the bedsit where he would use the skills learned in the camp in the Mansehra District of Pakistan, skills he had put to use so many times in the past. He knew generally what he would do. He had constructed the bomb the young Bosnian had used in Torino and al-Nassef had briefed him on what he would construct for others to use here. He would assemble the components on-site and place them into vests for two adults. He would attach the wires at one end to the C4 and run them down the inside of the vest and into a pocket where there would be a simple, battery powered detonator much like the one al-Nassef had used to blow up the young Bosnian — and the children — in Torino. The remaining plastic explosive would be molded to fit the sides of the carriage, leaving room for the child who would be placed inside. In that case, there would be no wires running from the charges in the carriage. He could easily have run the wires up through the hollow metal push handles and attached a button to the outer surface. But that would mean that whoever was pushing the carriage at the time would need to press the button on their vest and the one on the carriage handle at exactly the same time to make them both detonate the respective charges. It was possible they could do that but one could not rely on that kind of precision especially under the stress of the situation. In truth, it was likely, probable really, that the proximity of the initial explosions would set off the charges in the carriage. But there was also a chance they would not. So Mukhtar would place a barometric pressure switch in the carriage which would ensure detonation under the immense pressure resulting from the eruption of the other blasts.

When al-Nassef had begun to concentrate of Mukhtar's bomb-making skills and not his own martyrdom, the young Brit had become worried. So often he had begged to be allowed to be more than the constructor of a device. So many times he had pleaded with his leaders to be released to battle and his eternal rewards. Always, he would be denied, often with harsh criticism for his selfishness at putting his own glory ahead of the higher purpose of the *jihad*. He accepted the criticism with humility but, as time passed, he grew to feel more and more that he had made his contribution. Yes, he was very good at what he did but there were others who could do it as well. And many more waiting to make their contribution to the cause. Finally, over a long period of time, he had maneuvered himself into a position of close association with a cell leader who Mukhtar knew felt as he did: that to be allowed to be *shahid* was a reward that was earned for faithful service. After Mukhtar had imparted all his knowledge to another constructor, the leader gave the young Pakistani Brit permission to volunteer for a major undertaking that would utilize his skills one last time and bring him his coveted *shahadat*.

That would happen al-Nassef had assured him then. And now, in this email, al-Nassef promised Mukhtar his glory would come on Sunday. Building the devices for the others was necessary but when he was done there, Mukhtar was ordered to Col le Bermasse where, he was promised, he would construct the device he himself would use on Sunday to carry him to paradise. It would, al-Nassef's email assured him, be the crowning achievement of his life. It was not that its construction would be any more difficult or complex than the others'. One extra ingredient only. But it would cause the entire world to know of his glory even as they cowered in fear. It almost made Mukhtar happy that he had been required to wait until this moment for the martyrdom he had sought for so long. It made him glad and proud. He would leave this world in glory and arrive in paradise a martyr. A hero who would be spoken of and praised for years to come. For he had been chosen to carry the "*hadduta*" to the heart of the infidels.

Avenue de Sospel
Menton,
France

Rozafa Chani couldn't have slept if she'd wanted to. And she didn't want to. She had lain motionless for hours on her back, holding a sleeping Luan on her chest, the top of his head just under her cheek. She hadn't tossed and turned at all. That would have disturbed Xhelal who did not appear to have had any trouble sleeping. Now, in the middle of the night, she carefully climbed out of bed and carried her son across the room and out the door of the bedroom.

She sat down on the couch in the small living room still holding her son who was resting safely and contentedly in his mother's arms. "You are so sweet, my Luan," Rozafa Chani said softly to the sleeping little boy. "And so beautiful." Like the boys she had seen on the streets of Menton yesterday afternoon, she thought to herself. She had thought of nothing else the entire night. Not of the boys themselves. But of their laughing faces and carefree manner.

Luan stirred in her arms and a little clenched hand opened and for a moment rested itself on his mother's arm. Rozafa looked down at her son. Strangely, he looked up at her at that very moment and opened his eyes briefly and smiled before falling right back asleep.

"You trust me, my Luan, don't you?" she said sadly. "You feel safe with me and you know that I will never do anything to hurt you. Or allow anything to hurt you." She looked up and out the window into the blackness of the night. "So how can I do this thing to you?" She put her head back on the couch and listened in her mind to the exhortations of her husband who had decided

Rozafa had always felt she was a good Muslim. She worshipped Allah and recognized him as the one true God and she revered the prophet, Peace be unto him. But in her discussions with Xhelal earlier in the evening, she had realized with a sense of shock that she had doubts. Her fears for Luan were genuine but it had slowly entered her consciousness that, if she were secure in her belief in the afterlife promised, then she would want that for her child. Instead, she now questioned whether she wanted him to experience life because that was all there might be. Did that make her an apostate? She knew the penalty here on earth for apostasy was death. But if she died an apostate, her penalty would be an eternity of emptiness. Without Allah. Without Luan. How then, could she go to her death and take her son with her if such were to be the consequences. And would she be condemning Luan as well to a fate worse than what his father had for him. She was not afraid to die. At least she hadn't been until her fears arose. Now, she knew she could not make this act of *jihad* with Xhelal. Not now. Later, when she had cleansed her soul, talked to the Imam, found her way back to Islam, then would she consider a cleansing act for herself. But not for Luan. He could decide for himself.

She quietly gathered up some clothing for herself and her son and slipped out the door.

40

Saturday AM
4:30 CET
Castagnola,
Lugano

Manfred Rueger had assembled the FSS team quickly and then ordered everyone involved confined to their staging locations. He would countenance no leaks of their intentions to search Ottah Younis' villa lest the courts be given an opportunity to step in and rescind the suspension of the protective order. Technically, the order had not been "suspended". A single justice of the court couldn't do that. Rather, the single judge had issued the search warrant on his own authority, in effect superseding it. That was an act he did have the authority to take and, most importantly, was one that could itself be over turned only by a majority of the appeals court members.

It was still a risk and the Head of the Service for Analysis and Prevention would take full responsibility, he told his officers who were all concerned that they and their agency ran a real risk of being sanctioned after the fact. But Rueger was convinced it had to be done and would be done. And he was not the kind of man who would place his people in awkward or potentially untenable positions while he stood back. Rueger himself would lead the team. Gioele Nef would assist him. Neither man was sure whether that was a reward or a penalty.

At 7:30 AM, just before sunrise, the line of unmarked FSS cars sped up the long hill to the front entrance to the grounds of Younis' villa. Two men at the gate stepped groggily out of a small guardhouse as the first vehicle approached and attempted to prohibit their access. Rueger got out of the lead car and identified himself then demanded the gate be opened. One of the guards phoned the house as the other stalled as best he could. The phone inside was picked up by one of Younis' assistants/bodyguards who listened then made the painful decision to wake his employer.

It took a moment to rouse Younis from his deep sleep and his initial reaction was to dismiss the suggestion that his villa would be raided as ludicrous. He had far too many people in very high places for such a thing to occur. As he came more awake, however, he realized this particular aide wasn't the type to misrepresent or exaggerate and as the employee continued to insist he was speaking the truth, Younis threw back the covers and went to a front window. Seeing the line of cars outside the gate, he stormed back to a bedside table and picked up the phone.

Rueger wasn't about to wait for permission from the house — which probably wouldn't come anyway. At least not voluntarily. He quickly ordered his men to take the villa guards into custody and open the gates themselves. The convoy sped through and up to the front of the house where the members of the FSS force formed a perimeter around the entire structure as Rueger and several others made straight for the front door. After several moments of hard pounding and just as Rueger was about to order the door to be battered down, the door opened slowly. A small thin man, perhaps a servant, made a timid, somewhat half-hearted attempt to stall the official's entrance until a berobed Ottah Younis appeared at the top of a flight of central stairs.

"Are you insane, Signore Rueger?" Younis asked with bluster. "You are of course aware of the order preventing such actions as this, are you not? You will lose your job for this, I…"

"We have a search warrant, Signore Younis" Rueger said holding out the paperwork in front of him, "issued by a justice of the Appeals Court itself." Rueger held the papers out to the servant and flipped his chin toward the Egyptian. The servant took the papers and carried them up the stairs to his boss. After a moment, Younis looked down at the FSS officer with a mixture of disdain and bemusement on his face.

"I must tell you that I have already placed a call to Judge DiCiantis of the Federal Criminal Court and he has advised me he knows nothing of this."

"If he does not, Signore Younis," Rueger said politely, "he does now or soon will. Please know that we will be as non-disruptive as possible and be done as quickly as possible. But also know this warrant is properly authorized and will be properly executed."

Younis looked down at the paperwork again then up at Rueger. "And what exactly will you be looking for, Rueger?"

'As the warrant states, Signore Younis, any and all documents or other evidence that may pertain to the arrival in the Swiss Confederation of one Rashid al-Nassef who…"

"Al-Nassef?" Younis shouted incredulously. "He is dead for a long time. You are insane, Rueger. Out of your mind."

"With respect, I don't believe I am but that is what the warrant authorizes us to search for along with evidence relating to vehicles on the premises and any other materials that might relate to the Piazza San Giovanni bombing in Torino on Wednesday. The warrant also specifies we may search for explosives including but not limited to C4 as well as chemical elements and compound, in particular with relation to elements found in banned or regulated weapons of mass destruction."

"Weapons of mass…? The futile search for such things now extends to my home?" Younis fixed an intense glare on the Swiss official and bore in on him with his eyes. "I have armed men on these premises, Rueger, and I cannot be responsible if your presence on these premises results in an incident of some kind."

"To the contrary Signore Younis, you are in fact responsible for seeing precisely that such a thing does not happen. You would be very foolish to think otherwise. I dare say even Judge DiCiantis would not look kindly on such a matter. Now, we will proceed, as I said, as quickly and unobtrusively as possible so…"

"Unobtrusive? How is a search warrant unobtrusive, you fool? And for the record, I do not consent to this search and it is being conducted without my cooperation. I want that to be perfectly clear." Younis jabbed a finger in Rueger's direction.

"Your position is noted," the Swiss said politely.

"I am having my lawyers summoned as we speak. They should have been notified prior to your arrival." Rueger shrugged. "Yes, well" Younis continued," I see you know that. Rest assured, Rueger, that at the end of the day, I will not just have your job. I will have your head."

Rueger held the Egyptian's gaze for a long moment then turned away and pointed at three of his men to go in different directions around the house to conduct the search in accordance with the warrant. One went to the library and the other two went to Younis' office. One of them would search the files, the other the computer.

Outside the house, several men had been specifically directed to search the outbuildings in the villa complex. In addition to a four stall garage, there was a large shed and two smaller structures apparently used for storage. Rueger and Nef stood outside the front door where they could readily react to any discovery either inside or out. For almost a half-hour, nothing happened at all. The man who searched the library came down and shook his head in the negative. Nothing. A bit later, Rueger sent someone up to check on the computer search. The man returned with a message from the examiner that he had as yet found no suspicious files but there were hundreds of emails that would need to be scrutinized.

Out on the grounds, the other men had concentrated their initial efforts on the garage and its immediate surroundings. Two of the stalls were occupied — a Saab and a Mercedes — and the other two were empty. Keys were found for both vehicles and they were thoroughly searched without result. Along one wall of the garage was a workbench with a few auto parts and many tools spread around it. Above the bench and along the opposite wall were storage cabinets, also crowded with items that seemed to belong there.

Given the nature of the search and some of what they were looking for — *"...explosives including but not limited to C4 as well as chemical elements and compound, in particular with relation to elements found in banned or regulated weapons of mass destruction..."* the search warrant read — all were aware that, in addition to what they could see, they were also looking for things they wouldn't be able to see. For that reason, all of the searchers had been issued small key fob-looking devices that hung from their shirts and jackets. These were relatively simple but state-of-the-art NBC (nuclear/ biological/chemical) detectors that would signal the presence of many compounds and element. In particular, given the information in the Interpol alert that Sarin had been used in the Monaco bank attack, these had been specifically calibrated to detect even trace amounts of methylphosphonyl difluoride. But they would also detect many other things.

The garage was cleared, followed by the shed, which contained groundskeeping and landscaping tools and equipment and nothing of interest to the searchers. As the men approached the first of the two smaller sheds, the detector on the lead man chirped a single time. Instinctively all the men halted in place. The devices were detectors only, not identifiers. The 'chirp' told them only that one of many elements was present. They could also indicate the location and proximity of whatever had triggered the alarm by increasing the number and frequency of the 'chirps' as the device got closer and closer. One of the men took a step back and there was no 'chirp'. He then took a step forward toward the small structure and the device emitted its telltale sound. Another step and two chirps. One more step resulted in two more chirps but these were more rapid, closer together. That was enough. The men retreated and went to get Rueger and Nef.

Moments later a single man in a hazmat suit approached the shed. He wore one of the small NBC detectors which chirped more and more rapidly as he neared the small building. He also carried a handheld device similar to the one used by the Sapeurs-Pompiers sergeant to detect the Sarin at the Bank des Maritimes in Monaco. It registered nothing. And even as the man got closer and closer, the device remained silent. He checked the setting, then recalibrated, and even turned the device off and then powered it up again. Nothing.

But something was triggering the smaller detector. If it wasn't chemical... On a hunch, the man hooked the chemical sensor to his utility belt and unhooked a second device that looked a lot like a price scanner one might see in a supermarket. This was a portable isotope identifier which used lanthanum bromide to isolate and identify specific radioactive isotopes. He turned it on, waited for it to power up and go through its self-test. Then he stared at the small screen on the face of the device which would show a peaks-and-valleys graphic representation in the presence of radioactive isotopes. Immediately as the self-test ended, the graphic readout burst into life showing the presence of radioactivity. The graphic representation grew more distinct as the man neared and then entered the shed. The beauty of this particular device was that it had the ability to analyze and identify the specific isotope present. It took a few minutes to accomplish and the man stood silently waiting for the information needed. When it came, the news wasn't good. The device had found Cesium 137.

Cesium is a naturally occurring alkali metal with a variety of uses principally in research and development. There are 39 known cesium isotopes with atomic masses ranging from 112 to 151. All but one are unstable meaning they deteriorate by emitting radiation. How long it takes them to deteriorate — which is a function of how much radiation they emit and how rapidly they do it — is called a half-life. Cesium 137 has a half-life of 30 years which means, once released into the environment, it stays around for a very long time.

Cesium 137 is a product of nuclear fission, a by-product of nuclear power production and uranium enrichment. It is extremely toxic even in the smallest amounts. It is a gamma emitter meaning its emissions are stronger than alpha or beta rays and can penetrate many solid materials. Great care must be taken in its transport and handling. By way of contrast, Polonium, for example, is an alpha emitter. It is deadly if ingested — Polonium 210 was used in the poisoning death of the Russian expatriate Alexander Litvinenko by placing it in his food — but it could be handled unprotected without injury since its alpha rays are not even strong enough to penetrate the skin. Not so with Cesium 137.

So Cesium 137 is powerful, toxic, and long lasting. It is also the most "reactive" of all metals — meaning it combines readily with other elements and would easily combine with materials such as the concrete in buildings, the paving in the streets, and even the soil itself. Once the contamination occurred, it would be virtually impossible to clean it up. All of this makes Cesium 137 ideal for use in a "dirty bomb".

Dirty bombs — more formally called Radioactive Dispersal Devices (RDD) — are not nuclear bombs. They are conventional explosives mixed with radioactive materials. In some respects, the immediate death and destruction from an RDD is no different than that from a similarly sized non-dirty bomb. Except that, in addition, many of those not killed in the blast will die a horrible lingering death from radiation sickness. Those not so close will spend the next ten or twenty or thirty years waiting for cancer to develop. In many, it will. And the contamination of the surrounding environment is equally devastating in both physical and economic damage. It has been estimated that four grams of Cesium 137 and ten kilograms of explosives would contaminate and make unlivable two square kilometers for decades. That is an area just about the size of Monaco.

41

Castagnola,
Lugano, Switzerland

Rueger felt vindicated. And relieved. Cesium 137 was highly regulated and had no business being here. And it didn't just appear out of nowhere. This was more than enough to justify the search to anyone, Judge DiCiantis included. But they had found nothing as yet that would make a direct connection between the Cesium and al-Nassef.

"We need to report this to all the appropriate agencies — IAEA, etc. — as well as our government. You will need to advise your Italian inspector friend of what we have found here," Rueger said to Nef. "But based on what we know right now — or don't know — it's entirely possible the Cesium is unrelated to al-Nassef."

"But likely?" Nef suggested.

Rueger shrugged then waved at the technician who had been in the hazmat suit and called him over. "What do we know about this Cesium, Corelli? Can you tell how much was here. How long it was here. Anything further?"

"No, signore, I can't tell you any of that from the trace evidence the identifier found. Only that it was here."

"Well, can you tell me why there is trace evidence, then? Does that mean it was uncontained?"

"That is not likely, Signore. If the Cesium 137 was uncontained, we would find far greater concentrations of it and other evidence of its presence, like injury and perhaps even radiation sickness to the people here. If people here were exposed, depending on the extent and duration of the exposure, we would see some effects."

"Unless, they have been taken somewhere else for treatment. Or to die," Nef interjected.

"That is possible, I suppose." Rueger turned his attention back to the technician. "So you think it must have been contained? Was it leaking, then?"

"Perhaps," Corelli, the technician said. "But you must understand that the gamma rays of Cesium 137 can penetrate many materials. It is possible this Cesium was being kept in a reasonably suitable container but that some rays were able to get through. They would lose a good degree of their energy in passing through whatever the Cesium was being held in so that while the traces were readable, they may not be enough to have done any significant damage."

"Is it possible to trace the source?"

Corelli nodded. "We have the technology. But that requires far more time and far more sophisticated equipment than I have available to me here on-site, Signore. We will analyze what we can and I will advise you as soon as I know."

"How long?"

"It may be days, Signore. I'm sorry."

Rueger grunted, showing acceptance and annoyance at the same time.

"So all we really know is that there was some Cesium 137 here. Nothing else. Is that right?"

"I am afraid so, Signore. As of now."

Rueger turned to Nef. "And these men have not told us anything?"

"They say they know nothing about anything, Signore. To hear them, you would think they are strangers here. And they are not." Nef said. "But…" The sentence drifted off as Nef formulated an idea in his mind.

"But what?"

"Let me try something, Signore," Nef said pointing his chin at a group of three men who were hanging about in the open area in front of the garage. "They have been questioned and were shown the photo of al-Nassef and claimed complete ignorance of everything. The officer who had spoken to them initially, however, said he was certain from their facial reactions that at least two of them had recognized the photo of the terrorist."

"Whatever you have in mind, give it a try."

Nef discussed with Corelli what he was about to do and then crossed to where the men were standing. He nodded politely to them as he approached and held out a pack of cigarettes, offering it around. Two of the men accepted the offer with an unsmiling nod. Nef was under no illusion that he would suddenly be accepted as anything other than police but he still had an idea of how to perhaps get some information.

He said nothing for several moments as he and the others puffed away in silence. "My officer," he began finally, "tells me that you did not recognize the man in the photo he showed you." The others grunted their confirmation of that, one of them with a tell-tale smirk on his face. "You are fortunate, then, you know. That man is very ill. We know he was here. And we were quite sure he got it here but it appears not. We have found nothing." These men, of course, wouldn't have been told about the FSS' discovery of the Cesium traces but Nef was betting they knew it or something very much like it had been there before. "Lucky for you."

There was a long silence. Then one of the men said, "Got what here?"

"Radiation sickness."

Nef caught the look of concern between two of the men.

"The man in the photo," Nef went on with his bluff, "had some radioactive material with him in a container that was *supposed* to be properly sealed." He emphasized the word "'supposed" and followed it with a sad shake of his head. "But it wasn't. And now he is very, very sick. As anyone who handled the container would be. In time, of course."

"How much time?"

Nef knew al-Nassef had been there over a week ago so replied, "Oh, ten days, two weeks. A little more perhaps."

"Then why would this man in the photo be sick already?" the larger of the two men asked quickly.

"Gooaaalllll!" Nef thought to himself. Nothing had been said about *when* the man in the photo had been at Younis' villa. He continued the ploy. "Well, he was with it constantly for days apparently. The amount and length of the exposure controls how quickly one gets radiation sickness but anyone with even the slightest exposure will eventually get it." That last was not true.

218

There were parameters within which one could survive exposure unscathed but these men didn't need to know that.

"What happens with radiation sickness?" the second man asked.

Nef gestured to Corelli, the technician to come over. "Let's hear from the expert," he said. When Corelli joined them, Nef explained the nature of the discussion and repeated the other man's question.

"Well, depending on exposure, it may take some time for the symptoms to begin but they will arise unless treatment is begun as soon as possible. Preferably even before the onset of the symptoms. For sure, once the symptoms begin to appear, the treatment must be immediate. Every moment counts. Without it, the sickness will progress inevitably to death." That too was not necessarily true. "First," Corelli went on, "there is lightheadedness, then nausea and vomiting. The body begins to lose its immune system and becomes subject to many infections. Then the hair begins to fall out. The vomiting continues but the victim will begin to notice it now contains blood. A lot of it. And the stool will become bloody as well. In the end, the person exposed will die either of infection or from the failure of his organs to be able to repair themselves. It is a quite horrible way to die."

"You mentioned treatment," one of the men said. "Where does one go. Any hospital?"

Corelli shook his head. "No, only certain specialized locations can do this. And, as I said, the treatment must begin immediately once the symptoms appear. Preferably before."

If it weren't such a serious matter, Nef could almost have seen some humor in the looks of concern on the men's faces as they looked around like trapped animals. "Are we done?" the smaller man asked. "Can we go now?"

"Oh, no," Nef said. "We'll need to question everyone again." He looked at his watch. "We're just waiting for a van to bring you all to the station for further questioning."

"For how long?" the same man asked.

"Indefinitely," Nef answered. "We need answers to what went on here and as I'm sure you know the law allows us to hold you for up to thirty days without charges in matters of national security so…"

The larger of the two men shifted uncomfortably and looked at his colleague then back at Nef. He started to say something but the smaller man interrupted him. "Say nothing, Reto. We have no reason to believe this person. He is police." The man turned to Nef with a look of indignant skepticism on his face. "How do we know all you've just said isn't a trick?"

Nef shrugged. "You don't. But if you have information, perhaps you should decide if withholding it is important enough to take the risk."

The big man named Reto looked sharply at the other for guidance or a response but the smaller man said nothing. Nef looked back and forth between the two trying to will the large man to concede. But he didn't. For several more moments no one said anything. Nef thought he might be close and didn't want to give up quite yet. He walked away a few steps and took out his phone. This time he really did order a van.

42

Avenue de Sospel
Menton

Xhelal Chani had awakened just after dawn and thought nothing about Rozafa not being in the bed beside him. She was usually up before him attending to Luan, preparing breakfast, doing other womanly things. He was not overly concerned.

He made *fajr* in the bedroom and then went out into the central living/dining area expecting to see his wife puttering in the kitchen and his son somewhere close to her. It was a shock when he did not, the emptiness and silence somehow jarring. He quickly looked into the second bedroom which was unfurnished and held only the small bag left behind by Bleeker which he examined quickly, not understanding what it was or why it was there. But he quickly determined that it did not contain anything he recognized as his wife's.

For a time, he stood in the center of the living room doing nothing, thinking nothing. The situation was incomprehensible to him, that his wife was not here? Gone? In the middle of the night? With their son? In the context of Xhelal Chani's universe, this simply couldn't be. But it was. But it couldn't be. It was quite simply beyond his understanding.

Every morning one of the first things he did was to open the computer and check for messages. Out of pure habit, he did so this morning and found one from the leader. Allah be praised! It contained his final instructions. Forgetting everything for the moment, he read how he was to take the train to Monaco the next morning, Sunday, to arrive no later than 10:00 AM. The email went on to give him very specific directions to the location in the Ste-Dévote neighborhood where he would find the devices already prepared for him and his family. At the end of the message, the leader repeated his earlier admonishment in the sternest of terms that Chani must follow the instructions to the letter. No deviations, al-Nassef had written once again. None.

Chani's euphoria at finally being told the details of his mission was immediately offset by the realities of the current situation. He considered sending a return message explaining Rozafa's actions but rejected the idea. How could he speak of this shame to another man? Why would he broadcast his own humiliation, the insult to him as a man that his wife would do this thing? In the old country, he would not be able to live with this dishonor. He would not be expected to. Here it can be no different. Only by Rozafa's death, could he expunge the stain. It saddened him. But it was not his fault. Rozafa knows she cannot do this. And by her actions, she accepts the consequences.

Having fitted the situation into his own reality, Chani knew what he must do. He threw on some clothes and picked up the car keys, offering a prayer to Allah that he would find Rozafa. When he'd finished, he felt a calm assurance that it would be so. But just in case, he went back to the kitchen and took the largest knife he could find. Rozafa would die. It was just a question of when and how. It was his intention to bring her and Luan back to this place and he would not let them out of his sight until their act was done. Rozafa would die as he had decided she would die. In support of his act of glory. Either way, after her death, her true punishment would begin. He had made his decision on eternity. He would not serve her in Paradise. He would flaunt his virgins before Rozafa for all time to come.

But first he must find her.

It had been the most frightening night of Rozafa Chani's life. After slipping out of the apartment, she had made her way to the Avenue de Sospel, one of the main thoroughfares leading into Menton proper. In a yard on the corner, she saw what appeared to be a shrine of some sort with a granite cross as its centerpiece. Rozafa drew no comfort from it but rather wondered if it were a confirmation that she was in fact lost to Islam and vice-versa. She turned left and headed south in the direction they had come the previous day after Xhelal had returned from the café. It was not that she had a specific reason for going in that direction. Not that she was looking for anything in particular. It was all she knew. Pure and simple. The only frame of reference that she had.

There was little traffic at that time of night and when one of the few vehicles that were out and about at that time came down the road, its lights gave her plenty of time to withdraw into shadows and hide. Perhaps one of the cars would be Xhelal out looking for them. She felt that was unlikely. It was not impossible but he would usually sleep through until dawn. Then, she knew with absolute certainty, he would come looking for them. And what he would do. She was fully aware of how final her decision to leave had been and what the consequence would be. Must be. But even as she knew what she was running from, she had no idea what she was running to.

Eventually she came to the end of the Avenue de Sospel and stood facing the Casino. Even it was dark and shuttered at this time of night. She could go only left or right and, for no reason other than that was the direction they had taken the day before, she went left. Then she remembered that the shore was just one more block down and so she took the next right. Just as she'd recalled, there was a concrete wall that separated the street from the beach and she climbed over it and sat resting her back against it, cradling Luan in her arms in front of her. The night was cool but the breeze off the Mediterranean was light and she was able to bundle them both up in the clothing she had brought to keep them warm. Perhaps it was the sounds of the water gently rushing onto the shore but more likely it was sheer exhaustion that caused her to fall asleep.

It was the sounds of the early morning traffic that woke Rozafa as Menton began to rise to greet this late May Saturday. It was good that it did because the authorities frowned on people sleeping on the beach and, indeed, Rozafa and Luan had been fortunate not to have been rousted or even arrested by police. Like many Eastern Europeans, Rozafa had a visceral fear of the police but in her case, given her youth, it was more a function of horror stories heard than experience with forces such as the dreaded Sigurimi, the Albanian secret police of years past.

But she remembered her encounter with the Ventimiglia police on Thursday and how kind they had been to her. Nothing like the stories of insult and abuse she had heard from the elders at home. The woman police officer who had spoken with her had been very nice but even the men had seemed genuinely concerned for her safety and well-being and, most surprising of all, genuinely hostile to her husband. Even today in the old country, in her rural mountain region at least, the police would have been completely supportive of her husband and uninterested at best in whatever her plight might have been.

It was light now and as she walked away from the beach back toward the center of Menton, she watched the traffic closely, alert for any vehicle that resembled the rental car Xhelal would be driving. She briefly wondered if she should try to make it to the outskirts of town but decided she was better off in crowds. Unfortunately, it was still too early for any and she knew she had to find someplace where she could be out of sight until she could figure out what she would do.

She found a garden in a small square off a side street where she could sit on a bench and, through the shrubbery see the traffic, but was quite sure they could not see in. She and Luan remained there, feeling relatively safe for some time, an hour or more, then the boy stirred and emitted a short cry. He was such a good baby, Rozafa thought. She knew he would be hungry and, once again, she had nothing to give him. She berated herself for leaving without any money but Xhelal kept it all with him and she would not have dared to try sneaking into the bedroom to get some. She could have at least taken some yogurt with her but she didn't.

She felt tears of frustration start to build in her eyes and anger at herself for doing this, making such a foolish decision. She was alone and she didn't know how to be alone. Her entire life had been managed and dominated by others and she felt ill-equipped to take care of herself let alone her son. She was a fool. She knew it now. Perhaps her decision didn't have to be so final. Maybe Xhelal would forgive her. No, she knew, he would not. Could not. Her decision was final. Even if she wished, she could not take it back. Could she?

Rozafa looked around carefully and then left the garden area and walked down the street just a block or so from the sea. A black car that looked like the rental came slowly around the corner ahead of her. Rozafa instinctively stepped into the nearest open door which was a café just brewing its coffee and setting out its pastries. The smells were almost overwhelming and were perhaps the reason Luan started to cry now in earnest. Poor baby. What could she do?

There were only six tables in the café. Two of them were occupied by couples engrossed in their own conversations. A round, fifty-something man in a tall white cap with an apron tied around his waist came out from the back of the café and said something to Rozafa which she didn't understand. She'd had only a little schooling and knew not a word of any other language. She only knew Albanian. She drew away from the man and moved toward the door. Instinct again. Or more accurately ingrained behavior from experience. Men supported men. It was always that way. So even if she had been able to understand him — and even though the man seemed to be speaking kindly to her — she was reluctant and afraid to trust him. And if Xhelal ever saw her talking to another man outside his presence, she thought, he would… She stopped and almost laughed at herself, at her reflexive reaction to a lifetime of subservience. He could only kill her once.

Then an older woman came out the door leading into the back of the café. She looked at Rozafa and then Luan and gave her one of those sentimental smiles women always give another woman with a small child. The older woman, too, said something to Rozafa but she couldn't understand her either. Rozafa wasn't even sure where she was, what country she was in. Xhelal had spoken of Italy and France but since she didn't know either language, it didn't matter.

"*Shqip,*" Rozafa said pointing to herself. Often, a word in one language sounds similar enough to its counterpart in another language to be recognizable to others. Unfortunately, the word for "Albanian" in the Albanian language — "*Shqip*" — doesn't sound at all like "Albanian" to Western ears or anyone else's. The older woman thought perhaps Rozafa had given her name and pointed to the boy. Rozafa understood that and said, "Luan." Then she pointed to herself and said "Rozafa." The French woman understood as well. Though she still had no idea what "*Shqip*" meant.

"He is a beautiful child, my dear," the woman said in French. Rozafa gave no answer but returned the maternal smile with a hesitant one of her own. The woman then spoke to the man, her husband, and he answered her with a nod. "Are you hungry?" the woman asked. Rozafa shook her head to indicate she didn't understand. The woman pointed to her mouth and then rubbed her stomach and then pointed to Luan. Rozafa might have been tempted to politely decline for herself but she couldn't deny her son. She nodded yes even as she turned a palm up to the people hoping they understood she had no money. They did.

They sat her and Luan down at one of the tables and brought over a small soft pastry and some milk for the boy and a coffee and croissant for Rozafa. The two patissières smiled as they watched the mother and child eat.

"*Faleminderit*," Rozafa said, thanking the couple. The woman sat down at the table with them and again tried to communicate. "What language is that?" she asked.

Rozafa just shook her head. "*Nuk kuptoj*," she said regretfully. "I don't understand."

The café was a bit busier now with most customers taking their purchases with them. One of them, a dark-haired woman in her thirties was on her way out when she heard Rozafa speak. "*A flisni shqip?*" the other woman asked helpfully with a smile?

It was just three words but hearing her native language spoken so gently to her after the intensity of the previous night unleashed a flood of emotions in Rozafa and she burst into tears. Luan immediately followed suit. Both the younger and the older woman rushed to comfort mother and son and soon, with a native speaker to talk with, Rozafa had explained her entire situation in detail.

"We need to call the police," the male patissier who had been listening to the conversation said.

Unlike "*shqip*", the word for "police" may be the one word that sounds the same in virtually every western language and Rozafa looked up in fear when she heard it.

The woman customer who spoke Albanian put a hand on Rozafa's and patted it gently. "No," she said in French to the older couple, "not the police. Just yet." To Rozafa she said, "There is a place, a shelter for women here in Menton. I can take you there. You will be safe. They will help you and explain to you what you can do. When you are ready, if you are ready, only then will they involve the police."

"Will they be able to understand me, talk to me?" Rozafa asked with concern.

"Oh, yes," the other woman responded sadly. "They have helped many Albanian women there. Many."

43

Saturday Morning Practice
Grand Prix Course
Monaco

Even though the previous day, Friday, had been an off-day for the teams, the pit garages had been busy all day and, in many cases, all night with repairs from Thursday practice excursions off the road or mechanical or structural failures or, for the more fortunate teams, in tweaking and improving bits and pieces here and there in the never ending quest to cut thousandths of a second off lap times. It was Sir Robert Foster's principal duty and overriding responsibility to oversee every aspect of Team Sunbritech's race preparation and performance and he had done it to the exclusion of everything else. It was no different this Saturday morning of the Grand Prix weekend and he was back in the pit area very early to make ready for the days events which consisted of the last open practice session from 11:00 to 12:00 and then the all-important qualifying from 14:00 to 15:00.

It had been a good race weekend so far for the Sunbritech team. The cars were performing well — up to their potential at least. All formula racing cars are not equal. They are close but there are always one or two or three top level teams, then a grouping of what are called midfield cars, and then always a few up-and-comers or on-the-way-outers or never-will-be's referred to as back-markers. To be sure, the difference between the cream-of-the-crop teams and the rest of the field was measured in mere seconds but in world formula racing, a second is an eternity.

Sunbritech was, at this stage of development, one of the better midfield cars and hoped, as always, to score points here in Monaco and maybe even place one of their drivers on the podium. Foster was pleased with the state of readiness of the race cars, drivers, and support crew but not complacent. No one was ever complacent at this level of racing. There was always an improvement, a refinement, an adjustment to be made and Foster and Sunbritech and the rest of the teams concentrated on squeezing out the extra hundredth of a second and nothing else.

So John and Katherine had not seen Sir Robbie since Thursday and now it was Saturday. Even though they were two of the few who knew what was hanging over the Grand Prix and Monaco, they were determined they would not be cowed by the threat. And leaving wasn't even something they discussed. They got to the pit area just before 10:00 AM and were greeted by Foster who stepped away from his team duties for a moment to ask for and receive an update on the extortion situation and any related developments. He heard far more than he'd bargained for given all that had not been made known to the public at large. In addition to advising him of the initial email, John and Katherine briefed him on the Sarin attack at the bank yesterday, the ID on the attacker as one of the Torino "martyrs" and then their own sighting of Al-Nassef, and finally the new extortion demand. Foster listened shaking his head all the while. "It never stops, does it?" he said.

John and Katherine agreed.

"Will they pay this time?"

"They were going to meet on it earlier this morning." John looked at his watch. "Should be done by now. But Bazinet seemed to think it was likely. He wasn't happy about it, though."

"Problem is," Foster offered, "it doesn't do anything to deter it the next time. To the contrary, it encourages a next time."

"Right," Katherine concurred. "But the image of another Sarin attack, maybe a bigger one, during the Grand Prix weekend…" She threw her arm out toward the rapidly gathering crowd. "There'll be what, fifty thousand people here today? How many tomorrow?"

"Over a hundred thousand."

"A huge price to pay to stand on principle. I don't know. If it buys time." Even she hated the rationalization. But it was all they had.

"Yes, well…" Whatever Foster was about to say was cut off by a single screaming whoop as the mechanics in the garage raced the engine of one of the Sunbritech cars. The Sunbritech team principal excused himself and went back over to the bank of computers and monitors that gathered, analyzed and interpreted all the telemetry data from the cars for evaluation and, hopefully, improvement.

Katherine noticed Gamil Mukhtar sitting off to the side of the technical area and she and John walked over to the young aerodynamicist. "How is it that everyone else is running around like crazy and you get to relax like this?" she asked with a smile.

"My work is essentially done, Ms. Price," Mukhtar shrugged. "You recall our discussion about downforce?" Katherine nodded. "Well, the trick of most courses is to get the right balance for the track involved, You want the most downforce for the turns to keep the car adhered to the surface as it changes direction but, ideally, you want the least downforce when the car is going at top speeds down the straights. Here," he gestured out to Monaco in general, "it's all turns and almost no straights so we simply crank on the maximum downforce we can and let the drivers throw the cars around the turns with abandon." He gave a sheepish smile. "Well, perhaps not abandon but once I've determined the aerodynamic set-up all that's left for me to be concerned with is whether or not it behaves as the computer — and I — said it would. In the meantime, I'm surplus goods."

"Somehow I don't think Sir Robert would ever consider you surplus goods," Katherine said.

Mukhtar nodded acceptance of the compliment.

She and John walked outside and climbed a flight of temporary stairs to a viewing area on top of the garages. From there, they could see most of the race course from the tunnel in the distance to the left to the La Rascasse turn on the right. Beyond that, the harbor was packed almost solid with vessels small, large and enormous. To the right of the harbor where the Quais Albert and Antoine meet was the temporarily constructed modular race headquarters which was connected to the inner course by a raised enclosed passageway. John tapped Katherine on the arm and pointed to Director of Public Security Girard Bazinet who was just coming down the stairs of the crossover on the inner track side. He raised an arm in greeting and Bazinet responded in kind and came over to where they were. As he joined them on the roof of the garages, they noted Bazinet's slow pace and the chagrined expression on his face.

"Well, it's done," Bazinet said with a thoroughly Gallic shrug.

"The money's been paid?" Katherine asked.

Bazinet nodded, his mouth pursed in a classic moué. "His Highness is not at all happy about it but realizes we really had no choice given our responsibilities to all these people." He threw his gaze around the surrounding hordes. "Plus, France, as you know, has a great deal to say about Monaco's dealings particularly in international relations and such things like this and they were quite insistent that the demand be met. They actually provided a large portion of the funds."

"Still…" John commiserated.

Bazinet nodded. "One good thing is the DSGE is now involved directly and much more heavily than before," the Director said referring to France's premier intelligence and anti-terror organization. "They are on alert all over France for any sign of these *cons*." Bazinet bit his tongue as the word came out. "Pardon, Madame."

Katherine pretended not to hear the obscenity. "You really had no choice but to pay," she said trying to make Bazinet feel a little better.

"No, Madame," he demurred, "we had a choice. But the potential consequences were too severe to risk." His mouth tightened. "But make no mistake. I have every available officer looking for al-Nassef and this other man whose photograph we have. And we now also have photos of this Chani and his wife. Mastrota's colleague got her passport photo from the hotel in Ventimiglia."

"What about Katherine's sighting yesterday? And what we found on the surveillance? Al-Nassef? The bus routes? Any luck?"

"I'm afraid not. Each of the stops we saw — when he came in the morning and when he left around midday — has several buses with many routes and dozens and dozens of stops between here and Nice. A few go as far as Cannes. It was a good lead but so far we have nothing from it."

"Perhaps it is all over and they've already left," John said not at all convinced of that.

"They may have left, Monsieur," Bazinet stated formally, "but this will never be over for me. It is a stain on my career and I will not rest until it is expunged." The Director of Public Security took a few breaths and reined in his emotions. "But I do want to thank you for your help and offer to host you for lunch after the practice session. Have you eaten at La Rascasse yet?"

"We've started out to several times but never made it for one reason or another. I don't know that we could get a table today, anyway."

Bazinet clicked his tongue and smiled. "We'll get a table. I can promise you that."

Bazinet's cell phone rang in his pocket. He clicked it on and put it to his ear. "Bazinet, here." Both John and Katherine saw him straighten and focus in on what was being said on the other end. He listened some more interjecting only a few "mm-hmm's" and "oui's" then clicked off.

"Madame Chani has been found. She is at a woman's shelter in Menton. Apparently she has run away from her husband and has their child with her. The people at the shelter say she is very frightened of her husband and what he will do if he finds her. These people in the shelters are very protective of their clients. With good reason. But they are required to call the police particularly when there is violence or the threat of violence and they did so. Fortunately, someone at the Menton *gendarmerie* was alert enough to recognize the name from the Interpol alert and our office as the contact. So they are deferring to us in this. They've got people in place around the shelter but apparently Madame Chani is very afraid of the police and not trustful of men at all. So we will send a female officer over to question her. Apparently also the woman speaks only Albanian but we fortunately have a very good officer who speaks the language. The shelter has people who can translate for us but we prefer to have one of our own do it."

"I'd like to go with her," Katherine said.

John gave her a look of concern. "Why? You know Albanian?" He asked with a tinge of skepticism.

"Actually, I do know a little," Katherine countered but then she immediately backtracked. "Just a few words, though. Not enough to help." She spread her hands. "Okay, I confess part of me just wants to look into the eyes of a mother who would blow up her own baby. See if there's anything in there."

"I know, Kath," John protested gently, "but under the circumstances, I'd rather you stuck around."

Katherine smiled her understanding. "I know but…" She looked at Bazinet. "It's not very far at all, right?"

Bazinet shook his head. "Less than 10 kilometers."

"So, basically, I am sticking around, John. And let's face it. If the kind of thing we're worried about goes down, I don't know that 10 kilometers will make all that much difference."

"Oh, good," John said through twisted lips. "There's a comforting thought."

Katherine put her hand on his and smiled. "It'll be a matter of going there, seeing her and returning. I'll be back this afternoon. What could happen in a couple of hours?"

"Nothing, I hope but…"

"But you want to take care of me. I know."

"Yeah," John said earnestly. "As a matter of fact, I do."

"Thank you. Same here."

"You have. I know better than anyone how capable you are but that doesn't change the fact that I want to keep you close. And safe."

"I know." She kissed him on the cheek. "It'll just be a couple of hours."

"Well, what if I come with you?"

Katherine tilted her head and looked askance at him. "It's a woman's shelter. You heard Monsieur Bazinet say how protective the staff are." She squeezed his hand. "I know how wonderful you are but I doubt they'll be particularly receptive…"

John opened his mouth to object. "I know, John. I do. But they won't."

After a moment, John held his hands up in front of him, palms out in surrender.

"But…," he began.

Price stood up. "I know. Be careful. Right?"

John nodded.

"I will," she said. "You, too."

44

Federal Security Service
Ticino Canton
Switzerland

Nef had the two men from the Younis' villa placed in a single cell that was, of course, monitored with both video and audio surveillance. For the first hour or so, they spoke very little. Then Nef had the smaller man whose name was Marius brought into the interrogation room first leaving the larger of the two alone in the cell. The Swiss investigator made no progress whatsoever with the initial interrogation. He had Marius brought back to the cell and the larger man, Reto, was brought out. The two prisoners said nothing as they changed places but the hard look from the first conveyed that he had given nothing up and neither should the other man.

The second man, the one named Reto, was more nervous and Nef tried to take advantage of that. He'd refrained from discussing the radiation sickness ploy with the first man who appeared to be genuinely skeptical and probably wouldn't fall for it anyway. But this Reto seemed clearly concerned and Nef let the subject creep into the conversation again, not belaboring it but referencing it just enough to ensure it remained on the prisoner's mind. Even so, the man was either purely stubborn or cowed by his colleague and Nef couldn't break through and get the man to cooperate and provide the answers Nef felt sure he had.

They brought him back to the cell and waited. After a while, Reto finally spoke. "What if we do have this sickness they speak of, Marius. We know very little anyway. Is it so important to keep it to ourselves?"

"I don't know how important it is to us, Reto, but it certainly seems important to them and for that reason alone, we should keep silent. They can't hold us forever."

"No but the can hold us until we get sick, can't they," the larger man said almost sulkily.

"But we're not sick. And we're not going to get sick. Hold on and you'll see."

On the video screen that Nef and another interrogator was watching, Reto didn't seem convinced.

The interrogator assisting Nef looked up from the video screen he was watching. "It's time to separate them, Gioele. I have an idea. If the man, Reto, is afraid he is sick, perhaps we can help him."

Nef raised his eyebrows questioningly.

"It's against the rules, though. Very much so. But we are getting nowhere."

"Tell me," Nef said. After listening, he didn't really think about it for a long time. "Let's do it."

They went down to the cell and signaled for Reto to come out. As the cell door was relocked, Marius called out. "This is standard, Reto. To separate us. Soon they'll tell you that I've already broken. Don't let them convince you. It won't happen." Reto nodded as he was led down the hall out a door and into another hallway of cells. He was taken all the way down to a cell at the very end of the building which was no longer used. The reason for its disuse was that it sat directly over the parking garage in the corner of the building where vehicles were gathered and held for daily assignment. Some time ago, it had been noticed that when vehicles were left running directly below this cell, sufficient carbon monoxide would leak through the venting system into the cell above causing mild carbon monoxide poisoning. No one had been seriously injured but the cell was no longer used for that reason. What were the initial symptoms of carbon monoxide poisoning? Lightheadedness, nausea, vomiting.

Reto was left alone in the cell at the end of the hall and Nef and the interrogator went down to the parking garage and moved a number of vehicles as close to the vent as they could get. They left the vehicles running and went back to the monitors upstairs. Carbon monoxide is, of course, colorless, odorless, and tasteless so Reto would have no way of knowing what was happening. In a matter of minutes, Nef and the other man saw the prisoner start to sniff and then he shook his head a few times as though trying to clear it. They saw the man frown in confusion and watched further as the expression changed to one of concern. Then they saw the man called Reto put his hand to his mouth and swallow a few times. The other hand went to his stomach and the expression of concern became one of fear. The man in the cell started to look around anxiously and put his cheek up against the bars trying to see down the hall. After a moment, he shouted, "Guard!" There was no response and the man didn't wait long to shout again and then again. Nef looked at the interrogator and gave him a small salute as he went down to collect the prisoner. In a matter of moments, Nef had his answers.

Morning Practice
Grand Prix Course
Monaco

Bazinet arranged for Katherine to be picked up outside the race headquarters complex by the female police officer who would question Rozafa Chani in Menton. Cann and Bazinet remained on the roof of the garages and as they watched her climb the stairs and disappear into the raised passageway that crossed over the track and into the headquarters, Bazinet said admiringly, "Your fiancée is quite a woman, I think, John."

"As I've said many times, Girard, you have no idea."

"You are a fortunate man."

"I am," Cann agreed. "I am indeed."

Their conversation was interrupted by the screeching whine of engines from several of the teams as cars pulled out of the garages beneath then and proceeded at 50km per hour down to the entrance to the street course where they lined up waiting for the green light that signaled the start of the last practice session. For the better part of the next hour, the two men watched the practice and exchanged few words. When all of the cars were back in the garages and final preparations for the qualifying were being made, Bazinet turned to Cann.

"Well, I must tell you that I would have preferred to have the company of Madame Price as well but I did offer to host you for lunch." He extended his arm in the general direction of La Rascasse and John took the lead.

The food at La Rascasse is actually quite good and John decided that the reputation of the restaurant wasn't merely dependent on its location but equally on its cuisine. Somewhat playing against stereotype, Bazinet had a burger while Cann chose a salad. Both were delicious.

Bazinet's cell phone rang again. This time, it was Ispettore Pietro Mastrota.

"Where are you, Signore?" Mastrota asked abruptly.

Bazinet told him.

"May I come there?" the Italian asked.

"Not without race credentials, I'm afraid." Bazinet said. La Rascasse was within the confines of the limited access racing area and not accessible to the general public. "I can get them for you, Ispettore. It may take an hour or so, but…"

"There is no time for that."

"What's wrong?"

"I received a message from my *questura* in Torino that Gioele Nef — that is the FSS man who tracked al-Nassef for me," he reminded Bazinet — "called me with an urgent message. I have just spoken with him and I must speak with you at once. It is indeed urgent."

"What is it?"

"Not on the phone, especially a cell phone, Signore. We must meet immediately."

"Very well," Bazinet said looking at a very curious Cann who had sensed the tension. Where are you now?"

"Your office in Fontvieille."

"Go to the Place D'Armes. You know it?"

"Si."

"We will be there before you."

With the practice over and the qualifying not scheduled to start for some time, the track was empty. Bazinet held his credentials high for the track officials and security personnel to see as he and Cann darted across the Boulevard Albert I and quickly climbed the incline of Avenue du Port to the corner where the Avenue de Fontvieille meets the Rue Grimaldi. In a few moments they saw Mastrota coming almost at a run toward them. Both men noted the intense expression on his face.

Reflexively, the men shook hands as they met but even as they did so, Mastrota began his explanation, looking around furtively as he spoke.

"I explained to you before the story of how Ottah Younis is — or was — under the protection of the Swiss court and so forth," the Inspector began. Cann and Bazinet nodded. "Well, I've kept Nef informed of developments including the identification of al-Nassef." He nodded acknowledgement to John. "He was of course concerned about the connection of this terrorist to Younis but given the court's protective order and all, he was reluctant to discuss it. But then he saw the confidential Interpol alert about the Sarin attack yesterday and al-Nassef's connection and he felt he could no longer keep what he knew to himself. He brought the information to his superiors who deemed it actionable." He took a breath. "They raided his villa this morning. Based on what they knew, they were looking for information on al-Nassef but also for explosives or chemicals, particularly components of Sarin. They found explosives — a quantity of C4 — but no chemicals. They did however find something far worse than anything they'd expected. Traces of Cesium 137."

Cann blew air out through his lips. Bazinet realized he was holding his breath.

"With some persuasion, Nef got one of the men to talk about what had gone on there and he confirmed that a package had arrived in something he described that sounded like a diplomatic pouch. He said he didn't know the country of origin for sure but did say he recognized an Iranian diplomat who had visited Younis before. Apparently this man and one other had handled the contents of the package, a heavy metal box about the size of a large shoe box. They insist they didn't know what was in it. But they loaded it into the trunk of the car al-Nassef left in.

"We know al-Nassef has access to C4, Signori. That's what was used in Torino Wednesday. Now it appears he has Cesium 137. So you know what that means, then."

Cann and Bazinet looked at one another. They did indeed know what it meant.

Al-Nassef had the makings of a dirty bomb.

"So much for meeting the demand," Bazinet said bitterly. "50 million Euros. Let me tell you that I argued strongly that this is what could happen."

"Could?" John countered, then immediately stopped himself. Second-guessing served no purpose. "But what's done is done. Now we have the face the reality that al-Nassef has his hands on a dirty bomb. And I don't think there's any question that now that he's got it, he's going to use it."

"I agree," Mastrota concurred. "Terrorists all over the world have been looking to get their hands on a dirty bomb for years. I don't think they're going to go to all the trouble of getting it here and not use it. The glory, to them at least, of being the first is too great."

"And don't forget al-Nassef's history. He loves killing too much to pass all of this up," Cann made a sweeping gesture to encompass all of Monaco and the crowds.

Bazinet looked around at the enormous crowds and his beloved adopted city. Then he looked at Cann. "This man is a cancer, John. A cancer. I truly wish he really had died in your country's custody those years ago."

John nodded. "Me, too. But when you think about it, he's as much a symptom as he is a disease. Terrorism's the cancer. Al-Nassef is a malignant tumor."

"Yes. And what do we do with malignant tumors? We don't let them flourish and continue to grow. We cut them out. Which should have been done to this man long ago."

45

Du Cote des Femmes de Menton
Women's Shelter
Menton

Katherine Price and Chief-Corporal Jacqueline Tessier got on well. The French policewoman had been briefed on what this was all about and also on who and what Price was when she was ordered to bring her to Menton and was mightily impressed before she even met her. For her part, Price found the thirtyish Tessier to be bright, dedicated, knowledgeable and possessed of a wry sense of humor much like her own. Before they reached Menton, they had developed an easy sort of camaraderie that belied the short time they had known each other.

"So is your family's from Albania?" Price asked.

"My grandmother married an Italian soldier during the occupation in World War II. When Italy withdrew in 1943, she came back with him." Tessier paused. "The Albanian men would not have treated her kindly after her 'collaboration'." She gave Katherine a sidelong look.

"Anyway, they came back to San Remo and eventually settled here in Menton and while she fell in love with Italy and France she never lost her feeling for her homeland. So she made sure her children and grandchildren, including me, knew the history and learned the language." She smiled. "She's eighty-eight years old now and sometimes doesn't even remember where she is. I still speak Albanian with her every time I see her, which is often. It makes her happy. But I'm not as fluent as I'd like to be. That's why I plan to do this interview in French and let the shelter people translate. My Albanian is easily good enough to know how accurate the translation is and sometimes you get different meanings in different languages. Also, that way you can listen in as well." She and Price had been conversing in French so Tessier knew she was fluent.

They reached Menton and Tessier pulled the unmarked car into a parking space near the *Du Cote des Femmes de Menton* shelter where Rozafa Chani had been brought. Once inside, they were greeted by the manager of the shelter and the woman who had found Chani in the *patisserie.* The older of the two women, the manager, looked at Price and Tessier and even though she saw sensitivity and caring in their faces, she cautioned them sternly.

"Please approach this young woman gently," the manager said. "You must understand that she is very afraid, not just for herself but for her child. She has not told us everything about what she is doing here or was going to do but we can tell it was serious. We can tell that from your presence here as well," she said to Tessier and Price. "Normally we would let her story come out as she felt ready to tell it but... I request that, as you question her, please keep in mind that her life has been nothing short of slavery. And extended brainwashing. We have dealt with many of the rural people from the Balkans and Eastern Europe and we still sometimes find it hard to comprehend the difference in attitudes and development even in the 21st century. It is almost evolutionary. But, whatever she has done, she is here now and it is clear that it was her love of her child that made her do this — which she herself considers to have been a betrayal of her religion. She is very conflicted right now."

Katherine listened and accepted the lecture in the spirit in which she assumed it was given — concern for the client. But she still couldn't completely suppress the harsh pre-judgment of Rozafa Chani that had settled in her mind. She and Tessier were taken out a door at the rear of the main building and across a courtyard to a two-story building which could provide comfortable and private accommodation and shelter for half-a-dozen "residents"at a time.

Inside the unit on the second floor left, Rozafa sat uneasily in a corner of a comfortable looking sofa, her son Luan sleeping quietly beside her, easily within reach. The moment Price looked at the young woman and small child, her severe appraisal began to dissipate. Instead of the uncaring zealot she had been picturing, she now saw a frightened young woman not even out of her teens, almost a child still herself and one who had endured a life that was, as the shelter manager had said, "nothing short of an extended brainwashing".

Tessier crossed to an armchair that was facing the sofa and sat down opposite the young Albanian. Price sat in another chair further away. The French Chief-Corporal spoke in gentle measured tones giving Rozafa Chani assurances that she was safe now, that no harm would come to her or her son. The translator relayed the words to Chani who listened without apparent emotion then looked back to Tessier and gave her a small nod.

Tessier gently led Chani through the sequence of events beginning with the departure from Albania, the trip up through the Balkans and into Italy, first Torino and then Ventimiglia and then here to Menton.

Listening to the French translation back to Tessier, Katherine was struck by how little the young Albanian really knew. There was an obvious native intelligence to the young woman but it was clear that she had not been privy to any useful information and had no specific knowledge of what had happened. Or would happen. When pressed, she said her husband didn't know exactly what was to happen either. She had asked him only yesterday and he had said he didn't know, that it was not their decision. She thought it would be soon but they had not yet been told.

"How would you be told?"

A computer. Her husband would look at it often to see if there were messages.

Tessier suppressed the urge to look at Price.

"Your husband still has the computer?"

Chani assumed so. It was in the apartment when she left.

"Where was the apartment?"

Chani didn't really know. She wasn't allowed to look out of the car while they were driving. And she had left at night and walked to the sea and then ended up in the *patisserie*.

Could she find it again?

When that question was translated, a frightened look appeared on Chani's face. She did not want to go back to that place, the translator related. Please. Her husband will be very angry with her.

And required to punish her for…Rozafa looked around the room…this.

The translator gave Tessier a cautioning look but there could be no question this was something that had to be done.

"Tell her we will take her in an unmarked car with very dark windows. No one will be able to see her inside the car. We will protect her at all times."

And Luan?

And Luan.

Rozafa looked at Tessier and then Price. "You promise this?"

They promised.

Rozafa was afraid to take Luan with her and afraid to leave him behind. The two were quickly bundled out of the shelter unit and into the car Tessier had driven from Monaco. Tessier was at the wheel, Price was in the front passenger seat, and the translator rode in the back with Rozafa and Luan. Before leaving, Tessier made quick arrangements over the phone with the Menton *gendarmerie* to provide backup but at a distance from her vehicle so as not to alarm Rozafa.

Where to begin?

It was Rozafa who suggested they take her to the shore where she could get her bearings from the night before. They did and Rozafa recognized the place where she'd slept against the wall.

Straight up there, she said pointing up the street which ran alongside the casino. They stopped the car at the end of the short street and Rozafa peered out the front window looking left to right and back again. That way, she said pointing left, and then right and up the big street which was the Avenue de Sospel.

Tessier drove up the busy Avenue de Sospel as slowly as traffic would allow as Rozafa looked out the darkened windows at the buildings and sights along the right side of the road. Several times as passers-by and pedestrians would seem to be staring into the car as they drove by, Rozafa asked for reassurances that they could not see her inside.

"*Këtu!*" Rozafa spotted the granite cross she had seen the night before. "Here," the shelter worker translated. Tessier made the turn and drove up the side street. In the back seat, Rozafa withdrew into the seat, sliding down in an apparent attempt to disappear into the cushions. After a moment, she said, *"Atje"*, "there", her finger pointing at an apartment building on the right.

Tessier summoned the backup to stake out the building while more police units were called to reinforce an entry operation. Rozafa remembered which apartment within the building they had gone to and she described it to Tessier who moved the car away from the front of the building then got out to take part in the raid. Rozafa and Luan stayed outside in the car with Katherine and the interpreter.

The entry team was assembled outside the building and out of sight of the windows of the apartment to be entered. Before the team effected entry, a lone technician went into the building and up to the apartment designated by Rozafa as the one she and Xhelal had arrived at the day before. At the door, the technician used ultra sensitive sound detection equipment to listen for anything coming from within. He heard nothing. He then slipped a fiber optic camera under the door and maneuvered it to see as much of the apartment as was visible to the device. Still nothing. In the absence of any evidence or indication that there was anyone inside, the technician signaled to the head of the team that they should come up.

The door was flimsy and yielded to a single kick from a rather large police officer. The members of the team rushed in and cleared each room as they were so well trained to do. In short order, it was determined that the apartment was indeed empty except for furniture, some clothing, some food in the refrigerator. And a laptop computer set up on a low coffee table in the living room. Tessier and the head of the entry team approached the laptop gingerly, hoping against hope that there would be something on it that would take them to…somewhere. Anywhere. The computer was open and still connected to a website on the Internet. Tessier leaned down to see what was on the page. A message box was superimposed over the page itself and in the box were the words:

"For your security, this session has been logged off due to inactivity."

"Don't touch it!" Tessier said abruptly to the special unit commander who was just then reaching toward the keyboard of the open laptop. The man pulled his hand back sharply.

Tessier had her cell phone in her hand and was waiting for Gilles Patenaude, Monaco Public Security's computer security expert, to come on the line. When he did, he immediately asked for all the basic information — what kind of computer, operating system, etc. Tessier was no computer geek but she was easily knowledgeable enough to answer those kinds of questions.

"What's on the screen right now?" Patenaude asked.

"It's a website, 'charonportal.com'," Tessier replied.

"Proxy server," the computer technician commented. "Okay, and you said there's a 'logged off for inactivity' message on the screen?"

"Right."

"That could be a help. Don't close it."

"Can you log onto that site from where you are? Tessier asked.

"Already have." There was silence while the tech examined what he had. "Okay, I see where there are links to several clients servers. I can get to those but no doubt the individual users will be password protected. There's software for that. Maybe we'll get lucky and get some help from local system memory. And there's a very good chance there'll be some IP related verification as well. I need to work on the specific computer myself."

"Shall we bring it to you?" Tessier knew Patenaude was speaking from Monaco.

"You could but I'd hate to risk having it handled very much. Someone could drop it or just accidentally hit a key or anything. Leave it where it is. I'll come to you."

46

Roquebrune-Cap-Martin,
France

Rafiq Mukhtar looked around the room he'd occupied in Roquebrune-Cap-Martin since Wednesday and made sure he was leaving nothing behind. Unlike Bleeker, who'd been instructed to leave her belongings in the apartment in Menton, Mukhtar had things he would need for his assigned tasks. Also, unlike Bleeker, neither Roquebrune nor Ste-Dévote was to be his last stop. After constructing the explosive devices in the bedsit in Monaco, he would head for Col le Bermasse where he would build the final device. He suspected what the nature of the instrument would be from what the leader had said. But he couldn't be sure and, ultimately it didn't matter. So long as his act of sacrifice brought glory to him and the *jihad*.

As directed, he rode into Monaco by bus following essentially the same route Bleeker had taken the day before by bicycle from Menton. He got off not far from the Casino and walked the rest of the way down Avenue de la Costa to the bedsit which backed onto another building that had a spectacular view of the Ste-Dévote area of the race course where the Saturday afternoon qualifying session was just getting underway. He could see nothing of it but could hear the sounds of the engines and sometimes the crowds.

The engine sounds brought back memories. He knew of course that it was the Grand Prix weekend. Throughout his childhood the Grand Prix team had been the focus of their lives. His father had worked for the TerrentAll team for years and continued on when it was bought by Sunbritech. Initially, it had been expected, though not required, that he and Gamil would follow in their father's footsteps and for years, it had been Rafiq's dream as well as Gamil's. But he, Rafiq, began to outgrow it as he found himself more and more entranced by the words of the Prophet (Peace be Upon Him) and what he knew to be the touch of his heart by Allah. His pilgrimage to Pakistan and the madrassa at the age of eighteen and the words of the teachers had confirmed and ratified to him all that he had thought and felt before. He never returned to his home or family in England. There was no need. He'd wanted to feel badly or miss them but could not. They had drifted from the path of true Islam. They had "adapted" to the unadaptable and he was convinced the break had to be final. For a short time he kept the letters, especially the ones from his mother asking him to just please at least write and tell them he was okay. But he never did. And after a while, he simply threw them away when they arrived without even reading them.

He'd begun to realize, or surmise anyway, what the object of this mission was when he got to Torino. It was the last week in May and he knew he was only three hours from Monaco by car. When he was moved to Roquebrune, his suspicions were almost confirmed. Now it was clear he was constructing one bomb to be used in this location and there would be another — what al-Nassef had called the ultimate device tomorrow. His glory. At last. He set himself to his task.

But the screams of the engines, so familiar to him in his youth, kept reminding him of his family. Might they even be here? His father was probably retired by now but it was possible. The team was good to its people and often brought former employees to races as guests. And, he wondered, had Gamil gone on as planned and was he now part of the team from Chipping Crawford. Rafiq was a bit surprised to find that he hoped not. He would not be swayed from his task. But whether it was because he was here in Monaco or because he knew he was close to his end, he found he couldn't keep thoughts of his family out of his mind.

Avenue de Sospel
Menton

Outside the apartment building off the Avenue de Sospel in Menton, Katherine waited with Rozafa and Luan and the interpreter in the car. She had slid into the driver's seat and had her back to the driver's side window as she looked back toward the apartment building. In the back seat, she could see Rozafa slumped down holding her son close and pressing her face tightly to the boy's. Katherine tried to take the young woman's mind off her fears with a couple of off-hand neutral questions asked through the interpreter but Rozafa would politely answer in the most distracted fashion and then immediately go back into her defensive shell.

Behind them, at the end of the block, the black rental car driven by Xhelal Chani came slowly around the corner. He was distracted, angry and frustrated, both furious and fearful that the dignity and quality of his act of sacrifice had been compromised by Rozafa's dishonorable actions. As he neared the apartment building, he looked up at the front window and was shocked to see two figures standing inside the apartment he had left hours before. He drove on slowly and made two left turns until he was one street over from where the apartment was. He turned into a narrow alley that split the buildings on the block and pulled into a small parking area under a canopy. There were spaces for five cars but only one other vehicle was parked there at the time. He got out of his car taking the large kitchen knife and sticking it into his belt. Then he walked carefully down the alley keeping close to the side of the building on his left. At the end, there was a large trash bin. He stood behind it and peered across at the scene on the other side of the street. There were still people standing in the apartment window and he could now see that they were wearing uniforms. Clearly, the apartment was compromised. And the computer was still in there. He couldn't remember if he'd turned it off before leaving that morning but after an initial surge of panic, remembered it was set to break the connection after a short period of time.

As he watched, a woman in pants and a white blouse with a badge hanging from her pocket came out and walked up to a car on the other side of the street, bent down and spoke through the passenger side window to the occupants inside. Then the rear driver's side door opened onto the street and a woman — the interpreter — got out. The interior of the car was visible for only a few seconds but it was enough for Chani to be able to see inside where he recognized the figure of his wife huddled in the back seat. A sound that was something between a grunt and a growl came from his throat and his hand immediately touched the handle of the large knife he had inside his belt. Allah be praised! What greater sign of the righteousness of his mission could there be than this — Rozafa being returned to him just when he was at the point of despair. Then his anger returned as he realized what her presence in that car meant. Rozafa had not only left him but she was now working with the infidels to thwart his sacred mission. Was there no limit to her betrayal, he fumed?

He watched as the interpreter came around and joined the other woman. The two then walked back into the apartment building. He bowed his head and said a prayer of thanks for such a gift then raised his eyes and studied the scene around him. He saw no other people in the vicinity. He calculated the width of the relatively narrow street between him and the vehicle that held Rozafa and estimated he could cover the distance in seconds. He examined the car again. The windows were too dark to see inside and he realized he didn't know how many other occupants there might be. He had seen no others in the rear so there might be two at the most, he figured, in the front. Or perhaps there was just one, a driver. Or perhaps there were no others. Only Rozafa. He prayed for that to be so. That would further prove it was the will of Allah that he succeed. In any case, it was clear what he needed to do. And he would not delay.

He stepped casually out from behind the trash receptacle, the long bladed knife held tightly against the back of his upper thigh. He crossed quickly, taking a course slightly toward the front of the other car so as to keep his reflection out of the side view mirror for as long as possible. When he was close, he leapt the last few feet and grabbed the rear street side door handle and pulled. It was unlocked.

Rozafa let out a squeal of fright when the door opened and then she emitted a groan of despair when she realized it was her husband. In the front driver's seat, Katherine reacted quickly swinging her right hand in a backfist that missed Chani's head by inches. Already twisting in the front seat to get more leverage, she froze when the Albanian jabbed the knife into Rozafa's throat. The blade was also precariously close to his son's head as well. Katherine backed off immediately holding her hands in front of her, palms facing outward toward Chani.

"Who are you?" he asked her in Albanian.

She shook her head that she didn't understand.

"Who is she," Chani said to his wife without turning.

"An American," she answered with downcast eyes. "She came with the police. I don't know anything about her."

Xhelal looked at Price and gestured for her to turn her back to him and put her hands on the steering wheel. Then he turned back to his wife and son. "You have betrayed me. And you have betrayed Islam. How can you do this?"

"I was afraid," she admitted. "Afraid for Luan but also afraid for myself. I doubted."

"You cannot doubt. You know what that…" Chani stopped talking and looked toward the apartment building. Two uniformed police officers had stepped outside and were lighting cigarettes. They seemed engrossed in conversation but one appeared to be looking over at the car.

He sat without moving as he thought about the situation.

"Whose car is this?" he asked his wife.

"It is a police vehicle, I think. A woman officer drove it here."

Xhelal Chani gritted his teeth. He had convinced himself that Allah had given him this opportunity so that he could complete his sacred mission as he had planned. He would not kill them now. The woman in the front, perhaps. That would be easy, he was sure. But he saw a use for her. For a time. And although Rozafa deserved death, it must be as part of the plan, not here. As for his son, he looked at the boy and wished for him the glory he had planned. There would be no honor in killing him here and now. Luan had to die, of course, but properly.

"Drive!" he said to Price, again in Albanian. Again she indicated she did not know what he was saying. "*Parli Italiano*?" he asked.

"*Si*," she nodded.

"*Guida!*" He took the knife away from Rozafa's neck just long enough to jab it in a forward direction. The keys hung in plain sight in the ignition where Tessier had left them and Katherine regretted not having had the presence of mind to pull them out when the Albanian man had burst into the car. "*Dove?*" she asked him. Where?"

"To the corner there," he jutted his chin in a forward direction, "and turn left." She did as directed and Chani had her make another turn at the next corner and yet another into the narrow alley and into the space next to where his rental car was parked. When they were stopped, he grabbed Luan from Rozafa's arm and put the knife against the boy's neck. "Get her purse," he ordered his wife who leaned over and took it from the front seat. She handed it to him and he dumped the contents on the rear seat and sifted through them. To his satisfaction, he found a metal nail file that would suit his purpose. "Listen carefully," he said handing Rozafa the nail file. "Use this to remove the license plate from that car," he indicated the rental, "and switch it to this one. Do it quickly. Make sure no one sees you. If you run or cry out or do anything, I will kill Luan. Do you understand?" She nodded. "Then go."

Rozafa completed the task quickly and got back into the car. Xhelal directed Katherine to back down out of the alley on to the street away from the one where the apartment was. "Drive west," he told her. "Slowly and carefully. If you do anything to attract attention, I will kill you all."

Price had been in similar situations before and knew that the best time to strike back was at the start before things settled down — if they ever did. But the knife at Luan's neck argued strongly against any precipitous action on her part. And Rozafa was also easily within reach of her husband.

No. She would hold off and wait for a better opportunity. If one came. But for now, she would comply. For now.

47

Avenue de Sospel
Menton

IT expert Gilles Patenaude arrived at the Menton apartment carrying hardware, software, and most importantly an amazing brain chock filled with the intricacies and esoterica of computers and all related activities. That included an encyclopedic knowledge of all the legitimate processes in addition to a comprehensive and equally far ranging familiarity with hacking and cracking and phishing and every other illegitimate use of computer technology known to man. He was a fundamentally and compulsively honest man which was a very good thing for those who rely on the security of their computers for if Patenaude had chosen to go in the opposite direction he would certainly have found himself installed in the pantheon of hacking legends like Mitnick and Vladuz and only a few others.

He sat down in front of the laptop and looked at it closely. Without striking any keys, he inserted a CD into the side and let the computer become aware of it on its own. After a moment, there was a whirring sound and soon after the screen changed to a readout of numbers and letters and symbols that meant nothing to anyone in the room but Patenaude. The computer specialist read the data on the screen carefully and then gingerly moved the cursor along the toolbar at the bottom and clicked once. The first screen — the one with the charonportal.com and log off message reappeared.

Patenaude blew some air through his lips in relief. "That was the first touchy moment," he said to the room in general. "It was possible that we'd lose that page when I ran the CD but it had to be done. Okay, now I know what I'm looking for." He ran the cursor over the screen highlighting it in its entirety then hit a few keystrokes. Immediately, several words on the screen changed to bold print. "Client servers," he muttered. His fingers hit a few more keys and he stopped and watched what the screen would do. A few more keys, a bit more rapidly this time, and then another pause to study the result.

Tessier and the others stood behind him watching intently looking almost like they knew what was going on. They didn't. And they could only tell how it was going by the grunts or tch's that came out of Patenaude from time to time. But it was fascinating nonetheless to watch this electronic treasure hunt even if no one but the cyber-tech knew where they were at any given moment.

After some time, Patenaude leaned back in his chair and rubbed his knuckles and fingers. "Okay, here's where we are. The screen you found up in the first place was a proxy server intended to be anonymous but that's easy to defeat. I got past that and found the client servers of which there were several. Fortunately, the log out message told me which client server I wanted to go to and from there I was able to trace back to the specific site that had been contacted by this user. The next part got tricky because that location had a number of hidden links, some of which were decoys set up to sever the connection if they were clicked on. Fortunately again, I was able to get through the code and see which were real and which weren't.

"The good links on the initial destination page led to several different message boxes all of which require passwords and IP verification. Using a password hacking algorithm I developed myself, I was able to get the passwords for each of the message boxes but that does no good because of the IP verification requirement." He saw the questioning expression on Tessier's face. "What that means.' He explained, "is that the server holding the message for each user will only recognize that user's computer. Even with the passwords, we can't access the message boxes for anyone but the person using this one."

"Can you tell where the messages came from?"

"I can tell you the IP of the computer they were sent from. But there's no way I can tell you where that computer is at any given moment."

"And this computer. Are there any messages for this one?"

"One," Patenaude said as he turned to the computer and hit enter. He started to read the message and then said, "Merde." He looked up at Tessier who was already standing behind him reading over his shoulder the message giving Xhelal Chani very specific directions for where he was to take his family to a specific location in Monaco where the explosive devices were waiting already prepared for their "sacred explosion". The directions advised them to take the Monaco train in the morning making sure to arrive no later than mid-morning. That would give them a couple of hours to make their preparations. At 12:30, they were to go down the hill to the corner of the race course where the cars go up the hill toward the Casino. Do nothing as they to go by the first time, the message read. Wait until they come around a second time. Then perform your glorious act.

Tessier already had her phone out and was speed dialing Bazinet.

In Monaco, Cann and Mastrota were with Bazinet in his office where he was gearing up the organization of a renewed all-out search for al-Nassef and his people and, now, a radioactive dispersal device. At the moment, the Director of Public Security was on the phone with the head of the Sapeurs-Pompiers, the force tasked with all aspects of hazardous materials detection and handling. That included nuclear.

The call from Tessier came in. Bazinet put the Sapeurs Colonel on hold and took the other call with a curt, "Oui?"

Cann and Mastrota watched Bazinet's eyes widen and saw his body tense as he listened to the report from the Chief-Corporal on the other end of the line. "Bon. Bon," he said. Then, "Merde." He listened some more then asked, "Do we know when it was sent." A few more moments then, "Well, thank God you found this, Tessier. Well done." He clicked off that line and reconnected with the Sapeurs Colonel. He looked directly at Cann and Mastrota as he spoke into the phone. "It looks like we may have a major break here, gentlemen," he said. "Madame Chani led Chief Corporal Tessier to an apartment where the Chanis had been staying in Menton."

And Katherine no doubt went with them, John thought. Just a matter of going there and returning. Right. A couple of hours. He pulled out his cell phone and dialed Katherine's. It rang several times before it switched over to her voice mail. He left a message. "Give me a call, Kath. Let me know everything's okay." He clicked off.

"They found a computer there," Bazinet was saying. "One of our experts cracked it and found out how al-Nassef has been communicating with his people. And," Bazinet said, "there was an email giving Chani detailed orders on what he and his family are to do. Tomorrow. At the start of the race." Bazinet described Tessier's call in detail. "So it looks like our dirty bomb is in Ste Dévote."

"You asked your officer when the email was sent," Mastrota asked. "What was the answer?"

"Very early this morning," Bazinet replied. "Before the funds were paid," he observed pointedly.

"And the Menton apartment was empty when they found it?"

"Of people. There was food, clothing, the computer."

"Maybe they're bailing out," Cann suggested, not believing it himself. Hoping. Thinking of Katherine.

"No," Bazinet replied, "I don't believe that for a moment. And in any event, a dirty bomb is a danger even when it doesn't go off." He stood. "Let's go. The Sapeurs are already on their way to Ste Dévote."

Back in Menton, Tessier clicked off the phone feeling a sense of pride in a job well done and basking in the glow of the praise she'd just received from her superior. She could feel the tension of the previous moments dissipating as she walked slowly over to the front window and looked out on the street. It took a moment for it to register that something was not as it should be. Finally it dawned on her.

"Where's my car?" she wondered out loud.

Ste. Dévote
Monaco

His work at the bedsit done, Mukhtar looked around, gathered his things and went out onto the Avenue de la Costa. Strictly speaking, his orders were to go back to the bus route he had been on before and make his way across Monaco and east to Col le

Bermasse. Even though there was no indication he had been identified, there was simply no good reason for him to cross the principality on foot. An excess of caution perhaps but it was the small things that often made or broke an operation. This time, however, for one of the very few times in his life, Mukhtar would not follow instructions.

He walked down the hill toward the center of Monaco until he came to where the concrete and chain link barriers closed off the course and the abutting areas open only to ticketed spectators. He continued down the outside of the course along the Boulevard Prince Albert which served as the curving "straight" of the race course. On the other side of the Boulevard, he could see the rear of the individual garages each one clearly marked with the name and logo of the team. He stopped opposite the Sunbritech pit area and looked through the chain link fence. The rear wall of the garage area was partly open and just inside he saw Gamil standing with his hands in his pocket, talking calmly to someone. Rafiq looked away from his younger brother and up and down the street to see if he had drawn any attention to himself. When he looked back across the street, Gamil was staring at him, his eyes wide and mouth agape. The younger Mukhtar turned abruptly away from whomever he was talking to and started to cross the Boulevard. Rafiq considered moving off quickly but realized he couldn't be sure that his brother wouldn't shout for him to stop or do something else that might cause him to receive unwanted attention. Best to keep it calm and normal.

He raised his hand in greeting to Gamil who was in the middle of the Boulevard but walking off at an angle toward the nearest entry point to the course. For an instant, Gamil was out of sight as he exited the course but reappeared almost immediately just up the street from his brother. He slowed as he neared him and when he was close enough, threw his arms around Rafiq in a hug of greeting. The action made Rafiq uncomfortable and he was able only to return the gesture half-heartedly.

Gamil took a step back and looked at his older brother. At first he said nothing and could only shake his head. Finally, he spoke. "Rafiq. I...I don't know what to say. Where have you been? How are you? Are you coming home? Mom and Dad will be..."

"No," Rafiq answered more sharply than he would have wished. He softened his demeanor a bit. "No," he said more gently. "My home is in the heart of Allah and the Prophet (Peace be Unto Him). I need no home on this earth. My home is in Paradise."

Gamil inhaled and then sighed. He had no desire for a replay of the theological and ideological arguments that had consumed his family even all those years ago. "I'm happy for you then, Rafiq," he said sincerely.

"You should seek to find your home there as well," Rafiq said.

"My home is Islam, too," Gamil replied. "My spiritual home. On this earth, my home is still Chipping Crawford. It's yours, too, if you want it. Mom and Dad would love to have you back. To see you at least."

Rafiq shook his head firmly in the negative. "No. There can only be one home. Mine is with Allah. If you do not accept that, you are *kafir*." Rafiq spit out the last word.

Nothing had changed. It had gotten worse if anything. And Gamil hadn't taken it then and he wouldn't take it now. "Well, fortunately it's not for you to decide whether I am *kafir* or not, is it?" Gamil retorted. "I live a good life, I honor Islam and, unlike you, that doesn't prevent me from honoring my family as well."

"My family is my brothers in the *jihad*."

"*Jihad*? *Jihad* as in inner struggle. Or *jihad* as in killing. Have you gone that far, Rafiq. Do you condone killing now?"

"Yes. It is what the good Muslim will do when he sees his fellow Muslims being killed in the street? He defends them. And glorifies himself in the doing of it."

"By killing innocents? You actually believe if you kill women and children you will go to heaven. That's not religion, Rafiq. That's insanity."

"You blaspheme, Gamil," his brother hissed. "There are no innocents outside Islam. They are *kafir*. The only innocent people are those who are in Islam or accept living under Islam. Anyone else is *kafir*."

"You just called me *kafir* a minute ago, Rafiq. Am I an infidel, then? Will you kill me, too?"

"If you are *kafir* in the eyes of Allah. I look through the eyes of Allah and now I speak to you through the heart of Allah and…"

"Listen to yourself, Rafiq," Gamil challenged his brother. "*You* look through the eyes of Allah, *you* speak from the heart of Allah? It's you who blasphemes. Not me."

Rafiq reeled at the very idea of such an accusation and took a step back. "You were family before. You are no longer," he pronounced. Somewhere not too far away they heard the claxon sounds of emergency vehicles. Rafiq looked quickly toward Ste Dévote and then began to move off. "I do not know you, Gamil. You do not know me. But in the peace of Islam, I say this to you. Make your peace with Allah today or lose his blessings forever. Mark my words, you will not have another chance."

48

Ste. Devote
Monaco

The emergency vehicles that the Mukhtar brothers had heard in the distance had to do with a traffic accident on the outskirts of Monte Carlo city, and nothing to do with the explosive devices in the bedsit in Ste Dévote.

Bazinet's first instinct had been to order the cordoning off and evacuation of at least several blocks around the building where the explosives referenced in the Chani email were located. He was dissuaded by the blunt analysis of the NBC expert from the Corps des Sapeurs- Pompiers.

"Frankly, if there's an RDD in there, Monsieur le Directeur," the Sapeurs Lieutenant-Colonel had said, "evacuating a few blocks will make no difference. You would need to evacuate the entire Principality to be completely safe. And if as you said, it contains Cesium 137, then don't plan on coming back for a very long time."

That got a grunt of acknowledgment from Bazinet.

"Moreover, I believe you said the information you have is that the device was to be set off in the open outside the building. Of course we don't know what explosive is used or how much is involved but to some degree anyway, the building itself will contain some of the explosive power of the device if it were to go off.

"Which we don't plan on happening, of course," Bazinet said tightly.

"Of course, Monsieur. We never *plan* on that happening but we are discussing contingencies here. My point is, if it is a conventional device, there is, initially at least, no reason to risk creating panic among the general populace by overreacting."

"Overreacting," Bazinet repeated the word back. "I hardly think concern for the public safety is overreacting."

"No, Monsieur, of course not. But consider the extraordinary number of people we have in Monaco right now. A panic would be even more of a disaster than usual. And consider this as well. You told me that you learned of this device from an email to the person who was to be the principal bomber, no?"

Bazinet nodded.

"And you said that email came in early this morning so there is a chance — a very good chance, I would say — that the bomber has read it." Lieutenant-Colonel Allard held up a finger. "Now consider this please. Later in the day you learned of this location in Menton and conducted an entry. But the bomber wasn't there. There was food, clothing. The computer. It would seem he planned to come back. Assume that he did and found the apartment compromised? If so, where would he go? There may be alternatives but is it not most likely he would come to the Ste Dévote location early?"

"And therefore might be inside right now." Bazinet saw the point immediately. "If so, a show of force could very well cause him to detonate the device at once."

"Exactly. We must approach in stealth. See what we are dealing with."

Bazinet concurred.

They drove to the scene without sirens or lights and parked the marked units out of view of the building The same Sapeurs sergeant who had been at the bank Sarin attack scene arrived on the scene dressed in his utility uniform. Once inside the foyer of the building on the Avenue de la Costa, he put on coveralls and gloves and a face mask but not a full blown hazmat suit. Bazinet looked the question at Allard.

"He carries detectors for nuclear and chemical as well as explosives with him. They are on now and operating and getting no readings. Until he gets an indication of the presence of any such substance, it is simply easier to work without the hazmat suit. These detectors are quite sensitive and will alert him well before he is close to a dangerous exposure.

"Ready?" the Lieutenant-Colonel asked the sergeant who indicated he was with a thumbs up. Allard returned the gesture and the sergeant climbed the stairs to the second floor. None of the devices registered a reading as he did so. The sergeant went to the door of the bedsit and sat down on the floor just to the right of the jamb. The first thing he did was move the sensors of the NBC detectors over the surface of the door and around the edges. Nothing. He then took a highly sensitive microphone and carefully placed it on the surface of the door and heard nothing inside. Next, he took out a fiber optic cable with tiny lens at the end and slowly inserted it under the door. He was able to manipulate the tiny camera so that he could see most if not all of what he now knew to be a quite small space. He saw there was no furniture other than a table on which rested what looked to be vests. The only other thing he could see in the room was a baby carriage near the table. Satisfied that the bedsit was not occupied, he relayed his observations to Allard and Bazinet who had the rest of their forces move in closer and seal off the area to pedestrian and vehicular traffic.

Upstairs, the Sapeurs sergeant, having been briefed on the overarching nuclear concern, first inserted the radiation detector under the door in the same fashion as he had the camera. By adding segments to the cable, he was able to inch the sensor at the tip closer and closer to the table. He got no reading even with the detector set at maximum sensitivity. He did the same with the chemical sensor and got no reading for Sarin or anything else. Lastly he inserted the sensor developed for explosives detection. That got a significant hit.

Allard's transceiver chirped. "Oui, sergeant," he answered.

"There is no RDD here, mon Colonel," the sergeant advised. "And no chemicals. We do, however, have explosives inside. I will examine for booby traps and advise when I am sure."

"Very well, sergeant," the Sapeurs Lieutenant-Colonel said, adding, "Be very careful."

"Oui, mon Colonel," the Sergeant replied. He didn't need to be told.

The directions Xhelal Chani had memorized from the morning email told him how to get to the bedsit from the Monaco train station and nowhere else. So he had Price drive there. It was outside the restricted confines of the course and spectator areas and the streets around it were open to traffic. But the going was slow. Price continued to comply with Chani's instructions even while looking for an opening to resolve the situation. But at no time did Chani take the knife away from Luan's throat and so she continued to bide her time.

Price wasn't terribly familiar with the streets of Monaco either but knew generally what direction they were coming from and, by following the signs to "La Gare" was able to get them there. From there, Chani directed her to drive east on the Boulevard de Suisse which ran parallel to and to the north of the Avenue de la Costa. Then he told her to take a right and as soon as she did they were stopped in traffic. It was a short street and ahead of them about five cars were in line, not moving. She and Chani peered forward trying to ascertain what the hold-up was. At the end of the street, they saw a police officer requiring each car as it reached the Avenue de la Costa to make a three-point turn and go back up the street. Access to the Avenue de la Costa was obviously closed.

Chani leaned a little forward and told Price to stay in the line and follow the police directions. As well as his own. When they reached the intersection, Chani looked to his left at the building he was seeking and saw police and fire all around. That, too had been compromised. He looked through the windshield and could see the officer ahead gesturing for Price to turn around and go back.

"Do as he says," Chani ordered. "No eye contact. I'll kill the boy."

Price thoroughly despised the man in the back seat and was appalled at the irony — even that word didn't describe the incomprehensible disconnect that could cause a man to use his own son to force compliance with his demands — of her caring more about the boy's safety than his own father did. Perhaps he was bluffing but she wasn't prepared to risk it. She would do all in her power to bring this to a conclusion without harm to the boy. Or Rozafa.

She'd promised.

Katherine made the reverse turn and then went right on to the Boulevard de Suisse which curved slightly around to the right and intersected the Avenue de la Costa not far ahead. They would have turned left there except it was one-way in a westerly direction so they continued on and then doubled back until they were on the Boulevard des Moulins heading away from Monaco.

Xhelal directed her to pull into a supermarket parking lot so he could think. She was again ordered to put her hands on the steering wheel and look straight ahead. Rozafa was sitting straight up in the back behind Price with her hands folded in front of her and Luan was on his father's lap. Chani picked up Price's cell phone off the seat next to him. He'd shut it off when Cann had tried to call earlier and so they'd been unaware of Cann's subsequent attempts. Now the Albanian examined it closely, wondering how — if — he could use it to salvage his mission.

Out of the corner of her eye, Katherine could see Chani handling her phone. John was "2" on speed dial. If she could just get to it…

Chani knew he needed to contact the terrorist leader. He was tech savvy enough to understand the laptop he'd been carrying had the added protection of the IP verification and knew that meant he could only access the secure message board on that computer. But that was to pick up messages. He remembered the return email address from which the messages to him had been sent and wondered, could he send an email *to* that address from an unsecured location? Like making a bank deposit. Easy to put something in, much harder to get something out.

"What's the number of this phone?" he asked Katherine.

She gave it to him. She wanted him to use it.

Chani turned the phone back on. As it powered up, it briefly displayed "your number" on the face. He noted with some surprise that Price had told him the truth. He committed the number to memory just as the phone buzzed, saying there had been three missed calls. He ignored them and pressed the Internet button. He typed in the email address he had in his head and then put in as concise a message as he could think of. "Apartment in Menton compromised. Location in Monaco compromised. Contact this number." He punched in the number of Price's phone and sent the message.

Bazinet took the call from Tessier on his cell phone. His face sagged as he listened. Then he clicked off, took a deep breath and called an officer over. As much as he considered Cann a part of the team, Bazinet had insisted he and Mastrota wait on the periphery of the secured zone until the device inside the building was disarmed and the area cleared. "You know who Monsieur Cann is?" he asked the officer who nodded. Bazinet pointed up the Avenue de la Costa to where Cann and Mastrota were waiting with several police cars not far from the intersection where Katherine had been forced to turn around. Neither had seen the other.

"Please bring him to me," the Director of Public Security said.

When Cann came over, the look on Bazinet's face told him something was wrong. "In Menton," Bazinet began hesitantly, "Katherine was waiting outside the apartment where the Chanis had been while it was entered and searched. She was in Tessier's vehicle with Rozafa and Luan. I just received a call from Tessier that her car is gone. She just looked out the window just now and…it is gone."

"Gone?" Cann repeated the word dumbly, a knot forming in his stomach.

"With everyone in it." Bazinet confirmed.

Cann's jaw muscles tightened.

Bazinet put a hand on his shoulder. "We will do everything in our power to find her, John, I swear."

"Chani, you think?" Cann asked, his mind functioning on auto-pilot.

"Possibly. If he came back while they were inside the apartment. But I would have thought Madame Price would not have been so easy to…" He didn't finish the sentence.

"She probably wasn't," Cann snapped even as he knew the Director meant well. He was already reaching for his cell phone, again punching the #2 on it. Again there was no answer. He clicked off and immediately punched in the required international prefixes and added them to another speed dial number for the home office in Washington. Not #1. #1 speed dial on both John's and Katherine's phone was Arthur Matsen. That they hadn't changed it was a testament to the affection and esteem they both had for the senior partner. And it was that affection and esteem that caused him to call someone other than Matsen in Washington. Arthur was growing increasingly frail and John knew that, even so, if he thought Katherine was in trouble, the elderly man would want to be on the first flight to Europe.

Cann was calling Loring, Matsen and Gould's large and state-of-the-art equipped tech group. In years past, the lawyers/operatives for the law firm had worn watches with a GPS capability built in so they could be kept track of on assignment. Few did anymore and as the technology developed, there'd been talk of microchipping the people but that debate was still ongoing. What they did have, however, was a worldwide capability of tracking cell phone usage. It wasn't as precise as a GPS locater but it could track usage and identify the cell where the phone had been used anywhere in the world. Cann advised the tech people in DC of the situation and they immediately sprang into action.

49

Col le Bermasse
France

Following the confrontation with his brother, Rafiq Mukhtar had stormed up the Rue Princesse Caroline and then continued on up to the bus stops at the southern entrance to the Monaco train station. By now, he'd been given his ultimate destination so he studied the various routes for several moments before finding the shortest and most direct bus to Col le Bermasse. It was evening now and dusk was approaching by the time he arrived at the building where the BMW and the ambulance were stored. His instructions had included the combination to the lock on the over head door and he let himself in.

One of the side rooms appeared to be an old office from which the service station business had been conducted. On the old dusty desk was a simple walkie-talkie unit. More of a child's toy than an actual communications device. With a limited range of no more than a half mile. Mukhtar picked it up, turned it on and spoke into it. "Test, test," was all he said.

In his room at the Hotel Palais de Revere, Rashid al-Nassef heard the message on a matching handset and knew the Brit was in place. He looked outside and saw that the light of the day was fading and the streets were clear. He donned the mouthpiece and glasses and pulled a hat down over his eyes before going out even though he'd made a very thorough examination of the area and hadn't found any surveillance cameras. He'd been wrong about that before, he recalled.

It took only minutes for al-Nassef to join Mukhtar in the garage. After solemn formal greetings, they got down to business. The terrorist leader walked over to the ambulance and pulled open its back doors. Inside there was another 100 kilograms of C4 and all the other items Mukhtar would need for this, his final destructive assembly. All of the materials had also been secreted here weeks before just as the Sarin and explosive materials in Ste Dévote had been. The final ingredient, however, had been brought by al-Nassef himself.

He went over to the trap door in the floor and pointed down at it. "When the time comes," he explained, "pull this door open. There is a ramp down and at the end of the chamber, you will see a metal container. Inside that container is an element called Cesium 137. It is what will make this explosive device sufficiently radioactive to destroy all of Monaco. Not by the explosion but by the contamination it will spread. You understand this?"

Mukhtar did.

"Inside the container is another thick metal container. And inside that, you will find four metal tubes. Each of those tubes contains ten grams of the Cesium 137. I have not seen it but I am told it is in powder form, granular, like sand. And it has a blue glow. You will construct this bomb as you would any other and set it in the back of the ambulance. But wait to add the Cesium until the last minute when you will spread it on and around the device inside the ambulance. You understand the object is maximum dispersal." He saw that the young man did. "How long will it take to put the device together?"

Mukhtar looked back at the ambulance and then down into the trunk. "Not very long. It's quite simple actually."

"Even wiring it for detonation?"

Mukhtar gave a dismissive shrug. "I will place a detonator in each corner of the C4 and run the wires to a simple electrical switch in the cab. When it is time, I simply press it and it will explode. Very elementary. I can set all that up now."

"Do that," al-Nassef told Mukhtar. "Minus the Cesium, of course. You should wait until you are just outside Monaco for that." He looked at the young Brit. "You do know that when you expose the Cesium, you will be exposing yourself to its radiation." Mukhtar nodded. "So long as I reach my target, it doesn't matter."

267

"Good," al-Nassef said, once again impressed.

"The race starts at 1:00 PM," al-Nassef continued. "You know this." Mukhtar nodded. "Just as the race is to begin, the first strike will take place. A gas. You do not need to know what it is. But it is very effective. It will cause death and a great deal of panic. Then, at almost the same time, there will be an explosion on the other side of central Monaco which will cause further injury and death. And confusion. In the moments following, emergency vehicles will be summoned from all over. It will take a little time for you to reach the city but that will allow for more responders to be on the scene. When you are there, try to get as close to the center as you can although that is not critical." He gestured toward the trap door again. "There is more than enough to make Monaco a wasteland for many years to come."

"Insh'allah," Mukhtar said. "God willing."

Al-Nassef returned to the hotel while Mukhtar built the basic bomb and wired it. He was pleased. All seemed to be going according to plan at the moment. He had confidence that the young Brit would do well. Gallacher was in place and the leader had a good deal of confidence in the Scot as well. Not so with Chani but if the Albanian would follow directions and stay where he was until it was time to move tomorrow, that should also fall into place. Al-Nassef had received word that the money demanded had been paid — not that it mattered — and as a result he felt it likely that the authorities would have settled down just a bit. He was under no illusion that investigations and searches wouldn't continue, but his expectation was that the intensity of the efforts by the authorities would have been leveled off if not scaled back.

As he'd done several times throughout the day, al-Nassef checked his email box and saw there was a message waiting. His antenna went up immediately upon seeing a source address he didn't recognize. After a moment, he opened it. As he read Chani's cell phone post, both his anger and his confusion grew. "Chani. *La'anatullah!*. Again," he sputtered. "Can he do nothing...?" He read and re-read the message. "What does he mean 'compromised'? Menton? Monaco? Ste Dévote?"

Al-Nassef suppressed his growing fury and tried to focus on what this could mean. Depending on what exactly Chani meant by "compromised", it appeared that the Ste Dévote action may be aborted. It was not a critical strategic loss. The Chanis' part in the operation had been a "nice touch" but the plan wouldn't fail without it. His first instinct was to abandon Chani and his family and let them fend for themselves. The Albanian had been nothing but trouble and al-Nassef had grown more than tired of this man who he now saw as what the Americans call a "loose cannon". In the final analysis, though, it was precisely what al-Nassef saw as Chani's "loose cannon" tendencies that made him decide he needed to bring the Albanian in close where he could control his actions and make sure he did nothing further to endanger the operation.

Chani's message gave a phone number as a point of contact. Al-Nassef had no idea whose it was or where he had gotten it and had to assume it was not secure. The Albanian had texted him from it and al-Nassef could answer in kind. But he had far more questions in mind for this putative 'martyr' than could reasonably be answered by texting. He picked up the encrypted satellite phone and dialed the number.

They'd sat in the supermarket parking lot for an hour before Chani told Price to start the car and change locations. She drove back toward Monaco center and found a rare legal spot on the street and pulled into it just as the phone rang. "Pronto," Chani answered it anxiously.

"Chani," al-Nassef said coldly. "Answer only my questions and do so briefly. And be careful how you phrase things. I assume the phone you are using is not secure. Understand?"

"Si," Chani answered. Italian was also the common language between al-Nassef and Chani so Price would be able to follow that end of the conversation in the car. But there was little to overhear.

"Will you be able to attend the race tomorrow as planned," al-Nassef cryptically asked the Albanian.

Chani understood what was being asked. "No. It is impossible."

Al-Nassef started to ask why but checked himself. He would get the details later. For now, he had to get this troublemaker out of circulation. He needed to get him over to Col le Bermasse without revealing anything on this unsecured line.

"I assume you don't have your computer."

"Correct."

"Others do?"

"I don't know. I believe so."

Al-Nassef shook his head in disgust. "And this is a telephone you are on right now?"

"Yes. A cell phone."

Al-Nassef knew his satellite phone couldn't be traced. On the other hand, he knew the cell phone could. "Where did you get it?" he asked Chani impatiently.

The Albanian hesitated before he answered. "It belongs to an American woman…"

"American woman?" al-Nassef interrupted. "Who is she?"

"She was in the car with my wife and child when I found them."

"Found them? Where were they?" Al-Nassef caught himself. "Never mind." Would this idiot's mistakes never end? "This American," he asked. "Why would…" Then the thought struck him. "Is she still there? This American. Is she still with you?"

"Yes"

"Do you know how to take a photo with the phone?"

"Of course," Chani answered.

"Do it. Now. And send it to me."

Chani did so. Al-Nassef recognized Price immediately. He struggled to fit this into place but he couldn't connect the dots. It was enough, though, that there was a connection to this other American man whose path had crossed his twice before. Al-Nassef contained his anger. "Keep her with you. Bring her to me."

"Where…?"

"Quiet! Listen carefully," he said. "I am going to remove the IP verification requirement from the secure website so you can access it from where you are. But only very briefly. You remember your password?"

"Yes."

"All right, give me three minutes. I will post directions to where I want you to come. And pay attention to this. Even before you access the site, change your password. I will block the computer you had before from any further access to the secure website and then I will close the site down once you've retrieved the directions. Understand?"

"Yes."

"Then follow the directions. Without delay. You have diminished the mission already. I do not want any further problems. Do you understand?"

"Yes."

"Three minutes," al-Nassef repeated. Just before he clicked off, he added, "And then get rid of that phone."

The call ended.

Chani waited the requisite amount of time then did as directed, retrieving the directions posted on the website. Not two minutes after he'd done so, the cell phone rang again. Chani answered quickly again, expecting al-Nassef. "Pronto."

"Who is this?" the voice of John Cann asked angrily.

Chani hurriedly clicked off and the expression on his face gave Katherine no doubt as to what had just happened. "John knows," she thought to herself. "Good."

50

Department of Public Security
Office of the Director

Back in Bazinet's office, the search for Katherine Price was now one with the search for al-Nassef, the Scot, the Chanis and, the dirty bomb they hadn't found in Ste Dévote. There had been discussion about evacuating the principality but it was clear to all concerned it couldn't be done. It wasn't, as the cynics would say, just a matter of economics. It was more a matter of logistics. Word of the potential dirty bomb had come in just about twenty-four hours before the race was scheduled to start. Monaco emergency officials had long ago determined that in a non-Grand Prix weekend, it would take at least twenty-four hours to clear the area. This weekend, it simply couldn't be done. To their credit, the entire royal family remained in the palace as did virtually every other official who had knowledge of the situation. Bazinet certainly wasn't leaving his beloved adopted Monaco and even Mastrota rebuffed any suggestion he go back to Torino.

As for John, he wasn't going anywhere without Katherine.

His cell phone rang. It was Loring, Matsen IT. "We picked up four times Ms. Price's phone was used recently today," a tech informed him. "The first three times for several minutes. The last time for a few of seconds just a couple of minutes ago."

"The last one was me," Cann said. "Could you tell where the phone is?"

"Not the phone, sir, but the cell. That's in Monaco proper," the tech replied. "Northeast of the center." Cann used his index finger to draw an imaginary circle on the map spread in front of him indicating to Bazinet the area the tech had just referred to. Bazinet picked up another phone on his desk and spoke into it, scrambling all local units.

"What about the content?" Cann asked.

"I can't even tell you whether they were incoming or outgoing calls, Mr. Cann. We don't have the technology to intercept or listen in. Not from here. That's NSA level capability."

"Then get hold of them," he snapped impatiently. It wasn't as far-fetched as it sounded. Loring, Matsen and Gould's connection and assignments often placed them in contact — and cooperation — with the governmental intelligence agencies and capabilities.

"We have, sir, but it doesn't happen just like that. Even the President can't get an instant response. It takes time."

John blew air out through his lips. "I know," he said grudgingly after a moment. "Keep on it. Monitor Katherine's phone from here on out. 24/7. Got it?" He hung up and looked over at Bazinet questioningly.

"Anything?"

The Director of Public Security made an inconclusive face. "We have many units in the area, John. They have descriptions, photographs even of Price and the two adult Chanis. For now, we must operate on the assumption they are either in Chani's rental or Tessier's vehicle. If they've made a switch..." he gave Cann another of his classic Gallic shrugs.

Unfortunately, the authorities hadn't yet found the rental that Chani had left behind the building in Menton and, while it may not seem like much, the mix and match plate switch created enough of a disconnect between the respective car and the respective plate that it went a long way toward inhibiting a ready identification.

But what most defeated the scramble of units is the simple fact that by the time the call came in from the tech to Cann, Tessier's vehicle with Katherine and the Chanis inside had already left the quadrant they'd been in. When the cars and personnel swept in, the objects of their search were already out of the principality and into Cap d'Ail.

From where they were in Cap d'Ail, Col le Bermasse was only about three kilometers to the northwest. Price picked up the D6007

273

for a brief period and then quickly turned onto much more rural roads. When they were well away from the metropolitan area, Chani told her to slow down and pull over to the side of the road. When she stopped, he opened the door and put a foot outside the vehicle. He made sure the phone was off, then, standing half-in and half-out of the car and still holding Luan, he heaved it into a nearby field. Then he got back in and told Price to drive on.

Katherine was not happy with herself. She shouldn't have been taken by surprise in the first place and surely should have found a way to neutralize this guy by now. But she hadn't. At no point had he taken the knife away from the child and at no point had she detected even a slight lapse of attention on his part. She didn't have the impression that he was a trained professional but he certainly was a competent amateur. Competent enough to have held her at bay to the point that she could sense time was running out. It was all well and good for her to want to save the baby. And the woman. But she couldn't do it if she let herself get into an untenable situation. At some point — soon — she had to do something.

They came to a stop sign at a "t" intersection where she could go right or left. She waited for Chani to give her further directions. When he didn't she turned her head to the side and said, "Which way."

"Just wait," Chani said.

At that moment, she sensed something outside the car to her left. She turned and looked into the barrel of a large caliber handgun. The gun barrel moved up and then down ordering her to open the window. She did. At that moment, the passenger door opened and Rashid al-Nassef climbed in, also holding a handgun. Rafiq Mukhtar got into the back with the Chanis.

When they got to the garage in Col le Bermasse, Mukhtar got out and opened the overhead door. Price drove in and the door closed immediately behind them. The Pakistani Brit moved around to the driver's side to cover Price and then al-Nassef got out and came around and took his place. Mukhtar moved and opened the rear passenger side door. Rozafa Chani got out and al-Nassef waggled the handgun he was holding at her to move her toward the rear of the car. He then gestured for Xhelal Chani to get out and join her. Chani still carried Luan but wisely left the knife on the seat of the car as he got out and stood next to his wife leaning against the rear fender.

Mukhtar moved around to the rear bumper of the car just behind them.

Al-Nassef looked at the Chanis for a moment then turned back and beckoned to Price to get out. She did so, stood and looked directly into al-Nassef's face. He did the same to her.

"Hello," she said.

Al-Nassef dispensed with the niceties. "Who are you?" he asked.

"Katherine Price."

"What are you doing here?"

Price gestured with her thumb into the car toward the knife. "I really had no choice."

Al-Nassef looked contemptuously at Chani then back to Price. "I mean here in Monaco."

"We came for the Grand Prix."

Al-Nassef looked askance at her. After mulling her answer for a moment, he asked, "The man you were with yesterday. What is his name?"

"John Cann." Price saw no reason not to tell him.

Al-Nassef ran the name through his memory bank and couldn't find it. "I remember his face. I also remember where I have seen him. But his name means nothing to me." A cynical smile crossed his face. "He wanted me killed once."

Katherine refrained from expressing the thought that "more than once" was more like it.

"But that was long ago. What business does he have here with me?"

"None to begin with," she replied. "But now that you have me here. He'll make it his business, you can be sure."

Al-Nassef continued to study her for several moments trying to fit the pieces into a coherent whole. He couldn't. Finally, he decided he didn't need to figure it out. He only needed to make it to 13:00 tomorrow. "Very well," he said at last and started to turn away. Price took the opportunity and planted a hard front kick into al-Nassef's side that sent him slamming into the wall. The handgun he was carrying dropped to the floor and Price leaped forward and picked it up and held it on him.

"Stop," a young British accented voice said sharply. Price looked over at Mukhtar who had his gun placed against the back of Rozafa Chani's head. "Drop the gun or I'll shoot her," Mukhtar said.

Price stepped away from al-Nassef and swung the gun she was holding around and aimed it at Mukhtar's face. "You shoot her, I shoot you."

They stood looking at each other for a moment. A standoff, Price thought. She made a try at gaining some sort of control over the situation. "Listen. Don't get nervous. We both know if I drop this gun, you're going to shoot me. So here's the deal. You don't shoot her. I won't shoot you. We all just stay calm and figure out a way for..."

"Shoot the wife," al-Nassef said to Mukhtar who fired without hesitation. The front of Rozafa Chani's forehead burst open splattering bone and brain and blood in a spray that reached the wall ahead. Price didn't hesitate either. In the split-second after Mukhtar fired she did the same putting a bullet into the center of his forehead killing him instantly. Price whirled back toward al-Nassef but he had already regained his legs under him and charged hard into her side before she could bring the weapon around. They fell in a heap onto the floor, hands grappling for control of the gun and each other. Price managed to get a grip on the front of al-Nassef's neck and was trying to press her thumb deep into his esophagus when Xhelal Chani planted a vicious kick to the back of her head. The blow stunned her and she rolled onto her back losing control of the handgun in the process. Chani picked it up and held it on Price. He still held Luan who was dangling under his father's left arm.

Al-Nassef slowly got up on one knee massaging his throat. "Well done," he said to Chani. "You have redeemed yourself." He put out his hand. "Give me the weapon." Chani complied. "Now get his," al-Nassef said indicating Mukhtar who was lying behind the car. As Chani walked in that direction, he looked at his wife who was face down on the floor, the extent of the destruction to her face mercifully hidden.

"That was necessary," al-Nassef said to the Albanian and waited to see his reaction.

Chani looked at Rozafa for a few more seconds, then said, "Masha'Allah". God has willed it. He moved past and got Mukhtar's gun.

Al-Nassef stared at Price for a very long moment unconsciously rubbing his throat. "I don't know who you are," he said finally, "but clearly you are more than just this John Cann's companion. Yes?"

Price said nothing.

"Very well. It does not matter. Whatever you and he are doing here will end tomorrow. I will return you to him as part of my gift to Monaco and the world." Another nice touch, he thought.

Without taking his eyes off Price, al-Nassef told Chani that there were plastic ties in the desk in the office and to get them. When he came back, al-Nassef held on to Mukhtar's gun and covered Price from a distance while the Albanian bound her hands behind her and tied her feet. Then they propped her in a sitting position against the wall. She put her head back and closed her eyes willing the pain to go away.

51
Route de la Tête de Chien
Northwest of Monaco

One more time, Cann pressed the speed dial #2 on his cell phone and listened as the ring at the other end went unanswered.

"Shit!" he said as he clicked off, just as he had said every time before.

"Be careful you don't wear down her battery, John," Bazinet cautioned gently. "if she could answer,…" He stopped himself.

"Katherine's good at keeping it charged," he replied. "Anyway, it's all I've got." He pulled his hand back as if to throw his phone at the wall but didn't. "Damn it!"

They were in Bazinet's office where they could keep track of the efforts being made in the search. Throughout the evening and into the night, nothing had borne any fruit. The mobile units had missed Tessier's unmarked car and there was no sign of it or any of the people they were looking for. Foot patrols had been canvassing the entire principality and its environs since yesterday and those numbers had been augmented significantly since the information about the potential dirty bomb had come in. They had mobile radiation and explosive detection units out and others at the ready but with no specific locations to concentrate on, finding anything that way would of necessity be a matter of stumbling across it. Katherine's going missing added another dimension to the search but the entire force, and more, was already at maximum alert.

Ispettore Pietro Mastrota gave Bazinet a look of concern and the Director nodded his commiseration with Cann as well. At this point he knew he was reduced to willing something to happen that would get them off dead center.

Cann waited several minutes and then hit the speed dial #2# yet again. It rang and rang.

Nothing.

"Shit!"

Sunbritech Pit Area
Grand Prix Course
Monaco

Gamil Mukhtar was sitting atop the Sunbritech garages with his feet up on the rail. Ever since the disturbing meeting he'd had with his long lost brother that afternoon, he'd been playing the incident and what was said over and over in his mind. Initially, his reaction had been that of a family member. Sibling regret and also anger, followed by wondering what his parents would think of his having seen him after all this time. Should he even tell them he'd seen Rafiq? What purpose would it serve? They'd grieved for him over the years and still did but the loss had been more or less accepted, the pain internalized and suppressed under a layer of time. Rafiq was the same as before. Worse. And he wasn't coming back. He'd made that clear. Why open up old wounds?

After a while, Gamil had begun to focus more specifically on what had actually been said. Rafiq's commitment to *jihad.* His acceptance and rationalization of killing. His twisted definition of "innocent". And his warning at the end. Was it an idle threat? A violent but general admonition to accept Rafiq's version of Islam? But he'd not said "make your peace with Allah". He'd said "make your peace *today* with Allah". "Or lose his blessings forever". And "you will not have another chance." What did he mean by that?

He got up and went down into the garages. Sir Robert was there, as always, going over technical data with the race engineers and the drivers who would soon return to the hotels to get their requisite full night's sleep before a race. Gamil Mukhtar stayed in the doorway not speaking. After a moment, Foster noticed him. "Still here, Gamil?" he asked. "Please don't tell me you've suddenly conjured up some aerodynamic anomaly we've not thought of before."

279

Mukhtar gave a half-hearted smile and shook his head, then asked, "I know it's the night before a race but can I talk to you about something?"

Foster genuinely liked this young man over and above the immense respect and admiration he had for his skills. And the team was in good shape for the race tomorrow. So he nodded and came over. The two men walked outside.

"What is it?" Foster asked.

"I saw my brother today," Gamil said.

Foster had come to the Sunbritech team after Rafiq Mukhtar had gone off to Pakistan but he was aware, generally, of the what had occurred years before in the Mukhtar family and the circumstances surrounding it. "The one who left?"

Gamil nodded. "I was talking to Nelson today and I looked across the street and he was just standing there looking at me. I couldn't believe what I was seeing."

"Were you able to talk to him?"

"Yes. It wasn't a very good conversation though. Many years ago he left over his, how shall I put it, differences with the rest of us over Islam. And, well, let's just say he hasn't changed his views. As intense as he was before he left, now he's... extremist. And then some. He ranted about jihad and killing infidels — and to him that's anyone except him and those who feel as he does. Me included. I challenged him and he really went off. And made what sounded like some real threats."

Foster tuned in sharply at that. "Like what?"

"Make my peace today" he said. "Or lose the blessings of Allah." He looked directly into Foster's eyes. "I don't know how familiar you are with my religion but we don't have the Christian concept of hell. Rather, to be condemned is to lose the blessings of Allah. But one can only lose those blessings if one dies in a state of not being a good Muslim. I am a good Muslim but for Rafiq to assert that I will lose the blessings if I don't "make my Peace" today, tells me... he may be involved in something imminent." He made a frustrated gesture with his hands. "I don't know."

In other circumstances, Foster may not have taken the statements with such immediate seriousness. But knowing what he knew, he put a hand on Gamil's shoulder and said, "You need to come with me."

Foster made a phone call to Bazinet and was put straight through. He described what Gamil Mukhtar had told him and the Director of Public Security requested them to come over immediately. By the time they arrived, Bazinet had requested and received the digital files of the surveillance tapes of the area where the brothers had met and the surrounding environs for the relevant time period.

Gamil sat down at a computer station and began to run through the images taken by a camera on the corner of a building at Boulevard Albert and Rue Princesse Caroline. It was set high and pointed down giving a low bird's-eye perspective to the picture it displayed. The images showed the barrier separating the sidewalk from the track, the road course to the right of it and, in every frame, a number of people on either side. "There," he said abruptly after a short time. He placed the tip of his finger against the back of a head on the screen. "That's Rafiq."

Cann, Mastrota and Bazinet were all standing behind Mukhtar and they leaned in to peer more closely at what he was indicating. "We need to see his face," Bazinet muttered. "Please keep going." Mukhtar clicked and clicked his way through the ensuing sequence of images which showed Rafiq looking across the Boulevard then eventually turning toward the camera as Gamil approached. The image wasn't as full on as they would have liked but it was better than nothing and Bazinet had already ordered prints to be made. Then, toward the end of the conversation — it was obvious from the body language — Rafiq turned in the direction of the camera and looked up. "Why did he do that?" Cann asked. Gamil thought for a moment and then came up with it. "Just then we'd heard some sirens in the distance and he looked over in that direction. He got tense, more tense, and left right after that."

"He's looking in the direction of Ste. Dévote," Cann suggested. "And check the time," he pointed at the time/date stamp on the screen. "Just as we were arriving at the bedsit on the Avenue de la Costa." The others considered the implication. "I know," Cann said. "It's not much. But still…"

"But it's an excellent full face shot," Bazinet said and he directed a technician to capture the image and put it in the face recognition system. While they waited, they went back to the screen in front of Gamil Mukhtar and watched as Rafiq turned and went out of frame.

"Hit!" the tech said after barely a minute. "And another." The first shot the tech displayed showed Rafiq Mukhtar turning left at the corner of Rue Princess Caroline and Rue Grimaldi. The next shot was taken at the bus stops at the south entrance to the Monaco train station and showed Mukhtar with his head tilted up reading the bus schedules.

"Bus stops, again," Bazinet said testily. "Let's hope we get more than we did before." They did. Another shot taken from the same camera showed Rafiq Mukhtar boarding a bus that had pulled up in front of him. This time, the bus' route number showed clearly in the image. "#347," Bazinet announced. He turned to the tech. "Bring that up." The tech did so and Bazinet grunted. "Well, it's something anyway. At least this bus is local. It runs only from here to Col le Bermasse and back." He went to a street map on the wall. "Along this route," he said tracing his figure in an upward direction.

"Can we get people out there? Check this out?" Cann pressed.

Bazinet thought for a moment. "It's France. Outside our jurisdiction. And too small for a police force of its own but..."

"Then I'll go," Cann said.

Bazinet looked at him. "I understand, John. But to what purpose?" he said gently. "Yes, it is only a few kilometers long but..."

"I can't just sit here any more. I'll trace the route. Maybe see... something. Anything."

"I'll come with you," Mastrota said.

Cann nodded thanks to the Italian and looked back at Bazinet. "Can I have a car?"

"Of course. I will have one brought to the front. I would come with you but my place is here. Take copies of these new photos with you."

"Thanks."

"And, John," Bazinet said as he got up and crossed to a locked cabinet on the other side of his office. Taking out a key ring as he walked, he located a small key and opened the cabinet. It held a variety of weapons. Bazinet stepped aside and gestured for Cann to make a selection. He chose a duplicate of his own personal weapon, a Sig-Sauer P229 with Crimson Trace™ laser sighting. Cann was very much aware of how heavily restricted guns were in Monaco, France and the rest of Europe for that matter and was grateful. He looked at Bazinet. "Thank you."

"Use it wisely, my friend."

52

Col le Bermasse
France

Katherine was still seated against the wall with her head tilted back even though she had at last gotten past the effects of Chani's kicks. Behind her she moved her hands around as unobtrusively as possible and tried to expand the muscles in her wrists in an attempt to free herself or at least loosen her bonds. She was unsuccessful and, worse, the bindings first chafed then cut into her skin. After a while, she opened her eyes just a slit and watched.

Al-Nassef and Chani went over and lifted Mukhtar's body and carried it to the rear of the room and laid it down next to the trap door. Then they went and did the same with Rozafa's body. In doing so, the severe damage and distortion to the young Albanian woman's features became evident and Price looked for a reaction from Xhelal. There was none.

Al-Nassef lifted the trap door and swung it back on its hinges until it lay flat on the floor. He took a few steps back and kept his distance as Chani carried the two sets of remains into the space below. Before the Albanian came out of the hole, al-Nassef pointedly directed Chani's attention to the container at the back of the subterranean space.

Once they had put the trap door back in place, Al-Nassef led Chani to the ambulance and opened the rear doors. They spoke in Italian so Price understood what was being said as the terrorist leader pointed out the stacks of C4 in the middle of the floor and told the Albanian that he was a very fortunate man.

"You had lost your opportunity for glory through your series of foolish actions but this," al-Nassef jutted his arm into the rear of the ambulance, "means you will now carry the honor of striking the greatest blow ever against the infidel."

"Insh'allah", Chani said, outwardly humble but swelling inside.

Al-Nassef looked back toward Tessier's car where Luan was lying on the back seat. "What do you plan to do with the child?" al-Nassef asked. He had no intention of dealing with it.

"I will take him to glory with me," the Albanian said almost piously.

There was a pause then, "As you wish."

Al-Nassef then reminded Chani of the container stored in the underground space. "That will be the true instrument of your glory." As he had done with Mukhtar, he described the Cesium 137 and what Chani was to do with it. "The device in the ambulance is ready. All that is needed is for you to spread the Cesium before you detonate the bomb. Without the Cesium, you will destroy much. With it, you will destroy everything."

Rue des Remparts
The Rock
Monaco

In the apartment atop the Rock, William Gallacher had kept inside for almost thirty-six hours now. This despite the temptations arising from the sounds and smells and, when he peered out the windows, sights of the late night Grand Prix weekend partiers outside in the Palace Square and its environs. From his corner location, all he could see was the square on one side and the view out over the Rock and down into Monaco itself on the other. But, having walked through Monaco-ville on his way to the apartment the day before, he knew that the narrow streets and alleys all around him were filled with bars and restaurants in this central portion of Monaco-ville.

He knew there were at least two bars and two restaurants at ground level on the opposite side of the very building he was in on the Rue Basse. And, sitting quietly inside the apartment, the thought had occurred to him that perhaps there might be access to one of these from the inside — an interior entrance that would preclude the need to go outside at all.

He understood the need for operational security and was dedicated to performing his role in the operation perfectly. And while he was not the fanatical ideologue that Rafiq Mukhtar was, he was just as committed to his concept of jihad as the Pakistani Brit — except for the part about the lagers, perhaps. But he had made his accommodation with that restriction and felt secure that Allah was fine with it as well. So, he thought, if this was to be his last night on this earth, surely he would be forgiven one last taste of the spirit of Possilpark.

He forswore the disguise he had used on his way to the apartment. It would be pretty hard to enjoy his lager with the mouthpiece in. He did pull a hat down low over his eyes and vowed if he couldn't find a location dark enough to aid in his concealment, he'd come right back up.

He went down to the end of the hall and found stairs that ended in a central corridor on the ground level. Sure enough, as he walked along the hallway, there were a series of doors with names of what certainly sounded like there would be bars and bistros and such on the other side. One named "Côte de Barbarie" appealed to his more piratical instincts and he tried the door. It was open.

Inside he looked around. Glass and mirrors everywhere, polished wood, wrought iron decor. Given Gallacher's frames of reference in Possilpark, to him this wasn't a bar, it was a boutique. But it was dimly lit and crowded enough so he could be lost in it. It would do. He took a stool at the end of the bar closest to the entrance he had come through and ordered a McEwens, then a Tennants and finally "settled" for a Stella. He took a long, affectionate draught from a chilled mug and just enjoyed the taste.

Two stools over with no one in between, was a twenty-something young man who was with an attractive woman of about the same age. The young man was quite drunk. He said something to Gallacher that the Scot didn't catch and he was happy to ignore him anyway. The young man stared at Gallacher for a moment then stood and gave a back hand slap to Gallacher's upper arm. The Scot looked at him.

"Stella's horse piss," the other man slurred in a thick Scottish accent. Gallacher closed his eyes and shook his head. Unbelievable.

This far from home and he has to get a fucking hooligan next to him in a bar. He took a breath and looked at the younger man. "My mistake. I'll get something else next time."

The younger Scot seemed taken by surprise by the accommodating response and didn't say anything for a moment. Then he leaned into Gallacher again and said, "Ya need ta take yer hat off when there's a lady present, ya know."

Gallacher turned his head and looked the other patron directly in the eye. So much for enjoying his last lager. "Can't do it, son," the older man said, "but if it'll make you happy, I'll just leave." He threw back the last of his Stella and went to stand. At that moment, the youth reared back and threw a roundhouse right at Gallacher's head which the lawyer evaded with a simple pulling back of his head.

The punch had a lot behind it though and the youth's momentum carried him forward, very off balance and he ended up crashing into a table with two couples at it. One of the men at that table wasn't in a mood to be as gracious as Gallacher had been and he lifted the hooligan off the floor by his shirt and shoved, sending him stumbling across the room into another table. That table reacted and in a moment there was something of a mini-brouhaha in progress. The owner was quickly on the phone and in the confusion, Gallacher slipped back out the door he had come through and made his way back up to the apartment for the last time.

The police arrived quickly and as they began to sort things out, the youth who had started it all complained loudly that it had been this other guy at the bar who started it all. The sergeant of the patrol that had responded asked the owner about it and was told, "No. There was a quiet man there at the end of the bar just trying to mind his own business and enjoy a lager." He pointed at the offending youth, "It was that one who started the whole thing. No one else." The young Scot was taken away in plastic cuffs to spend the night reflecting on his transgressions in a cell.

53

5:00 AM
Sunday
Route de la Tête de Chien
Northwest of Monaco

John Cann was unshaven and bleary-eyed. He and Mastrota had covered the entire length of the bus route from where it began in Cap d'Ail all the way to the little village of Col le Bermasse and back. Several times. More accurately, Mastrota had driven the entire length. John had walked some of it dialing and redialing Katherine's number, hoping against hope she would answer or — hell, that anything would happen that might help. They had branched out to other roads in the general area as well. In some places where there was habitation, where there were still lights on in a house, Cann had even knocked on some doors despite the late hour. Surprisingly, only one or two of the people he disturbed showed irritation at the intrusion and even those mellowed when he explained what he was doing. But it was all just as futile as everything else had been so far. No one had seen a lovely auburn-haired lady alone or in the company of others and no one recognized the photograph of Rafiq Mukhtar or anyone else.

They were pulled over to the side in the pitch darkness. John was seated in the passenger seat of the car with Mastrota behind the wheel. Both men had their heads back against the seats but while Mastrota was in danger of nodding off, Cann's mind was racing.

"What am I missing, Pietro?" he asked. "There has to be something."

"You have done what you can tonight, John," the Italian responded. "I don't know what else we can do."

"I can't give up."

"I know that. I am not suggesting it. But clearly we need something new, some piece of information or data that will give us some kind of different perspective. Some other line of approach." He looked at his watch. "In about an hour it will be sunrise. People will be up and about. Then we can ask around, show the photographs we have. See if anyone has seen anything." He rolled his head to the right. "And it would help to get a little rest in the meantime. You cannot think so clearly when you are this tired. Me also."

John had to accept the logic of what Mastrota was saying and nodded slowly. "I know," he said grudgingly. "Listen, I do appreciate your being out here with me all night. Get some sleep." Mastrota raised his brows in a question. "Yeah," Cann said interpreting the expression correctly, "I'll try, too."

He did try but failed. When he closed his eyes all he could see was Katherine's face and in his mind he heard her voice. Her laugh, too. But her voice, especially. Things she had said to him. He was afraid. For her. More afraid than he had ever been in his life. He was afraid for himself, too. Very. He couldn't lose her.

He had his cell phone plugged into the car cigarette lighter to keep it charged and, because he had nothing else he could try, he pressed the speed dial #2 again. Still nothing. Maybe he had in fact run her phone battery down. He put his head back and, in spite of himself, drifted off.

He slept for less than an hour but the dark was already beginning to thin when he awoke with a start. He looked over at Mastrota who was still sleeping. Then he ran through the mental checklist of what they had already done and tried to think of something new. There was still nothing. He picked up his phone and hit "2" yet again.

Katherine's phone rang five times then there was a click and a male voice said, "*Allo?*"

John bolted upright. "Who is this?" he almost shouted. Next to him Mastrota lurched awake.

"My name is Raymond Cormier," the deep voice answered. "Who is this?"

"Where are you, Monsieur Cormier?" John asked desperately.

"I am in my field, But you have not answered my question, Monsieur," the voice said calmly. "Is this your phone I am on? You have lost it?"

"Yes, Monsieur Cormier. It's my fiancée's phone. She's missing."

"Oh, Monsieur, I am sorry. What can I do?"

"Tell me where you are." As he spoke, he was gesturing for Mastrota to turn the key and start the car.

"I am at my farm. Where are you located right now, Monsieur."

"We are on the road they call the Dog's Head about one kilometer north of the route 6007."

"Eh, bien, Monsieur. Then you need only continue north on that road for another kilometer and a quarter or so. I am in a field off to the right. I will look for you. What are you driving?"

Cann told him as Mastrota put the car in gear and drove off. In short order they came upon a man on the side of the road in overalls and boots. He waved them down. Cann got out and ran over. The man held out the phone and Cann took it as Mastrota began to show the farmer the photos they had.

For a moment, John held the phone in both hands and just looked at it. Right then it was much more than a mere communications device. Just as he was about to open it, his own phone rang. It was Loring Matsen IT in Washington.

"We got another hit, Mr. Cann," the tech said," north of Monaco about…"

"I know," Cann interjected. "I'm holding it now."

"You have it?"

"Yes. Now what can we do with it."

"Open up the 'recent calls' screen. At least now we can see who was calling who."

"Okay. Done."

"Go to "dialed calls". See what's there.

He did that and examined the screen. "There's two."

"What's the number?"

"Not a number," Cann replied. "It's a URL." He read it off to the tech who recognized it. "Damn. That's the website the guy in Menton found on the computer. The French police have given us all their information. And we already tried that URL but it was shut down." Barely missing a beat, the tech then directed Cann to go to "received calls".

He did. "Two there as well. The last one was mine. The next one before it is a bunch of characters — gibberish." He read the letters and symbols to the tech.

"That could be an encrypted satellite phone."

"What if I hit 'send'? Call the number back?"

"I doubt it'll go through. But try it."

John did so and after a series of clicks and other sounds, there was silence. "Shit," he said yet again.

"It gets blocked at the satellite," the tech told him.

"So we've still got nothing?" He was angry and afraid at the same time. "There's got to be something we can do to find her."

"*We* can't," the tech emphasized the pronoun, "but NSA can do wonders with what we've got on the phone. Keep it charged and ..."

"We've got NSA on it?" Even though he had pressed for that very thing earlier, it wasn't a certainty they could get this kind of help. And so soon.

"Yes, sir. Mr. Matsen got wind of what's going on and he started making calls. I think he actually got the President to order it."

John knew it was after midnight in the States. "How did Arthur find out about this?" he asked, concerned for his elderly mentor's health.

"How does Mr. Matsen always find out?" the tech countered.

That was when John finally lost it. He was exhausted and not only from lack of sleep. The throbbing visceral fear for Katherine had threatened to suffocate him all night. And now, the image of the elderly, increasingly frail Arthur Matsen working the phones, staying up all night, putting his health at even further risk...again...for them.... He put a hand over his face and a sob burst from his throat. Mastrota and the farmer shuffled and looked away for a moment, as men will often do, but then the Italian stepped alongside and put his hand out and squeezed John's shoulder. They waited.

Cann regained his composure and muttered a quick, "Sorry." Both men dismissed the need for an apology out of hand. The farmer spoke first. "If I may suggest, Messieurs," the man said holding the stack of photos, "everyone in this area attends the Sunday masses at l'Eglise de St. Gabriel in Col le Bermasse. Perhaps if you show these photographs around, someone may have seen something, no?"

Cann and Mastrota agreed immediately and the farmer gave them directions. "What time are the masses?" they asked.

"7:30 and 9:00."

John gave the farmer his sincere thanks and he and Mastrota got in the car and drove to Col le Bermasse.

The farmer stood by the side of the road and watched them drive off. Then he turned and, as he walked, home, he said a little prayer for them.

The church of Saint Gabriel in Col le Bermasse is set on the opposite end of the village from the garage where Katherine and the "hadduta" were being held. Cann and Mastrota drove down the road and came to the stop sign where al-Nassef and Mukhtar had intercepted the car the night before. Where Katherine and the others had turned right, John and Mastrota, following farmer Cormier's directions, went left.

They arrived at the church early enough to meet with the parish priest before the 7:30 mass. Over much needed coffee and pastry, they explained what they were doing. The priest was sympathetic and promised to help and did so during his homily by strongly requesting the assembled parishioners to wait after mass and speak to two gentlemen who were on very important business. As far as they could tell, most of the churchgoers complied but still it did no good. None had seen Katherine or any of the people in the photographs. The priest tried to be encouraging advising that the people at the early mass were the rural folk, used to getting up early for farm work and other things. The people of the village would be at the later 9:00 o'clock mass. Perhaps they had seen something.

John hoped so. Prayed it would be so. Once more, yet again, it was all he had.

Fort Meade
Maryland, USA

The NSA people had a shot at finding Price's phone. Using algorithms developed specifically for the purpose, they'd run the encrypted access number for al-Nassef's satellite phone through a super computer and reduced the possible combinations to a manageable number — manageable being in the millions as opposed to the trillions. Then these possibilities were beamed up to the satellite system at a rate of thousands per second. They dodged one possible bullet when it became clear the satellites themselves didn't have any sort of automatic cutoff based on multiple attempts.

The idea was for the unencrypted combination of numbers to access the satellite and then be passed on down to the phone unit to which that number was attached. When that happened, the computer could track the specific signal(s) by use of what are called inter-packet delays (IPDs). Digital information, including a telephone number is sent in packets — think of it as the cars on a very long freight train. Between each packet is a minuscule but very definable and *regular* interval. The NSA computer programmed the slightest anomaly into that interval, measured in nanoseconds, and recognizable only to the computer as the signal it had sent. With that, the computer was able to track that specific signal to the specific phone unit the satellite was attempting to access.

The problem, however, was that any number of the unencrypted combinations that got through could be actual numbers assigned to other satellite phones. This issue was obviated by programming into the supercomputer the original encrypted number that had been on Price's cell phone. In the instant, the nanosecond, the satellite signal hit the object phone that unit's number immediately backtracked up the line to the satellite which re-encrypted it and passed it back down to the NSA computer which rejected it as not a match and did it quickly enough to prevent the object phone from even ringing. The owner of that phone would never know it had been called.

But they needed to find the right number and the right phone and have the supercomputer make the match and let the ring go through. Then they'd have found the phone but would still need something more.

Someone had to answer it.

54

Grand Prix Race Course
Monaco

Sunday, race day of a Grand Prix week, starts early. Most of the garages in the pit area had been locked and quiet all night. According to the sporting regulations, with some relatively minor exceptions, the teams are not allowed to work on the cars between qualifying and the race itself. To do so without a very good reason and only with permission will incur a penalty, usually a demotion on the starting grid. So the only garages open and occupied during the night were those of teams dealing with issues of actual damage or serious mechanical failure.

The rest of the Principality was already filling up as the morning progressed. Almost every seat in Monaco is a reserved seat and there were already people streaming in to take their places. In many other venues for Grands Prix, there are camping areas at or near the track but in Monaco the only thing resembling open space is the side of the Rock facing down on the city. The earliest arrivals there didn't really arrive at all but had spent the night on the slope in order to claim the best viewing spots. Those prime spots would be along the walls that lined the zig-zagging walkway while other daring souls actually slept in sleeping bags tethered to trees on the side of the Rock which sloped as much as 75°.

The main race — the Grand Prix — does not start until 13:00 but the morning is by no means idle. On the track, there are several preliminary races: street cars, supercars, other formulae, stepping stones to the "big league". And off the track, parties galore, many just beginning, some that never ended. And everywhere, people rise from their night's sleep — if they've slept — at varying times, and converge on the tiny area that surrounds the track until it is a tightly compressed mass of human beings looking forward to the day's events. By race time, there will be well over one hundred thousand people in the area. Already there were tens of thousands and the number was growing by the minute.

One person who had slept little but not because he had been partying — well, not directly because he was partying — was one Tommy Sutherland. He was the young "hooligan" who had parlayed an attempt at impressing a young woman he had just met by trying to pick a fight with Gallacher into a night in Monaco's House of Arrest. And while Monaco may be Monaco, jail is jail and he'd spent the night on a concrete bench with the mattress removed due to his "resistance". He was tired, grumpy, cold, and not a little hungover when the guard banged on the cell bars at 8:00 to rouse him. A not totally unpalatable breakfast was provided which Sutherland couldn't have held down even if he'd wanted to. A short time later, he was advised to make himself as presentable as possible and was taken to a hearing room where he took a seat with dozens of other revelers and/or miscreants and waited for his turn before the magistrate.

Less than half an hour later, unshaven, unkempt, and unbowed, Tommy Sutherland stood sullenly before a magistrate who listened as Tommy said he wasn't guilty and then promptly found him so. The fine was three hundred Euros. Not excessive by Monaco standards and that was mostly because the authorities didn't want offenders to opt for taking up space in the jail. Tommy, whose father owned several automobile dealerships in the Perth area, signed the bond to cover the damage to the "Côte de Barbarie" then pulled out his Gold Card and readily albeit resentfully paid his debt to Monaco society.

Once the financial aspects of the transaction were completed, Tommy Sutherland was taken down to the main desk where his effects were returned to him in a manila envelope. As the desk officer read off the items to be accounted for, Sutherland looked around, his eyes falling on a bulletin board just to his right with flyers and posters and alerts prominently displayed. He looked closely at one more than the others and muttered to his police escort,

"That there's the one you lot should have pulled in. If it wasn't for him, there'd been no fight, ya know."

The officer glanced at Sutherland and then over at the bulletin board. "Which one is that?" he asked almost casually. Sutherland extended his arm and put a finger on the photo of William Gallacher. "That one right there. That was him last night being disrespectful to me and the lady I was with. You lot should have…"

"How sure are you?" the desk officer asked reaching for his phone. Every member of every unit and force in Monaco had been made aware of the importance of finding the man in the photo and even as Sutherland was saying, "Oh, I'm sure, all right. That's him, for sure," the call was being put through to Bazinet.

Bazinet knew, of course, that just because the man had been spotted in Monaco-ville the night before, it did not mean he was still there or staying there. But the fact that Gallacher had been spotted at all did. The Scot's image had been circulated throughout the principality for days now without a single hit which indicated he'd been lying low, staying out of view which, in turn, was a further indication that where he'd been seen was likely where he'd been hiding.

Definite? Not at all.

But enough to justify a broad directed response.

Bazinet ordered all available units including the Sapeurs-Pompiers NBC unit to the top of the Rock. Bazinet himself headed directly to the House of Arrest where an even more sullen Tommy Sutherland sat indignantly protesting he'd paid his fine and should be allowed to leave. Bazinet silenced the young Scot with a threat that he would hold him for as long as he wished if the man didn't answer his questions right now. The Director of Public Security quickly established the basic facts and satisfied himself as best he could that the ID of Gallacher was good. Then he headed for Monaco-ville and the Rock.

Inside the apartment, William Gallacher had risen early and would prepare himself for his martyrdom throughout the morning. He'd given little thought to the events of the previous night other than a measure of chagrin at his own foolishness. He'd eaten nothing and would not. So far, he'd spent the morning in prayer and reflection and all in all felt ready for his sacred act.

He got up from the couch in the living room and once again felt drawn to the bedroom that contained the Sarin and the mechanism for its disposal. He was standing in the doorway just reviewing the actions he would take in a few hours when he heard the first of the sirens. Initially, for just a moment, he dismissed them as distant but as the sounds grew louder and closer, he went to the bedroom window and peered out through the side of the drawn curtains. The Place de Palais was packed with police and other emergency vehicles. He crossed the room and looked out the window onto the Rue des Remparts and saw the same was true out there.

He quickly went back in to the living room and opened the laptop. His message to the leader was brief. Something was wrong. Very wrong. The area was crawling with police and the apartment building was virtually surrounded. Gallacher concluded the post by saying if he didn't receive instructions to the contrary, he would assume there was a serious breach and would, if necessary, implement his act of *jihad* prematurely rather than risk failure.

Bazinet had sealed off the area and cleared the nearby stores and shops in Monaco-ville to facilitate the search. An evacuation of the residences, including the apartment building where Gallacher was, was considered and rejected as unwieldy and ineffectual. Similarly, on the other side of the wall leading to the steep slope of the Rock, the spectators closest to the top were being held back but had not been ordered to leave. Ultimately, as the NBC officer had said previously, if a dirty bomb went off, nothing short of a total evacuation of the the principality would suffice. And, as also noted, that was simply not possible.

Everyone's mindset was directed toward a dirty bomb. At the moment, Bazinet had the Sapeurs personnel in full hazmat suits saturating the area with radiation detectors at their most sensitive setting. As a secondary precaution, they placed small NBC detectors on the ground at intervals as they passed. When done, they'd found nothing. The Sapeurs sergeant walked back to where Bazinet stood some fifty or so yards from the corner of the apartment building and shook his head.

"Is it possible the detectors are faulty?" Bazinet asked the sergeant.

"All of them, Monsieur?" He pursed his lips and shook his head. "And I have recalibrated and retested and all appear to be fine."

Bazinet nodded. "Then we must do an interior search. Door by door. If there is something here, we have to find it." He flipped his chin in the general direction of Monaco-ville.

"Go." He pointed at the sergeant's radio. "And stay in constant contact."

Inside the apartment, Gallacher watched through the edge of the curtains. He could only observe what was on the two sides at his corner of the building but was able to see the Sapeurs in protective gear fanning out, heading in the direction of his building. He went into the living room and checked the laptop one more time for an answer from the leader.

Nothing.

It was time, he decided.

He went into the bedroom where the Sarin was waiting, took the time to say the prayers he had chosen for his last moments on earth and then opened the spigots on the drums of chemicals. There was no sound as the two elements ran through their respective tubing and into the stainless steel tank where they would mix. Gallacher then flipped the switch that started the pump that discharged the compound that was now Sarin into the vaporizer in the A/C unit in the window. Lastly, he walked over and turned the vaporizer on.

That was it. It was done.

Outside, Bazinet and others became aware of a chirping sound from one of the multi-range NBC detectors the Sapeurs had placed outside the building. It was one on the Rue des Remparts side and Bazinet started up toward it to pinpoint the location. As he neared the building, he saw two officers who had been stationed on the corner where Gallacher's apartment was begin to exhibit signs of discomfort and stress. Bazinet stopped and watched as first one, then the second officer progressed from sniffling to coughing to difficulty breathing. After a moment, progressively in a direction away from the corner, other officers started to react. Sniffles, coughing, Then some clutched their chests in pain. Some began to gag and vomit.

This, he knew, was not radiation. It was too fast. And he remembered the Banques des Maritimes. He shouted into his radio. "Switch to chemical detection! Not radiation! Switch to chemical!" He heard sounds off to his left and saw spectators at the top of the slope beginning to exhibit symptoms as well.

Bazinet turned back to the apartment building and examined the scene looking up above where the first two officers to be stricken had been standing. His eyes settled on the A/C unit on the corner. He turned back to the men who were still standing by the vehicles where he had been moments before and signaled for one of them to drive the car forward. Then he immediately changed his mind and ran back to his car. He would do this himself. He opened the trunk of the vehicle and pulled out a tarp and duct tape then ran to one of the police vans parked nearby in the Place de Palais. He ordered the driver out and jumped into the front seat, started the van and drove to a spot under the A/C unit he suspected was spewing the deadly poison. In his heart and mind he knew the consequences of what he was doing. But he could do nothing else.

Bazinet got out of the van and climbed up onto its roof. As he did so, he knew he was breathing in the mist and even felt several drops on his skin. But he was just able to tape the tarp over the grille of the A/C unit before he began to feel the symptoms. When he was done, he sat down on the roof of the van, pulled his knees up to his chest and pressed his face against them. He felt no pride, no sense of accomplishment or even heroism. Rather he was consumed by a profound sense of regret. He thought of his wife, his children, grandchildren to come. Why had he done this? Surely there must have been some other way. The nausea was overwhelming and the physical agony was beginning to match the emotional. He cramped up and twisted on to his side as the paramedics reached up and pulled him off the top of the van and put him on a gurney. Precious time was wasted as one of the medics first called out for atropine and then ran back to one of the hazmat vans to frantically search for the antidote. But Bazinet had both inhaled and absorbed many times the lethal dose and there was nothing to be done. They knew it. He knew it. Bazinet's death wasn't mercifully quick but it was over in moments.

Gallacher had been standing back from the window a bit where he could still see the gas beginning to take its toll on people outside. He'd been quite startled when he saw a head appear outside the window just above the A/C unit and begin to shroud the unit with a tarp. The Scot knew that even if some of the Sarin still escaped, much would come back into the apartment. He glanced over at the gas mask in the corner. No, he thought, this is what he had come to do. He reached down and grabbed the hose leading out of the stainless steel tank and yanked it off. The mixed liquid poured out of the hole where the hose had been.

Inside the building, the Sapeurs sergeant had switched to a chemical detector and, at first, hadn't gotten anything. Then there was a faint hit and guided by a strengthening signal, he found his way to the second level and turned in the direction of the apartment. By the time he reached the door, the chemical detector was going off the scale. The Sapeurs sergeant ordered everyone out of the building. When they were gone, he turned back and awkwardly kicked at the door until it smashed open. He ran inside and quickly assessed the situation. Using a spare glove that was part of his uniform, he managed to plug the hole in the tank that was releasing the Sarin thus stemming the flow of the deadly liquid onto the floor. There was still an excessive amount of the poison in the room which he knew would eventually evaporate. He went into a bedroom and pulled the sheets off the bed and used them to block the space under the door which he closed behind him. He gave no attention to Gallacher who, the Sapeurs sergeant would later recall, was still moving when he left.

55

Col le Bermasse
France

Inside the garage in Col le Bermasse, Rashid al-Nassef looked over at Katherine Price who was still bound hand and foot and sitting on the floor. Neither al-Nassef nor Price nor Chani had slept during the night. The terrorist leader checked his watch yet again. Not long now.

A sound pricked his ears and he turned his head side to side before recognizing it. It sounded like his satellite phone was beeping. He crossed to the office where he'd left it and confirmed that's what he was hearing. That was not right. No one should be calling him, especially right now. None of the "martyrs' had the satellite number and only a few other people in the world did and they knew — or should know — not to try to contact him. And certainly not on that phone. It was encrypted, yes, but measures and countermeasures constantly overtook one another and he was not going to take any chances. Aside from security, his biggest concern was that for some reason the operation was being called off. If so, he didn't want to know. He stared at the beeping phone but didn't move. He wouldn't answer.

The phone rang for about a full minute then stopped. Al-Nassef tried to dismiss it as an aberration but couldn't. You don't generally get 'wrong numbers' on an encrypted phone. But more than anything, why would it be going off now? Never believe in coincidence.

After about another minute, the satellite phone began to beep again. Al-Nassef felt increased annoyance and increased apprehension. Why was it doing that? He'd brought a small television into the office to watch the events as they unfolded later in the day and walked over and turned it on. He froze at what he saw.

The scene was clearly the top of the Rock and it was one of a building under siege. The commentators had little information to impart to the viewers and so were spending much of their air time complaining about that very fact. Al-Nassef turned to his laptop but quickly remembered he had closed down the contact website the night before. Gallacher was on his own. Al-Nassef had a fair amount of confidence in the Scot lawyer and hoped he knew that a piece of the pie was better than none at all.

He, al-Nassef, certainly felt that way and immediately told Chani to go down into the old service ditch, now covered, and retrieve the container and wheel it around to the passenger side of the ambulance.

"We must move the timing up," the leader advised. "You will go now. Take the small container out of the larger ones and bring it with you. Inside is the Cesium itself. Before you get to Monaco, pull over and spread the Cesium over the explosives in the back. Then get back into the driver's seat and put your thumb on the detonator on the steering wheel. Get as far into Monaco as you can but if you are stopped or impeded, then detonate the explosive wherever you may be at the time. It is big enough to accomplish its purpose even on the outskirts."

Chani nodded acknowledgment.

"Now," al-Nassef said, "help me with this one." The two men walked over to where Katherine was sitting on the floor. As they approached, she lashed her legs straight out catching al-Nassef in the knees and knocking him back. It was a futile gesture of resistance. Al-Nassef came back and unleashed a vicious right fist to the side of her head, stunning her while Chani followed with a series of full force kicks that rendered her completely unconscious. Then they picked her up and threw her into the back of the ambulance. Just then al-Nassef heard the satellite phone go off again. He went and got it, shut it off and threw it in the back of the vehicle as well. Then he threaded a length of chain through the rear door handles to prevent them from being opened from the inside. He left the main area as Chani went around and got out the small container of Cesium and put it on the passenger seat in the ambulance. Then the Albanian went and picked up his son and settled himself into the driver's seat, the boy on his lap.

Cann and Mastrota had waited impatiently for the 9:00 o'clock mass to end. The priest had again made a strong heartfelt plea to his parishioners and as he told them to "go, the Mass is ended" the first of the communicants started to leave.

John was close to despair as parishioner after parishioner stopped and, as much as they clearly wanted to help, failed to recognize the men in the photos. Then the manager of the Hotel Palais des Revères pointed at the original Ponte Tresa surveillance photo of al-Nassef and said, "I believe this man has been a guest at my hotel."

"When?" Cann and Mastrota almost shouted in unison.

"The hotel manager looked a bit startled. "Now, Messieurs. He is still checked in as of this morning."

Adrenalin jolted John back to full alertness as he turned for the car. "Please come with us, Monsieur?" he said quickly, his hand already tugging the man's arm. "Take us there. Please!"

"Of course," the manager said as the three of them ran to the car.

Cann, Mastrota and the hotel manager took the most direct route from the church to the hotel. As they neared it, an ambulance pulled around the corner and quickly sped past them. While the sun reflecting off the windshield made it difficult to see inside, it was apparent that the driver held a small child on his lap. That seemed odd enough for Mastrota to ask the hotel manager, "What's down that road? Is there a hospital or clinic?

"No, Monsieur. It is a dead end. An abandoned garage at the end."

Mastrota turned into it and accelerated the short distance to the end of the street from which the ambulance had emerged in time to get a glimpse of a man who could very well be Rashid al-Nassef just closing the garage door. Close enough for Cann. "He's mine," he announced forcefully as he instinctively touched the Sig P229 Bazinet had loaned him. Mastrota braked the car, nose against the double garage doors. As Cann exited, Mastrota turned to the manager in the back seat and directed him to get away from the area and call Monaco Public Security — ask for Bazinet — and tell him about the ambulance. Then Mastrota joined Cann outside the vehicle and they approached the garage building from either side.

The roads into Monaco from every direction rise and fall and switch back virtually every half kilometer or so. As a result, there are many spots when the route ahead is visible from a distance. At one such vantage point, Chani saw a roadblock off to his right and below. There was a small dirt road leading off to the left and he took it. He was anxious to spread the Cesium, anyway, knowing it would help him to paradise no matter what. He reached over to the passenger seat and picked up the small container that held the tubes of the lethal radioactive material.

The front of the vehicle was separated from the back by a solid partition so, still carrying his son, he took the small container off the passenger seat and carried it around to the back and removed the chain. He opened the doors carefully and checked to make sure the woman was still unconscious. Then he climbed in and knee-walked up to the stacks of C4. He opened the small container and reached in for one of the tubes. He didn't expect it to be as hot as it was and pulled his fingers back sharply. He looked around the rear of the ambulance and found a blanket which he used to hold the bottom of the tube as he unscrewed the top.

For a moment he was captivated by the soft blue glow that came from inside but then he quickly got back to business, shaking and spreading the contents atop and around the explosives. He did the same with the remaining three tubes and then, ironically gently, spread the blanket on the floor between the explosives and the front partition and laid his son in the space. He exited out of the back, replaced the chain, and got back into the front of the vehicle.

He was not at all familiar with the roads in the area but decided to stay on the dirt track as long as he was still heading in the general direction of Monaco. He would get as close as he could before he detonated the bomb. But he would detonate it. This day, he knew, he would be in paradise. Muttering his final prayers, he drove off.

Al-Nassef had seen the vehicle come around the corner as he was closing the garage doors. He couldn't tell who was inside but the speed with which it approached was cause for concern. He'd watched from a corner of a window as it nosed up to the front doors of the building and wasn't even surprised when he recognized Cann getting out. He grabbed his Glock 29 and ran to the rear of the building where he opened a window in an attempt at misdirection. Then he crossed to the trap door, lifted it and went quickly down the ramp. He pulled the door back down over him as he did so, resting it on his head so that he would be able to see out into the garage area through the small opening.

Cann and Mastrota each sidled all the way down the two sides of the building ducking under and then peering into the windows as they went. At the rear, they gingerly, tentatively inched an eye around the corners until they saw each other and nothing in between. They both noticed the open window and turned their attention out into the woods beyond. They heard nothing and saw no evidence of an intrusion such as footprints, broken branches, scuff trails, or even the sounds of animals being disturbed. They turned their attention back to the building, silently indicating to one another their agreement that entry would be necessary. Each went back along a wall to a window, checked inside very carefully, then made an entry. On Cann's side, the window was unlocked and he slid it up quietly. Mastrota's window was locked and he had to use the butt of his handgun to break a pane to get in.

Once inside, each man was in one of the small side rooms off the main area. The one Cann was in was the office al-Nassef had used. The small television was still on, the sound turned low. Cann had to use a lot of will power not to focus on what was on the screen. Something was happening on the Rock. Something big.

Cann, like Mastrota, laid a shoulder against the frame of the door that led into the main area and then rolled his head around until one eye could see what was out there. He looked across at Mastrota who jabbed a thumb at himself indicating he would make the move into the room. Cann raised his Sig to eye level and pointed it around the corner and then around the room, his eye following wherever the front sight went. Mastrota dropped down low and started to come around the frame. Out of the corner of his eye, Cann saw the slightest movement as al-Nassef raised the trap door with his head. All Cann could see was just the tip of the barrel of a handgun barely visible in the tiny crack between the door and the floor. Cann was a good shot, an excellent, skilled shooter but he knew the scenes in movies of shooting guns out of people's hand was, almost inevitably, pure theater. Except for the Crimson Trace™ laser sight. He pressed the button on the butt of the P229 and the red line shot out like, well, like a laser. Cann braced his hands against the door frame for support and squeezed the trigger. The shot was true and the weapon flew out of al-Nassef's hands into the darkness around him.

The trap door dropped when al-Nassef did. There was no sound from within. Cann and Mastrota slowly approached at different angles and waited and listened. After a moment, Cann called out, "Come out! Now!" Below the surface, al-Nassef stayed quiet. He'd considered that they couldn't know if this was a just a hole and might think this could be a tunnel and would go outside to check. They'd both thought of it but didn't have the manpower to check anyway. The best they could do in that regard was to periodically glance out the windows and otherwise hope it wasn't a means of escape. Mastrota moved over to Cann without taking his gun off the trap door. In a quiet voice, he advised Cann he was going out to check the trunk of the car Bazinet had given them. Police vehicles often carry the most useful things.

He was back in a couple of minutes carrying two canisters with the marking "CS" on them. Cann nodded immediately and went over and straddled the trap door. He reached down and grabbed the ring as Mastrota pulled the tabs on top of the canisters. Cann pulled up on the door, Mastrota instantly tossed the CS gas into the space beneath and Cann dropped the door back down. Both men then went and stood on it and waited. It wasn't long before they felt pressure under them followed by thumping from below. Neither man above felt a pressing need to release al-Nassef and the longer they waited, up to a point, the more debilitated he would be.

After a few more moments, Mastrota moved off to the side and pointed his weapon at the trap door. Cann reached down and pulled it up a few inches shouting, "Show your hands! Show your hands!" Al-Nassef snaked his hands out the opening and Cann raised the door all the way up moving away as quickly as he could so as not to be affected by the gas himself. Al-Nassef stumbled up the ramp and fell forward on to his hands and knees gasping for air and scrabbling at his burning and temporarily blinded eyes.

Cann had no sympathy. "Where's Katherine?" he shouted.

Al-Nassef waved his hand about indicating he couldn't talk. Cann took a step forward and tightened his finger on the trigger of the Sig.

"Where's Katherine?" he repeated.

56

In the back of the ambulance, Katherine was slowly regaining consciousness. She first tried moving her neck and head but even small motions caused disproportionate stabs of pain. She kept her eyes closed and lay still for a moment mentally surveying her body for any other damage. Slightly contracting her various muscle groups, she noted numerous aches but no apparent severe damage. In doing so, she became aware that she was still bound hand and foot. Finally, she tried moving her head again and found that the pain was a bit less severe but still significant.

Nonetheless, she opened her eyes and assessed her situation. She was lying more on her side than back in the rear of what she assumed to be the ambulance that had been in the garage in Col le Bermasse. She was facing toward the front of the vehicle and realized that she was looking at the stacks of C4 al-Nassef had told Chani about. Then she noticed the blue glow and went cold as she recalled al-Nassef's description of the Cesium 137.

She tried to move her fingers behind her but realized the way she had been laying had cut off the circulation to her hands. She shifted her weight to relieve the pressure and then wiggled her fingers as much as she could until the pins and needles signaled the beginning of the return of sensation. When enough feeling had returned, she bent her wrists as sharply as she could in an attempt to check her bonds by feel. She learned little from the act other than that the plastic ties were very secure indeed.

Katherine put her head back and rested her eyes for a moment then opened them and examined her immediate environment more closely. She saw that she had been placed just inside the ambulance with her back toward the rear doors. She shifted her position so as to place her weight on an elbow and gasped at the searing pain that shot up her arm. Might be broken, she thought, then immediately dismissed the concern. Whether it was or not, she had to continue. She continued the painful shifting of her position until her feet were toward the door. Then she extended her legs out and up and tried to get the tip of her shoe behind the inside latch. The act of extending the muscles caused painful cramping but she persevered until she managed to lever the latch outward. The doors separated but barely an inch, prevented from opening any further by the chain.

Partly out of stubbornness, mostly out of frustration, Katherine pulled her knees up to her chest and then slammed them out against the doors. The shock from the impact coursed up her spine almost causing her to lose consciousness again. The chain held.

She let her head fall back against the floor and looked around again, this time at floor level. In the corner, she saw the satellite phone. Despite the pain, she didn't hesitate. She twisted her body and snaked across the floor until her fingertips were almost touching the phone. But she couldn't get a grip on it. She took some breaths and tried to consciously relax the tension in her muscles and joints. Then she concentrated on stretching her arms as much as she could and began to inch them past her hips until her hands were behind her thighs. After that, it was a matter of bringing her knees up toward her and forcing her hands down the backs of her legs and over her feet. Her hands were still bound but now they were in front of her.

She saw that the phone was turned off. She leaned over so that her wrist pinned the phone and kept it from moving while she extended a single finger and turned it on. Almost instantly, the phone started beeping. Using the same single finger, she answered it and leaned her ear over it, but heard nothing but chirps and beeps at the other end. Not knowing what it was, she ended the call and painstakingly punched in John's cell phone number. In Maryland, the NSA caught the activated signal.

Al-Nassef continued to go through the motions of a man in distress from the tear gas. Cann wasn't inclined to be patient. "Knock it off and talk to me," he said. Al-Nassef ignored him and so he walked over and threw a front kick into al-Nassef's shoulder knocking him over.

"Where's Katherine?"

Al-Nassef got back up to his knees and looked up. Even as he was still gagging and coughing from the CS gas, he somehow managed to give Cann a condescending sneering smile. "The beautiful lady?" he asked gratingly. He shrugged. Cann kicked him again. Harder. This time in the head. Al-Nassef went down again. From his back, he still sneered up. But still he said nothing.

John's cell phone rang. He answered. It was Katherine.

"Hi," she said. Even the one word somehow sounded strained.

John's first reaction was profound relief. Just to hear her voice. Know she was alive. That she was able to call. He allowed himself to hope.

"Kath!" he almost whispered her name. "Where are you?"

Katherine told him she was in the back of an ambulance. John remembered the one they'd seen driving off. That had to be the one. And he'd let it drive right past. He ached with the realization. "But first, listen, John," she said. "Al-Nassef's in a garage in a small village north of Monaco. *Col le* something. I only got a glimpse…"

"I know, Kath. Don't worry. We've got him."

A brief silence. "You've got him," she repeated back, dully.

"Right here in front of me."

"He has to be stopped." John heard her struggling to take a breath. "He's pure evil, John. I know you know that but… now I've seen it. Felt it."

"I know," he said again. "He's not going anywhere. But what about you? How are you?"

Katherine sounded exhausted. "Not good," she said. "The ambulance is packed with C4 and," she hesitated, not knowing John knew about the Cesium, "he's spread Cesium 137 all over it. A dirty bomb. I don't know how long I've been exposed but…"

The hope John initially felt was overwhelmed by a deep abiding dread. It felt like his soul was being drained from his body; like he was becoming an empty shell. "Do you feel it?" he asked gently. "Can you feel any effects?"

"I don't know. I was pretty banged up even before I got thrown in here so… It's hard to tell." She told him about the beatings she'd received in the garage. As she spoke, John's eyes went to al-Nassef and stayed there. But he had to think about Katherine. His mind raced, looking for an answer.

"Can you get out of the ambulance?"

"I've been trying to. There's no access to the front and the rear doors are secured from the outside."

"And you don't know where you are?"

"I can't see outside. Somewhere between where you are and Monaco. It's not much but…"

John controlled his growing sense of desperation and forced himself to concentrate. Then he remembered he had her cell phone with him. "Wait a second, what are you calling me on?"

"A satellite phone. It was in here with me."

He felt a small resurgence of hope. "If it's al-Nassef's, NSA's been trying to find it. Whatever you do don't break the connection. It'll be like a beacon to you."

"Okay," Katherine said. To John her voice already sounded weaker than before.

There was no way he was breaking the connection so he explained the situation to Mastrota and gave him the number of the Loring Matsen IT. In a moment, Mastrota put the call through and handed his phone to Cann.

"NSA has the signal," the tech advised. "It's moving."

Cann quickly explained it was the ambulance with a dirty bomb in it. And that Katherine Price was in it.

He turned his attention back to his phone in time to hear Katherine utter a low, startled, "Oh," at the other end.

"What, Kath?"

There was only silence.

"Kath? What is it" he shouted desperately.

Nothing.

Katherine had just seen the tiny foot of Luan Chani sticking out behind the stack of C4. To get to him, she realized she would have to crawl past the C4 and get very close to the glowing particles of Cesium. She hesitated only for a second then got up on her hands and knees and, holding her breath, not even knowing if that mattered, crawled forward trying to stay as close to the sides of the vehicle as she could. She reached the child who was lying quietly between the explosive and the partition and with her still bound hands pulled her to him. She moved him to the back where she had been and positioned herself between the boy and the bomb. It probably wasn't much protection but it was better than nothing. She hoped.

Suddenly she realized that while she was getting Luan, she'd seen the simple four wire detonation scheme of the C4 assembly. Four simple detonators pushed into the four corners of the C4. Easy in, easy out. Once the wires were disconnected, Chani could push the detonator all he wanted. She'd already been very close to the Cesium and didn't know how long she'd been exposed. She thought about it only briefly and then decided fatalistically that there was a good chance she'd already received a lethal dose of radiation, so…. What was that movie? You only die once?

She crawled forward again and one by one pulled the detonators out of the C4. Twice she actually came into contact with particles of Cesium and felt the burning sensation on her skin. In short order, the device was effectively disarmed. She went back to the rear of the vehicle and picked up the satellite phone. She could hear John calling her name. "I'm back," she said quietly.

"What happened?" John asked with apprehension. "Where'd you go?"

Katherine told him what she'd done.

"You disarmed the bomb?" he said looking directly at Mastrota. "Are you sure?" He nodded at the Italian who immediately relayed the information to the authorities.

"But what about you?" John asked trying to keep the fear out of his voice. "How close did you have to get to the…?" He didn't want to say the word.

"Close," Katherine told him. "I got some on me."

"Oh, Kath," was all he could say for a moment. Then, "It'll be okay, Kath. It will."

"I know," Katherine replied slowly. Neither of them really believed that.

"You know," she said sadly, "I meant it when I said I didn't want to be just a memory when you're in your eighties. Now…" her voice trailed off.

"Don't you give up on me, Kath," John said almost harshly. Then he softened his tone. "Just don't. We'll get there. We'll be there together."

From inside the ambulance Katherine heard sirens. Very close. She felt the vehicle suddenly brake sharply and stop. There was banging from the cab on the other side of the metal partition and a good deal of shouting all around. In moments there was relative quiet. Then she heard voices outside and the rattling of the chain securing the rear doors.

"They're here, John. I think. I guess I'll have to go."

"I'll find out where you are and be there right away."

"I love you, John. Please don't ever forget that. No matter what."

"I love you, too, Kath. More than you know. More than I thought possible. Wait for me. I'll see you soon."

John listened to the commotion on the other end of the satellite phone and stayed on until someone at the other end told him that Katherine and the child were on their way to the Princess Grace Hospital Center in Monaco. He clicked off the phone and turned to al-Nassef. He stared at the terrorist leader for a long moment then turned the Sig in his hand, popped out the magazine to check there were still rounds in it, made sure there was one in the chamber and then pressed the button to see that the laser sight was still working. He looked at al-Nassef.

"This ends here," he said flatly.

Al- Nassef huffed and shook his head. "No, it doesn't." He spoke calmly. Confidently. "What you'll do, as always," he said, "is take me away in shackles and say all kinds of bad things about me and also talk about how evil men like me will see justice. And then you will tie yourselves in knots being fair to me and when all is said and done, in perhaps a few years, I will be set free to do what I do best. And I will." He smirked. "You see, I remember you, Mr.....Cann, is it? I didn't at first, you know. But then I remembered Nahariya." He sneered when he mentioned the name of the Israeli town.

"I should have killed you then."

"But you didn't, did you? I recall you suggesting it to the Israeli's." The smirk became a grin. "It's what I would have done, of course. But that's not how you do things. We all know that."

"Not this time."

"Because of the woman?" al-Nassef said the last word with undisguised contempt.

In a movement that barely took a second, John raised the Sig and put the red dot just on the edge of al-Nassef's left ear and pulled the trigger. It barely nicked the lobe but it shocked al-Nassef enough so that he cringed and leaned sharply to his right. For the first time uncertainty appeared in his eyes. The terrorist licked his lips and turned his eyes to Mastrota.

John followed the look. "Maybe you should wait outside," he said calmly to the Italian.

Mastrota looked at him and then at Al-Nassef who was now looking back and forth between the two of them. Images of the tiny sneaker and the carnage at the bombing in Torino came into the Italian inspector's mind.

"I'll stay," he said simply.

John nodded and pointed the gun at the terrorist's torso and pressed the laser sight so that the red dot appeared in the middle of al-Nassef's chest. The terrorist looked down at it and then up again. He shook his head, trying to maintain his pose of arrogance. He opened his mouth as if to say something but nothing came out.

John fired. Not where the dot had been a moment ago. That would have been instantly fatal. So he'd lowered the Sig and the shot instead went into al-Nassef's stomach. Painful, ultimately fatal without treatment but not immediate.

He wasn't just being cruel. That *was* part of it, though. He wanted al-Nassef to suffer. But more importantly, he wanted al-Nassef to have time to absorb the fact that he was going to die. To feel what so many of the terrorist's victims had felt in the past. To feel what Katherine was feeling.

Al-Nassef grunted when the bullet hit him and he looked down at the blood beginning to seep through his shirt. Then he raised his head and there was genuine fear in his eyes. John raised the Sig and put the dot in the center of the terrorist's forehead just above the bridge of his nose. Al-Nassef slowly raised his hand in supplication. He knew he was about to die.

"Please…," al-Nassef started to plead.

Good. He would die a coward.

Consciously prolonging the moment, John slowly squeezed the trigger of the Sig until it exploded a second time. The bullet left a small black hole on the terrorist's forehead precisely where the red dot of the laser had been. It created a much larger opening when it exited out the back of his head.

Rashid al-Nassef was dead.

Finally.

Both men looked at the body for several seconds. Then Mastrota walked over and gently took the Sig from John's hand.

"Go," the Italian said quietly.

John didn't speak at first, then said, "I'm not going to let you..."

Mastrota interrupted him. "Go to Kathcrine. I'll take care of this."

John looked at him for a long moment then nodded. Mastrota watched him leave the garage and get into the car Bazinet had lent them and drive off.

Mastrota took out his cell phone. He would not involve Catrone, his direct superior, in this business. Instead he placed a direct call to Capo della Polizia Marco Tridente who took the call and listened as Mastrota described what had happened.

Exactly what had happened.

Tridente kept Mastrota on the line as he called Tonio Argente, his head of the Divizione Investigazioni Generali Operazioni Speciali (DIGOS), the Special Forces/Counter-Terror unit of the Italian State Police. Together they teleconferenced in Argente's counterpart in the French Direction Gènèrale de la Sécurité Exterieure (DGSE). Within minutes, a team of *décapants* — cleaners — was on its way to the scene.

57

Le Centre Hospitalier Princesse Grace
Avenue Pasteur
Monaco

John sat in a special waiting room with his head in his hands. He'd been there for several hours and still hadn't been allowed in to see Katherine. No one would tell him anything other than that she was radioactive. Literally. Not just sick with radiation sickness. She was actually emitting radiation to a degree that she presented a danger to others. She was in isolation. One doctor and one nurse were assigned to her and they had to suit up before they went near her and go through extensive decontamination after.

He didn't care about the danger. Not for himself anyway. He just wanted to be with her. But that tiny part of his brain that could separate logic from his feeling for Katherine told him he would do no one any good, Katherine included, if he forced his way in. He'd never felt so helpless in his life.

His cell phone rang and at first he didn't even look at it. When he saw the DC Loring Matsen office number, he clicked on.

"John?"

He immediately recognized the concerned voice of Arthur Matsen.

"Arthur."

"How is she?"

"I don't know, Arthur. Not good from what little they've told me and the sense I get from people's attitude. I just..." His voice cracked.

"They've got good people there, John. And we've reached out from here to find the very best in the world. I just wish we could have gotten to her sooner."

"We wouldn't have gotten to her at all if you hadn't stepped in, Arthur. How...?"

"You have friends in high places over there. As does Katherine. A man named Stanley Appel called me. Said he was calling for the Prince."

"You know him? Appel?"

"No. We operated in different spheres. Different theaters entirely in World War II. Let's just say we have some interesting mutual acquaintances though. But you should have called me."

John had had this conversation before. More than once with Arthur. Also with Katherine. It happens a lot when people care about each other.

"I didn't want to make things any..."

"I know," Arthur cut him off gently. "You still should have told me."

There was a commotion at the door to the room he was in and John looked up to see Prince Albert standing in the doorway. Behind him stood a cadre of doctors and nurses. He could also see Appel in the background. They all wore serious, somber expressions.

Prince Albert stepped into the room and crossed to him. He started to extend his hand but instead reached out both arms and gripped John's shoulders and looked into his eyes.

"I am so very sorry, Mr. Cann," His Serene Highness said. John returned the gaze but couldn't speak. "That such things like this should happen while you are guests in my country is...unthinkable."

"Katherine?" John managed to croak out.

The Prince exhaled heavily. "I'm told she has only just begun the vomiting which is a good sign. Relatively speaking. The longer the time from exposure to the onset, the better a sign that is. She is in pain from burns, most severely on her hands and arms but also where she was covered by clothing. They are doing as much as they can in that regard. As for the radiation, they know it was Cesium so they've begun giving her Prussian Blue which will attach to the Cesium and help flush the body and they've begun drug therapy to try to deal with any marrow issues. The doctors tell me it will be a long and difficult process and there may be long term effects...but she will recover."

For the second time in twenty-four hours, John broke down. The pure relief that he hadn't lost Katherine overwhelmed him. Prince Albert pulled Cann into him and held him until the emotions passed. "She will have the best possible care. I promise you."

"Can I see her?"

The Prince nodded. "Yes. I have prevailed upon the medical staff to allow it as soon as possible. You will have to wait a few more minutes then you will need to be prepared and suited up for it. It's a bit unwieldy but necessary."

"Anything. I just want to see her."

"And you will."

After a moment, John asked, knowing Katherine would ask him, "How's the little boy?"

The Prince shook his head.

John did the same.

After a pause, the Prince looked him directly in the eye. "Monaco owes you and Madame Price a debt of gratitude. As do I. As does the world. We've averted a terrible tragedy." He described the planned second Sarin attack and what Bazinet had done. "There were several deaths, unfortunately, and many others are quite ill but, if not for Bazinet, it would have been much worse."

John was awed and saddened by the Frenchman's incredible act of heroism.

After another brief silence, the Prince spoke again. "I've been briefed on what happened in Col le Bermasse. I want you to know there will be no repercussions of any kind."

"This is Monaco. Col le Bermasse is in France."

His Serene Highness nodded. "Girard Bazinet had many friends in France also, many of those in very high places indeed. Rest assured, John, there will be no repercussions for what happened today. After all," the Prince shrugged, "everyone knows Rashid al-Nassef has been dead for years."

A few minutes later, an orderly came in to get him to be prepared for his visit with Katherine. On the way out of the waiting room, he stopped and shook Stanley Appel's hand and thanked him.

"My pleasure, my boy. My pleasure," the gracious older man said. "Give her a kiss for me, if you will."

John said he looked forward to it.

Katherine lay under a tent of cloth that rippled from the air being blown across her body by cooling fans set at her feet and sides. John looked at her from inside the hazmat suit and ached with the need to touch her and hold her. The best he could do was lay a hand enclosed in a thick rubber glove on the side of the bed as near her as he could without making contact.

"Hi," he said, his voice sounding metallic through the microphone that passed it to the outside.

Katherine gave him a smile that was more evident in her eyes than in her mouth.

"Hi," she breathed. Her voice was a little raspy but it sounded like her. To John it sounded like music.

"You look good" John said after a while.

Katherine's looked at him. Even through a grimace, there was a glint of humor in her eye. "You always said I was hot but this is ridiculous."

John shook his head and had to fight hard not to lose it again. He didn't just love this lady. He was awed by her. Amazing. Simply amazing was all he could think.

After a moment, Katherine asked, "How's the little boy?"

John hesitated. There would be time later to tell her. But Katherine understood right away and nodded. "He was so little," she said sadly. "And that animal put him right in the middle of the Cesium. How could…?"

John said nothing for a while then, "You're going to be okay, you know."

Katherine's shoulder's shrugged almost imperceptibly. "I don't know." She looked into John's eyes. "I did so want to be Mrs. Cann."

"You will be."

"I hope so. If there's time."

The thought came fully formed into Cann's mind in an instant. "There's no time like the present," he said.

Price stared into his eyes and understood. "Now? Here?"

"Why not?"

She didn't answer right away. Then a small smile appeared. "Arthur will kill us," she said. "He wants to give us a huge wedding."

"So we'll do it again when we get back."

Katherine's smile faded just a bit and she looked away.

"And we will get back," John insisted.

She said nothing for a long time. Cann waited. Finally, Katherine returned her eyes to Cann's. "Yes," she said softly. "Let's."

It didn't take very long to organize. Cann told the Prince what they wanted to do and His Serene Highness took it from there. Less than two hours later, the most unlikely looking wedding party was gathered in Katherine's room. All except Katherine were in protective suits. John stood beside the bed holding his hand just above hers, not touching. Sir Robert Foster stood on John's right as best man. On the other side of the hospital bed stood Chief-Corporal Jacqueline Tessier who had been hurriedly summoned to the hospital to act as Maid of Honor. Stanley Appel and Inspector Mastrota stood by as the required two witnesses. His Serene Highness Prince Albert of Monaco insisted on performing the ceremony personally.

When they were pronounced man and wife, John and Katherine still couldn't touch so they kissed with their eyes. Then, even before the congratulations were finished, the doctors came in and shooed everyone out. They gave John a few more minutes along with a stern admonition that she needed to get her rest.

"I'll be right outside," John told her as he prepared to leave.

"I know," Katherine smiled weakly at him. "Say it."

"I love you," he said misunderstanding.

Katherine shook her head slightly. "I love you, too, John. But that's not what I meant. Say my new name."

Cann cherished saying the words. "I love you, Mrs. Cann," he said.

"Mmm," Katherine let her head sink into the pillow, her lips still holding the smile as she drifted off to sleep.

www.ingramcontent.com/pod-product-compliance
Lightning Source LLC
Chambersburg PA
CBHW031543240626
47153CB00002B/362